A PIECE OF GLASS

A Piece of Glass

R. Chauncey

Printed in the United States of America
ISBN 978-1-64133-901-8 (hardback)
ISBN 978-1-64133-650-5 (paperback)
ISBN 978-1-947352-09-4 (ebk)

Library of Congress Control Number: 2021911032

Sci-Fi; Action and Adventure

MainSpring Books
5901 W. Century Blvd
Suite 750
Los Angeles, CA, US, 90045

www.mainspringbooks.com

A PIECE OF GLASS

Lyle Morton, an employee of the Department of Information in Crown City, the capital city of the united world leaves work on June 1, 3075 and disappears with a glass disk that contains information that could destroy the five most powerful and richest men in the world. The five hire Lee Adams and Evelyn Summers, who've worked for them in the past to find Lyle. Lee and Evelyn know once they've found Lyle and turned him over to the five, they will all be killed. If they fail to find Lyle, their families will be killed. They must find Lyle, find out what he's got, and reveal it to the world to save themselves and their families. When Lee and Evelyn fail to keep in contact with the five, they send their special killers out to find them and Lyle. What Lee and Evelyn eventually learn at first shocks them and then nearly destroys them.

CHAPTER 1

June 1, 3075 10: p.m., Friday, Department of Information

Lyle Morton was afraid because what he was doing could not only result in the end of his life but those of the wife and three children, he hadn't seen in twenty-two years because he had to abandon them in order to protect their lives and to preserve his so he could do what he had to do. Tell the world the truth.

He looked at the computer on the desk he sat at and watched carefully as the information he had managed to steal from the secret files hidden among the classified files in the Department of Information's classified section was downloaded on the glass crystal in the DVD drive. He felt uncomfortable about what he was doing, because he was not a thief by nature. What he was doing offended his sense of right and wrong to steal. His theft of the information downloading on the glass crystal went against every concept he had of an honest, law abiding citizen. But the world needed to know what had been happening to it over the last five hundred years, or it would happen again and soon this time. He had inadvertently stumbled across the Information more than twenty-three years ago when he worked for the Department in its Hong Kong office.

It took him two months of research to accept what he had uncovered was the truth, and not someone's idea of a cruel and vicious joke. And when he did it had upset him so much he lost ten pounds in five days. He had been trying to lose ten pounds for the past three years without success. It was only when his wife and three daughters had begun to comment on his loss of weight that he realized the danger he had put them in with his discovery if the monsters found out.

Lyle had thought about ignoring the information and continuing with his life, until he realized his unintentional discovery might by discovered by someone analyzing data as he had been doing and reported. If it was the men who had hidden the information among the Department's classified section would know instantly he'd discovered it because his identification number was on the file where he'd discovered the information and come for him and his family.

The information was so dangerous he would have to die and anyone he'd come in contact with would have to die, too. Family, relatives, friends, even neighbors would all have to die to guarantee the information would never be released to the world. If it was, then the men who wanted it to remain hidden would be destroyed. He knew instantly his life would have to change to protect those he loved and respected. Even his coworkers he came in contact with daily would face horrible deaths to guarantee the information remained safely hidden.

So, a little over twenty-two years ago Lyle Morton arranged his death in an automobile accident that guaranteed his body would never be found, and there would be no question his death was an accident. It sickened him to do what he had to do to protect his family—his death would hurt them deeply, but he did it anyway and disappeared.

Then he reappeared a few months later as a new man with a new identity and started working as a clerk in the Department of Information's ten story two blocks long two blocks wide headquarters building in Crown City, the capital city of the United World Government. It was easy for him to acquire a new identity for himself.

Lyle Morton knew how the Department of Information worked with information having worked for it for five years before he disappeared and how to acquire the paperwork that helped him develop a new identity for himself. One so well put together no one would question it because there were plenty of documents within the Department of Information to prove who he said he was. Even his DNA matched that of the person he had become. He had simply switched his health records with those of a man who had died in Honk Kong the same week he'd died, and taken the dead man's health records for his. And then eliminated all information indicating what he'd done.

Once that was established he started the slow work of climbing the ladder of success in the Department to his present position. A position that allowed him to access any information in the Department he wanted as long as the proper paperwork had been made out. It took him fifteen years to get into his position, and once there he began to gather the information he knew the world needed to know. Now seven years later he was ready to release what he had collected to the world. All he had to do was find a place where he couldn't be found and release the information.

The world was no longer the world it had been in the late twenty-fifth century. It was now a united world with one government ruling the planet. The individual nations still existed with their unique cultural customs, languages, and religions. But national competition between the nations of the world had ended on May 1, 2575 when the United World Government was proclaimed and established with Crown City just northeast of the city of Denver, Colorado, as the capital of the world. Crown City, originally a small town in the state of Colorado, was chosen as the world capital to avoid arguments among the nations that their capital cities should be chosen as the world's new capital.

War was a thing of the past. As was starvation, disease, and ignorance. Everyone had the ability to acquire a clean comfortable place to live with free medical and dental services available. Education was available to everyone. The world was certainly a better place to live for the common people, but no one, not even the rich and powerful, knew the events of the past that had led to a united world was the work of five men who made the brutal Nazis of the twentieth century pale in comparison. Nowhere in the history of the human race were there people as monstrous as the five men whose information Lyle was downloading on the glass crystal in the DVD drive of his computer.

The world had become a better and safer place to live for everyone, but no one suspected the horrible cost of unifying the world and keeping it unified was the work of five greedy men who cared for no one but themselves. A cost the human race did not have to pay to achieve world peace and unity, but a cost it did pay because five men benefitted.

Lyle heard noise of footsteps in the corridor outside his secretary's office and calmly looked in the direction of his office door. He had learned the advantage of acting calm. It put suspicious people off guard and allowed him to do what he wished without them suspecting anything. He looked back at his computer and saw the information being downloaded on the crystal paragraph by paragraph every five seconds. He looked at his watch. *Another thirty seconds and all four thousand pages will be on the crystal with room left over for another four thousand pages.*

He heard the door to his secretary's office open. The hydraulic door openers always made a mild whooshing sound when someone opened or closed a door on one of the many corridors in the building. No one paid any attention to them.

The sound of footsteps ended when the guard, he knew it was a guard, they always made their rounds every hour on the hour, stepped from the hard tiles in the corridor onto the soft gray carpeting of his secretary's office.

Every office in the Department of Information's building had gray carpeting, because it was a neutral color and easy to clean. That was the explanation the Government Accounting Office gave people when they asked why the government couldn't buy carpeting with color in it.

Lyle leaned back in his chair and waited for his office door to open as he watched the information being downloaded.

A moment later the frosted glass door to his office opened and the head a guard poked into the semi-dark room. The guard scanned the room with his eyes before he looked at Lyle.

Lyle ignored the guard.

"Good evening, sir," the man said. As a night shift guard he wouldn't know Lyle's name as the day guards did.

Lyle looked up at him and nodded as he said, "Good evening."

"Working late, sir?" the man asked.

"Unfortunately, yes."

"Who are you, sir?" the guard asked him as he entered the office.

"Lyle Morton, data analyzer second class," he said as he started to reach for this wallet.

The guard walked over to the desk and stopped in front of it.

Lyle removed his ID from his wallet and handed it to the guard to prevent him from coming around behind the desk and looking at the computer screen. He didn't want him seeing the bright red letters at the top of the computer that read 'Classified. Not For The Public'. The guard might ask why the information was classified, since classified information was extremely rare in a united peaceful world.

The guard took Lyle's ID and looked at it and at Lyle for a few seconds before he handed it back to him saying, "Doing work for the political big shots, huh?"

Lyle smiled as he returned his ID to his wallet and his wallet to his pocket. "Someone in the capital building requested this information at four, and unfortunately I was given the assignment to find it. I just located it half an hour ago."

The guard looked at the drape covered windows behind Lyle's desk and around the room before he said, "Don't forget to swipe out before you leave, Mr. Morton."

"Oh, yes, thanks for reminding me," he said.

The guard turned around and walked toward the door saying, "Good night, sir."

"Good night, Officer," Lyle responded.

When Lyle saw the guard's shape walk out the outer door to the corridor and heard the whooshing sound of the hydraulic door opener opening and closing the door, he allowed himself a few seconds to tremble before he got control of himself and looked like nothing more than a data analyzer second class doing his work.

Ten minutes later the download was complete and the glass crystal, an eighth of an inch thick, and three inches in circumference, slid out of the DVD slot and he picked up a plastic case lying on the desk in front of him and put the glass crystal in the case and closed it. He picked up his canvas laptop briefcase, opened it, and slid the plastic case into a pocket on the left side of the briefcase and zippered it closed. He looked at the clock on the wall above his office door.

Ten fifteen.

He stood up and walked to the closet in his office, opened the door, and removed his suit coat from a thick plastic hanger hanging from the rod and his hat from the shelf above the rod and put them on and closed the closet door.

I mustn't do anything unusual.

He walked to his desk, picked up the canvas briefcase, and turned around and walked out of his office. He didn't turn his computer off because it had an automatic off switch. After ten minutes it would go into sleep mode and after an hour shut down. Only the special code word he had put into it would allow someone after starting it up to get into his files, which were nothing but general department information.

Lyle didn't worry about the five men getting his finger prints. Those that were on file belonged to a man who had died the day he'd moved to Crown City and taken a job as a regular clerk in the Department. Those he'd left on the keyboard of his computer would be wiped away by the cleaning robots that would clean his office now that he'd left it.

Lyle walked to the elevator section on the floor he worked on and pushed the down button on the brass plate between two of the elevators calling an elevator. As he waited for the elevator he thought about how the five monsters would catch on to what he'd done. *But not before I've put the information on the Internet.*

Every government building in the federal world government had one person working for the five working in those buildings. They were hired as regular workers but their real jobs were to monitor what went into and out of the buildings' computers they worked in, and they were capable of doing that because of a secret special program entered into all the computers and servers in the government that allowed the five's loyal people to know whenever anyone had doing something that would be of interest to the five.

Lyle knew that special program would analyze everything the government computers and servers did, especially those in the Department of Information where the five had hidden their dirty secret. And that special program would detect what he'd done within minutes once it got pass the firewall he'd built to protect his actions.

All I need is a few hours to reach my cabin in the wilderness where I can finish my work and destroy those five monsters. If my firewall can remain undetected for two or three hours, I'll be safe.

The elevator behind him and to his left signaled its arrival with a ding and the doors opened.

Lyle turned around and walked into the elevator like a tired government employee and pushed the button on the elevator panel for the basement garage. The elevator doors closed and started its downward movement.

Lyle's calm, bored exterior hid the turmoil of fear in his stomach.

Two years ago he'd located the cabin he was heading to when he accessed the Interior Department's computes. The cabin was listed as nonexistent because it had been there over a hundred years and apparently someone scanning for abandoned property in the wilderness had assumed after a hundred years the elements would have destroyed the cabin. But the stone cabin was as secure as it was the day it had been built. All he had to do was repair the roof. It was an easy job for him doing his vacation time. Even the outhouse, protected from the elements by a covered wooden hallway, was in good condition. Once he repaired the roof over it. The computer he'd acquired from a junk yard and put in the cabin was over twenty-five years old, an antique by today's standard, but still in working condition and almost impossible to trace because of its primitive program.

He had stocked the cabin with enough dry nonperishable food to last him a year and the spring half a mile from the cabin provided him with all the water he needed. He didn't trust the well sixty feet on the other side of the cabin from the outhouse. All he had to do was get outside the city limits away from the street cameras that monitored traffic, and he'd be safe and he could expose the five monsters to the world within ten days.

The elevator stopped at the garage level and Lyle walked out of it, stopped to look at the garage chart on the wall next to the elevator to locate the computer he needed to swipe out and walk to it and swipe out with his ID card, and from there to his late model car four hundred and forty feet away Five minutes later he was approaching the exit. The electric eye above the steel exit barrier scanned the government sticker on the left hand side of his car's windshield and raised the barrier.

He drove pass the barrier onto the apron that lead to the boulevard in front of the apron and stopped, as was his habit, and looked both ways. Though he knew there was little traffic on the boulevard at this time of the night. There wasn't anything around the Department of Information's headquarters building but a large park anyway. And the only people who'd be in it on a cool June night would be lovers and horse mounted police officers making sure anyone screwing in the park was a willing participant and over the age of consent.

Lyle drove out onto the boulevard and turned right heading north. He relaxed a little but kept his guard up while not acting as if he was being observant of everything around him.

The world was a computerized world where every vehicle, even bicycles, had computers attached to them, No one had privacy from the five even though the World Supreme Court had ruled that the right to privacy was a basic human right if people were to be able to exercise the other five freedoms that had been adopted from the United States Constitution and made a part of the New World Constitution over five hundred years ago.

He looked at the dashboard of his car and knew if the five were aware of him, and he hoped they weren't, they would be watching his every move.

If I can make it to the city limits and the forest preservers, where I've hidden my other car, I'll be safe.

He stuck to avenues and side streets as he drove toward the forest preservers just north of Crown and obeyed every traffic law. The last thing he needed was to attract the attention of a traffic cop. The cop would stop him and take down his license number after warning him and let him go. Basic human rights were an everyday thing in the world of the thirty-first century. But they meant nothing to the five whose only goal he'd learned over the years he'd read their secret documents was to live as rich, powerful men accountable to no one but themselves. Only power for themselves mattered to them. Fuck everyone else.

As soon as he was deep within the forest preserves, he hid his car among thick brush—knowing it would be located within a few hours or a day at the most by the forest preserve employees who constantly checked the forest preserves for garbage left by people. He walked the mile and a quarter to where he'd parked his other car. He got into it, started the electric engine, and drove off knowing he couldn't be traced by the five monsters, because the car had no tracking chip in it and its computer program was so primitive it couldn't be tracked even by the most sophisticated satellites.

What a world we live in. A world dominated by five monsters who have created the greatest horrors against the human race humans have ever known. Well, with luck I shall expose them to the world for the monsters they are and end their reign of terror.

Luck was still with Lyle, but not the sort of luck he expected.

CHAPTER 2

11 p.m. Friday

Paul Simpson was smiling at the joke Fred had told, because smiling was the best thing he could do to be polite when Fred told a joke. Fred Hammer's jokes were not only dull, but stupid and they never made sense because they either had no punch line or it was stupid.

The dinner party he'd given in his spacious one hundred million dollar home in the northwest section of the outer circle of Crown had been a success and his thirty year old beautiful mixed blood dark haired wife was happy. He was glad for that because Sunday morning when she drove to the cabin they had next to a lake fifteen mile east of the city in her million dollar cherry red sports car for a day of rest the bitch was going be drowned in the lake she loved swimming naked in with her young twenty-two year old lover. The stupid bitch didn't understand that when he acquired something, including a woman, it was his until he grew tired of it. Cheating on him had been a foolish mistake on Janet's part. Cheating on her was a privilege he, as a leader of the five, was entitled to do whenever he wanted and with whomever he wanted. He knew he deserved that privilege and she didn't because he was, in his mind, better than her. He was better than everybody except the four men attending his party.

Her lover would also be drowned and their deaths would be blamed upon the cocaine found in their systems—neither of them took drugs of any kind. But that didn't matter. His people, completely loyal to him, would make sure the cocaine was put in the food they ate before they went swimming.

Her funeral would be a nice quiet affair with only his fellow members and their wives and girlfriends present and the parents and relatives of the bitch. As for her lover's funeral, they could dump his body into one of the cities forty incinerators to be burned along with the rest of the city's garbage for all he cared.

His lawyers would handle the complaints of Janet's family and her lover's family. He'd have to give the bitch's family a few million dollars to keep them happy. But so what? He was worth over two hundred billion dollars and that didn't count the hundreds of billions more he had under assumed names and social security numbers in seven banks around the world. Banks that he and his four friends had controlling interest in.

He and his eleven guests were sitting in his library around a handmade glass coffee table with empty handmade China coffee cups and hand blown brandy glasses on it. The walls of the library had paintings hanging from them that were valued at only thirty million dollars and the carpet was a handmade Persian carpet made by Iranian artists. The wooden handmade shelves had over ten million dollars in first edition books on them. The sixty-five by fifty foot room was his favorite room in the thirty room house. Only his fifty by fifty foot study compared with the library.

Paul could have lived in a billion dollar house if he had wanted to, but he saw no reason for faulting his unlimited wealth and power. Not that he was concerned about the scandal sheets of the press writing about him. He, like his four fellow members, was as invisible to the press as they were to the rest of the world. To the world he amounted to no more than a successful businessman who loved giving to charities privately, and he insisted they not tell anyone about his generous gifts of money or they wouldn't get any more money.

Invisibility was a rule his ancestors and the ancestors of the other four men had obeyed without question—as well as they, because their lives and everything they possessed depended upon them remaining invisible to the world.

The com-cell in his left pants pocket vibrated.

He reached into his pocket and pulled it out and looked at the screen.

"Not another business meeting, darling," Janet said as she touched her husband's left hand with her right.

"No, my love," he said as he pushed a button on the screen and put the com-cell back in his pocket. "At least not until nine o'clock Monday morning."

"Hay, have you heard this one," Fred said as he waved his hands to get everyone's attention.

"No, we haven't," Steve Gamble said. "And I for one don't want to hear it."

Fred a short man with muscular hairy arms and thick black hair and a face that always looked sunburned looked at Steve, tall, thin, handsome with a comb over hair style that hid his bald spot, and said, "Steve you have no sense of humor."

"We've had a wonderful dinner with excellent wine, and a very nice dessert, and Ithink we're wearing out our welcome with our host and his lovely wife," Bruce Yearly said. Bruce was just as ruthless as the other four even though he looked like a Hollywood version of an accountant with his long face, short brown hair, and long thin fingers that didn't seem to go with his five foot seven frame. "So I should like to say thank you to Paul and Janet, and wish them a good night."

There was something in Paul's expression that told him the call he'd received wasn't just a business call.

"Bruce is right," Lilly, his present girlfriend, said as she stood up. "It has been a lovely night, and I think it's time to go."

"I agree," Denise Davis said as she looked to her left at her husband who was fighting the desire to go to sleep and losing the battle.

"Must you?" Paul asked them.

"Yeah, it is time to go," Larry Davis said standing up. His dark blond hair and somewhat square face gave him a very common look. He was only five ten with an average looking physique. "We've all got a busy Saturday tomorrow."

"Yes, ladies," a woman said. "We must get our husbands home so they can wake up early enough to tee off at the country club before the other members arrive."

The five men laughed and said nothing.

Within five minutes everyone had gathered at the front door and were saying long good-byes and making polite statements about hairstyles, evening gowns, jewelry, and what they were going to do over the week-end. Within another minutes Paul and Janet were closing the front door.

"To bed," Janet said as she walked toward the stairs leading upstairs to their bedroom.

Paul silently followed her.

Cleaning up was for the seven live-in servants they hired Twenty minutes later they were in bed making love. An hour and twenty minutes later Janet was in a sound sleep and Paul was downstairs in his study looking at his computer. The faces of his four male dinner guests were staring back at him on the divided screen as his face was staring at them on their divided computer screens and the faces of the others at each of the five men. This eliminated the need for using names.

"Is this important?" Steve asked.

"Our lives depend upon it," Paul said.

"What's happened?" Larry asked.

"A man working for the Department of Information managed to learn about our lab and download information about us," he said.

"Maybe we shouldn't be talking over the computer?" Bruce said.

"Don't worry," Fred assured him. "No one can access our computers. The fire walls change every thirty seconds."

"How was this done?" Larry asked. "Learning about the lab is impossible. No one knows it exists but us. And the people working there are one hundred percent loyal. They never leave the lab so no one could have learned of the lab from them."

"I don't know, but I suggest we find out as soon as possible," Paul said.

"Who is this man? And are you sure it's a man," Fred asked him.

"I don't know who it is, but it's a man," he said.

"And how do you know this?" Steve asked. He wasn't the leader of the five, Paul was, but he was the most intelligent of them.

"Three men left the Information Department around ten and a little after tonight each by a different route," Paul explained. "All three had worked late and had access to sensitive information. All three are also experts with computers, and one of them managed to get information as to where our lab is and got the information about us from the files we put in in the Department of Information."

"We must locate and kill these people as soon as possible," Fred said.

"No," Larry disagreed. "We must find out which of them stole the information then contact him and tell him the consequences of not returning the information immediately. Once we've got the information then we can have him killed in some accident."

"No, we can't do that," Steve said in a thoughtful manner.

"And why can't we?" Paul demanded as he looked at Steve.

"Because we need to first find out how he got the information. Information about the lab is in that information."

"That can be done after we have them," Bruce said.

"The last thing we need is three government employees disappearing or dying in accidents at the same time," Steve said.

"The press would begin to ask questions and so would the police. Not to mention insurance company investigators."

"So what do you suggest, Steve?" Larry asked him.

"We put our best people on this and make sure they don't to tell anyone what they are doing," he said. "We also have our computer people at the Department find out how this person managed to get into the Department's servers to get the information."

"We don't have to worry about our people talking," Paul assured them.

"Who are our best people?" Fred asked.

"Evelyn 102740 and Lee 801943," Paul said.

"Are they loyal?" Steve asked him.

"Not like our people, but they are the best hunters we've ever had," he said.

"Had?" Larry asked.

"Yes, had," he said. "They both retired ten years ago."

"What are they doing now?" Bruce asked.

"Living normal lives," he said. "They even have families."

"I thought we disposed of such people when they were no longer useful," Fred asked.

"We did," Paul said. "But with these two it was decided to see if they were capable of retiring to normal lives. And they have."

"How can you get them to come back and work for us?" Larry asked them.

"As I said, they have families," Paul said.

"They well not suspect anything?" Larry asked him.

"They have never suspected anything," Paul said.

"So when do we make contact with them?" Bruce asked.

"Our wives and girlfriends won't expect to see us until late afternoon around three or four I should say," Paul told them. "That gives us more than enough time to play eight holes of golf and contact them and meet them off club grounds in a safe spot."

"And you sure they will answer our call for a meeting?" Steve asked him.

"I can assure you they will answer," he said as he reached for the off switch on his computer. He sat staring at his computer for a few seconds before he picked up his com-cell on his desk and pushed a button.

"Yes, sir?" a male voice asked. There was no need for the man to ask who was calling. He knew only the five men had access to the com-cell he answered.

"Postpone the event at the lake tomorrow until a later time," Paul said and hung up.

He didn't bother thinking about what would happen to them if their secret got out. For five hundred years their secret had been safe and he couldn't imagine anyone exposing it.

CHAPTER 3

June 2, 12 p.m.

Lee Adams, a tall black male with a bald head and a hard body, had been living the life of a widower for five years and he still had not adjusted to the loss of his wife, nor did he have a desire to replace her with another woman. Two women had tried replacing her, but he'd refused their attempts to convince him to marry them which resulted in an immediate end to their relationships. But that didn't bother Lee. His son and daughter more than made up for the emptiness in his life when his wife had died of a sudden heart attack. Even in the thirty-first century heart attacks accounted for a large number of sudden deaths among people over the age of fifty.

He didn't see his grown children more than once a week. Sometimes only twice a month, but he called them twice a week to find out how they were doing and if they needed anything. They were both working good jobs and had no need of financial assistance from their father, but his investments and ample private pension fund had made him financially comfortable, and he liked spending money on his children. He also liked taking ocean cruises when he had a girlfriend, reading history, mystery novels, and taking long walks in the Brookline Zoological Park just outside Crown City. He was even trying his hand at writing a book on the history of world in the twenty-fifth century. A century he found interesting because of the great political and economic changes that had occurred within that century in the last thirty years, changes that had forced the nations of the world to unite and create the World Government during the last years of the twenty-fifth century.

Lee was interested in answering the question what had caused the events of the last quarter of the twenty-fifth century to force the world to become politically united? He had the feeling that if he could answer that question the historians of the world would hate him for doing what they had failed to do, and admire him for doing it. He would not be forgotten when he died.

Lee was in the study of his four bedroom brick townhouse looking out the window at the attractive redhead who lived across the street from him wondering if he should be friendlier to her. She was on her knees with her back to him planting flowers in the bare dirt area between her house and lawn. So far he hadn't done more than have a few short talks with her about how to fight crabgrass and grubs that ate the roots of plants and killed them.

That wide ass and thighs and hips of hers say I should be more of a polite neighbor.

The old fashion twentieth century phone on his desk ran and he reached for it.

"Lee, speaking," he said.

"Glad to see you're still alive, Mr. Adams," Paul said.

Lee immediately recognized the voice, and said, "Fuck you!" and hung up.

The phone rang again and he picked it up.

"I suggest you don't hang up again, Mr. Adams," Paul said. "You know what I am capable of doing."

"What do you want, asshole?" he asked in as nasty a voice as he could summon.

Lee was more than aware of what Paul Simpson could do to him. He'd worked for him for twenty years framing people for crimes they didn't commit simply because they got in Paul's way. It was a part of his life he never told his wife about or talked about. It was a part of his life he wished he could forget, but couldn't because of the pain he'd caused people who had never done anything to him.

During that time he'd amassed enough information to prove he was innocent of doing anything wrong, though he wasn't, and that Paul was guilty of numerous crimes that could put him in prison for life. Where Lee hoped he would one day end up.

But it was information he couldn't use without the Justice Department asking how and why had he gotten the information? A question he didn't want to answer. Its only value was insurance that Paul would never move against him.

That asshole Paul must know I've got information on what he had me do in the past. So why hasn't he moved against me. He looked out the window at the redhead's ass and thighs and thought, *because that piece of filth doesn't know where I've hidden the information. He can't afford to move against me until he finds out.*

"A meeting with you at 2333 West Bright Road at one o'clock," Paul said. "And don't tell me you don't know where that's at. Knowing your abilities at finding things it will be no problem for you to find the place. Come alone and don't bring a weapon." Paul hung up.

Lee placed the receiver back on the cradle and trembled a little. There were few things, and no man or woman in the world he feared, but Paul Simpson was the exception. He was the only human Lee had ever met who didn't have an ounce of humanity in him, and probably no soul, though he did an excellent job at pretending he had both. And Lee knew that better than any man or woman on Earth because he'd spent twenty years working for that inhuman asshole. And he'd cursed every moment of those twenty years when he was in Paul Simpson's employ. It was also doing those twenty years he'd amassed the information to protect himself.

He looked at the clock on his desk and decided he'd better get going. He got up and walked out of his study and up the stairs to his bedroom. He opened the closet door and walked into the back of the closet and knelt down and pushed one of the floor boards.

A three inch wide six inch long section popped up to reveal a lever inside. He reached in and pulled the lever up. A section of the scared wall right in front of him dropped down and he reached inside it and removed an electric twenty-four hundred volt semi-automatic hand gun. It had a range of six hundred yards and had a muzzle attachment underneath the barrel that could be quickly snapped into place, and that could reduce the loud cracking sound of firing it to no more than the sound of him cracking his knuckles. The muzzle attachment also eliminated the bright flash produced when the hand gun was fired. The muzzle attachment was his own invention and no one knew about it.

When Paul said don't bright a weapon that meant he'd be a damn fool if he didn't. Paul was not the sort of person you met alone without bringing a weapon because Paul was never alone.

He closed the wall section after he made sure the weapon was charged, and then closed the floor section. Five minutes later he was in his car following the directions his computer-cell (com-cell) phone had given him.

Attached to the dashboard just below the clock was an alert monitor, another of his inventions. It was a simple electrical detecting unit that could detect the presence of police radar cars and speed detecting cameras on light poles. Such devices were easy to acquire in the thirty-first century except his didn't scan for radar and cameras because the electrical current the scanning ones gave off enabled the police to detect them. His looked like a cell phone charger, which it was, and didn't flash. If it picked up radar impulses a small map appeared on the small screen under the monitor showing where the impulses were coming from more than a mile away. It was also designed by him to burn up the chip inside it if it was removed from the dashboard without first entering the three digit code. His com-cell possessed the same ability, which is why he hadn't bought a new com-cell in over twenty years.

He drove faster than normal when he was sure there were no cop cars or speed detecting cameras around. He had no intention of arriving at exactly one o'clock. He wanted to arrive at least ten minutes earlier so he could look over 2333 West Bright Road. He had never heard of the address, but he knew it had to be someplace isolated and comfortable. Paul wasn't the sort of man who'd go someplace common people went. Lee knew the thought of being common sickened Paul.

Lee arrived with eleven minutes to spare.

Bright Road turned out to be a single lane road leading into a section of the forest preserve at least two miles from the nearby building which was a part of a private country club.

Lee parked his car among some bushes on the road facing out toward the main road and got out and walked quietly through the woods until he saw a faded white house with six cars, five were luxury cars, parked in front of it. The sixth car was a beat-up looking four door minivan that had large all terrain tires on it. He moved around the back and sides of the house to make sure there were no guards with weapons hiding in the wood. If there had been he would have backed off and gone home and dealt with the consequences later.

Appears safe, he thought as he walked back to where he packed his car.

A minute later he parked on the road facing out and got out and walked up to the door. He started to knock, but decided banging on it was better. If nothing else, it would piss Paul off. He knew Paul hated loud noises. He had very sensitive ears. He stepped back and kicked the bottom of the door as hard as he could.

"Who's that?" Fred asked in a surprised voice as he turned in his seat and looked at the door.

"Lee Adams," Paul said in a cold voice. He was sitting behind a card table playing solitaire with a new deck of cards and didn't bother looking at the door. On the card table was a small leather bag about the size of a paperback book. They had again become popular among readers.

"How do you know?" Steve asked him as he stood up and backed to a wall. He wanted to make sure that whatever came through the front door had to come face to face with him.

"That man is arrogant," Paul said. "One of you let him in."

Bruce got up from his position next to a window and walked down the short hall to the door and opened it. The hard expression on Lee's face surprised him and he backed away without saying anything.

"Come in, Lee," Paul said, without looking up from his game of solitaire.

Lee, with his hands behind his back like he was in a relaxed position, his weapon was in a holster in the small of his back under his loose fitting pale black shirt looked pass Bruce and saw only four other people in the well-furnished living room. He looked at the door on the wall of the hall near the front door and said, "If you were going to have six people here, you should have told the sixth person to hide their car in the woods."

The closet door opened and a good looking woman with reddish brown hair and a weathered face wearing jeans and a white blouse with short sleeves stepped out of the closet.

"I told them I should have parked my car in the woods," she said as she closed the closet door and walked into the living room of the house.

Bruce stepped back to allow Lee to enter.

"Go," Lee told him.

Bruce released the door knob and walked back into the living room and returned to his seat near the window.

Lee followed him. He left the door open He moved to the wall to his left and looked around the room.

Paul glanced up at him for a few seconds and returned to his game saying,

"As cautious as ever I see."

"You're Mr. Lee Adams," Larry asked him.

Lee nodded as he took a step from the wall and put his hands behind his back as he looked at the door across the room to the right.

"You don't have to worry, Mr. Adams," Fred said. "There's no one here but us."

He looked at the woman and added, "And her."

"Nice of you to include me," she said with a smirk on her face.

"He knows that, Fred," Paul said in a calm voice as he stopped playing solitaire and looked up at Lee. "Like Evelyn he looked around the woods before he knocked on the door." Then he quickly added, "Oh, sorry, before he kicked on the door."

Evelyn gave Lee a nod of approval of his action.

"Why am I here?" Lee asked.

"We want you to find a man who works for the Department of Information," Steve told him. "Why is our business? You will work with Ms. Summers. And we don't have a lot of time. So you will begin immediately."

Evelyn looked at Lee with eyes that said she was experienced at whatever she did.

Lee looked her over noticing her firm shape and the fact she carried a wallet in her front pants pocket and a com-cell in a pouch on the left side of her belt. He noticed her jeans fit loose enough for her to hide a weapon on the inside of one of her legs. He assumed she was carrying a small electric semi-automatic.

"Don't bother asking them what's important about this man?" Evelyn told him. "I asked that ten minutes before you got here and got the same answer."

"Your salary will be five million dollars, plus an expense account," Paul said, picking up the leather bag and holding it out for Lee to see.

"Both of you will receive five million dollars," Larry said. "And that bag contains keycards that will allow you to go anywhere you wish in any government agency."

"Does this man have a name?" he asked.

"If we knew that, Lee," Paul said. "We wouldn't need you."

"Why do I need a partner?" he asked as he looked at Evelyn.

"Because two heads are better than one," Bruce said. "One of you might overlook something the other won't."

"Is that all?" he asked.

"That's all," Paul said. "Other than notifying us when you've found the man."

"How will we know when we've found him?" Evelyn asked him.

"Trust us," Steve said. "You'll know."

Paul laid the bag on the table and stood up. "Let's go, gentlemen, we've better things to do than talking in this little house." He walked toward the door with the others following him.

Evelyn followed them and stopped at the door and watched as each got into his car and drive off. Lee stayed in the living room watching her. As soon as they were gone she closed the door and turned to face Lee.

Lee picked up the bag from the card table and walked pass her, opened the door, and walked out of the house. He didn't stop until he was in the woods across from the house.

Evelyn stared at him for a few seconds before she followed him.

He stared at her without saying a word.

"You don't like those assholes any more than I do, do you?" she asked him.

"We have to talk," he told her and walked away from her into the woods.

Evelyn followed him making sure to remain on his left side and two feet behind him.

CHAPTER 4

1:20 p.m.

They had walked over a hundred feet into the woods before Lee stopped and put the leather bag carefully on the ground and walked a hundred feet from the bag before he stopped and spoke to her in a soft voice.

Evelyn had followed him.

"Tell me about yourself." He told her.

"You don't want to know about me, and I don't want to know about you," she said. "What you want to know is why they picked me to work with you."

"Okay," he said.

"I'm' what they use to call a hacker," she said. "I can get into any computer or server in the world. I understand them like I've got some sixth sense. That is why those five assholes picked me to work with you."

"You use to work for them?" he asked her.

"Your turn, Lee," she said.

"I'm a tracker," he said. "Not of animals but of people. I'm good at finding people who don't want to be found. Like you, I've got a sixth sense about finding people."

"So, you can find people other people can't find, and I can get into their computers," she said. "Together we should be able to find this man they want found."

"There is a question," he said.

26

"I know," she said with a nod. "Why do they want this man found?"

He looked in her face and said nothing.

"Because he has something they don't want anyone to know about," she said.

He nodded.

"And once we've found this man and gotten what they don't want anyone to know about they're going to kill us and this man. They can't afford the luxury of assuming we didn't read or listen to what this man has on them. What's that old expression from the twentieth century? Dead men tell no tales."

"Do you have family?" he asked.

She stared at him for a few seconds before she answered. His question disturbed and frightened her. "Two daughters, four grandchildren, and an ex-husband I don't give a damn about but my daughters and grandchildren like him."

"I've a son and daughter. I'm a widower."

"Sorry to hear that," she said.

"There is another expression from the twentieth century," he said.

She looked at him and said nothing.

"We're up shit creek without a paddle, there's a hole in the boat, and a storm's coming and we don't have life preservers."

"So what do we do?"

"We, my dear Evelyn, do our jobs," he said as he turned around and looked at the bag lying on the ground. "But we use our own resources."

"Can we trust each other?" she asked, looking at the bag.

"Considering the power those five have, do we have a choice?"

"Have you had lunch?" she asked.

"What has lunch got to do with our problem?" he asked.

"I have a place where we can eat and talk in private and there are things there we can use," she said as she started walking toward her car.

Lee turned to get the bag.

"Leave it," she said.

He turned and followed her.

She walked to the trunk of her car taking a set of keys out of her right pants pocket.

"What's wrong with an electric key?" he asked her.

"Computer locks are too easy to override," she said as she stuck the key into the trunk's lock and twisted it. "Learn one thing now, Mr. Adams," she said as she locked the trunk and raised the lid.

"Lee," he said. He wanted this woman to feel relaxed around him better to figure out if he could trust her.

"Okay, Lee, I'm Evelyn," she replied. "Electric locks and computer locks are easy to get pass. All you have to do is confuse the code."

"They shut down," he said.

"No, the code in them shuts down and the lock opens up."

"Why is that?"

"Because the code in the lock interprets the confusion as a new code being installed and opens the lock's chip to accept a new code. So stick to dead bolt key locks. They've been around over ten thousand years and the locks open only with the matching key."

She reached into the trunk and took out a plain wooden box seven inches long, five wide, and three inches thick and lined on the inside with metal. "Follow me and be quiet," she said as she turned around and walked back into the woods.

Lee followed her.

She stopped next to the leather bag and knelt down and opened the box and covered the bottom of the box with dirt. Then she picked up the leather bag sat it inside the box and covered it with dirt and closed the box snapping the brass catch in place.

"Now we can talk," she said, standing up with the box in her left hand.

"The metal inside the box is lead and the dirt is an extra blocking device for any signals from entering or leaving the bag," he said. He still wasn't sure he could trust her, but so far she'd proven she didn't trust the five men. But that could mean she was only a very careful, but loyal, agent working for them.

"The more electrically complex our world becomes the easier it is to blind the electrical equipment."

"So where to from here?" he asked her.

"To a hole in the ground," she told him.

"They can track us using the travel chips within our cars," he said.

"Don't tell me you don't know how to get around that?" she asked him.

"Place a nine volt battery next to it to scramble the signal," he said.

"Slip one in the pouch you carry your com-cell in," she said. "It'll do the same thing to the chip in your com-cell."

He nodded and asked, "Where's this hole in the ground?"

"Know where Barrel Road is?" she asked him as she started walking back to her car.

"In the inner city," he said as he followed her.

"Go to 1723 East Barrel Road," she said. "Park in the lot across the street, and don't worry about them seeing us."

"They have other people out watching us, you know," he said.

"Which is why we're going to 1723 East Barrel Road," she said.

"You should know one thing, Evelyn," he said as he walked beside her. "I don't trust those five assholes. If I decide I can't trust you, I'll kill you."

"And I you," she said.

Lee always carried three nine volt batteries in his car just in case he didn't want the police or anyone else knowing where he was going. It took him less than two minutes to place one next to the travel chip in his car's engine and one next to his com-cell. Then he left five seconds after Evelyn did for Barrel Road.

The parking lot across the street from 1723 Barrel Road was part of the neighborhood park with mothers sitting around talking while their children made as much noise as they could playing. No one paid any attention to him as he parked his car in the lot facing the street and walked across the street to 1723 which was an old three story apartment building in excellent shape. Evelyn was waiting in the lobby for him as he walked up the steps and entered the lobby. She turned around, opened the glass and wood door, and walked through it and down a hallway to a door which she opened with a keycard and entered. She stood to one side as Lee entered the dark room and closed the door.

"You think they're watching us?" she asked him.

"No, but they've got someone watching us," he said as he stopped and waited for her. "And they're probably loyal killers."

"What do you know about them?" she asked as she walked pass him through the dark room.

"What's in here?" he asked as he followed close behind her. The darkness disturbed him. He didn't know if there was someone in the room with them.

"Nothing. I rent this room through a company in Asia that doesn't know it exists."

"Then why are we here?"

"We're going to the hole in the ground," she said. "Answer my question."

"Paul Simpson, the guy playing solitaire is wealthy, I don't know how wealthy, and has contacts all over the world among the politically powerful and rich. Laws don't concern him because he can get around all of them probably because he's got something on all of those politically powerful rich people he knows. He's like an ancient Roman Emperor. He's got absolute power and as far as I know unlimited wealth. Or at least access to unlimited wealth. But he doesn't live like he does."

"What about the other four men?" Evelyn asked him.

"They're like him, rich and powerful, and they stick together. Why I don't know."

"How long did you work for him?" She stopped in front of another door and took some keys out of her pocket and opened the door.

"Twenty years," he said.

"What did you do?" she asked as she opened the door.

"I got information on people he wanted me to get information on once I found them."

"What sort of information?" she asked as she walked through the door into another dark room.

"Dirty secrets. How do you know him?" he asked, wondering where the hell he was going.

"I don't know him that well because I worked for Steve Gamble," she said as she closed the door and reached for a light switch on the wall to her right and turned on a single light bulb in the center of the ceiling. "My job was getting into the computer systems of people he wanted to know things about. Mostly about investments."

"So, like me you were violating the law for him and the others," Lee said.

"For Steve, but he probably shared what I gave him with the others," Evelyn said.

"And like you I didn't like doing what I did so after thirty years I quit."

"So why aren't you dead?" he asked as he looked about the closet size room.

"Because like you, Lee, I developed a life insurance policy," she told him. "I end up dead, Steve Gamble and the other asses end up with the law breathing down the backs of their necks with information that could put them away for life."

"So why did you answer their call?"

She walked to the back of the closet size room, knelt down and pushed against the sideboard at the back of the room.

He heard a soft clicking sound and the room moved downward.

"I was afraid not to," she said as she stood up.

"This building is centuries old, isn't it?" he asked.

"About three hundred years. It was originally a storage building for equipment for the subway system," she said. "Two hundred years ago it was renovated into an apartment building and has remained one since."

"How did you find out about this elevator?" he asked.

"Twenty years ago, Steve wanted me to get information on a man whose company was renovating the subway system. He wanted to sell the man's company the building material they'd need, and get a fat bonus from the man. I found out about this building's original purpose and about this elevator."

"But the man was honest," he added.

"I got the information, and the man ended up dying two months later of a massive stroke even though the man's family had no history of strokes."

"And Steve Gamble convinced the heirs to do business with him," Lee said.

"I don't know how he did it, nor do I care," Evelyn said. "But everyone came off with a lot of money in their pockets and I rented this apartment with this elevator."

"And nobody but you knew about it," he said.

"And I made sure no one would ever find out, because I wiped out or altered the old blueprints of this building and its original purpose," she said. "Why did you answer Paul's call?"

"Like you, I was afraid not to," he said. "Does the subway still run under this section of Crown City?"

"No, not for the last two hundred years. But don't worry it's in good shape."

"How do you know?" he asked as he felt the room stop moving.

"Because I know how to access the robots that maintain the subway system," she said. "And the city always buys more building material to maintain the subway than is needed. I just take a little to keep the part under this section of the city in safe condition."

"Your hole in the ground," he said.

"Exactly," she said. "Tell me, Lee, do you trust me?"

"I don't know," he said, remembering the gun in the holster in the small of his back.

"Well, don't shoot me with that gun you're carrying and I won't shoot you with the one I'm carrying," she said as she walked to the door and opened it.

He followed her out of the closet into a concrete room ten feet long and half as wide. "It appears, considering who we're working for, we have no choice but to trust each other."

"Why were you afraid not to answer Paul's call?" she asked him.

"For the same reason you answered their call," he told her. "I have children."

She closed the door and pushed a button on a metal panel that turned off the light in the closet and sent it back up. "So what do you suggest?"

"We find this man and what he wants and go from there," he said.

"Good plan," she agreed.

"How much experience have you got in dealing with killers?"

"I'm a computer hacker, Lee," she said. "Not a killer."

"Well, be aware of one thing," he told her. "We're being watched by people who are killers."

CHAPTER 5

Lee followed Evelyn through an old subway tunnel that had a carpet of dust on the tracks and the platform in which they left tracks.

"We're leaving tracks," he told her as he looked behind them.

"Don't worry," she told him. "The robots will clean the platform and remove our tracks."

"You can program subway robs to clean this abandoned line?" he asked as he followed her.

"That I can," she replied.

"And the subway people won't know about it?" he asked her.

"No, they don't, because they've got a hundred or more robots cleaning the subways every day, and they don't always know where they are, or care as long as the parts of the subway people use are clean," she answered.

They walked half a block before she stopped in front of a steel door, raised the metal lid on a keypad to the right of the door, and punched three numbers into the keypad. A clicking sound came from inside and the door opened on silent hinges. Evelyn walked into the corridor with Lee behind her and the door automatically closed and locked after them. Lights came on in the corridor as they walked.

"Where is this hole in the ground?" he asked as he followed her down the corridor.

"Hungry?" she asked him as she stopped in front of another steel door.

"Yes, and I don't like being someplace I don't know about," he said, stopping behind her.

"Evelyn Summers," she said.

The steel door in front of her opened and lights came on inside the room beyond the door. She walked into the room with Lee behind her.

Lee was amazed. He had expected some dirty room filled with dust and spiders and roaches and scurrying rats. Instead he was looking at a room that looked like the living room of an expensive condo. The pale blue carpet on the floor went well with the four white concrete walls and the dozen colorful paintings on the walls and the clean comfortable looking furniture. Light came from a glass chandelier hanging from the ceiling.

"What do you think about my hole in the ground?" she asked.

"No one knows about this place but you?" he asked as he looked at a lighted hallway fifty feet in front of him.

"Just me," she said, noticing him looking at the hallway. "That leads to a study and two bedrooms each with their own bathrooms and a kitchen and a dining room."

"And that way we came is the only way in and out of here?"

"One of them," she asked. "Let's go get something to eat then get busy on our assignment."

"Are there any traffic cameras in the neighborhood above?"

"One of the north corner," she told him. "Why?"

"Because I'd like to see if anyone is watching the building we entered," he said.

"Then let's get some sandwiches and coffee and go to my study," she said.

Twenty minutes later they were sitting behind her desk in her study looking at a six foot wide four foot high sheet of glass on the opposite wall that became a TV screen as she soon as said 'On'. Underneath it on the desk was a computer keyboard without a computer.

"The computer is built into the keyboard," he said, looking at it.

"Basic computer," she said. "With a simple firewall and very hard to get into unless you know the code."

"Get into that traffic camera on the north corner you said was there," he told her.

Evelyn used the keyboard to get into the camera. "Okay, what now?" she asked.

"Scan the neighborhood, especially the park and parking lot," he said.

She used the mousy next to the keyboard to do as he said.

"Stop," he said.

She stopped the scan on a park bench under a tree with low hanging branches.

"See that guy?" he asked her.

"Yeah, the one in the park maintenance jacket sitting on the bench. What about him?" she asked.

"He's right where we can't get a clear shot of his face, because of the low hanging branches."

"So what?" Evelyn said.

"Scan the cars in the parking lot," he told her.

She looked at the information on the screen about the camera and said as she started scanning the cars, "Not enough magnification for a close up of anyone in those cars."

"Stop," he said. "See that car parked twenty feet away from the man on the bench?"

"Yeah, I see it," she said, looking closely at it. "There's someone in it."

"Wearing sunglasses, and looking around as if she's looking for someone," he said.

"How do you know it's a woman in that car?"

"Because male and female killers working together attract less attention than two men," he said. "Two females would have been better, but those five guys aren't good at picking killers no one would notice."

"I didn't notice them as we entered the buildings," Evelyn said. "Why did you?"

"That's a small neighborhood park where mothers take their children to play. Such a place wouldn't require any maintenance unless the swing sets, teeter-totters, and slides were being replaced. Cleaning is done at night by robots monitored by humans. And notice there's no one in that park but mothers with their young children. Those two are as out of place as shit on a dining room table at dinner time."

"We're being watched?" she asked.

"Yes, and soon as we get what those five assholes want, we'll be killed."

"But I walked around that house just like you did, Lee," she said. "And I saw no one in the woods around the house."

"Because they were deep in the woods across the road where we weren't supposed to see them," he said as he looked at the box on the small table near the wall.

"Don't worry," she said, noticing where he was looking. "They can't track the box." She looked at the box then looked up at him. "If those two in the park aren't really park maintenance how did they track us to the house?"

"They used the old fashion way," he told her. "Visual. They kept us within sight."

"So what do we do?" she asked.

"Paul and his thug buddies won't move against our families until they've got what this man from the Department of Information has," he said. "So they're safe. But they're being watched."

Evelyn leaned back in the chair and ran her hands through her hair. She was afraid even though she didn't show it. "So what do we do?"

"Can you duplicate the cards in that bag?" he asked. "But removing the tracking chips inside them?"

"Yes, that's easy," she said.

"And the cards will still work?" he asked.

"Yes, they should, but I can check them to make sure they do."

"And there's another way out of here?"

"Yes."

"How many? And where?"

She didn't answer.

"Listen to me, Evelyn. We're both dead if we can't avoid the killers they've assigned to watch us and so are our families," he told her. "We trust each other and work together, or we die and our families, too. And rest assured our families won't have quick painless deaths. I've worked for Paul before and I know the kind of vicious man he is. He is capable of anything."

She leaned forward and typed on the keyboard.

A diagram of the subway tunnel they were in appeared on the monitor along with the entrances and exits from it.

"It won't take them long to find out about this place, Lee, once they find that elevator," she said. "And this is the only hole in the ground I've got."

"I've got two others but they're not in the ground," he said. "How good are you with this weapon you've got strapped on the inside of your left leg?"

"How do you know it's on the inside of my left leg?"

"You're wearing baggy jeans with a slit on the inside of the left leg and you're right handed," he said. "But you could be ambidextrous."

"I'm not," she said. "But I can shoot well enough, but I've never killed anyone.

Like I told you, I'm a hacker. Not a killer."

"Well, I've killed before in the service of Paul before, and I can hack into computers, too."

"So we leave and go to one of those holes in the ground you've got?"

He gave her a hard, cold look. His brown eyes were almost as lifeless as dead wood. "Can I trust you?"

"Yes, you can. Can I trust you?"

He stared into her gray blue eyes and said, "My word on it. And I don't like giving my word to anyone except my children."

Evelyn extended her right hand. "My word on my trust of you."

He took her hand and shook it. She had a strong reassuring grip.

"Let's see what I can do with those cards it that plastic bag," she said as she released his hand and stood up.

Lee watched her as she walked to the table and picked up the box and returned to the desk and sat down. He put their coffee cups and plates on the far side of the desk, as she leaned over to her right and opened the bottom drawer of the desk and took out a small plastic box that contained a tool kit. She placed it on the desk next to the box, and started to open the box.

Lee grabbed her hand and stopped her. "Won't they pick up the signal those cards are sending out?" he asked her.

"Too much concrete and steel around us for them to pick up any signal," she told him.

"How are you going to duplicate the cards?" he asked her.

"See that metal box on that table the cards were on?" she asked him.

"Yes," he answered.

"Bring it here," she said.

"Tell me exactly what you are going to do, before you do it," he demanded.

"Inside that metal box are blank cards and a machine I can use to make exact copies of the cards in the bag in this box," she said. "They'll look and work exactly like the cards in the bag, but they won't be traceable."

He nodded his understanding and got up and walked to the table and picked up the three foot long one foot wide ten inches thick metal box and brought it to the desk and sat it next to the wooden box.

Evelyn opened the metal box and took out a machine that looked like a key cutting machine, but with slots in both ends for inserting plastic cards. She noticed him looking around the machine.

"If you're looking for a cable to plug into an outlet, forget it. This machine is battery operated, and the battery is self-charging." She pointed to a small light bulb on the top center of the machine. "When that's red, it means the batteries have to be replaced."

"You come down here often enough to do that?" he asked her. He still had the feeling he couldn't trust her, but he also realized he was in a position where he had no choice but to trust her.

"The battery can last five years," she answered. "They can be found in any electronic or general store."

She turned the machine on, opened the small box, and picked up the leather bag and shook the dirt from it before she placed it next to the machine on the desk. She opened the bag and took out four plastic cards, two with their names on each, and placed them on the desk next to the metal box.

As soon as Evelyn removed the four plastic cards from the case, they began to emit a signal.

The woman in the car took her com-cell from her left pants pocket and pushed a button and said, "They've taken the cards out of the bag, sir?"

"Continue listening," Paul said into the com-cell lying on the table. He was sitting at a table in the lounge of his private country club with his four friends around him. They heard what the woman had said.

"Do you know where they are?" Fred asked the woman.

"Inside the building in front of me, sir," she said.

"Why didn't they just get started on the assignment?" Larry asked.

"I do not know—," the woman began.

"I'm not speaking to you!" he snapped at the woman.

"Keep watching the building," Paul said in a calm voice. "Report any movements they make." He reached out and touched a button on the com-cell that turned off the sound. "You must understand Lee, Larry," he said. "He's man who doesn't trust us."

"Neither does Evelyn, apparently," Steve said. "Or she would have reported their movements to us."

"And we wouldn't have lost the signal after they left the cabin," Bruce said. "Choosing them may have been a foolish mistake on our part, Paul."

"No," he said as he smiled. "Evelyn's an excellent hacker, and Lee's an excellent trackers and hunter of people. Together they will find what was taken, how it was acquired, and who took it."

"What we need to know is how this person managed to get the information in the first place," Steve said.

"That we will find out before he or she dies," Paul assured them.

Evelyn took a Phillips screwdriver from the plastic tool case and scratched under their names on the cards.

"Why not scratch the logo where the chips are?" Lee asked her.

"The tracking devices aren't there," she said. "Take four blank cards out of the box please. Don't worry about the bank names on them when we use them the banks won't know about it, but the private accounts of our five employers will. But the five won't know when or where we use them or what we're buying with them. All they'll know is what it will cost them."

"Why won't they know what we buy?"

"Only if they know the store we shopped in."

"Good," he said as he removed four cards from the box. "We will travel first class." He placed the cards on the table next to the machine.

Evelyn took one of the scratched cards and stuck it into the left slot of the machine and a blank card into the right slot and pushed the button to the right of the bulb.

Both cards entered the machine and three seconds later came out the same slots. The blank cards had their names on them. She repeated her actions three more times before she said, "All done. Clean un-traceable cards." She picked up the cards with his name on them and handed them to him. "Now take out your com-cell, open it up, and remove the chip inside, and smash it."

He did as she said, dropping the chip on the carpeted floor and smashing the heel of his left foot down on it. "What do I do with this?" he asked, holding his com-cell.

"Toss it into the trash can," she told him as she did the same with her com-cell. "It's not worth a damn without that chip."

"I've got personal information on my com-cell," he said.

"Getting another one won't be hard and you can put your information on it," she said. "And they won't be able to track it."

Lee nodded as he said, "I know where I can get two more com-cells."

She leaned back in her chair and looked up at him. "What now?"

"We get out of here," he said.

"Let's eat first," she said. "I'm still hungry."

"No," he said. "It could be the last meal you'll eat."

"You think they know what we've done?" she asked him with a surprised look on her face.

"Those two across the street wouldn't be there if they didn't know where we were," he said. "It won't take them but a few minutes to figure out how to get down here once they've entered the building."

Evelyn stood up saying, "Follow me. But where we're going after we leave my hole in the ground, I haven't the slightest idea."

"I do," Lee said as he started for the door.

"Sir," the woman said as she looked at the static on the screen of her com-cell. "We are no longer receiving the signal from their com-cells or the cards."

Damn, Paul thought.

"So what do we do now?" Fred said.

"Get into that building immediately," he ordered the woman. "And find out what's going on."

"Isn't it apparent?" Steve said as he looked at his four friends. "They suspected they were bugged, and now they've destroyed the bugs."

"It doesn't matter," Paul said. "The two we assigned to watch them will find and track them. We may not be able to hear what they're doing, but we will still have eyes on them."

"I don't know about that," Steve said thoughtfully.

"What the hell does that mean?" Bruce asked him.

"If they were smart enough to destroy the cards and their com-cells they may be smart enough to get out of that building without being seen," he said.

Larry chuckled and said, "Does it really matter? They will have to go to the Department of Information to start their hunt for who has our information. We can assign more people to look for them in addition to our man at the Department."

Paul looked up at him and nodded his agreement. "Let's go home. Our people will report on those two as soon as they show up at the Department."

❧

CHAPTER 6

4 p.m.

Getting out of Evelyn's hole in the ground wasn't as hard as Lee had thought it would be. She decided to use the third exit out of the hole which went through the main sewer in that section of the city. When she suggested it, Lee imagined himself walking through miles of raw, stinking sewage with rats as big as small dogs and cockroaches as big as mice running around them trying to attack them as a source of fresh food. Instead she took him to an exchange section where two main sewer lines intersected next to an automated storage station where automated inspection carts the size of small trucks were located. One of the four carts at the station was automatically activated every five hours by computers at the main sewer center, located under city hall which many people in Crown thought was the appropriate place for it to be, and sent on an inspection of the section of the sewer it was located in. The inspection cart moved at a speed of two miles per hour and did a thorough job of inspecting the sewer looking for cracks in the concrete foundation and using its laser ray or wide beam to kill rats and cockroaches. Which Lee thought was a good thing since he didn't like cockroaches, and he wasn't fond of rats, either.

Fortunately for them there was an open cargo area on the back of the cart which they hitched a ride on sitting side by side.

"Where are we headed?" Evelyn asked him.

"As soon as we reach an east-west line, we get on a cart heading east," he said.

"And from there?"

"We go east on an inspector's cart."

"How do we get one of them?"

"Leave that to me," he said.

"Where do we stop?"

"We get off under police headquarters," he said.

She looked at him like he was a little crazy and said, "You know those five assholes have people in the police department?"

"Just one," he said.

"How do you just one?"

"Because I know who the person is," he said.

"Someone you use to work with?"

"No, that person died years ago. Of what I don't know."

"You know his replacement?"

"Her replacement not his. The five prefer using women. Plain looking women who are good workers and don't attract attention."

"How do you know this person?"

"I make it a point to keep my information up to date."

"Why?" she asked then quickly added. "I know you use to work for Paul."

"I learned one thing working for Paul," Lee said. "Know who you're working with, and don't let them know anything about your private life. Paul likes to keep detailed records on people."

"He knows a lot about you, don't he?"

Lee nodded and said, "More than I'd like him to know." He didn't want to admit he suspected Paul knew more about him than he knew about himself, and that he had spent his life wondering exactly what it was. What frightened Lee was he had the feeling he didn't want to know what it was that Paul knew about him.

"That includes those other four?"

"You noticed he was the leader of them," he told her.

"Yes, I did," she said. She rode in silence for a few minutes before she started speaking. "I started working for them when I was twenty and in college. I proved to be very good with computers, and I was hired the year I graduated. I was paid three times the salary my fellow graduates started earning when they found jobs. My expense account was equal to their starting salaries. I lived a very comfortable life and travelled to every major city in the world during the thirty years I worked for Steve Then, I quit one day and walked away from the job."

"What type of job?" he asked.

"Just what I told you. Getting into every computer system in the world they wanted me to get into," she said. "I felt like a slave. Doing as I was told without asking questions."

"Why did they let you go?"

"As best I can figure out, they had a replacement for me."

"And they didn't kill you?" he asked, looking at her out of the corner of his right eye. His face held a hard expression of doubt and confusion. Never in Lee's life had he felt like he had a question he couldn't answer. A question he really didn't want an answer to.

"What about you?" Evelyn asked him.

"Like I said, I was a tracker. I found people they, especially Paul, wanted me to find and got information on them. What happened to them after I found them and got the information on them I don't know."

"And don't want to know, do you."

"Are you any different from me?" he asked her.

"Identical," she said. A second passed before she started laughing.

"What's funny?" he asked her as he looked at her.

"You and I," she said.

"There's nothing funny about me," he said and added, "Or you either."

"We both spent years working for two of five men we hated, we quit the jobs, then years later here we are back where we started. Working for the five people in the world we like the least."

They rode in silence for a mile before Lee spoke.

"I fell in love with a wonderful woman I wanted to spend the rest of my life with ten years after I started working for Paul," he said. "That was my main reason for telling Paul to take the job and shove it up his ass after we had two children." He thought for a few seconds then said, "It was my only reason for quitting."

"I didn't fall in love until fifteen years before I walked away from the job," Evelyn said. "Unlike you, though, I married a man I shouldn't have married. So I kicked the bastard out of my life and raised my children on my own."

"Didn't he try for partial custody?"

"I'd made a lot of money working for Steve," she said. "I knew where to invest it to get rich, and I knew the only thing my husband cared about was money. So I gave him two-thirds and got complete custody of my children and never saw or heard from him again."

"Ann died of a heart attack," he said. "I spent a year investigating on my own to confirm it was natural. Because I suspected Paul was behind her death, but he wasn't. She had died of a heart attack while driving. When I confirmed it, I accepted it, and became a widower. Both my children were in college and old enough to accept the death of their mother, though it took them a year to get over it."

"What about you?" Evelyn asked him.

"I think I finally accepted Ann's death about a year ago," he said. "But I didn't want to. I've always felt like I was deserting her by accepting her death. But considering the mess I'm in now maybe it was for the best."

"Lee," she said.

"What?" he asked looking at her.

"We must find this person those five want and find out why they want him. Then we must take what this person has and hide it somewhere the five will never find it. It is the only guarantee of a safe life we can give our children."

He lay back in the cargo area of the cart on his back with his hand behind his head and said, "We may have to do a bit more than that, Evelyn."

CHAPTER 7

3 p.m.

Fred, Steve, Bruce, and Larry were arguing among themselves. As if doing so what help them find Evelyn and Lee. Paul looked at them with almost lifeless eyes and said nothing. He didn't have to. He knew both Lee and Evelyn quite well. He had never hired Evelyn, but Steve had told him everything about her. The five never kept secrets from each other to guarantee they would always have to work together. He knew Lee and Evelyn would do the jobs they were assigned and then report in to him.

"Have you nothing to say?" Bruce asked him.

They were sitting in the private office of the country club manager around a conference table where they had gone to have privacy. The manager didn't object because Paul owned the club.

"What would you like me to say, Bruce?" Paul asked him.

"They've been working for us less than three hours, and we don't know where they are?" Bruce said. "Even those two people we sent to watch them said they somehow got out of that underground hideout of Evelyn's without passing them and disappeared."

"Yes, they have," he said in a soft calm voice.

"More is required, Paul," Larry said.

Paul's hands were lying side by side on top of the wooden conference table. He raised his hands and said, "Yes, they've managed to evade the two people we sent to watch them."

"I thought you said you knew them," Fred said.

Paul looked at him as he folded his hands together and said nothing.

"You didn't know that bitch Evelyn had a secret hideout in an abandoned subway tunnel, did you?"

Paul stared at him and said nothing.

"What exactly are you thinking, Paul?" Fred asked him.

"Wherever they are they are going to do the job we've assigned them," Steve said. "They have no choice, because they have children and grandchildren they love. And they know we know where they live."

"And that my dear brothers, is the leverage we have over them," Paul said.

"We may not know where they are, but we do know they will do as we've ordered them to do," Steve said.

"Tonight we will know where they are," Paul said, standing up. "I, therefore, suggest we all go home, have a pleasant time with our wives and girlfriends, and meet at midnight in the chamber."

"Why, will we know tonight?" Fred asked.

"Because they'll go to the Department of Information," Larry said with a smile on his face as if a bright light bulb had come on in his head.

"And how do we know that?" Fred asked.

"Because, Fred," Steve began. "That's where they have to start looking for the person we want them to find."

"Oh, yes," Fred said remembering Larry had said that.

"Until midnight," Paul said as he walked toward the door. "Good afternoon, gentlemen."

CHAPTER 8

8 p.m.

As soon as they reached an intersection of the sewer system which was a large east-west sewer line, Lee led the way to a small underground garage a few hundred feet from the intersection where four small inspector carts were parked. Evelyn had worried aloud that it would be hours before they reached his hideout under police headquarters. Lee told her not to worry and opened the garage door and got into one of the carts and punched a code on its computer keyboard into its computer.

"That code you put into the cart's computer will blind streets and sanitation's computers to this cart's movements?" she asked him getting into the passenger's seat beside him.

"It should," he said. "Unless they've changed the codes which I doubt."

"Why do you doubt they've changed the codes?"

"This is the sewer, Evelyn," he said. "Who the hell would be interested in anything in the sewers of Crown City?"

"Homeless people," she said.

"Don't be an ass, woman," he replied as he buckled his seat belt. "There haven't been any homeless people in the cities of the world for almost three hundred years. The World Government does an excellent job of providing for people who don't have or want jobs."

"What about hermits?" she asked.

"They live in the wild far away from cities and towns," he said as he started the electric engine. He turned and looked in her eyes.

"What?" she asked staring back into his eyes.

"Let's assume whoever stole what they want us to find from the Department of Information isn't in the city," he said as he started driving the cart. "Buckle up. We're going to be doing eighty miles."

She buckled her seat belt and chest belt around her and asked, "Why does a cart that only robots use have seatbelts?"

"Because every now and then streets and sanitation people use them, and the city doesn't like getting sued because there weren't any seat belts in these carts if someone is injured in an accident. So they all have them."

He used the keyboard to open the overhead door, and as soon as the cart cleared the garage the overhead door it started to close.

"Whoever this person is they'd have to be a fool to remain in the city. Finding people in any city or town, is easier than picking your nose."

"So what we've got to do is find out who took what from the Department of Information and where they went," he said as he increased the speed of the cart.

"That shouldn't be too hard," she said. "All the government departments keep very accurate lists of their employees."

"Let's not be stupid, Evelyn," he said. "Let's assume whoever we're looking for knows someone's looking for them and have done a good job of covering their tracks."

"Fake ID?" she said.

He nodded as he drove and thought. "Or this person has no ID at all, or ID that belongs to someone who really exists but doesn't work for the Department of Information and lives in another city on another continent."

"I don't get you," she said.

"The best way to disappear is to prove you've never existed before," he said. "Or have been dead for years."

"So we're looking at a difficult job," she said.

By eight-thirty they were walking into Lee's hideout under police headquarters.

As soon as they entered the hideout the lights came on lighting up every room.

"A bit austere," Evelyn said as she looked at the bare walls and plain furniture in the living room of the hideout. "How many rooms have you got?"

"Two bedrooms with matching bathrooms, a kitchen without any food in it, I haven't been here in years, a study, and a workroom with a weapon's cabinet."

"It looks like you haven't been here in years," she said as she ran her right index finger over the dust covered cocktail table. "Why don't you have robots to clean it for you?"

"I do whenever I think about it. I use police robots. There are quite a few of them, and the police seldom knows where they all are," he said as he walked toward the workroom. "Police officers are a macho bunch of men and women and don't like relying on robots to catch the bad guys. We're going to need new com-cells that can't be traced, another set of ID's, a vehicle that can't be traced, and more weapons."

"What was this place before you took it over?" she asked him.

"Centuries ago, about four, was it a series of storage rooms with bathrooms for the people who worked down here for the police department. Then for some reason the city decided to close it up and move their storage rooms up next to police headquarters where it was easier to get the equipment they needed," he said as he stopped and turned toward her. "I discovered it one day years ago while working for Paul just after I got married, and over a period of a year I converted it into what you see now."

"You thought it would be a good place to run and hide with your wife if things got rough between you and Paul," she said as she looked for a place to sit down.

"By then I knew Paul wasn't going to move against me because I cease to be of value to him," he said. "I kept it as a hideout, or hole in the wall, just in case I needed it."

"Why did Paul let you retire?" she said as she sat down on a wooden chair and a small cloud of dust rose up around her.

"Probably for the same reason Steve let you go," he said.

"He found a replacement for you," she said as she brushed dust off her jeans.

"Yes."

"I've always wondered why he did that," Evelyn said.

"Me, too," he said. "Paul isn't the sort of person that lets a good tracker go."

"Maybe because they had information on us, they could use against us any time they wanted to," she said in a thoughtful voice.

"Yeah," he said as he turned toward the workroom.

"How do we get into the Department of Information?" she asked, changing the subject as she stood up. "The place closes down at three o'clock."

"Through one of the five kitchens," he said as he walked into the dusty workroom. "We're going to need clothes, too." He pointed to a door on the far left side of the room. "There should be something in that closet that can fit you. Our problem will be evading all the security systems in the Department."

"Leave that to me," she said as she walked toward the door.

"Good." he said. "We get what we need and then get a few hours of sleep." He looked at his wrist watch on his right wrist. "One thirty should be a good time to start. I figure there'll be fewer guards on a Saturday night, and thieves aren't interested in breaking into government buildings with only information in them."

CHAPTER 9

Midnight

The five men had gathered at the chamber.

"It's midnight and there's no evidence of them entering the information building," Fred complained.

"It's nice to know you can tell time, Fred," Larry said. He was sitting in a wide brown leather chair looking at a four foot wide two foot high screen hanging on the wall of their chamber.

"Insults I don't need, Larry!" Fred yelled at him without turning to look at him from his comfortable chair.

The chamber was a private room at the top of the Diamond Bank Building in the downtown area of Crown. The room wasn't listed on the bank's list of conference rooms because no one knew it existed. Not even the bank president or the board of director or the building engineer. Only the architect who designed the building and built the room knew it existed because he had been paid millions to build it using only construction robots, and he was killed in an accidental fall from another building three weeks after the Diamond Bank Building opened twenty-one years ago. On the computer blueprints it was listed as part of the air-conditioning room at the top of the building. Even the bank's maintenance crew never entered the room because there was no door that led from the air-conditioning room to the chamber. The room was kept clean by the two robots that were permanently assigned to the room. Access to the room was through an elevator that had been built into the north corner of the concrete and steel support beam. There was a single bathroom for their use, and it was the only place where they could get water.

"They're doing this deliberately," Steve said as he stared at the empty hallways on the monitor.

"I would agree with that," Paul said. He had a bored expression on his face as he sat still in his chair. "But sooner or later they will show up."

"Do we have the time to wait," Fred said.

"We have always had all the time in the world, Fred," Paul said. "So be patient."

"Time may not be something we have a lot of," Bruce said. "What if the person who has our information decides to release it on the Internet? We don't control that, you know, Paul.

"No, we don't," Paul agreed. "But our people can remove anything from the Internet without leaving evidence it was done."

"Maybe we should have one of their children kidnapped to let them know we want to know everything they're doing," Bruce said.

"Do that, Bruce," Larry said. "And our problems will double."

"How so," Bruce asked.

"They will find this person and join him against us," Larry explained. "We've no choice but to let Evelyn and Lee do what we've hired them to do without any interference from us."

"They know what we are capable of, gentlemen," Paul said. "So don't worry about this annoying game they are playing on us."

"Making us blind and deaf to their actions and words is not a game they're playing, Paul," Steve said. "We must know everything they are doing and saying, because everything we have is dependent upon it."

"Including our lives," Fred added in a worried voice.

"Patience, patience," Paul said softly in a calm voice. "They will eventually show up. And when they do, our people will follow them and hear everything they say and do."

You hope thought Steve.

CHAPTER 10

1:30 a.m.

"I'm hungry," Evelyn complained as she followed Lee down the dark sewer under the Department of Information Building. Only the use of night vision goggles made the sewer look as if a bright summer sun was shining into it made their walk down the sewer easy to the southwest kitchen. The masks they wore over their heads contained miniature microphones and filters that enabled them to talk and hear each other and to avoid the foul smell of the sewer.

"Me, too," Lee said as he slowed down and took another look at the map on his com-cell.

"You sure they can't see or hear us?" she asked him as she looked at the screen of the I-pad she held in her left hand.

"Every piece of equipment we're using is over a hundred years old," he said. "The high tech equipment they're using to search for us is too advanced to pick up what we've got. Even the electrical impulses given off by our equipment is too primitive for their equipment to pick up. They won't even pick up the static coming from our equipment, because the equipment they're using to look for us is designed to eliminate static electricity no matter how primitive." He stopped and looked up and saw a manhole cover directly above him. He looked at his com-cell, checked his position, and said, "We're here."

Evelyn didn't say anything. She was busy working with the keypad on the hundred year old I-pad she carried. The I-pad enabled her to hack into the building's security system and see everything without the system knowing it had been hacked. Thirty seconds passed before she said, "The computers and security cameras in this building and even in this sewer are blind and deaf to us."

"Good," he said. "Because Paul and his four thug friends have their people looking and listening for us at this very moment."

"Let them," she said. "They will see and hear nothing." She checked her I-pad again and saw the location of the guards in the building and said, "We can go up. All the guards are in the guards' lounge over three hundred feet away watching TV."

Lee turned to the wall and saw a steel ladder that led up to the manhole cover. "Give me a minute," he said as he put his com-cell into his pants pocket and started up the ladder.

The manhole cover was made out of cast iron, no sense in using good steel for a manhole cover inside a government building. He put his back against the cover and pushed up expecting to hear a loud rusty squeaking sound. All he heard was the sound of the manhole cover moving against the concrete it was resting on. The robots that cleaned the Information Building did a very thorough job. It took him less than twenty seconds to move the cover to the side far enough for him to enter the kitchen.

"Is it clear inside?" he asked Evelyn.

"No one's in the kitchen looking for a late night snack," she replied.

He breathed a sigh of relief as he climbed up high enough into the dark, silent kitchen and looked around to make sure no one was around looking for a late snack.

"All clear," he told her.

"I told you it was," she said.

The large kitchen was empty and appeared to have been thoroughly cleaned before the kitchen crew left for the week-end. He looked at the floor and noticed it was clean. That meant they'd leave tracks unless they wiped away their tracks before they left, and they'd still leave evidence of their tracks being wiped away. He ignored them.

"Remember where you step," he told Evelyn. "We're going to leave muddy foot prints."

"Not many," she said. "All we have to do is get to the kitchen's office and use their computer."

"Going inside," Lee said as he crawled into the kitchen on his hands and knees. "Give me a few minutes. I want to make sure there's no one here." He slide on his knees to a stainless steel cabinet and looked around for a few seconds before he stood up and began to move silently through the kitchen, looking carefully for any signs of a human moving around. Satisfied there was no one in the kitchen he moved to the double swinging doors that led to the cafeteria, turning down the brightness of his goggles as he moved. He stopped on the right side of the double doors and looked through the window in the right door into the cafeteria. The large cafeteria with it fifty tables was empty.

"Okay, Evelyn, all clear," he said.

Evelyn came through the manhole into the kitchen and looked around for the kitchen office. When she saw a glass enclosed corner with venetian blinds covering the glass walls and the word 'manager' on the glass, she moved toward it as quickly and quietly as she could. "I'm opening the door," she said as she grabbed the doorknob with her right gloved hand and twisted to her right. "Be ready to run if you hear an alarm."

The door clicked and opened without setting off an alarm.

Lee took out his com-cell and turned it on and got a picture of the hallways leading to the kitchen they were in. He scanned four other hallways before he was satisfied not even a silent alarm had been set off. He decided to scan the entire first floor of the Department of Information just to be sure.

"I'm at the computer," Evelyn said as she sat at the desk that held the computer.

"Just get the information," he told her as he looked at the screen on his com-cell.

It took her less than ten seconds to use the computer to get into the basement servers of the Department and less than thirty seconds to get pass the firewalls and codes to the files that held the information she and Lee wanted. She took a flash drive out of the left pocket of her jacket and stuck it into one of the USB ports and pushed enter on the keyboard. The drive could hold a billion pages of information with three hundred six letter words per page.

Lee stopped his scan of the hallways when he saw a man dressed in a guard's uniform walking in a hallway a few hundred feet away from the cafeteria. The slow careful way the man moved caught his attention. He moved in an easy loose manner, turning to his right every few feet to look back as if he wanted to make sure no one was following him. The man walked a foot away from the left wall, and looked as if he was listening for any sounds.

Lee saw the holstered weapon on his right hip and saw the man's right hand was only a few inches in front of it and thought, *he wants to make sure his gun hand is free to move forward or backwards with the wall protecting his back. A guard making his rounds would just walk down the center of the hallway with his hands swinging by his sides. This man's right hand doesn't move from his holster.* He looked at the man's belt and noticed he didn't have a radio then at his head and saw there were no earphones in either of his ears. He wished he'd brought a weapon instead of leaving it back in his hideout. "How's the download going?"

"Another minute," she said.

"Hope we have the time," he said.

"What are you talking about?"

"There's man approaching the cafeteria, he's dressed in a guard's uniform, but this guy isn't a security guard," he told her.

"How do you know?" she asked.

"His uniform fits him like it was tailored for him, and from the way his chest doesn't move when he breaths, I'd say he's wearing body armor. Plus he moves in the loose manner of a man skilled in hand-to-hard combat, and his hair is short so it can't be grabbed and used against him."

"Maybe he's an ex-World Security Forces Soldier."

"No, he's medium tan in color, short black hair, and about six feet with large strong looking hands. This guy has experienced hired gun written all over him."

"What has his hands got to do with him being a hired gun?" Evelyn asked him.

"Better to strangle someone," he said. "How close are you to finishing?"

"Another ten seconds," she said.

"Good," he said. "Because this guy I'm looking at is about a hundred feet from the cafeteria."

The man stopped a few feet from an intersecting hallway and looked up at a TV screen in the center of the ceiling of the intersection hallways that showed the four hallways. Then, apparently satisfied no one was around, he walked pass the intersection heading for the cafeteria.

"No guard making his rounds would do that unless he was alerted to danger," Lee said more to himself than to Evelyn.

"Finished," Evelyn said.

"Make sure you leave no evidence of being there," he told her.

"I'm not new at this, Lee," she reminded him.

Lee continued watching the man until Evelyn told him she was at the manhole and going down.

"Right behind you," he said, noting the man had just pushed open one of the swinging doors of the cafeteria and entered the cafeteria, and quickly moved to the side putting a wall behind him. Lee moved quickly and as quietly as he could toward the manhole, he went into the manhole, slid the cover back into place, and climbed down the steel ladder to the sewer.

Evelyn was moving away in the direction they'd come.

"Stop! Stand still and turn off your I-pad, and don't make a sound," Lee told her.

Evelyn stopped and moved against the wall of the sewer turning off her I-pad.

Lee moved two yards from the manhole cover and looked up and listened. He didn't hear a sound, but he knew what was coming next. When a bright light came through the holes on the manhole cover, he knew he'd done the right thing. Even though he hadn't seen a flashlight hanging from the man's belt, he knew he probably had one in his pocket. After a few seconds the flashlight went out. Lee waited for a minute before he turned to Evelyn.

"Move fast," he told her.

She turned and started running down the sewer asking as she ran, "Why didn't he see the muddy tracks we left on the kitchen floor?"

"He will once he turns on the lights in the kitchen," he said, running behind her.

"And when he does, he's going to sound an alarm and come down the sewer after us."

"Let's hope we make it to the car first," she said.

Lee didn't want to tell her it wouldn't make much difference if they did if the man came down into the sewer. He'd pulled out his electric pistol and start shooting, moving the automatic weapon back and forth at a low level to hit whoever was in the tunnel.

They had just made the car and jumped into it when Lee looked back and saw light from the kitchen coming through the holes in the manhole cover.

"Did you cover your tracks on that computer?" he asked her as he flipped the switch starting the electric engine and shifted the car's gearshift into drive.

"Yes," she said. "But they'll know I was on the computer from the tracks I left in the office."

"Can't be helped," he said as he floored the accelerator.

The small electric car shot forward with a jump and raced down the sewer. Within a few yards in reached seventy miles an hour. Too fast for the man to catch them no matter what shape he was in, but they'd be close enough for the electric bullets he'd fire at them to reach them. The damn things moved more than eighteen hundred feet a second. But unlike metal bullets from the twenty-first and twenty-second centuries gravity didn't have much of an effect on electric bullets. They just dissolved into stray electrons after a hundred and fifty yards if they didn't hit anything.

Lee was hoping they'd be farther away than a hundred and fifty yards by the time the man came down into the sewer.

Two minutes passed before he heard the cracking sound of the man's semiautomatic being fired.

"He missed," Evelyn said, looking back.

"No," Lee said as he drove. "We were too far away."

"He'll notify the police about us," she said.

"No, Evelyn, I think he's going to call our employers."

"They'll know where we are," she told him.

"Yes, they'll know we're in the sewer line under the Department of Information," he agreed. "But they won't know exactly where we are or where we're going."

"That gives us maybe twenty seconds before they send their killers down here looking for us," she said.

Lee didn't say anything because she was right.

$$\backsim$$

CHAPTER 11

2:30 a.m.

"Are you sure?" Paul asked the caller.

"Yes sir, positive," the caller responded.

"Continue with your regular job," Paul told the caller and hung up. He looked at his four fellow members with a concerned expression on his face.

"Well," Fred asked him.

"The expression on Paul's face says they got away," Steve said.

"How the hell did they manage to get pass our security devices?" Bruce demanded. "We control the best security systems in the world."

"Apparently not," Larry said in a soft voice.

"Tell us what our man in the Department of Information told you, Paul?' Fred demanded.

"They managed to get in the building by way of the sewer, and got into the kitchen," he said as he stood up and started pacing about the room.

"Is that all?" Fred demanded.

"The security guard we have there noticed muddy foot prints on the floor of the kitchen and traced them to a manhole cover in the kitchen floor. He noticed it had been moved and got down into the sewer and saw a sewer car driving off."

"Then they didn't get anything," Fred said, watching Paul.

"They did," Bruce said.

"How do you know?" he asked Bruce.

"What would have been the purpose of getting into the kitchen then leaving if they didn't get something," Steve said.

"What a quart of milk?"

"No, Fred," Larry said. "They used the kitchen's computer to get what they wanted."

"To use the kitchen's computer they would have had to get into the kitchen office," Steve said. He turned and looked at Paul. "Did the guard say he saw evidence of them getting into the kitchen office, Paul?"

"Yes," Paul replied. He was silent for a few seconds before he said, "The guard saw muddy foot prints on the floor leading into and out of the office."

"So they managed to get into the Department's computers and servers," Larry said.

"They got information on the thief who stole our secrets," Fred said.

"I don't think so," Paul said as he stopped pacing.

"Not enough time?" Steve asked him then yawned deeply and loudly.

Paul gave him a disapproving look. He didn't like people to display their physical sounds around him. It made them seem like animals, because humans kept such sounds to themselves. "Knowing Evelyn as I do, I suspect she left something in the computer's hard drive that allows her to get into the Department of Information's servers and every computer in the building." He looked at Steve and said, "You've used her many times, Steve, what do you think?"

"I agree with you," he said. "The woman's a genius with computers."

"Then what we should do is have our computer people to wipe out whatever she put there, and leave a message demanding they contact us as soon as possible."

"No," Bruce said. "We get our computer people to find out what they put in the computer and wait for Evelyn to contact the computer and trace the contact back to her, and grabbed them both.

"That's impossible," Steve said. "Evelyn's an excellent hacker. She can get pass any fire wall, and leave a program in a hard drive no one would find in years. That's why she was chosen for this special job."

"Let's just have our enforcers grab their families and contact them through an ad in the papers or over the radio or TV telling them to report in or their families will die horrible deaths," Fred said. He was tired and wanted to go home to bed. Over twenty hours had passed since he'd had any sleep.

"We can't do that," Paul said as he started pacing again. "If we do, they may find the person we want them to find and what he stole about us. And blackmail us."

"They won't do that," Fred said. "They can't."

Paul stopped pacing and said, "Gentlemen, we must accept a fact. We assigned two outstanding people to do a job for us, and they know that once the job was done they will die because we can't afford to let them live. We won't have a guarantee they will not have read and copied the information this person stole from us. We're in a position where we can't trust anyone but ourselves. Our lives and future depend upon it."

"So what do we do?" Bruce asked him.

"We can't harm their families, because if we do and they find out we've harmed their families it will only enrage them, and force them to seek revenge against us," Paul explained.

"We shouldn't have put the information about us in the Department of Information anyway," Fred complained. "We should have realized it was only a matter of time before someone stumbled across it."

"The Department was the safest place to hide our information," Larry reminded him. "There are trillions of pieces of information in the Department that go back thousands of years. The only way someone could have found our information was by accident."

"Placing our information in the Department was the best place because we could quickly get to it," Steve said. "Leaving all that information in the lab was risky."

"Why was it risky?" Fred demanded. "No one knows about the lab."

Steve turned around and looked at Fred and said, "Fred, what would have happened if an accident had occurred to the lab. Explosive chemicals are used in the lab."

"Spilt wine," Paul said. "What we must do is to assign our two best computer experts to go over all the information in the Department of Information. Somewhere in those servers in the Department is a clue to who stole our information."

"Isn't that why we chose Lee and Evelyn?" Fred asked.

"Of course it is, Fred," Paul said. "We just made the mistake of choosing two people who aren't as obedient as we had hoped they were, and are more intelligent than we suspected."

"We just made the mistake of choosing two people who are like us," Steve said. "Now what we must do is look carefully among our people and chose six who are intelligent and obedient, and send them out to find and kill Evelyn and Lee."

"Once they've located the thief and our information," Bruce reminded them.

"We've one advantage," Paul said.

"Evelyn and Lee must use computers to locate the thief," Larry finished for him.

Paul looked at him and nodded as he said, "You are correct, Larry." He looked at Steve. "Now I suggest we all go home and get at least ten hours of sleep. When we meet again we do it at the lodge, and be sure to tell your wives and girlfriends you'll be going on an extended business trip of at least ten days."

CHAPTER 12

Sunday morning, 6 a.m.

Lyle stared at the ceiling of the bedroom in the cabin he was hiding in and thought, *their killers will eventually find me, but by then I hope it will be too late. I've hidden my identity behind faked names, social security numbers, and addresses. It will take them days to discover who I really am, and by then I should be able to upload the information I've got on those four monsters to World Internet. But I've got to be very careful. They will have their experts looking for any information someone is trying to put on the Internet about them. And their experts have the skills to block any information going on the Internet long enough for them to trace the information to the source.*

He closed his eyes and wished he'd never come across that information. It had shocked him to think someone in the world of the thirty-first century could do the horrible things they'd done to the human race for last five hundred years.

Lyle was like everyone on the Earth. He had thought the barbarism of the past had died with the creation of the United World in the twenty-sixth century. Little did the people of the world know that the United World and the World Democracy had been deliberately created by events to hide and protect those five monsters. He had never liked it when his history teachers in high school and college had told their classes that no matter how far the human race advanced, the blood thirsty beasts we had evolved from still existed in every man, woman, and child on Earth. It was only through education that it was possible to control those beasts hiding within us, and use the beasts' desires for blood and destruction for useful purposes.

Now he realized they were right and that made Lyle wonder if he had been foolish in doing what he'd done. Maybe he should have just ignored what he found that day over twenty-two years ago. If he had done so, he wouldn't have had to create a fake identity for himself and fake his death and leave his wife, whom he still deeply loved, and his children whom he thought about every time he was alone.

But he hadn't ignored the information and he was now hoping that what he intended doing—had to do since there was no other recourse, would not destroy the World Democracy and the World Congress. The world had advanced too far scientifically to go back to the old days of violence six hundred years ago. The weapons the various states could produce would destroy all human life in a matter of months if those nations went back to fighting each other.

Lyle wiped his mind clear of the horrible things he was thinking and tried to get some sleep. Monday was going to be a busy day for him, and maybe the beginning of the

end for the human race. And if not the human race certainly him if he wasn't careful and not leave a trail the five monsters could follow back to him.

You're a damn fool Lyle for being so civilized. You should have just ignored that information you found and let someone else find it and do what you intend doing. He allowed his mind to go blank for a few seconds before he thought *maybe someone found it years before I did and tried doing what I'm trying to do and died because of it.*

CHAPTER 13

6 a.m.

"So what have you done?" Lee asked Evelyn. He was standing behind her chair in the study of his underground hide out.

"Simple," she said as she stopped working on the keyboard. "I've put my own special program in the main server in the Department of Information's computer servers. And no one can get to it, but me."

"How's that possible?" he asked as he leaned over and looked at the screen on the desk.

"I've put in a code word that has to be entered a certain way every time someone wants to get into my program, or my program goes into hiding."

"Those five assholes have experts who'll find your code in a matter of hours," he told her.

"Maybe," she said. "But a lot of good it'll do them."

"What do you mean?" he asked her.

"My code has a self-destruct code written into it," she said.

"What does that mean?"

"Even if their experts do manage to find my code and figure out how I let my code know when I'm the one using it, it still won't help them."

"You put a code cover over your code?" he asked her.

"No, I put in a code support that has to be put in within five seconds after my code has been used, or it destroys itself."

"Well, you might be a little slow putting in your code and the damn thing will self-destruct," he said. "That's not smart."

"You're not listening to me, Lee," she said. "I said the code has to be entered a certain way each time it's used."

"And so does this code support."

"Exactly."

He straightened up and stretched his back muscles and legs. "Are you finished?"

She pushed the enter button on the keyboard and watched as the information on the screen downloaded onto her I-pad. "Yes," she said.

He looked at her I-pad. "Can that thing hold the information you've put in it?"

"All it has to hold in its hard drive is my special code." She pushed her chair back and stood up. "I'm starved. And I'm bone tired."

"Let's get some breakfast and go to bed," he said as he looked at the clock on the desk.

"Do we have to remain in this underground hideout of yours, Lee?" she asked, looking around at the bare walls. "I'd prefer working someplace that's a bit more-homey than this place."

"I've got another place," he said. "But we'll have to go to the surface to get to it. And once we do that they'll have every camera in the city programmed to look for us."

"Don't worry about that, Lee," she said. "I can blind every camera to our movements."

"That's exactly what they're experts will be looking for," he told her. "Someone or some vehicle they can't see or get inside of."

Evelyn turned to face him. "Will there be shooting?" she asked him.

"And killing," he replied as he stepped away and moved toward the door.

"Then let's get breakfast, some sleep, and prepare for battle," she said as she followed him.

"Follow me," he told her as he walked out of the study in the direction of the kitchen.

CHAPTER 14

9 p.m. Sunday

Lee was sitting on the faded green couch in the sparsely furnished living room of his hideout watching a TV program he wasn't interested in and wasn't paying any attention to because he was thinking.

"Boy, am I well rested," Evelyn said as she walked into the living room. She was dressed in clean jeans and a matching shirt and underwear and socks. Even the black jogging shoes she wore were clean. "Nice collection of clothes you've got in this hideout of yours—but fashionable they aren't."

Lee glanced over his left shoulder at her and said, "I've prepared dinner for us. All of it is out of cans unfortunately. I thought of going on the surface and getting us hamburgers and fries but decided it would be too dangerous."

"Can food is okay with me," she said as she took a seat next to him. "As long as it's hot. So what do we do today?"

"We leave here about midnight and head for my second hideout. On the way we may be able to stop and stock up on fresh food at one of the All Night Stores."

"Isn't that dangerous?" she asked. "By now our employers know about us getting into the Department of Information computers and servers. And while they won't be able to stop us from getting back into the Department's servers they will have accessed every camera in the city."

"When we leave here we'll go to the city's underground garage," he said as he thought. "There'll be cameras there, so we'll have to disguise ourselves. I've clothing we can use in one of the bedroom closets and what may pass for a makeup kit. And we'll have the weather on our side. According to the weather report on the news it should be foggy outside with drizzle coming down until morning."

"Where is this other hideout of yours?"

"Just beyond the city's western boundary a few miles pass the forest preserve."

"You got a car down here?"

"No."

"We going take public transportation?"

"No, we're going to steal a car."

"Lee, those garages are heavily guarded with all sorts of security devices," she said.

"I know that," he said as he stood up. "Let's go eat and get ready."

"They'll have killers out looking for us," she said.

"Probably those two who followed us to that apartment building of yours that led to your hole in the ground. But their orders will be to take us alive. The five want to know what we've been doing." He walked toward the door. "Come on. Let's get dinner. It's a little after nine now. Take what you'll need from the equipment I've got here to get us pass the security systems in the underground."

"Tell me, Lee," she said, following him. "Why would a tracker need hideouts? If you're a good tracker no one would even know you're following them."

"The same reason you have holes in the ground," he replied.

"Even a half ass hacker needs a place to run and hide when he's realizes someone's onto his game."

"You know, Evelyn, in addition to finding this mysterious person they want us to find, I suggest we get something on our employers."

Evelyn reached forward and patted Lee on his left shoulder with her right hand. "You think like me, Lee."

∾

CHAPTER 15

The lodge 11:45 p.m. Sunday

"Sir," the pale face man was sitting in front of eighty inch computer screen hanging on the wall he was facing said in a flat emotionless voice.

"What is it?" Larry said as he swung the club as hard as he could and hit the stationary golf ball on the floor to the ceiling TV screen which doubled as a wall mirror. The golf ball on the screen flew off in the direction of the green four hundred feet away. The speed at which the ball was traveling and its height were listed under the ball. Computer golf was so much better when one had a wall screen. The player actually felt he was on a golf course playing golf. The vents on the wall above the screen even blew air on him that smelled like the wind coming off a golf course. Everything was so real like.

"There are two people in the downtown underground garage stealing a car."

"People steal cars from the city's underground garages every day," Larry replied.

"But sir," the man said as he looked down at the right hand corner of the screen which contained a smaller screen. "The security cameras in the underground garage aren't displaying the theft."

Larry watched his electric golf ball land twelve feet from the hole and roll to a stop after a few feet. The display under the ball indicated it was nine feet seven inches from the hole. "Damn," he exclaimed.

"I was hoping to get within two feet of the hole. You caused me to slacken my swing just a little when you spoke to me."

"Sir," the man said. "You should look at this."

Larry turned toward the man and snapped, "You're the computer expert, Sam, not me."

"Yes, sir," the man said. "The thieves are taking a gray Honda passenger car that's five years old."

"So damn what?" Larry turned to the wall screen and said. "Put me on the green."

The screen immediately changed and he was on the green facing the hole. He pushed a button on the electric golf club he was holding and the driver was replaced by a putter.

"The car the thieves are taking is a Honda G-4. A very powerful and fast car with wide wheels and an excellent suspension system for making sharp turns."

"Just find those two people you were told to find," he said angrily. He leaned over and concentrated on making the put.

"Yes, sir," Sam replied. "These two thieves are the same height and weight of the people I was told to look for."

"Be quiet! I'm putting. I want to make this hole in two swings," Larry told him.

Sam said nothing as Larry hit the ball with his putter and watched as the golf ball rolled to the cup and rolled around the lip of the cup and stopped two feet beyond it.

"Damn!" he yelled angrily. "I was hoping to be three under par on this hole. Now I'll only make two under par."

Sam said nothing.

The next scene on the screen showed Larry standing next to the ball getting ready to make another put. This time he put the ball in the cup.

"If I could have made this hole in two swings, I'd be at level ten on this game," he grumbled. "But because you spoke to me I slacken my swing and I'm still at only level nine. Now I'll have to make the next hole with only two swings and that's almost impossible on this computer course." He pushed a button on the club he was holding and the screen when blank becoming a mirror. "I'm going to bed." Larry started walking toward the door and stopped before he got close enough for it to automatically sense his body heat and open. He turned around and looked at Sam as he asked, "What did you say about their height and weight?"

"They matched the weight and height of the two people you told me to look for, sir." Sam said.

Larry walked over to the chair Sam was sitting in and stopped behind it. "Are you sure?"

"An ultraviolet scan of their bodies indicate they are of the same weight and height, and one of the thieves is a female."

"What else has the scan revealed about them?" A Larry saw the garage with cars scattered about it.

"The female's body function and musculature, indicates she is between sixty-one and sixty-two. The male's body says he is between sixty and sixty-one. The female is five ten in height. The man is six feet two."

"Is the man black and the woman white?" he asked.

"Impossible to tell, sir, their faces are hidden by hoods and dark glasses and they are wearing black gloves."

"Why would they be wearing gloves in this weather?" Larry asked. "It must be sixty degrees outside."

"To avoid leaving finger prints, sir."

"Where are they? I can't see them."

"They have left the garage."

"Did you get the license number of the car?"

"Yes, sir," Sam said.

"Give the number to our people on the street," he ordered Sam.

"Yes, sir," he said as he typed on the keyboard and pushed enter.

$$\sim$$

CHAPTER 16

12 p.m.

"So far so good," Evelyn said as she looked around at the empty streets. She was sitting in the passenger seat next to Lee.

"Bullshit," he said as he drove. "Keep your eye out for a dark side street with at least two exits."

"You think we were spotted?" she asked as she looked around. "Slow down. There's a narrow side street just ahead on your left."

"You know this area?" he asked her as he reduced speed.

"There's a nice lady's dress shop that sells fashionable clothes half way down on the street coming up. There's a big wide alley next to the dress shop that lets out onto a four lane street. Two of the lanes head north the other two head south. Very few stop lights on them before the exit."

"Any traffic cameras on the street or in the alley?"

"No, none. Good place to put on our phony plates," she said.

"Get ready," he said. "We'll have maybe thirty seconds to make the plate changes."

Lee turned onto the street, moved down it till he saw the alley, and turned into the ally and stopped after thirty feet. They were out of the car in less than three seconds with the phony plates in their hands. Lee took the front plate and Evelyn took the back plate. It took them less than twenty-five seconds to remove the original electrically attached plates and put the phony ones in their places, and get back into the car taking the replaced plates with them.

"Get the weapons out of the bag on the back seat," he told her. "I figure we got maybe twenty minutes before they check every Honda G-4 on the streets in the city and realize our plates aren't what they expected."

Evelyn laughed as she said as she turned around and grabbed the tan canvas bag on the back seat, "Smart move on your part remembering the plate numbers of one of the cars parked in front of that cabin we reported to two days ago."

"I don't think I got the numbers right," he said as he drove. "But it'll take them some time to find that out."

"Let's hope by the time they do we'll be long gone and disappeared." She opened the bag and took out two electric semiautomatics. She checked both to make sure they were fully charged and handed one to Lee and put the other one in her belt.

Lee pushed the weapon into the belt of his pants with his right hand said nothing as he drove. He avoided the expressways because they were too easy to check. The regular streets, avenues, and boulevards were harder to check because of the number of side streets and alleys, and many didn't have traffic cameras. But with the number of men he thought the five had working for them they could block off any street in Crown City within minutes, but only if they didn't care about attracting the attention of the police.

Fifteen minutes passed before Evelyn spoke. "What are you thinking?"

"They're going to come for us with everything they've got, but they won't throw up any road blocks," he said. "To do that they'd have to shut down the traffic cameras on the street they want to block, and that'll attract the attention of the traffic department's computer people. And they'd send in a patrol car to check out the area."

"So its killers only we've got to worry about," she said.

"Killing us isn't the goal of our employers. Grabbing us and forcing us to do as they wish in some hidden place is what they want."

"Because they realize now that they can't find us they made a mistake in hiring us," she said.

"I don't think they had much choice in hiring us, Evelyn."

"Why you say that?"

"Because if they could have found this person who has the information they want without our assistance they would have done so."

"Which means whoever this person is they've done an excellent job of hiding their identity," she said as she looked out the window to her right.

Every building they passed was either dark or had dim lights coming from them.

Crown City appeared to be asleep for the night. Waiting for the sun to rise and call its inhabitants to work or play. The only lights on the streets were those of a few cars they passed, or the defused lights of street lights caused by the wet mist that had descended upon the city an hour ago.

Lee turned the windshield wipers to slow and looked in the rearview mirror then glanced quickly at the left side mirror, then to the mirror on the right side.

Evelyn noticed his actions. She turned to her left and looked out the rear window. "So far we're alone."

"I wonder what information this person has on those five they couldn't use regular methods of looking for him. Why hire us?"

"Because the last thing they want is attention."

"So we're looking for someone who is a very dangerous threat to them and has something on them that could destroy them," he said.

"Lee," Evelyn said.

"What?"

"There's car about a block behind us."

"Let's see if it's interested in us," he said as he took his feet off the accelerator and let the weight of the car slow it down. He saw an intersecting street a little more than a block ahead of them, and moved into the left hand lane without using his turn signals. He looked into the rearview mirror and saw the car remained in the right hand lane and draw closer to them. "Make sure you're buckled up."

"I am."

He waited until he was a few yards from the intersection before he suddenly turned sharply to the right, the tires squealing in protest, and hit the accelerator with his right foot. The Honda G-4 shot ahead.

"The car picked up speed, Lee," Evelyn told him.

He saw an alley off to his right and quickly turned into it without touching the brakes as he turned off his headlights. He saw a large parking space off to the left side and turned into it and turned the Honda around and stopped so he could leave the alley by the same way he entered.

The following car turned into the street with its tired squealing and shot pass the alley.

"They're onto us," Evelyn said.

Without a word Lee shot out of the parking space made a sharp left turn and headed back toward the street they had turned off. As soon as he hit the intersection he turned right and slammed his foot down on the accelerator. The Honda went from fifteen miles an hour to ninety within twenty seconds.

"You said this hideout of yours is in the forest preserves pass the city's western boundary?" she asked him as she looked out the rear window.

"A few miles pass the forest preserves."

"Two blocks up is Wood Boulevard. It heads directly toward Route 90 which borders the forest preserves."

"Got that I-pad of yours?" he asked as he saw a car two blocks down the street heading directly for them. He reduced speed to forty miles an hour.

"Sure right here on the side of the seat between us," she said, turning around to face the front. She saw the car coming toward them.

"Now would be a good time to blind the city's traffic cameras to us," he told her.

"You think that one heading for us is partners with the one we just ducked?" she asked as picked up her I-pad.

"I certainly do," he said as he moved to the right lane. He looked into the rearview mirror and saw the car they had just ducked turning back onto the street after them and increasing its speed.

Evelyn powered up her I-pad and got into the city's main traffic control center and quickly found the cameras on the street they were on.

"Brace yourself," Lee told Evelyn as he prepared to make a tricky move that if it failed to work, they would both be dead or seriously injured.

"Do what you got to do. I'm ready," she said as she worked on her I-pad.

He waited until the car ahead moved into the left hand lane then dropped his speed to twenty miles per hour allowing the one behind to catch up to them. When the headlights of the car behind him filled the rearview mirror and flooded the interior of the Honda with light, Lee braced himself and slammed his foot down on the accelerator pushing the Honda to sixty miles an hour within seven seconds leaving the car behind them forty feet behind. Just as he hoped it increased its speed to catch up with him just as he moved into the lane of the on-coming car and hit his bright lights blinding the driver. When the car behind him was only a foot away, he swerved into the far lane just before he collided with the on-coming car.

The sudden move took the driver of the car behind by surprise and the driver foolishly made the same move without considering the car ahead of Lee had heading for him. When he realized his mistake, the driver immediately turned back to the lane on his right. But he wasn't fast enough to avoid the on-coming car, because that driver instead of moving into the lane to his right, where the Honda was, moved to the lane to his left. The head-on collision was loud with the sounds of breaking safety glass and smashing metal.

The sudden move caused the Honda to spin in a circle on the wet pavement. Lee took his foot off the accelerator and gently pressed down on the brake. The stop-start brakes immediately went into action causing the Honda to slow down allowing Lee to get control of the Honda. He brought the Honda back to the direction they were heading and moved off at sixty miles an hour toward Wood Boulevard. As soon as he saw Wood Boulevard, he dropped his speed to five miles per hour and made a safe left hand turn.

"Did you blind the traffic cameras?" he asked Evelyn.

"That I did, but I can assure you that collision has awakened a number of people in the apartments along that street."

"Good. Right now some responsible citizen is calling the police."

"It may not matter, Lee," she said. "Considering the power of our five employers, if they witnessed the collision, they probably have a cleanup crew on the way."

"Or a pickup crew for the men in those cars," he said.

"Think the people in those cars are dead?"

"I could care less," he answered. "But our troubles for the night aren't over."

She understood what he meant. "If they saw that collision, they've probably sent more people out after us."

"Yes," he said. "The last thing those five assholes want to do is lose us again. But if I have my way they will."

CHAPTER 17

12:20 a.m. the lodge

Larry didn't like what he'd seen on the screen but he knew he couldn't afford to let the police pick up the men in those cars. "Send a van to pick up the men in those cars," he said as he removed his com-cell from his pants pocket and pushed a button notifying Paul, Steve, Fred, and Bruce. "And give the police the wrong address for the accident."

"I have a pickup van on the way, sir," Sam said in his flat voice. "And I am giving the police the wrong address for the accident."

"Can the plates and sticker numbers on those cars be traced back to us?" he asked.

"No, sir," Sam said. "The numbers are all fakes. The men inside will leave no prints."

"What about that Honda?"

"The window sticker is probably legitimate, but the plates are probably fake and can't be traced."

"Did you get the plate numbers on that Honda?" Larry asked him.

"Yes, sir, I did," he said.

"Trace them," Larry ordered him.

Sam began to trace the numbers on the plates.

"What will they do next?" Larry mumbled out loud.

"They will have to abandon the Honda, sir."

"Can you follow it?"

"No, sir," Sam replied. "The traffic cameras are not showing it on Wood Boulevard."

"Why is that?"

"Because the cameras have been programmed not to show it."

"How can they do that?" Larry asked in an angry voice.

"The traffic cameras on Wood Boulevard as well as those on Train Street have been programmed to run the previous recorded scenes."

"How can they do that?"

"They got into the traffic department's main control room and put in a program to tell the computers to show previous scene."

"Get into those computers and find and eliminate that program," Larry ordered Sam.

"Yes, sir," Sam answered. "But it will take at least twenty minutes to get into the traffic department's main server and find the program."

"Do it!"

"Yes, sir."

"Send two of our people to Wood Boulevard and tell them to find that Honda."

"Yes sir."

"Find out if the people in those two cars are still alive, Sam," Larry said.

"They are not, sir," Sam said. "The power of the impact of the collision was enough to kill them."

CHAPTER 18

12:30 a.m.

"We've got to dump this car, Evelyn," Lee said as he drove.

"Right now whoever they've got on a computer is getting into the traffic department's main server to eliminate my short program."

"Can they trace the program to your I-pad?"

"No. Once the program is located it will dissipate into a lot of electrons. But they are going to know I put it there. Steve knows my skills with computers."

"They'll also have someone on Wood Boulevard looking for this Honda," he said as he increased his speed. "How long do you think we've got before they locate your program?"

"Twenty minutes at the very most," she said. "So I suggest we dump this Honda within the next ten minutes."

"More than enough time for us to be in the preserves," he said.

"And after that?"

"We drive to the western end of the preserves."

"And what do we do after that?"

"We walk to my hideout."

"How far is it?" she asked.

"About twenty miles maybe a little more."

"That'll put us well outside the preserves that are the city's boundary if we keep going west."

"Where there are no cameras or electrical devices to spy on us."

"You know they're going to send a squad of killers to look of us," she reminded him.

"I certainly do," he said. "That is why I, like you, have a safe hole in the ground no one knows about."

"With everything I need to get into the Department of Information computers?"

"All of it low tech, but you can bounce messages off the satellites into the Department of Information computers."

"Good," she said. "Even our five employers aren't stupid enough to mess with world satellites."

"I don't know about that," he said. "If they're desperate enough to get back what this mysterious person stole from them, they'll do whatever they have to do, and they won't give a damn about what the government thinks."

"You know what we forgot, Lee?" she said.

"What?"

"To buy fresh food."

"So we'll have to live on canned foods and the coffee I've got in my hideout."

Evelyn shook her head as she said, "I was looking forward to breakfast of bacon and eggs."

"Considering the mess we're in, I wouldn't complain about canned food," he said. "It's better than being in their hands."

Seven minutes later Lee turned off the headlights of the Honda and turned off Wood Boulevard onto a muddy dirt road and drove a few miles east down the road before he stopped among ten foot high brush.

"From here we walk?" Evelyn asked Lee.

"From here we walk," he replied.

They got out of the Honda, took their backpacks out of the back of the Honda, and wiped it clean of their prints. A minute later they were walking through the dark preservers heading west with their backpacks on their backs.

"The rain's increasing," Evelyn said in a voice that indicated she was not happy with the thought of walking through mud.

"That's good," Lee told her as he walked two feet ahead of her. "The rain will wipe out any tracks we leave. Try not to break off any branches. They might send someone after us who is a good tracker."

"We should have brought night vision goggles with us," she complained.

Lee stopped and took his pack off his back. "Thanks for reminding me," he said as he sat the pack down on the ground and opened it and took out two sets of night vision goggles. He handed one pair to Evelyn. "I forgot I had packed these."

She slipped the goggles over the hood that covered her head, and down over her eyes, and adjust the vision of the goggles.

"Ready?" he asked her after he'd done the same thing.

"Yeah, let's go to your hideout," she said. "And I hope it's safe, because if it ain't we and our children are all dead."

"Don't worry, Evelyn," he told her as he started walking. "It's safe, because no one knows where it is."

"How can you be so sure of that?" she asked him as she followed a few steps behind him.

"Because we live in world with a population that's less than half the size it was a thousand years ago," he answered as he carefully walked avoiding thorn bushes and depressions he could fall in and break an ankle or leg. "Watch your step. You don't want to fall and break something out here. Not with those killers chasing us."

"That's because of all those terrible plagues that attacked the human race over the last nine centuries. Plagues cause by all of the pollution the people put into the air and water. If the damned greedy fools who owned the industries that polluted the world had listened to the environmentalists' warning those plagues would never have happened," Evelyn complained as she followed as closely in his footsteps as possible.

"You're right there, Evelyn," he agreed. "But one of the benefits of all those plagues was a smaller population where more than ninety-eight percent of the people live in one of the one hundred clean safe cities, and the other one and one-third percent live in agricultural zones producing food for those in the cities."

"What about those two-thirds of one percent?" she asked.

"From what I've read those are people who prefer to live in small isolated communities far from the cities and towns and agricultural zones," he told her.

"You sound like someone trying to sell a townhouse or condo in an inner city," she said.

He smiled and said, "You know at one time the term inner city meant a place within a city that had large numbers of poorly educated seldom employed minority groups with high crime rates."

"Is this a history lesson?" she asked.

"Don't knock history, Evelyn," he told her. "Because of history we know where we come from, where we are, and where we're going."

"Because of history, and the lessons we've learned from it, the inner cities of the world today are clean, safe places, with excellent schools, hospitals, and apartments and townhouses as well as condos," she agreed with him. "And all of them are surrounded by the outer rings where the rich and powerful live who control the city governments and the state and world governments, too."

"Yeah, I agree with you there, but political power is still in the hands of the common woman and man," Lee reminded her. "And surrounding those outer rings

outside those cities is what, Evelyn?"

"Forest preserves that turn into muddy forest preserves when it rains like this one has," she complained. "And as a mother of children who did a wonderful job of getting their clothes muddy when they were young—which I had to clean up—I don't like mud."

"And beyond those muddy forest preserves is what, Evelyn?"

"I don't know. I've seldom left the city except to go on a vacation and when I did I went to four star hotels with all the comforts of home except I didn't have to cook or clean. And where I met really nice men, especially after I dumped that worthless crap, I was a damn fool for marrying." She looked down at the mud covering her shoes and complained. "Doesn't grass ever grow in this damned preserve?"

"The trees in these preserves grow so close together their branches and leaves block out most of the sunlight. Only shade plants grow under them," he told her. "So what's beyond those forest preserves that surround every city in the world today?"

"We've got to walk through twenty miles of this mud?" Evelyn complained. Even the squishy sound of her feet in the mud annoyed her.

"That we do," he said. "Beyond those forest preserves, my dear Evelyn, is the wilderness which the major expressways by pass, and only dirt roads cut through them. And most of them are overgrown with weeds."

"And there isn't a decent laundry mat for miles," she added. She glanced down at her shoes and said, "These shoes cost me three hundred dollars and they're ruined by all this mud."

Lee laughed a short laugh and said, "I think I've shoes that'll fit you at my hideout."

"If it's anything like that Spartan one we left, I seriously doubt it." She noticed the legs of her jeans. "Do you also have jeans that'll fit me? My jeans are ruined."

"They cost three hundred dollars, too?"

"They're designer jeans," she told him in an angry voice. "This spring's jeans design by Wilcox."

"What's that mean? They look different from last year's jeans?"

"Yes, they do. The stitching makes them look great on me."

"What about the stitching on last year's jeans? They've gone bad or something?"

"No, they still look good on me. It's just that I like to be in fashion. Don't you?"

"That's why I haven't bought a pair of jeans in twenty years. My old ones are still in fashion."

"I'll bet you keep your cars a long time, too, don't you?"

"A minimum of ten years. I also drive carefully, too."

"After seeing what you did with those two cars, Lee, I'm sure your insurance company loves you."

He turned around and looked at her and smiled as he said, "I haven't had an accident in fifteen years which is why I haven't bought a new car in fifteen years." He turned back to the front.

"When was the last time you got a moving violation?"

"Twenty-two years ago, but I did manage to get a parking ticket five years ago."

"Can we stop and rest?" she asked. "The straps of this backpack are cutting into my shoulders."

"In another two miles after we've crossed the river," he told her.

"I don't suppose there's a bridge we can use?"

"Not where we're going to cross. The nearest bridge is a mile south of where we're going to cross. And we don't want to go to that."

"Why not," she asked him.

"By the time we reach that river the Honda will have been discovered by the people the five have out looking for us," he told her. "They'll know we're walking through these woods and they may have someone near, or on that bridge waiting for us."

She walked quietly for an hour before she spoke.

"Why are we going into the wilderness? I have another place in the city where we could have hid, and is far more comfortable than your hideout."

"Because like this preserve there aren't any surveillance equipment of any kind in the wilderness. Our employers won't be able to find us like they would have eventually done had we gone to one of your holes-in-the-ground."

"They wouldn't have found us in my other place," she said.

"Don't kid yourself, Evelyn," he told her. "There's no place in Crown City they can't see into. And that goes for every other city in the world and the small farming villages and towns, too. If there's one thing I learned while working for that ass Paul is there is no such thing as privacy from those five in a computerized world. No power lines penetrate the wilderness. To keep the environment safe from pollution the Department of the Interior makes damn sure no modern equipment penetrates them."

"Then how is it you have a hideout in this wilderness we're going to?"

"It took me ten years to renovate it after I discovered it," he said. "And I made damn sure no one knew I was renovating it, too."

"How far are we from that river?"

"We're coming up on it now," he said.

"We're going to wade across this river?"

"The only way across. Don't worry it's narrow and only chest deep, but with the spring melt off it might be a little swift."

"I'm not as tall as you, and I'm not a good swimmer," she warned him.

"Don't worry, just hang onto my backpack, I'll get you across."

His words didn't give Evelyn any assurance.

$$\infty$$

CHAPTER 19

1:45 a.m.

Paul, as usual, was looking unconcerned as he watched the screen. He was sitting in a leather chair looking like he was the gentleman he liked to pretend he was with an expression of complete confidence in the successful outcome of any project he had started. His hair was neatly combed and he wore a dark red silk and cotton dressing gown with wide deep pockets. Three thousand dollar handmade black leather slippers, to match the dressing gown, were on his feet and a matching scarf, neatly tied, was around his neck. He wore matching pajamas of equal value. His hands were folded together on his lap.

Steve was dressed in slacks, expensive of course, brown slippers, and an open at the neck white shirt with the cuffs unbuttoned. He was pacing back and forth behind the chair Paul was sitting in. He had an expression of worry on his face.

Fred was sitting in a chair next to the desk Sam was working at dressed similar to Steve looking at Larry with an expression of anger on his face that said he wasn't satisfied with Larry's conduct of the problem.

Bruce was on couch against the wall looking at the mirror and thinking.

"I don't know how they could have gotten away from us," Larry said in a chair on the other side of the desk.

"Explain how that happened, Sam," Bruce said.

"I told Mr. David I saw two people with hoods hiding their faces in the downtown underground garage stealing a Honda G-4, and that the underground's cameras couldn't see them."

Bruce looked at Larry and asked, "And what were you going, Larry."

"My job," he snapped at Larry. "What else?"

"Playing electronic golf comes to mind," Bruce said. His tone was accusatory.

Larry spun around so fast to face Bruce he nearly fell off the chair he was sitting on as he angrily growled, "What the hell are you saying?"

"That you were playing electronic golf when you should have been paying attention to what Sam was telling you," Steve said, stopping his pacing.

"Go on, Sam," Bruce said.

"The two people who stole the Honda then left the garage and headed north. One of our vehicles caught up with them on Ball Street, but the Honda took a sharp turn onto a side street and our vehicle lost them until it turned around and returned to Ball Street where the Honda was seen turning from Ball Street onto Wood Boulevard heading north.

Another vehicle we'd sent was heading south and encountered them. But the driver of the Honda made an unexpected move and caused both of our vehicles to collide."

"I sent a pick up van for our people in the cars, and two tow trucks to remove the two cars," Larry said, turning around to face the monitor. "They were gone before the police arrived."

"Were the police slow in arriving at the accident scene?" Steve asked Larry.

"I had Sam send them the wrong address for the accident," he said. "By the time they realized they were on the wrong street and got on the right one our people had picked up the two cars and left."

"But the police found evidence of an accident," Fred added.

"So what," Larry snapped.

Paul cleared his throat to get their attention and asked in a calm voice, "Did you see where the Honda went after the collision, Sam?"

"No, sir," Sam said. "I was using the traffic cameras and all that I saw was our two vehicles colliding with each other."

"Why was that?" Paul asked in a calm smooth voice.

"Someone in the Honda had managed to blind the traffic cameras to the Honda by having the traffic cameras' servers replay the same scene over and over."

"So how do you know the collision was caused by the Honda?"

"Considering the two people in the Honda knew they were being pursued it is the only logical explanation, sir."

"And you did a complete scan of all the streets and alleys in that section of the city?"

"I told him to do that," Larry said.

"Yes, sir," Sam answered.

"We didn't pick up the Honda again," Larry said.

"You didn't see the Honda as it was being stolen and after it left the underground garage, Larry," Fred said. "And you didn't see the collision, so for all you know the collision could have been the result of Snow White driving a carriage down Wood."

"Listen all of you," Larry said in as calm a voice as he could manage. "While you were sleeping, I was working."

"No," Bruce said. "You were playing electronic golf and paid no attention to what Sam was telling you."

"I don't have to take that crap from you," Larry hissed at him in a voice filled with a challenge to fight.

Paul stood up. "Quiet! All of you!" he said in a loud voice.

The four men fell quiet and looked at him.

Paul put his hands behind his back and folded them together as he lowered his head and thought.

They looked at him and said nothing.

Paul put his hands into the pockets of his dressing gown and said in a slow even voice as he raised his head, "Wood Boulevard is the only four lane street on the western edge of Crown heading north and south. I doubt if they headed north after the collision or went south. Even if they could blind the city's traffic cameras to their movements, they would have wanted to avoid any more traffic cameras and those are on major streets."

"Which means they would have headed west for the forest preserves," Steve said.

He was still pacing but not in the same aggressive way.

"And they would have taken the closest street to go there," Paul continued as if Steve hadn't spoken. "And that street, if memory serves me well, connects with Wood Boulevard." He stopped speaking and waited for one of them to say something. But no one said anything. "But they wouldn't have remained on any connection streets very long because of traffic cameras. They would have remained on it just long enough to get outside the city limits and find a place to dump that Honda." He turned to Sam and asked, "Did you see the Honda on Wood Boulevard?"

"No, sir because the servers at traffic control kept replacing the same scene over and over again," Sam replied.

"I sent two of our best people to look for the Honda," Larry said as if it made his mistakes seem unimportant.

"All our people are the best," Paul said.

"So now they're in the forest preservers hidden somewhere from us because there are no traffic cameras there doing God knows what," Fred said.

"Did you manage to get the license number of the Honda, Sam?" Paul asked him.

"Yes, sir," he replied.

"Put it up on the screen, please," Paul told him.

The license number appeared on the screen.

"Damn," Bruce said.

"You recognize that number?" Fred asked him.

"Yes, it's my license number," he said.

Steve laughed.

"What's funny?" Paul asked him as he looked at him.

"Lee remembered that number from one of our cars parked in front of that house where we met him," he said. "The man knew we'd get the license number of the Honda, and he gave us one we wouldn't expect to get."

"Those plates look legitimate," Larry said. "I wonder how they managed to make them."

"Wherever they were hiding at when they left that kitchen in the Department of Information," Paul said.

"It matters little," Fred said. "When the Honda is found in those preservers, there won't be any finger prints or anything found in it to indicate Lee and Evelyn stole it from the downtown underground garage."

"Sam, are you looking for the program in the traffic servers that prevented you from seeing the Honda?" Paul asked him.

"Yes, sir," Sam replied. "But I have not found it."

"And you won't," Steve said. "Evelyn put it there and since they are in the forest preserves that program has probably self-destructed."

"Do what you can do, Sam, to find that Honda," Paul told him. "But I doubt if you will find it."

"Yes, sir,"

"Send someone in to relieve Sam within the hour, Larry," Paul said as he looked at his watch. "In the meantime, I suggest we all retire to the breakfast room for tea before we return to our beds." He walked toward the door.

The four obediently followed him.

Sam continued working at the computer without turning to see where they had gone.

As soon as they were in the breakfast room, Paul motioned to Bruce to close the door.

"Gentleman, I know where Lee and Evelyn are going," he said.

"Where?" Larry said.

"Into the wilderness where we can't find them no matter how hard we search for them."

"Then we kill their families as punishment for failing to do as we ordered, and find two other people to find this person with our information," Bruce said.

"That we can't afford to do," Steve said.

"And why can't we?" Fred said. "In order for us to maintain our positions of power and wealth we can't afford to let them get away without punishment."

"Because they are the two best people we've ever employed," Paul said. "We're responsible for those skills they possess. And killing their families won't stop them from locating the person with our information. If we did that and they found out it will only make them more determined to find this person and reveal our information to the world."

"But they've run away. They've abandoned their families and deserted us, and that we cannot permit," Bruce said. He was sitting at the table.

"They have not run away, or abandoned their families," Steve said as he took a seat at the table in the brightly colored room with a partial glass roof to let the rising sun into the breakfast room. "What they've done is put us in a position where we can't harm their families, and they know that. And they will find this person with our information. And when they do, they will use that information against us and we will be finished."

"Where in the wilderness have they gone?" Larry asked. He was standing next to the door with an expression on his face that was a mixture of worry and fear.

"Some place where they can work on finding the person with our information," Paul said as he raised his eyebrows as a thought came into his mind. "Once they find this person and the information he has they will have to verify the information and there is only one way they can do that."

"Go to the lab?" Bruce asked as if it was a place none of them knew about, but they all did.

Paul looked at him and nodded.

"They would be exceedingly foolish to go there," Fred said, looking at Paul. "It's the most guarded place in the world. They'd never get pass the automated security robots or the laser weapons."

"Oh yes they would," Steve said. "Whoever stole our information has the secret codes to get into the lab."

"Then we change the codes," Larry said. "And lay a trap and wait for them."

"Waiting is a luxury we don't have, Larry," Paul said. "Once they find who has

our information they will learn about the lab, Evelyn will start working on a program to get pass any new codes we put in place. Remember, Gentlemen, we chose her because of her outstanding skills as a hacker. Look at what she did with the city's traffic computers. And Lee will find this person we want. The man has the tracking skills of a leopard."

"There is one thing we haven't thought of," Bruce said.

They all turned and looked at him "Whoever stole our information must know we're looking for him and that we will kill his family when we find out who he is," he said as he looked at the mosaic pattern on the table and thought aloud. "This person is probably preparing a way to release our information to the world. And considering how skillful they were in getting the information I don't think we have the luxury, as Paul said, of waiting. At the most we have maybe three or four days before the information is released. After that we will be investigated by the government, and none of the people we control will stand by us no matter what we offer them."

"Excellent assumption, Bruce," Paul said. "Wherever Lee and Evelyn are hiding in the wilderness they won't be far from the city. But they won't be around any electrical sources, because they know we can use them to find them. They will use what equipment they've got to search for this person using satellites." He turned to Larry and said, "Assign the best computer people we've got to access all information coming from every satellite that passes over this county."

"We have two others down stairs in their quarters awaiting orders, Paul," he said.

"Good. Next we send out a half dozen of our people to watch grocery stores in small towns in the county because Lee and Evelyn will need food."

"I'd suggest every county bordering this one," Paul said. "Lee is smart enough not to stick to this county when buying supplies."

"How many people have we got left?" Fred asked.

"Fifty-six. The four in those two cars were killed when their cars collided."

Paul was in deep thought for a few seconds before he spoke again. "Anymore suggestions, Gentlemen?"

"None at the moment," Steve said.

"Then let's go to bed and get a good night's rest, because getting a lot of rest isn't something we're going to be able to do for the next few days." He turned and walked toward the door.

CHAPTER 20

7 a.m. Monday morning

As a rule Lyle wasn't an early riser when he didn't have to get up to go to work especially on Monday morning. He was like most working class people. He hated Mondays even when they were beautiful Mondays winter, spring, summer, or fall. But today was different just as all his days had been different since he uncovered the information about the five, and would continue to be until he managed to find a way to put the information, he had on the Internet without the five monsters learning his true identity.

In the thirty-first century world of computers and servers that should have been easy. But it wasn't. The world had changed drastically since the beginning of the computer age in the late twentieth century and the new age of electrical gadgets of the twenty-first century. People did everything with computers then as if they were an important part of their lives and they had a right to do as they wished with computers. Today there were strict laws governing the use of computers. What a person did with their own personal computers in the privacy of their homes was their business as long as they weren't using the computer to violate the various computer laws.

Hacking into other people's computers, and that included company computers, was against the law everywhere in the world. And government computers at the local, county, state, and federal level were off limits unless one had a code which was hard to get, or if a person was just looking around at government agencies that served the public. Then a person could browse the various government agencies to their heart's content.

Computer porn was strictly controlled but not outlawed. There was a lot of money in the computer porn business and that meant a lot of taxes for the federal government and the various state governments. So the government permitted it as long as it was for adults only, and only adults over the age of twenty-one were involved in the computer porn business. It was the responsibility of parents to control the computers and cable TV service that came to their homes. All the government Communication Department had to do was make sure cable companies, network TV had died out centuries ago, strictly followed federal law regarding content and quality.

Child porn on the other hand was illegal everywhere in the world and punished with many years in prison including the confiscation of all money made from the business and of all possessions bought with the illegal money—even if legally bought.

Since there were no longer any competing national states, the arms industry had declined and using a computer to sell weapons was against the law even though each state made its own laws regarding gun ownership. America had centuries ago ended its stupid romance with guns and America were longer thought of as a wild-west society with cowboys shooting it out in the streets of dusty western towns.

While computers had become as common as leaves on a tree in the summer, and a user could go anywhere including contacting the scientific colony on Mars and the three Pluto Space Stations a billion miles beyond the orbit of Pluto they were also easy to trace by someone who knew how to run a trace. And what was disturbing about that was a user could be traced and not know he/she was being traced, even though it was a violation of federal and all state laws to trace someone's computer use without a warrant, until everything he or she had done was known to the tracer. The only way to avoid that was to go through the servers of corporations. And that could be dangerous since every company and corporation in the world had a UUIP—Unauthorized User Identification Program. It was a simple program that looked for anyone not authorized to use the company or corporation's servers. And that was Lyle's problem.

Somehow Lyle had to get into some corporation's or company's servers without them knowing about it and release what he had on the five monsters. And he couldn't use one or two companies or corporations. He needed to use hundreds of them, preferably thousands and at the same time, so he could release his information in bits and pieces from each corporation or company without the five's experts finding out about what he'd done until it was too late for them to locate him, identify him, kill him, and then kill his family if they managed to learn his true identity. Time was both with him and against him.

Lyle knew the five had their people out looking for him. So he didn't have a lot of time to waste. Waste too much time and the five's killers would find him, learn who he really was, and his family would die horrible deaths. But release the information he had before they found him, and he had won and they had loss.

As Lyle sat down at the desk in the living room kitchen of the cabin he was hiding in, he trembled with fear as he looked at the fifty years old laptop on the desk. He sat staring at the laptop for fifteen minutes before he started typing.

CHAPTER 21

June 4, 2:03 a.m. Monday

When Lee said narrow river Evelyn thought it would actually be a narrow river and easy to cross. As for hanging onto Lee's backpack that was easier said than done. Not only was the water in the river colder than she had expected, the current was also swift and strong. Even Lee was pushed a few yards south by the strong southerly current as he waded across the narrow chest deep river. Evelyn didn't want to imagine what would have happened to her had she tried crossing the river on her own. The water, which was at Lee's chest, would have been at her neck and she wouldn't have been able to maintain her footing. She would have slipped under the surface and drowned within minutes. Even Lee had a little trouble maintaining his footing and staying upright.

Even the width of the river surprised Evelyn. When Lee said it was narrow she thought it would be only five or ten feet wide. Instead she estimated the river to be more than forty feet wide, and that wasn't her idea of a narrow river but a wide river.

Lee was glad she was hanging on to his backpack. He didn't think the river's current would be so strong or the river so deep and the muddy bottom so slippery. Until he realized the last time he had waded this river alone was twenty-two years ago when he was not only much younger but stronger, and that was in late August when the river was shallow and slow not early June when melting snow farther to the north was still pouring into every river and stream in the country and heading south to the Gulf of Mexico. And the rain, though light, added more water to the narrow river.

He had hoped their combined weight would make him sink deeper into the muddy bottom thus making for a more stable footing for them to wade across the river. But the swift, strong current negated their weight. Twice he slipped and fell to his knees plunging his face below the cold, dark water, and dragging a frightened Evelyn down with him. He had to struggle with all his energy to rise to his feet and pull Evelyn back up with him. Keeping his mouth shut and exhaling through his nose was the only thing that kept water out of his mouth and nose. He was glad Evelyn didn't cry out when they surfaced. There was a chance it would have attracted the attention of the killers he was certain were on the bridge even though the bridge was a mile away. Who knows the damn butchers could have had com-cells with sound detecting ability.

Lee had thought it would take only two minutes to cross the river. By the time he crawled, breathing heavily, up on to the muddy bank, which was easy to reach because of the high level of the water, he estimated it had taken him all of twelve minutes to cross the forty-five foot wide river that was deeper than he thought. He collapsed on the bank to catch his breath.

"Next time," Evelyn gasped between breathes as she lay next to him. "Next time we use the fucking bridge."

"No more rivers to cross from here on out," he said between breaths. *Boy, do I need to do some exercising. Or at least get off my ass and do more walking.* He turned his head to the left and looked at her and thought, *No sense in telling her about the two creeks we've got to cross before we reach my cabin. I hope they aren't very wide.* He got up on his feet and pulled Evelyn to her feet. "A few more miles and we can rest."

"And bathe," she said as she moved her hands down her body to push as much water off herself as she could. She stood up and looked around the woods. The night vision goggles made the dark forest look like day. She saw a small herd of deer looking at them like they were crazy. "I'll bet they use the bridge when they want to cross the river."

Lee looked at the herd of deer and said, "They can afford to. Hunting is not permitted in these woods."

"How far have we to go before we're in the wilderness?" she asked.

"We've been in it for the last hour." He looked up at the sky at the dark clouds and said, "Looks like it's about to start pouring down."

"Well, that won't bother us since we're already soaking wet," she said.

He started walking. "Hope it comes down heavy and hard. It'll wipe out any tracks we've left."

"Hell, maybe we should have brought some soap with us," she complained falling

in beside him. "We could strip down, carry our clothes on our backs, and taken a cold spring shower. Even wash our fucking muddy clothes."

"You going be one really surprised woman when you see my hideout," he told her as he looked at her and smiled.

"I'll bet. It's probably some dusty, Spartan hole under some damn mountain with nasty ass animals running around inside it."

"Save your breath for the walk and think about how you're going to use those excellent computer skills of your to find the mysterious person we're looking for."

They walked for almost an hour before it started to rain. In ten minutes it was coming down in a steady down pour. It stopped after twenty minutes and became a sprinkle that didn't seem like it would let up for hours.

Lee stopped at four a.m. and looked at the endless trees in front of him. The trees went up the side of the mountain they were facing like they were toy soldiers marching to some Christmas marching song. The terrain had changed a little, more brush was growing in those areas the trees hadn't claimed, and the area looked like it hadn't had a human in it for almost a century. He hadn't been away from it that long, though.

"You ever wondered why when the World Democratic Government was created in 2452 the state of Colorado was chosen as the spot for the capital?" he asked Evelyn.

"No, and I don't care," she replied, standing next to him. "Have we gone twenty miles?"

"Just fifteen," he said. "Colorado was one of those western American states that still had a healthy clean look about it. And the new World Congress and President wanted a new place to establish the capital of the first united world government. New York City had too much of the old world of greed about it. So did the other major old cities of the world. So the town of Crown in Colorado was chosen to be the world capital. And from that we ended up with Crown City the capital of the world. Thirty-two million people living in a state that is still beautiful with a healthy clean look about it. Let's go."

"Where," she asked.

"Over there in that direction," he said as he started walking toward a tree covered hill.

"What's over there? I don't see anything that looks like a hideout."

"If it looked like a hideout, Evelyn, it wouldn't be a hideout."

He walked over to the small tree covered hill and climbed up it and looked down it into a long narrow valley. It was only a hundred feet wide and a mile and a half long that had six different ways into and out of it. Then he started walking down it as if he was taking a stroll in a park.

"Where is this hideout of yours that doesn't look like a hideout, Lee," she asked him. "I'm cold, hungry, and still wet."

"Be patient," he told her.

"I have been patient, Lee," Evelyn complained.

An hour later he stopped in front of wall of trees and thick brush in front of two hills that were joined together by a smaller one between them.

"Wait here," he told her and took off his backpack and dropped it on the ground next to her. "I'll be back in a few minutes."

She smelt a strong unpleasant odor. "What's that odor? And where are you going?"

"Bat guano. Through that wall of thick brush and trees directly in front of us.

Don't go away."

"Bat guano?" she said as she thought about the word 'guano' as he disappeared into the brush. "That's bat shit."

Lee didn't hear her because he'd penetrated into the brush and was forcing his way toward a cave he could clearly see. He didn't worry about running into any bats. After a long winter in the cave with little to eat they were out fattening up on insects foolish enough to be flying around in the rain. He stopped at the edge of the cave and looked inside at the floor. There was over three inches of fresh guano on the floor of the small cave with maybe a foot or more underneath what he could see. He smiled when he saw the large ten foot high seven foot wide, double thick heavy canvas that hung like a curtain from a three inch round seven foot long steel rod by heavy steel rings that went from one side of the rear of the cave to the other side and to the floor of the cave just beyond the guano. He looked up and saw the heavy steel screen that started an inch below the steel rod and went to the top of the cave.

Lee wasn't surprised to see the heavy canvas and screen were still in place. He checked on this place as well as his hideout every three to five years, but never on the same day or in daylight. The canvas and screen kept the bats out of the rear of the cave.

He walked through the guano to the canvas curtain on the right side of the wall and pulled the canvas curtain back and saw the covered hump at the back of the cave. He looked at the ground and saw no guano on the dirt floor, and moved toward the hump thinking he'd have to get rid of the shoes he was wearing when he reached his final destination. Evelyn would complain like a mad woman with the smell of guano in his hideout. He wouldn't like it either because he couldn't stand the stink either, but he needed what was under the thick canvas cover.

As soon as he reached the large lump, he pushed back the canvas from the left side to reveal a forest colored dust free four wheeled all-terrain two seat vehicle with wide tires. He knelt down on the left side of the vehicle and pulled out a handle next to the engine and began to pump the handle back and forth. He hadn't been here in almost five years but he knew the battery was still good. A few seconds of pumping and the electrolytes in the dry cell battery would come alive with just enough energy to start the electric engine. After that the running engine would recharge the battery enough for him to travel around the world in the vehicle for years. That was the nice thing about electric powered engines since 2050. There was no foul carbon monoxide odor resulting from burning gasoline or dangerous gasoline and no need to plug the engine into some electrical socket like the early electric powered engines.

Lee pushed the handle back into place, removed the canvas from the rest of the vehicle, climbed into the driver's seat, and pushed the start button. The engine came to life like it had been driven only yesterday. He got out of the vehicle pulled back the canvas curtain and drove out of the rear of the cave into the guano dominated part. Then he got out of the driver's seat and walked back and closed the canvas curtain to keep the bats out of the rear of the cave. Then he got back into the driver's seat and carefully drove the vehicle out the cave trying to do as little damage as he could to the outside brush and trees. He maneuvered the vehicle around the trees and stopped in front of Evelyn, and said, "Put the backpacks in that bed on the back and hop in.".

"This isn't your hideout?" she asked with a surprised look on her face.

"Of course, not," he said.

She picked up his backpack put it and hers in the bed and got in the seat next to him.

"Two more creeks to cross and we'll be at my hideout," he said. "Forty minutes at the most traveling through this forest. Buckle up. Bumpy ride ahead."

She put the seatbelt around her waist and chest and sat back in a relaxed manner. The long walk had taken a lot of her energy.

He took off at a slow two miles per hour. Any faster and the ride would be bumpier than she'd like.

Thirty minutes and two shallow fast running creeks later, they stopped in both to wash their shoes off—Evelyn was complaining about the stink of bat guano on Lee's shoes, and the tires and the driver's foot well of the vehicle and he stopped in front of solid wall of trees.

"There's nothing here," Evelyn said, looking at the wall of trees.

"Twenty-three years ago in Crown City's main library I read about a rich guy who two hundred years ago divorced his cheating wife, gave his spoiled children half his money and moved into these woods." He got out of the vehicle and walked toward the wall of trees saying, "Drive the car into the opening when I tell you." He disappeared behind the wall of trees and ten seconds later the trees move to the left side revealing a garage with two cross country vehicles with large fat tires parked inside. "Come on," he said waving her forward.

She unbuckled her seatbelt and jumped into the driver's seat and moved the car forward into the garage between the two vehicles. She turned around in time to see the wall of trees closing again without so as much as a squeak. She heard a soft metal snapping sound and the lights in the garage came on. She looked forward and saw a car with roll bars over the roof and plastic sides and four foot high wheels parked in the back of the garage. Next to it was a four wheel bike.

"This rich guy built this place?" she asked as she got out of the two seat car.

"That he did but he didn't want to live like some backwoods hermit," Lee said. "So he made sure to put all the comforts of modern life in this house—which is now my best hideout."

"House?" she asked, looking around the clean garage. "I didn't see a house just a hill with this garage in it."

"Originally there were three small hills around a small lake fed by an underground stream. The guy who built this house built it between the largest of those hills right over the lake. Over the centuries after he died, the place was neglected because no one knew it was here. The forest grew up between the hills blocking access to the front and back doors hiding the house. Centuries of dead leaves provided the brush with plenty of fertilizer to grow and they filled in the cracks between the trees and the gaps between the three hills."

"So anyone flying over can see the roof of this place. Some hideout," Evelyn said.

"The guy who built this house gave it a roof of stone eight feet thick resting on the hills on each side of it. Strong enough to support a hover craft landing on it, and dirt landing on it from the wind and grass and small brush growing on top of it," Lee told her. "This place looks from the top like nothing but a hill covered with trees like hundreds of other hills for over a thousand square miles."

"This isn't a hideout, Lee," she told him. "If you found out about this house in the Crown library, the five will also find out about it from the same source."

"No chance of that," he said with a grin on his face.

"You found the blue prints and destroyed them," she said.

"And I erased it from the library computer and server I found it in," he said.

"Smart move," she said.

"Come on," he said as he walked toward four steel stairs to the right of the garage. "I'll show you around the place."

"How do you know there aren't copies of the blue prints in the city office of records?" she asked as followed him.

"The guy who built this place didn't have any blueprints or computer diagrams made to register with the city, county, or state," he told her as he walked up the stars to a door and stopped. "This whole area was off limits to construction then, as now. The guy owned a small construction company and built this place himself without filing a permit or blueprints of any kind." He pushed a button on the brass pad to the right of the door and waited.

"So how did you find out about this place?" she asked standing beside him.

"The story I read about the guy who built this place said he liked building unusual homes for people in odd places. This house wasn't mentioned in the book I read about him, but it did say he'd disappeared somewhere into this wilderness. Now I assumed a guy who built homes in odd places wouldn't live in a cave or a tent. So out of boredom I went looking for this place and after a few weeks of searching found it. I took the book I'd read on him without checking it out of the library."

The door withdrew to the left side exposing a carpeted elevator.

"Take off your muddy shoes," he told Evelyn. "I don't want mud or bat guano tracked onto the carpet."

They both took off their shoes and left them on the metal landing. Lee walked into the elevator and pushed a button marked 1 when Evelyn had entered. The door closed with a soft hiss of air and the elevator rose. Above the door were two square markers with the number 1 on the one on the left and 2 on the right next to it. The door opened three seconds later on a lighted foyer with soft white light that brought out the beauty of the medium red and blue carpet and the beige walls that had two landscape paintings on each wall.

Evelyn looked at the paintings and the carpet and walls and noted they were clean and not dust covered like everything was in Lee's hideout under the police station.

"This way," he said as he walked out the elevator and turned to his right.

She looked to her right as she left the elevator and saw a steel wall at the end of the foyer. "What's behind that steel wall?"

"Dirt," he said as he walked. "I had it put there to keep the dirt from getting in."

"Then there's a record of the work done," she said as she followed him into a spacious living room as the ceiling lights and lamps on the tables went on.

"No," as he walked over to large wooden globe of the world that set to the right of fireplace that had a gold fire screen in front of it. "Twenty years ago I found a guy who'd stolen twenty million from Fred. Paul told me to find him. He was with his family—a wife and four young children—and he begged me not to turn him in. I didn't like Fred any more than I liked those other four assholes. I knew if I reported his whereabouts to Fred, he'd have him killed along with his family, rather than file charges against him. The money the guy stole was drug money Fred was extorting from a drug dealer. Would you like a drink?"

"So you lied and said you couldn't find him."

"No, I told him to fake his and his family's death, and I'd be in touch with him."

"Scotch. Single malt. And this guy helped you restore this place?"

"No. He helped me get four robots and they helped me restore this place, and now they keep it clean and perform maintenance on themselves and this house when necessary." He opened the top of the globe and fixed her a drink, and walked over to her and handed it to her. "Don't sit down, please, Evelyn. You're pretty muddy."

She took the drink and downed it in one swallow and shuddered as the heat of the alcohol passed down into her stomach. She looked around at the clean plush furnishings and said, "This place looks great, Lee. Got a place where I can clean up?"

"This floor consists of this living room and a dining room, kitchen, breakfast room next to the kitchen, a large pantry with loads of can food; a study where you can work, a library—with mostly history and fiction in it—a lounge, and believe it or not a swimming pool with a steam bath that also acts as a sauna on the other side of the garage, plus two small bathrooms at each end of the hallway. The second floor has six bedrooms each with its own bathroom and dressing room."

"The guy who built this place liked living well even if he was in the wilderness," she said as she looked around the living room at the paintings on the wall.

Lee grinned and said, "He sure did."

"Where does the electricity come from?" she asked as she looked around the living room.

"It comes from batteries under the floor next to the garage. A solar disk pops up on the east side of the stone roof whenever the computer attached to the three generators register energy levels at only half. Even on a cloudy day it can absorb enough solar energy to keep this place heated in the winter and cooled in the summer for thirty days."

"It's rather chilly in here now," she said as the heat of the scotch left her body.

"I haven't been here in almost five years," he said. "The automatic thermostat is programmed to detect living objects and increase the heat. It should be about seventy degrees in here in a minute."

"Very good," she said. "Now how do I access the servers in the Department of Information without electrical lines?"

"Satellites."

"Which ones? There are five hundred still up there even after the Space Admiralty got rid of all those left over from the twentieth century."

"What satellites are constantly sending information down to the Department of Information?"

Evelyn thought for a few seconds before she answered. "Those receiving information from the Mars Scientific Station and those Pluto space stations."

"Think you can hitch a ride on one of those messages?"

"Piece of pie," she said.

"Cake," Lee said correcting her.

"I like pie."

"The big bedroom at the far left is mine," he said as he started for the hallway. "Choose any of the others."

She walked over to the open globe and fixed herself a double scotch.

He stopped and watched her. "You going get drunk?"

"No, I'm not, but if the bedroom I choose has a bathtub in it I'm going to soak in a hot bath for an hour, and warm my insides with this scotch. Got any clothes I can change into?" She walked back toward him.

"Yeah, of various sizes but no dresses or bras or panties," he said as he looked at her wet socks. "There are shoes, too, but I suggest you use the slippers even if they are a bit large for you."

"Then we're going to have to get me some clothes that fit," she said as she walked out the living room pass him and walked toward the stairs she had seen earlier.

"Give me a list of what you want and the sizes," he said as he followed her. "I know just where to go for them, and how to shake any tails I'll pick up."

"I work in the lounge or library?" she asked.

"No, in the computer room in the attic right under the stone roof, the equipment in there is only five years old so you should be able to do a lot of work."

"You said the stone roof was eight feet thick," she said. "How am I going to get a signal through eight feet of stone?"

"The solar disk has an antenna attached to the side of it," he said. "That'll work, won't it?"

"Just fine, but first a hot bath and sleep," she said. "Lots of sleep."

"Make out a list of what you want in the way of clothing and leave it on the coffee table," he said, pointing to it.

Two hours later after a hot bath and shower they were both asleep in their separate bedrooms.

CHAPTER 22

June 4, 9 a.m.

The five of them were sitting on the veranda of the lodge which was ten miles south of the city on a mountain overlooking the forest preserves. Their breakfast dishes had been removed by a silent but obedient servant. Only a half filled glass pot of coffee sitting on a heating pad with a sugar bowl and creamer remained on the table alone with their coffee cups. Their breakfast had been silent because they all were reading foreign stock reports from their I-books.

"We must do something about this damn Frenchmen," Fred said breaking the silence. "He keeps complaining that the Department of Health is not spending enough money on bacterial research. He's been warning every news service in the world that if the government doesn't increase spending on bacterial research the world will face another plague like the one two hundred years ago that killed over half a billion people and made another three hundred million sterile."

"At the moment, Fred," Steve said. "Complaining Frenchmen are not an important issue with us."

"If I was Lee and I needed supplies I wouldn't shop at some nearby county store," Paul said as he looked up from his I-book. "He'd expect us to have such places watched."

Larry placed his I-book on the glass topped table and said, "Somewhere far outside the county. Maybe even in another state."

"No," Paul said. "He won't go to another state. Wherever he's hiding, he'll want to be able to get back to it quick."

"Our computer can keep an eye on any unusual purchases at every major department grocery stores in the world," Larry said.

"I wouldn't go to a department or grocery store for what I needed if I were him," Bruce said. "I'd stick to the small mom and pop stores. Those big stores have servers that keep accurate records on all purchases. But the small stores keep their information on the hard drives of their computers. They probably order replacements once a month."

"Very good, Bruce," Paul said. He looked at Larry. "How many people have we got who are not already on assignment?"

"Just six," he said. "We're spread pretty thin, Paul."

"They went west," Steve said as he helped himself to more coffee. "I'm willing to bet they didn't go that far from the city. So if he's going to be shopping for food he'll stay close to where he's hiding. Larry, you should send out two people to check on every mom and pop store in the surrounding counties."

"Just the counties west of the Crown County," Paul said. "And tell them not to stop him, or even make contact with him. Just watch him and follow him. If we can get a general area of where he's hiding, we can conduct a sweep of the area."

"I'll also have our computer people look for the credit cards we gave him," Larry said. "I doubt if he or Evelyn will use their own credit cards."

"You think they're still working on the assignment we gave them?" Fred asked.

"Oh, most certainly," Paul said. "They are as curious as to why we want this thief as we are determined to catch him."

"And finding this thief and protecting him from us guarantees the safety of their families," Steve said as he added one teaspoon of sugar to his coffee.

Paul looked at him and asked, "Why do you think that, Steve?"

"They know now we would have never assigned them the job of finding this person with our information if that information wasn't a matter of life and death to us," he began to explain.

"I don't agree with that," Larry interrupted him. "I don't think they're that aware of how important the information is to us."

"The measures we've taken to catch them, Larry proves we're desperate to get the information back," Steve said to him. "They're not stupid, you know. They know now that their lives and those of their families are dependent upon them finding this person with our information and protecting him and reading the information."

"Are you suggesting blackmail, Steve?" Fred calmly asked him as if he was afraid of the answer.

"Yes," Steve said in a strong voice. "Find this person with our information, contact us and tell us they've got the information, read some of what's in the information to us to confirm they have the correct information, and then issue us an ultimatum. Back off for good or we'll release this information to the world."

"They won't tell us to back off for good once they've read the information, Steven, because they'll be shocked by what they've read and will immediately understand the value of releasing that information to the world and to protecting their families," Paul said.

None of the others said anything because they knew Paul was right.

"Once they've read part of what's in the information they'll release it to the world because they'll have no choice," Paul repeated in a quiet voice.

"And we'll be too busy running and hiding to even think of harming their families," Bruce said. His voice had the sound of fear and defeat in it.

The others looked at him and though they didn't say anything they knew he was right.

CHAPTER 23

June 5, 7:30 a.m. Tuesday

Lee would have preferred to sleep late, but he wanted to stock up on fresh food and get the clothes Evelyn needed as soon as possible. He had plenty of clothing and shoes and boots in his hideout for himself even if they were somewhat out of fashion. So he had gotten up at seven and left twenty minutes later after a cup of coffee. He had taken the four wheel bike after he'd had one of the robots cleaned it up a bit and put a trunk on the back big enough to hold a ton of food and clothing. He didn't intend buying a ton of food and clothing with the altered credit card Evelyn had given him from the cards in the pouch the five had given them. A month's worth of food would be just fine.

If It took them more than a month to find the person who'd stolen the five's information, then they were going to be out of luck as well as their families, because it certainly wouldn't take the five a month with the resources available to them to find him and Evelyn.

And when they did the five would vent their rage against him and Evelyn because of their conduct in evading them. While the five knew they didn't know what information the thief had on them, the five now knew from their conduct since they were given the assignment against their will that whatever they found also meant they must die, too.

Lee slipped the biker's helmet over his head, put on the black leather gloves, climbed on the bike, and started the bike and rode it out the garage. He'd made sure, using his com-cell to access the computers in the attic to scan the area, before he opened the garage door there was no one around for at least a mile to see or hear him leave the garage.

That's what Lee liked about the wilderness. Like its name, it was an area most people avoided. The forest preservers around Crown and every other major city in the world was the closest most people wanted to come to being in the wilderness. Camping out in the cabins, they had all the modern conveniences people enjoyed in their homes, apartments, and townhouses, in the forest preservers was as close to roughing it most people wanted. The few that did enjoy going into the wilderness usually chose places hundreds of miles from the city where they could feel like mountain men challenging the wilderness.

The bike's engine didn't roar like those bike engines did before the government issued a federal order outlawing internal combustion engines in 2701. But it did emit a purring sound that wasn't normal for the wilderness—though it couldn't be heard more than a few yards away. But why take a chance? Being watchful and careful is what had made Lee such a valuable tracker for Paul. He had prided himself on developing those two skills years ago, now he was sorry he'd bothered developing them. He would have been better off as a loud, clumsy oaf. Paul wouldn't have wasted a second on him had he been like that. He wouldn't have even been approached by Paul to be a tracker when he was twenty-three if he'd been a loud, clumsy oaf.

Lee had decided on a small country market a hundred miles away he'd located on a map on his com-cell while he was having coffee. The note he'd left on the kitchen table next to a coffee cup told Evelyn not to worry about him, that he'd be back before sundown.

A half an hour later he'd made it through the semi-dark forest to a dirt road that zigzagged through the woods for forty miles before reaching a single lane black top road used only by farmers and country people from a small town twenty miles north. He headed south on the road making sure to remain as close to the trees that lined the road to make satellite detection of him hard and to make it difficult for any low flying aircraft to see him. He doubted the five would have planes searching for him and Evelyn. That would attract the attention of the World Aviation Administration, and he knew they didn't want any government agencies, local, state, or federal asking questions about low flying planes.

Twice he turned off on dirt roads that cut through thick forests to give anyone who might be watching him the impression that he was no more than a bike rider out for a long ride. Both times he doubled back to the black top road, and continued south. When he was twenty miles away from his destination, he cut into a wooded area and reduced his speed to less than mile an hour to convince any tails he might have picked up he wasn't anything but a bird or animal watcher riding around looking at animals. He used the binoculars he carried in the pouch on his left side to look around himself when he stopped. He knew there were no tails following him, but it didn't hurt to play it safe.

Anyone tailing him would have to keep him within visual distance since the bike didn't have a tracking chip, and he'd spot anyone on a bike suddenly slowing down long before they realized they'd been spotted. Better safe than sorry as the old saying from the twentieth century went. He left the wooded area five miles from his destination and headed directly for the country market.

Twenty-five minutes later he pulled into the gravel parking lot at eleven-thirty and parked next to the main entrance facing out toward the road. Always be ready for a fast getaway. He got off the bike, pushed the wind visor on the helmet up into the slot on the top of the helmet, put his gloves in his back pocket, and walked into the store in a casual manner. The store was typical of many country stores close to wilderness areas with wide thick glass windows for shoppers to look through, and a wide revolving glass door.

A shopping area with nonperishable foods stacked neatly on ten different thirty foot long shelves sat parallel to each other with space between them for shoppers to walk about pushing shopping carts. None of the shelves were higher than five feet so a buyer could look around at the other shelves and see something they needed or wanted but wasn't on their list. At the far end facing the revolving doors was another section of the store with the word clothing in large red letters on the wooden frame above the wide door. A smaller glass enclosed store was located to the left of the grocery store. It contained liquor, beer, and tobacco. To the right in the front next to the window was an eating area with ten tables covered with clean red and white checkered table clothes large enough for four adults.

He stopped a few feet to the left of the wide revolving glass doors, and turned around and scanned the parking lot like he was taking a breather before he bought something. The black two door sedan parked to the left of the store with dark sun screened windows was the only vehicle of the nine pickup trucks and three four door sedans in the parking lot that stood out.

It was wider than the other vehicles with wide tires and sat lower than the others.

It's either some teen-ager's car, built for speed and sharp turns or it belongs to a tracker working for the five, he thought. He heard some talking coming from his left and turned and saw four teen-agers, two girls and two boys, sitting at a table drinking soft drinks admiring the car with envious statements. *Well, it don't belong to them.*

"May I help you?" a female voice behind him said.

He slowly turned around and saw a woman who looked to be in her late forties with short black hair and a friendly smile on her square dark face. She was dressed in a country dress with penny loafers on her feet. There was a penny stuck in the front of both shoes. She had the full healthy figure Lee associated with country women.

"Yes, you can," he said as he zipped open the thin black leather jacket he wore and reached into the left inside pocket and pulled out a slip of paper. He opened it up and held it out to her. "My wife and two of our friends are on a two week camping trip and we need some provisions."

The woman took the slip of paper, opened it up, and stared at the list for a few seconds before she said, "We've got all of this."

He took the list of clothing Evelyn had left on the coffee table out of his jacket pocket and held it out to the woman. "Can you fill this list of clothing, too?"

The woman took the list and read it and said, "We've everything on this list, Mister."

"Oh, good," he said. "I didn't want to try another store."

"Follow me, sir," the woman said.

"Do you mind getting that stuff while I look around?" he asked her.

"Not at all if you trust me to pick the best for you?"

"Frozen vegetables and the best steaks and meat you've got," he said. "And could you put it all in a box. I came on a bike with a freezer compartment on the back."

"Meet me at the express checkout counter in about half an hour," she said, pointing to it.

"Will do," he said, smiling at her. "Got a tobacco store in here?"

"Through that door on your left," she said, pointing to it.

"Thank you," he said as he nodded and walk toward the tobacco store.

Tobacco in the thirty-first century was back in fashion, now that the tobacco companies were growing hybrid tobacco without nicotine in it. But it still wasn't good for you. But Lee occasionally liked to smoke a pipe when he read or wanted to think, alone.

He walked slowly toward the tobacco shop looking at the nineteen other people in the store in an uninterested manner.

Nine of the ten women in the store looked exactly like what they were. Middle-aged women in colorful country dresses or skirts and blouses or dressed in jeans that were designed to show off their shapes wearing shoes that were either low heel walking shoes in brown or black color or two inch strapless heels for the warm spring weather. Of the nine men in the store eight were following one of the eight women and talking to them as they looked at the various products and looked like the husbands of the women. One of the women was dressed in black loose-fitting jeans and a dark blue long sleeve blouse—the sleeves were buttoned—that allowed freedom of movement and provided minimum protection for her arms.

He deliberately walked down the aisle and passed by four of the women making sure they saw him. Three looked at him with a friendly smile and nodded a greeting or just looked at him with pleasant expressions on their faces. The women in the loose fitting jeans avoided looking at him. He noticed the top button on her blouse was buttoned, and he saw the outline of body armor under the blouse. He looked left at the window as if he were looking out it and saw her reflection. She nodded at a man who was a few yards away from her on the other side of a shelf and dressed in a similar fashion.

Lee walked into the tobacco store and bought two hundred dollars' worth of tobacco and a pipe, plus a lighter. While he paid with the credit card Evelyn had created, he looked through the glass partition and saw the similarly dressed woman and man standing close to each other speaking. The man was looking at him with a hard expression on his face as if he was trying to remember what he looked like. When he saw

Lee looking at him, he quickly turned away.

Lee took his purchases and left the tobacco store and walked over to a large magazine rack and picked up four magazines and walked to the express counter and waited for the woman to come with the things on the two lists.

Three of the couples in the store left with the four teen-agers jabbering away and got into two of the four door sedans and drove off. The couple dressed alike watched him for a few minutes then the man left the store and headed for the two door sedan. He opened the passenger's door and got into the car and closed the door.

Lee knew he was making a call to the five if his suspicion about the couple was right. He knew they had been told of what happened to the four trackers in the cars last night, and wouldn't make a move on him as long as he didn't run or do something foolish. Such as pulling out the gun he carried under his jacket on his right side near his back. He knew better than to do that. Those two weren't just trackers. They were merciless killers who wouldn't think once about killing everyone in the store to take him alive.

"Lee Adams is here," the man said into the com-cell in his left hand.

"Could you be more specific as to where is here?" Larry told him.

"Clear Water Market on South Land Road," the man said.

"I have his position, sir," said Troy another of the five's computer experts.

Larry looked at the screen on the wall and saw a flashing light that indicated the man.

"What type of car is he driving?" Larry asked, knowing the man would hear him over the computer speakers.

"He came on a four wheel overland bike," the man said.

"Are there any people in that store?" Steve asked, staring at the screen, too.

"Two women and two men," the man said. "Plus, the owners and their employees."

"Don't do anything," Steve said.

"Why not?" Larry asked him as he turned and looked at Steve. "If we grab him, we can make him tell us where Evelyn is."

"We don't want any innocent victims," Bruce said. "Innocent victims attract the police, and we don't want or need them."

"Wait until he leaves," Bruce said to the man. "Then both of you follow him."

"Yes, sir," the man said.

"He will, of course, spot them following him," Steve told Bruce.

"Yes, he will," Bruce agreed. "But he's on a bike with no protection around him. Lee isn't stupid, is he Paul?"

Paul was sitting at a table near a wall watching the TV screen. "No, he isn't. But he's resourceful and intelligent. Tell our trackers to be alert for any unusual moves he makes once he leaves the store."

Larry told the man what Paul had said.

"I hope I've gotten everything, sir," the woman said as she approached the counter pushing a shopping cart loaded with the supplies on the two lists she held in her hand.

"Well, let's see," Lee said in a cheerful voice as he began to look over everything in the shopping cart. "Yep," he said after twelve seconds. "You got everything on those lists. Right sizes in clothes and shoes?"

"Exactly what you had on the list, sir," the woman said.

"Very good," Lee said. "Then I'll check out."

"Put this in a box for him, Eva," the woman said to the young woman at the checkout counter.

"Okay," the young woman said as she turned around and picked up a large, heavy cardboard box on the floor behind her.

Lee glanced at the woman in the loose fitting jeans every few minutes as she wandered about the store looking in his direction occasionally and looking out the window at the two door sedan.

Eve scanned his selections over a glass in the counter and carefully wrapped the frozen vegetables, meat, and flour and sugar in plastic bags before she placed them in the box. When that box was filled she turned around and got another box after pushing the full box to the end of the counter. She did the same thing with the rest of his selections until they were all packed in the box.

"That'll be seven hundred and twelve dollars, Mister," Eva said, looking at him with a blank expression.

Lee took out the credit card Evelyn had changed, and handed it to her while he looked about the store as if he were trying to remember something.

The woman in the loose jeans suddenly walked out the store and got into the sedan on the driver's side and slammed and locked the door.

Lee looked as unconcerned as he could because he knew what they were going to do.

Wait until he left the store and loaded his purchases in the trunk on the back of the bike, and leave. They would follow a hundred yards or more behind him to avoid arousing his suspicions until he was in an area on the road where no houses were close by. Then they'd make their move.

Lee wondered if they were aware that he was ready for them, probably not. Tracker-killers like them the five used didn't think their targets were smart enough to be aware of them and prepared for them. They tended to be single minded. Do as ordered.

"Come again," the young woman said as if it was just an empty statement she said to everyone as she handed him the credit card and the receipt.

"Will do," he said as he pushed the receipt and credit card into the right-hand pocket of his jacket.

"Would you like some help?" she asked him as he put the two boxes on the cart.

"No, thank you," he said. He was positive the killers wouldn't move on him until there was no one around and it was safe. But there was no sense in endangering Eva in case they got jumpy and decided to make their move.

He pushed the cart out to his bike, raised the trunk and put the box with the perishables in the refrigerated section of the trunk and closed it then put the other box into the other section and closed the trunk. He pushed the cart back to a cart rack and walked back to his bike, lowering his face plate and putting on his gloves. He got on the bike, started it, and rode out of the parking lot heading south not north. He didn't look at the sedan as he passed it. He didn't have to. He knew it would follow him within a minute after he left the parking lot.

CHAPTER 24

The lodge 11:03 a.m.

"He is leaving the store's parking lot, sir," the man sitting in the passenger's seat of the two door sedan said into his com-cell.

The woman was looking at the clock on the dashboard waiting for the proper time to move out after Lee.

"Okay, just follow him and move to grab him when there's no one around to see you," Larry told him.

"Yes, sir," he said. "He's just driven out of the parking lot of the Clear Water Market. He's heading south."

"Very good," Larry said.

"What direction did he come from when he entered the lot?" Steve asked. He was sitting in a chair next to the table the speaker box was on.

"He came from the north, sir," the man said.

"Then why is he heading south?" Bruce asked.

"He's no fool," Paul said. "He probably spotted them and is heading away from where he and Evelyn went last night."

"Follow him, and grab him when you can do so without arousing attention," Larry ordered the man. He turned toward Troy and said, "Display their positions on the screen."

"The large red dot is them," Troy said in the same emotionless voice Sam had used.

"Who is them?" Paul asked.

"Our two people, sir," Troy said.

"There is no dot for him," Larry said.

"There is no tracking chip on him, sir."

"Check and see if he used a credit card to pay for what he bought," Steve said.

"One moment, sir," Troy said as he quickly accessed the Clear Water Market's computers. Within ten seconds Lee's purchases were displayed on the lower left hand section of the screen with the credit card number, the fake name, and the name and ID number of the issuing bank.

"If he's carrying that credit card that was in the leather bag we should be able to get a blip on him," Fred said.

"He didn't use the card we gave him," Paul said, softly.

"It's the same card," Fred snapped at him. "Look at the numbers."

"You remember the numbers on the credit cards we gave them?" Paul asked Fred.

He didn't so he turned to Troy and asked, "Are those the numbers of the credit cards we gave them, Troy?"

"A moment, sir," Troy replied as he got busy accessing their servers in the lodge to get the credit card numbers of the credit cards that were given to Evelyn and Lee. A few seconds later he said, "They are the same numbers, sir."

"Then why can't we get a red blip on Lee?" Fred asked.

"That's a new card Evelyn made from a blank," Paul said. "They knew we'd keep an eye on them. That's why they somehow managed to conceal the tracking chips on the cards we gave them as soon as we left that house."

"How the hell could they do that?" Fred yelled angrily.

"A few inches of dirt around them in a lead lined box would do that," Steve said in a voice that indicated he was bored with Larry's and Fred's stupidity.

Larry and Fred turned around and looked at him with questioning expressions on their faces.

Steve noticed their expressions, and explained. "A few inches of dirt on the top and bottom of the cards in a lead lined box would be more than enough to cut off the tracking signal sent out by the chips in the credit cards and ID cards we gave them."

"Well, it didn't do them any good," Fred said. "We have him."

"Why is he going south?" Bruce asked again.

"He probably came from the south and circled around and came to the market from the north," Larry said.

Bruce watched the dot that represented their two trackers as it moved over the road map. "I don't think so," he mumbled from his position on the couch.

Paul looked over at him and asked, "Why don't you think so?"

"Convert that map to a terrain map, Troy," Bruce said, ignoring Paul's question. "Show all nearby towns and cities on the map."

Troy did as he was told. Uninhabited wooded areas appeared in dark green with uninhabited open country appearing as light green and the road as a single black line. No mountains or hills appeared on the map. No towns or cities appeared on the map.

"There's nothing around him for at least two hundred miles, but flat open country."

"Heavily wooded flat country," Steve said as he looked at the map on the screen.

"Can that map show dirt roads?" Bruce asked Troy.

"No, sir," he said. "This area is not a map of a wilderness tourist area. Only they show dirt road."

"Grab him now," Bruce demanded.

Lee had traveled over a mile pass the wall of forest on his left before he saw on the bike's screen in the center of the handle bars behind the wide headlight a terrain map. The map revealed what he wanted a hundred yards ahead of him. He moved the bike to the right hand side of the road as if he was going to stop and slowed down.

The car behind him did the same thing.

Lee saw them make the same move in the left hand mirror on the handle bars of the bike. He looked to his right at the ground and saw the bike's front wheels were only a few inches from the dirt safety lane. The bike's right rear wheel was on the dirt safety lane throwing up dirt because he was riding at a left angle.

I wonder what those two think of the dirt I'm throwing in their faces. He thought.

When he was less than ten feet from where he wanted to go, he sharply turned the bike to the left, and increased his speed to nearly a hundred miles an hour. The bike shot toward a grass and weed choked dirt road, invisible to the car following him because of the dirt clouding their vision but clear to Lee, tilting on its left tires almost as if it were about to turn over on its left side. Lee compensated by shifting his weight to the right and the bike's right rear wheel made solid contact with the pavement as it shot into the woods.

The woman jammed her foot down on the accelerator and the car shot forward reaching more than a hundred miles in a ten seconds. When she spotted the dirt road, she realized where Lee was going and moved her right foot to the brake and brought the car to a screaming stop. But not before it was twenty feet pass the dirt road.

Lee shot into the forest following the dirt road as carefully as he could, avoiding rocks and branches lying in the road that could flip the bike over. The last thing he needed was to hit a rock or branch and flip the bike. He'd be thrown off and would hit the ground with enough of an impact at the speed he was traveling to break his spine or pelvis and that would be it for him. He looked around for someplace where he could get off the bike and take cover and wait for them. He knew he had only seconds. Maybe fifteen if he was lucky, and Lee wasn't going to rely on luck.

He looked to his left and right and saw fallen trees and thick brush on the left. He turned the bike to the right and headed for a group of three trees growing close together. He raced over to the group of trees, went behind them, stopped, and jumped off the bike and ran to the left around the trees toward the fallen trees and brush. If he could reach the trees and brush, the odds would be in his favor. But the odds would be very thin. He'd never met those two trackers, but he had the feeling one was experienced.

The woman rapidly turned the car around, giving Lee the seconds he needed, and shot into the woods like a bullet out of the barrel of a gun. She didn't worry about branches or rocks in the road, and she hit two knocking the car up and to the right then to the left making her lose temporary control. That gave Lee another five seconds. She quickly brought the car back under control and raced forward. The man was looking out the window for Lee unconcerned about the damage done to the car.

They were a little slow.

Lee reached the spot he wanted and threw himself over a fallen tree surrounded by brush. He landed on his left side and flipped over on his stomach a few feet from the tree and crawled to the tree and pushed some of the leaves aside making a small hole in time to see the car bouncing over rocks and branches.

"The bike's behind those trees to our right," the man said to the woman as he saw the bike.

She stopped the car a few yards from the trees and opened her door and jumped out of the car. She landed on her left side and rolled a few feet from the car to a firing position on her stomach with her electric semiautomatic in her right hand. The man did the same thing on the right side of the car.

Lee saw them.

The woman looked to her left. The car was protecting her right side. He couldn't see the man because the car blocked his view of him. But he knew he was probably looking to his right. That told Lee these two weren't just trackers but well trained killers. He reverted to a lesson he'd learned over twenty-five years ago. Never go to someone who is expecting you. Let them come to you. He would wait for an opportunity and he knew one was coming his way.

The woman and man lay on their stomachs for a minute before the woman looked under the car at the man and made a signal to him with her left hand.

Lee waited, watched, and controlled his breathing.

Both of them got up slowly at the same time, the woman looking to her left and the man looking to his right. That was a smart move. Separated as they were even if he had an automatic rifle, he wouldn't be able to take down both of them at the same time. And the one he didn't kill would have more than enough time to kill him.

Lee waited until they started moving. Walking on dead leaves and stepping on twigs under the leaves. The snapping sounds of twigs and the crunching sounds of the leaves they stepped on as they walked covered the sound of him moving the muzzle attachment under the barrel of his semiautomatic pistol into place with a soft metallic snapping sound.

The woman immediately stopped and listened.

"Hear something?" the man asked her more than thirty feet away.

She waved him silent with her left hand with an angry expression on her face as she dropped to her left knee making herself less of target. That told Lee she was the smarter of the two, and the one he had to kill first.

He made as little noise as he could as he aimed at her throat. He didn't know how impenetrable her body armor was, thickness didn't matter with the type of body armor used today. If it had a tight weave and a rubber and fiberglass backing it could stop an electric volt, so a throat shot was the only guarantee of instant death. Because wounding her would only make her angrier.

The woman rose to her feet and scanned the woods before she looked on the ground.

Lee knew it wouldn't take her long to pick up his tracks in the soft, leaf covered floor of the forest. He knew she'd see they ended four or five feet in front of the log he was hiding behind, and she'd know instantly where he was. He held his breath and squeezed the trigger. Just before he felt the gentle recoil of the weapon he released his breath.

The electric bullet hit her just where her neck joined her chest slicing through her throat and electrocuting her spinal cord and brain. She dropped lifeless like a rock.

The man showed Lee how inexperienced he was no matter how well trained he was. Instead of dropping to the ground like a professional he ran toward the woman as soon as he heard her body hit the ground. Then he foolishly stopped next to her body and looked down at her lifeless body. A stupid act for a trained professional even if he wasn't experienced in killing in the field.

Lee's electric bullet hit him in the face right between his eyes. It was the best shot Lee had ever made in his life.

The man dropped dead.

Lee remained in position for thirty seconds just in case they had had back up even though he hadn't seen any. Then he moved slowly to his left from behind the fallen tree and stood up scanning the forest around him as he did so. He listened and heard nothing but the sounds of the forest. Birds and insects busy in the warm spring weather. He walked toward the woman's body and knelt down on both knees as he put away his weapon. He removed the com-cell in the belt pouch on the left side of her belt then stood up and walked over to the man's body, a foot away, and did the same thing. He knew whoever was operating the computer tracking these two would know they were dead within a minute or so. The warmth of their bodies would keep any tracking chips on their clothing or in their bodies operating for at least a minute and a half. After that the heat sensitive chips would stop working as their bodies grew cold.

He walked to the car and looked through the open driver's door. He couldn't see anything inside that indicated it was booby trapped. They never were anyway. Two much of a chance the killers could trip the booby trap and kill themselves. He reached inside and pushed the trunk button popping open the trunk. He walked to the back and looked inside the trunk.

"Thank you, very much," he said as he reached into the trunk and opened the brown leather athletic bag inside. "So very nice of you, lady and gentleman, to give these to us."

Inside the athletic bag were two pairs of the best night vision goggles money could buy. Far better than the old ones he had. Not only did they turn night into day, but they also had flash protection for the wearer's eyes in case a bright light was flashed at them, but they were also telescopic with small mirrors on the sides that allowed the wearer to see anyone six feet behind them. There were also two assault rifles with barrel extensions for long range shooting and telescopes on them which looked like the kind that could give the user a range of close to two miles. Attached to the left side of both rifles were silencers. There were also four magazines apiece not counting the two in the rifles, and two small electric scanners for detecting tracking chips in the athletic bag.

"All this ammo just for me," Lee said softly to himself. "What a waste of ammo."

He closed the bag and took a pen knife out of his pocket and opened it up. He placed the two com-cells on the floor of the trunk and picked up one of the com-cells and removed the back and located the tracking chip in it and flipped it out. Without a tracking chip it was just a piece of silicon with a tiny light tube in it and it could be used as a regular com-cell without being traced. He did the same thing with the second com-cell. He put the backs back on the com-cells and put the man's com-cell in his pocket. He left the woman's com-cell on the floor of the trunk because he knew both of them would start ringing in a few seconds. He opened the bag again and searched the weapons, ammo, and night vision goggles for tracking chips. There were none.

Sir," Troy said, looking at the fading red dots on the large wall screen. "I have lost them."

"Our trackers?" Larry asked him.

"Yes sir."

"How could you lose them?" Larry asked him as he looked at the map on the screen.

"Their tracking chips are no longer operational, sir," Troy answered.

"Are they defective?"

"No, sir, if they were I should have detected it on the screen or on their responses. The chips are not working, sir."

"What about the chips in their com-cells?" Steve asked. He was bored with sitting in the computer room of the lodge watching blinking red lights on a TV screen.

"They are not working either, sir."

"When did they stop working?" Fred asked.

"One minute thirty-one seconds ago," Troy answered.

"The trackers were following Lee, at that time," Bruce said. His flat expression didn't convey his deep concern.

"Yes, sir," Troy said.

"If their implanted chips aren't working it means their dead," Paul said. He was looking at the map on the screen. "If the chips in their com-cells aren't working it means they've been removed or the cells have been destroyed."

Larry turned and looked at Paul. "You think he managed to kill both of them?"

"Yes," Paul said in a calm voice.

"The son-of-a-bitch is a tracker not a killer," Larry said. "That's all he is, isn't he?"

"Call both com-cells," Paul said, ignoring Larry's question. His hatred for Lee was growing with every incident and there were already too many incidents.

Lee was walking rapidly toward the bike carrying the athletic bag from the trunk of the car in his left hand and his weapon in his right. He had no desire to remain in the area since he knew the five and their computer experts would know his general location once they realized their trackers were dead and com-cells and tracking chip immobilized. When the com-cells started ringing, he knew they were calling him. Losing visual contact with the location of their tracker-killers had probably upset them. Lee put the athletic bag on the back of the bike behind his seat and strapped it down with the leather straps and got on the bike before he answered the com-cell with his left hand.

"What is your location?" a male voice said.

It sounded angry, and Lee knew the computer experts they had wouldn't be emotional. They were just emotionless geeks on computers doing as they were told. Lee had worked with enough of them during the decades he'd worked for Paul and his four friends to know how they were. The call was from one of the five. He decided not to say anything.

"Answer me 23," the voice said.

Lee said nothing.

"Damn you, 23, I know it's your com-cell that was answered," the man said.

"Who are you?" Lee asked.

"Who are you?" the man asked him.

"23's dead," Paul told Larry. "You're speaking to Lee."

"Mr. Adams," the voice said. "It's so good to hear from you."

"Ah, fuck you, asshole," Lee said. "Don't give me that good to hear from you shit. Which one was 23?"

"That's not your concern, Mr. Adams," Larry said.

Lee closed the com-cell ending the call.

The com-cell rang ten seconds later.

Lee answered it.

"The man's number was 29," Paul said. "Is that important to you?"

"Why don't you give these people names?" Lee said. "Don't they deserve that considering what they do for you?"

"I doubt if you care about their names," Paul said, trying to keep his voice calm even though he wasn't.

"I've got a surprise in store for you and your asshole friends," Lee said then ended the call.

"What does he mean by that?" Fred asked with concern in his voice.

"I haven't the slightest idea," Paul said. "But knowing Lee as I do I would imagine it's something we wouldn't expect him to do."

"Call that fool back," Larry ordered Troy.

Troy started to type call back on the keyboard, but stopped and stared at the lower right hand corner of the screen.

"Well, do it!" Larry demanded of him.

"Sir," Troy said. "The man Lee is calling the police in Wilmot a town twelve miles away."

"Why is he doing that?" Fred asked.

"Oh, for Christ's sake," Bruce blurted out. "To cause us trouble. If the police find those bodies and that car they'll be traced back to the lab."

"A lot of good it'll do them," Fred said. "The lab's not listed anywhere. No one knows it even exists."

"Those bodies will cause the local police to alert the state police and an investigation will begin," Bruce said. "We can't have those bodies found. Troy, send out a cleanup team to pick up those bodies immediately."

"To hell with them," Fred said.

"Have the bodies picked up as soon as possible, Troy," Steve said.

"Yes, sir," Troy said as he sent a message to another team to pick up the bodies.

"That's nothing but a waste of time and energy, Steve," Fred said. "We've more important things to tend to."

"Fred, the last thing we want is to have those bodies picked up by the police and an autopsy done on them," Steve explained. "They have no identification records on them anywhere in the world. Once that gets out we'll have the FBI and the World Police Force asking questions we don't want asked."

Fred nodded that Steve was right. He didn't turn around to acknowledge to Steve he was right.

Paul smiled and gave out a short laugh while Troy was giving instructions to the other team as to where to find the bodies of their two dead trackers.

"I don't see what's so damn funny, Paul," Bruce said.

"While we are trying to remove those bodies before the police arrive Lee will make his get away," he said. "Are there any satellites over the area?"

"Not at the moment, sir," Troy said. "One will pass over in forty-three minutes."

"Get into the computers of that police station and find the patrol car that is closest to that area. Then get into the car's computer and misdirect it. That should give the other team enough time to reach the area and remove the bodies. The car is of no importance."

"Yes, sir," replied Troy.

Paul stood up and walked toward the door of the computer room.

"Where are you going?" Steve asked him.

"To lunch," he replied.

"At a time like this," Steve asked.

Paul stopped before the door and turned to face the others. "At this moment Lee is probably a half a mile away heading back to wherever he came from with two com-cells we can't trace. In addition to the weapons our trackers had. Possessing a credit card, an identity card we can't trace because the tracking chips have been removed, or he has new cards that will do exactly what the originals we gave him and Evelyn were supposed to do."

"What do you think Evelyn's doing?" Bruce asked him.

Paul stared at him and thought for a few seconds. "If I were her, I'd be tracing every employee who works for the Department of Information." He turned around and continued toward the door.

The door opened silently and he walked through it.

CHAPTER 25

4:35 p.m.

Lee had been as thorough as he could be as he rode back to his hideout.

He had doubled back three times each time hiding in some heavily wooded area, in a different part, for a few minutes each time waiting for a vehicle to come along moving slow to indicate it was looking for him. He had taken side roads that he knew dead-ended in forests or next to streams because of the terrain maps he brought up on the bike's computer screen. He had avoided being in the open as often as he could. The vast number of satellites that had once ringed the planet like the rings of Saturn had been reduced to only five hundred—which every nation in the world had access to—and he knew the five would also be able to access them, too if they wanted to. And even though he wasn't certain, he knew they probably had a general idea of the direction he was heading in. The man, 29, had certainly told them the direction he came from when he entered the market's parking lot.

By the time he reached the forest his hideout was located in, forty-five miles away, he was pretty certain they hadn't seen him even if they did know the direction he was heading and he was tired and hungry. But still he rode in circles, doubled back twice to check his trail to see if he was being followed and prayed for rain to washout the tracks, he knew he'd left.

By the time he rode his bike into the hidden garage he was near exhaustion, and ready to drop. The years of soft living had caught up with him, and Lee didn't like admitting it. He was sitting in the saddle waiting for exhaustion to knock him out when he heard the door at the top of the stairs open and Evelyn walkout on the platform.

"You look like you've been through quite an ordeal," she said as she came down the stairs.

"I killed numbers 23 and 29 over four hours ago," he said as he looked up at her.

"Two of the five's killers," she said as she walked up to him.

"Yes," he said as he climbed off the bike. "23 was a woman and she was the pro. Taking her out required some shooting skill. Glad I haven't lost it."

"Can you make it upstairs to the living room?" she asked as she looked him over noticing the exhaustion in his face.

He wasn't covered with dirt even though the dirt on the bike's tires and lower frame indicated he'd spent some time riding on dirt roads and through the woods.

"Yeah," he said as he walked toward the stairs. "There's fresh food and frozen vegetables in the trunk of the bike's freezer compartment, and the clothes you wanted. I had a woman in the store pick them out for you."

"Don't worry. I'll unload it and put everything away. If you can make it to the kitchen you'll find some hot vegetable canned soup on the stove and coffee. The coffee I made isn't bad even if it is five years old. I got it out of the freezer."

"See you in the kitchen. Or living room," he said as he started up the stairs.

Half an hour later Evelyn walked into the living room and took the chair facing the one Lee was sitting in in front of the fake fireplace.

On the table next to him was a rock mug of hot coffee and an uncut cigar.

"I didn't want to start smoking it until I got your permission," he said.

"Thank you," she said. "I'm not fond of the smell of tobacco even though I like the occasional smell of a pipe."

"You won't like mine," he said. "I smoke a very rich mixture of tobacco."

"You go in for expensive tobacco?"

"Rich in pipe tobacco and cigars means strong flavor. I'll stick to my study next to my bedroom where I have an exhaust fan that blows the smoke out of the house."

She nodded her acceptance of that as she said, "I've been rather busy since you left. By the way what time did you leave?"

"Seven-thirty this morning," he said. "I've ridden over two hundred and seventy miles. I'm positive no one followed me." He looked at his jacket on the couch and said, "There are two extra pistols in the pockets plus two com-cells. I removed the tracking chips from the com-cells and checked both weapons for tracking chips and removed them. They're clean. Did you see the bag on the back of the bike behind the seat?"

"Very smart of you, Lee," she said. "Those com-cells have probably got directories in them, and we will probably need the extra weapons even if you do have an arsenal in this house. What's in the bag behind the seat?"

"Two assault rifles with scopes, night visions goggles, and extra ammo. You've been looking the place over?" He picked up the mug and finished the coffee.

"Top to bottom," she said. "But it's what I found out about the employees of the Department of Information that's important."

"What did you find out?"

"Every employee is accounted for. They're either working or on sick leave or vacation. But there was something unusual about a man known as Lyle Morton."

He sat the mug back on the table and closed his eyes and asked, "What about him?"

"Lyle Morton left work late Friday night. Around 11 p.m. and hasn't shown up."

"So, one of the employees of the Department of Information is missing."

"No. None are missing. Lyle Morton doesn't exist."

Lee opened his eyes and turned his head to the left and looked at her with an expression of confusion on his face.

"Everything about Lyle Morton is a fake except his social security number which belongs to a seven year old girl who was given the number by the Department of Social Services thirty days after she was born. And, Lee, she lives on a wild life preserve in Tanzania which her parents own. They raise rare exotic wildlife which they sell to zoos since it's illegal to catch game in the wild in Africa these days."

"Lyle Morton's our mysterious person," he said as he looked back at the fireplace.

"How did he manage to keep the Department from learning his social security number belongs to someone else?"

"He made sure two numbers of the girl's social security number kept changing," Evelyn said. "And since she's been listed as a dependent on her parents income tax returns since she was born, no one at the Internal Revenue Bureau bothered checking since the numbers only changed twice in the last seven years."

"The IRS people assumed the parents had simply made mistakes," he said. "Then Lyle Morton does exist as far as the Department of Information is concerned as long as no one gets curious about the girl's social security number."

"And that's probably not going to happen until she files an income tax return herself years from now," she said.

"Mr. Morton didn't return to work because he's gotten what he wanted," Lee said in a thoughtful tone of voice.

"I also learned there are one hundred and seventy-two classifications of information in the Department of Information. And one labeled special information because the information in that file comes from the Martian Scientific Station or on of the Pluto Space Stations or one of two hundred deep space telescopic probes twelve billion miles beyond the Oort Cloud that circles the solar system."

"So if you were going to hide information you didn't want anyone to find where would you hide it, Evelyn?"

"Most people aren't that concerned with space exploration. If it wasn't for our unified world there wouldn't be any Martian Station or Pluto Space Stations or electronic telescopes orbiting our solar system billions of miles beyond that Oort Cloud ."

"You didn't answer my question."

"I'd hide it in the file labeled space exploration."

"I'll bet that's where we'll find out about the non-existent Lyle Morton."

"That's exactly where I've got my special program looking," she told him.

"And what have you found?" he asked before a deep yawn.

"A lot of stuff about planets that may have life on them and possible supernovas," she said. "And two asteroids that are on a collision course with Earth. The closest one is about the size of a bus and is mostly ice. It'll burn up the moment it enters the Earth's atmosphere. The other is a small mountain, but not to worry the Martian Station already has it lined up to be pushed away from the Earth when it reaches the orbit of Jupiter, which is about three hundred years from now. The smaller one will be here in three weeks."

"Interesting," he said as he stood up. "I'm going to take a hot shower and go to bed."

"You ever heard of a special lab the Space Admiralty has?"

"I know very little about the Space Admiralty, Evelyn," he said as he walked toward the door.

"I found that term 'special lab' among the files listed in special information," she said as she watched him leave.

He stopped at the door and turned toward her. "So, what about it?"

"Most of the information I found in that special information file is just boring information about space. And all information about space labs are listed in the file labeled Scientific Information, and that's available to the public. Every lab in the world doing work on space is well known, and there are only four of them. All of them are located in areas miles away from cities so they won't be bothered by a lot of crazy people opposed to space travel."

"I'm tired. See you in the morning, Evelyn," he said as he turned and walked out the door of the living room.

Evelyn stood up and walked toward the door. If there was a special lab someplace nobody knew about it would have to be supplied with food, water, scientific equipment, and it would need a source of energy. If Lee's hideout was any example of a hidden lab, its source of energy would be solar. And would be located some place no one would ever bother looking at. Some place no one would even knew existed because it hadn't been used in centuries. The question was where would such a place be?

CHAPTER 26

5:30 p.m. Tuesday

Evelyn walked toward the stairs to the computer room thinking where to look for someplace that hadn't been used in centuries and as a result no one knew of its existence? She stopped in the hallway and thought, *wait a minute, I'm going about this the wrong way. Instead of asking myself where to look for someplace that hasn't been used in centuries I should be asking myself where would such a place be?* She started walking again. Her mind was wrestling with the question of where would such a place be?

"Close," she said softly to herself. "If it was far away, those five monsters wouldn't have had Lee and I meet them in that house in the city. They would have arranged for us to meet them close to where this place. Assuming, of course, whoever's got their information—."

She stopped speaking and walked slowly toward the stairs leading up to the computer room in the attic letting her mind sort out the facts. She stopped at the foot of the stairs and thought.

Instead of looking for a special lab and it's probably close, I should find out all I can about Lyly Morton. A person who creates a fake identity always puts some of themselves in it so they can be comfortable with it and move around with the identity without being seen, but not enough to attract attention to themselves. She started up the stairs walking slowly. *Mr. Morton has a family and wants to protect them. Because the information he has on the five shows them to be ruthless enough to kill his family to get back what he has on them.* She stopped on the stairs.

Mr. Morton's on vacation with his family. At least that's what listed in the Department of Information files on Mr. Morton. But he'd not with his family. So I look for a family of an employee that's on vacation without the husband. She rushed up the stairs to the computer room and got busy as soon as she sat down behind the computer.

The problem with the Department of Information was that it had one hundred and one branch offices scattered about the world. The democratic world was obsessed with letting the people of the world know what was happening in the world. Secrecy among the nations in the world before 2500 had led to suspicion and distrust and that for thousands of years had led to wars, and an intense desire on the part of the defeated nation for revenge against the victor. And that had only led to more wars. And every new war had resulted in better weapons and more dead. Only the atomic bomb had prevented another world war in spite of a statement by the foolish President Ronald Reagan in the late twentieth century that a limited nuclear war could be fought and won.

Because everyone with anything resembling common sense and a working brain, which Ronald Regan apparently didn't have, knew once atomic bombs started to fly about the world there wouldn't be any limited war, but total war in which each side would try to exterminate the other side in order to survive.

So, all of the nations in the world in 2449 sent representatives to The Hague in the Dutch province of South Holland where the first united world democratic government was formed on Earth and war became a thing of the past. Because by then everyone with anything resembling intelligence knew wars didn't solve problems, but only created more problems. The only thing that had plagued the human race after that was reoccurring plagues that cost the lives of billions of people over the last six hundred years. Some complained the plagues were deliberately caused by the rich to keep control of the world government in their hands, but there had never been any evidence of such a thing found. Anyway political power was in the hands of the voters, and there were more common voters than rich voters.

And all of that meant the Department of Information was the largest government department in the world. Over thirty-five million people worked for it using over forty million computers and servers. Which meant over a hundred billion pieces of information was constantly being moved about the world every second. Most of it was seldom read by the general population, and all of it was filed away in the Department of Information's headquarters building in Crown City. That made Evelyn's job both easy and complicated.

Easy in the sense she could move freely among all that information without anyone knowing she was doing it because of the special coded program she put in the servers when she was in that kitchen in the Department's building as long as she was careful, and careful was Evelyn's middle name.

Complicated in the sense she had to know what to look for and where to look for it in order to get what she wanted. And what she wanted was a list of all the employees of the Department who were on vacation, which ones were married, and where they had gone for their vacations with their families, and most important, which one of those vacationing male employees wasn't with his family.

She started by hacking into the employees information files where her special program allowed her to go anywhere she wanted to without anyone in the Department of Information knowing she was in those files. All their servers would show was another employee going through employee files. And that was done every day every minute of the day by one of the one hundred and one branch offices scattered about the world. Within twelve minutes she had a list of every vacationing employee of the Department of Information working at the headquarters building. Within another ten minutes she knew where they were vacationing and if they were with their families. Then she hit a brick wall.

Every vacationing employee was accounted for along with their families.

Evelyn leaned back in the high back padded wooden chair she was sitting in and thought for a few seconds. Then she leaned forward and typed, 'what employees on vacation aren't at the usual vacation spots?'

A list of two hundred thousand employees popped up on the screen.

Evelyn printed out the list.

Then she typed, 'which ones work in the Department's main headquarters'.

Lyle Morton had put a special program in the servers in the Department of Information to alert him if someone started asking about employees on vacation not at the usual vacation spots. The screen on the laptop on the desk began to emit a ringing sound that couldn't be heard outside of his cabin.

Lyly jumped up from his chair and rushed to his desk and leaned over and looked at the information on the monitor.

'Twenty-two employees working at main headquarters aren't at the usual vacation spots.'

They're getting close, raced through his mind.

But he knew that it wouldn't take the computer experts working for the five very long to determine his true identity. It meant he had less time than he hoped he had. He straightened up and walked back to his chair and sat down.

I could just dump the information I have on the Internet, and hope for the best, he thought. But he knew the influence of the five was so great it would be laughed off as a hacker's joke, even though the five weren't very well known outside of the highest political and economic circles of the world. No, he'd have to release the information when he had the final proof, and so far he wasn't even close to getting that.

Evelyn was surprised at the short list that appeared on her screen. Only sixteen people, seven women and nine men. She typed, 'Are they married?'

'None are married,' was the response.

She leaned back in the chair and put her hands behind her head and looked at the screen. She wasn't going about this the right way, and she knew it. Anyone smart enough to steal the information the five wanted back would have been smart enough not to use their real identity. So who among the twelve thousand people who worked at the Department's main headquarters wasn't who they were listed as being? *I'm stupid,* she thought as she leaned forward and started typing on the keyboard.

Lyle Morton had left the Department at ten-thirty p.m. on Friday night. He could have walked away or taken public transportation. Buses stopped in front of the Department every ten minutes during the day during the working week and after six p.m. every twenty minutes. On Saturdays and Sundays the buses stopped every fifteen minutes during the day and every twenty minutes at night and the same on holidays.

She got into the Department's security system and asked to see recordings of everyone leaving the building after four p.m.

One car was seen leaving the building's underground garage at ten-thirty three p.m.

I hope this is the one, she thought as she magnified the tail end of the car and got its license plate number. Then she hacked into the Department of Vehicle Registration for the state of Colorado and got the name and address of the person who owned the Dodge Dart knowing it would be registered to Lyle Morton. Next she got into the traffic department's street cameras and watched a recording of vehicles on Friday night driving pass the Department of Information and saw Lyle's Dart and watched as it drove north on Storm Highway to Danner Woods the forest preserve area that was north of Crown City. The Dart disappeared into the woods of the preserve.

"So he'd not in the city," she said to herself as she brought up a map of the Danner Woods and told the computer to show all houses in the woods. There was only one and it was listed as belonging to the forest ranger who was the overseer of Danner Woods, and it was seven blocks from the road Lyle had driven from Storm Highway. Evelyn knew Lyle Morton wasn't hiding there—too obvious.

That meant Lyle had to be in the wilderness area north of Danner Woods and if he was like Lee he was probably hiding in some cabin no one knew about. But just maybe he wasn't exactly like Lee, and he was hiding in a cabin connected to a power line.

Evelyn got her computer into the servers of the Colorado Power Company and asked to see power lines running through the wilderness area north of Danner Woods.

There was only one and it dead-ended at a small dam across the Fork River. The power line was what was called a double power line in that it had a generator at its end that took power from the dam and provided the Colorado Power Company with extra power at the expense of the public. She wondered what politicians in Colorado got campaign contributions from the Colorado Power Company. The world may have been unified under one world government, but politicians still did favors for businesses in exchange for cash. And the people still got fucked.

There weren't any houses or buildings in the area around the dam, which meant it was probably automated with computers and robots to make sure it remained in working condition. But that didn't mean there wasn't a cabin hidden among the dense woods that surrounded the dam.

Evelyn printed a map of the area, and turned off her computer. *If I know you're somewhere around the Fork River Dam, Mr. Morton, the five will quickly know if they don't already know.*

CHAPTER 27

6 p.m. the lodge

For two hours Troy had been trying to find a program hidden among the thousands of programs in the servers of the Department of Information, and he hadn't found anything that shouldn't be there.

"Well, why the hell can't you find it?" Larry angrily demanded. He was standing behind Troy with his hands in his pants pockets feeling helpless.

Steve looked at Larry shook his head and thought, *and he is supposed to be the computer expert among us.*

"There are many reasons, sir," Troy replied.

"Aw, bullshit!" he spat out. "You and Sam are supposed to be the best computer people we have, Troy. You should be able to find a hidden program regardless of the reasons."

"You haven't figured it out yet, have you, Larry," Steve said in a calm voice that hid his disappointment in Larry.

Larry spun around to face him. "What the hell does that mean?"

"Troy is looking for a program that's designed to detect when someone is looking for it and hide." Steve didn't bother looking at him. He was looking at his feet and feeling very bored.

"Or, sir, it's bouncing program," Troy said.

"Bouncing program?" Bruce asked.

"A program that constantly moves around among the programs in the servers," Troy explained.

Larry turned around again and said, "So this bouncing program remains stable for a few minutes?"

"Maybe, sir," Troy answered.

Larry pulled his right hand out of his pocket and raised it to strike Troy on the left side of his face.

"Don't do that!" Paul said in a sharp voice. He was reclining on the couch in the computer room watching Larry.

Larry lowered his hand and turned to face Paul. "And why shouldn't I? He's not doing what he's supposed to do."

"It would solve nothing," he told him. He hated when a superior struck an inferior, because it was bad manners. And superiors were never supposed to display bad manners toward inferiors.

"Like hell it wouldn't!"

"Then don't do it, because I said not to do it," Paul said in a nasty tone of voice.

"We'll be finished if that information gets out, Paul," Larry told him as he approached him in a menacing manner. "We've got to use extreme methods to save ourselves. No matter how extreme they may be."

Paul got up off the couch and took two steps toward Larry.

"When were we notified about the theft of our information?" Fred asked. He was sitting in a chair next to a table with an unfinished drink on it, and he wasn't interested in stopping a fight between Paul and Larry.

Larry stopped a yard from Paul and looked at Fred.

"Why do you ask?" Bruce, who was sitting in a chair next to the wall with his legs stretched out and looking relaxed.

"The man we have in the Department of Information was put there to keep us informed of any information of an unusual nature leaving the Department," he said.

"So what," Larry snapped at him.

"So he had to notice something unusual was going on at the Department to notify us," he said, looking at Paul.

"I got the call a little after eleven," Paul said.

Fred was staring at the far wall thinking.

"Have you thought of something, Fred?" Paul asked him.

"He knew there was information we didn't want getting out to the public," he said as he continued to stare at the wall. "How do we know he didn't take it?"

"If he did, we wouldn't be here," Steve told him without bothering to mention the man had been disposed of right after he reported the break-in in the Department's kitchen. Failure was one thing the five didn't accept from their people.

"Whoever has the information had to get it just before our man in the Department called you, Paul," Fred said.

"And he would have left immediately after getting the information," Paul said, realizing what Fred was getting at. "Troy, go back to Friday night around ten and list all employees in the Department of Information who left between ten and ten-thirty."

Troy did as he was told and put the list on the screen on the wall in front of him.

Larry turned around and looked at the screen.

Eight names appeared on the screen.

"The Department had internal and external cameras, Troy," Paul said. "Show those eight."

Troy obeyed.

Eight people left the garage in their cars.

"One of them took it," Larry said.

"Troy, did anyone leave after ten-thirty?" Steve asked him.

"One moment, sir," he said as he accessed the cameras of the Department of Information.

Only one car was shown driving out of the garage.

"Show the plate number and run a check on it," Steve said.

Troy did so.

'No such license plate number is registered with the Department of Vehicle Registration,' appeared on the screen.

"That's our man," Larry said.

Steve shook his head in frustration at Larry's stupidity. "Find out who that car was registered to in the Department."

Lyle Morton appeared on the screen.

"Show all information on that man," Steve ordered Troy.

It appeared on the screen in seconds.

"Now, Troy run a check on Lyle Morton's social security number," Steve told him. "And have the computer compare that number to every social security number that closely resembles it."

Troy did as he was told.

"You're correct, Larry," Paul said as he read the information. "Lyle Morton's social security number is one number different from that of a seven year old girl living in Africa."

"The first three numbers of everyone's social security number indicates where they were born," Steve said. "And Lyle Morton's birth certificate indicates he was born in America, but the first three numbers of his social security says he was born in Tanzania."

"Access the traffic cameras and follow that car," Larry told Troy.

The traffic cameras showed the car disappearing into Danner Woods of the forest preserves.

Larry slapped his hands together and exclaimed in a loud voice, "Now we're getting somewhere."

"Not necessarily," Fred said.

"What on Earth do you mean?" Larry asked, turning around toward him.

"If Lyle Morton's social security number is faked and the license plate number of his car is fake, then Lyle Morton is probably a fake name, and that car is still somewhere in the Danner Woods. And Lyle Morton isn't."

"How long have you been working, Troy," Paul asked him.

"Twelve hours and fifteen minutes, sir," Troy answered.

"Have Sam replace Troy in half an hour, Larry," Paul told him. "And I suggest we go to dinner. It's probably awaiting us now, and I dislike eating cold food. In the meantime, Troy, find out everything you can about the Danner Woods and the area beyond it."

"Yes sir."

Paul turned toward the door.

"No one would steal our information unless they weren't going download it on the Internet," Steve said as he stood up.

The four looked at Steve.

"Wherever Lyle Morton is he'd have to be next to an electrical cable to use it to download the information."

"Unless he has a computer than can access one of the satellites," Bruce said. "And computers have been capable of doing that for the last five hundred years without the use of an electrical cable."

"Let us discuss that at dinner," Paul suggested. "I also suggest we freshen up and change for dinner. It will make us all feel a bit better."

CHAPTER 28

June 6, 7 a.m. Wednesday

Lyle Morton knew he was in trouble. He was still far from finishing his work to expose the five, and now someone was aware that he was hiding in the wilderness north of the city. He estimated he had less than two days left before his hiding place was discovered, and he was killed. Death didn't bother him though. He had done a clever job of hiding his real identity, and his family was quite safe. No one would ever connect them to him no matter how much checking they did. What did bother him was he wasn't close to discovering where the lab was the five had used to create the horrors they have been visiting upon the Earth for the last five hundred years. Without the location of the lab the information he had on the five amounted to no more than dirty gossip.

He knew it had to be somewhere close to Crown City. For five hundred years the five had been born on the North American Continent, and always ten or twelve years after a new plague had killed hundreds of millions of people. It was the perfect way for them to reintroduce themselves into the world. While the people of the world would be recovering from the terrible loss of life, they would quietly appear re-inherit their wealth and in ten or twelve years reestablish their powerful political and economic contacts. They were godless monsters who had to be exposed, and he wasn't even close to locating the lab he needed to find to convince the people of the world what they were.

And now they were onto the general area where he was hiding.

Such a lab, he thought. *Would not be located above ground but below ground with solar crystals to provide it with the power it needed. And those crystals would be camouflaged to blend into the surrounding terrain. But where would such a lab be?*

Lyle got up from his chair and walked into the kitchen of the cabin to make a pot of tea. He'd been up for almost twenty hours and he was tired and needed sleep. Sleep which would let his mind rest so he could awake refreshed and ready to look for the lab. He sat at the old wooden table and looked at the ancient electric tea kettle. It had been made back in 1993 during the era of the Cold War when men thought atomic weapons would protect them from a third world war. Such foolishness to think weapons of mass destruction could prevent another world war when nearly every nation had the ability to build such weapons, or could acquire the technology and nuclear material to build them by buying them.

His mind drifted back to his days in school when he had loved working in the school library reading newspapers and news magazines from the twentieth century. It was such a violent century. Millions were killed in wars that accomplished nothing except giving the loser a reason for starting another war against those nations that had defeated it.

Lyle refocused his eyes on the tea kettle and decided tea wasn't going to help him fight off sleep more than an hour. Eight hours of sleep is what he needed and wanted and he'd be ready to continue his search for the five's lab. He stood up and walked over to the kettle and pushed the off button. That wasn't necessary since once the water was hot the kettle would automatically turn itself off.

He walked to the kitchen door and stopped and turned around and looked at the kettle and thought, *there's something about the kettle that should make me remember something I read when I was in high school about the twentieth century.* He stared at the kettle for five minutes before he shook his head and started for his bedroom. *Can't remember what it was.*

$$\sim$$

CHAPTER 29

June 6, 9 a.m. Lee's hideout

"I've made breakfast," Lee yelled as he knocked on Evelyn's bedroom door. "There's bacon, eggs, buttermilk biscuits, coffee, and orange marmalade."

Evelyn didn't respond.

"Better hurry up before I eat it all myself," he said. He was in a good mood. He had sleep till six in the morning, gotten up and shaved and taken a long hot shower. He had even watched two hours of the Morning Show.

It was one of those weekday morning television programs with smiling hosts who tried to look handsome and heroic in their expensive suits, and hostesses dressed in expensive short skirts to show off their shapely legs. All of whom only managed to look like human dolls and act as they didn't have a care in the world. And they shouldn't have since most were making more than thirty million a year with all sorts of perks for six months of work in a world where the dollar was actually worth a dollar.

"Don't!" Evelyn responded. "Give me fifteen minutes."

"I'll be in the breakfast room," he said and walked off.

Thirteen minutes later Evelyn walked into the breakfast room drying her hair with a white towel and sat down at the table.

The food was on glass plates covered by glass dooms that kept the food hot. The coffee was in a glass coffee pot. Even the dishes were of glass.

Evelyn tossed the damp towel on a chair and started helping herself to the food while Lee poured coffee for both of them. "Guess what?"

"Just tell me, Evelyn," he said as he added sugar and cream to his coffee.

"Lyle left the Department of Information a little before eleven on the night of June first and drove to a spot in the Danner Woods preserves where he abandoned the Dodge Dart he drove and disappeared." She started eating.

"The plates of the car were fakes as was the sticker in the window and the car was registered to someone else," he said as he began eating.

"I didn't bother checking out who the plates and sticker were registered to," she said before she took a swallow of coffee. "Waste of time."

"Lyle Morton's somewhere in the wilderness like us," he said.

"Yes, and I think he's somewhere near a power line that gets power from a dam across the Fork River."

"Hiding close to a dam isn't very smart," he said. "Somebody working at the dam may spot him."

"The dam is an automated dam serviced by robots. Electricians from the Colorado Power Company probably check on it a few times a month."

"Still not smart," he said. "By now the five's computer people have discovered he left the Department near eleven in that Dodge Dart, and they've probably found it.

They'll know he's somewhere in the wilderness north of Danner Woods and they'll send their killers out to search the woods and they'll start their search at that dam."

"Which means we've got to get to that dam and start searching for Lyle before they send their killers out," she told him.

"They'll be looking for us, too, Evelyn."

She finished her breakfast and poured more coffee in her cup. "Because they'll know we've located the Dart and know Lyle went into the wilderness near that dam."

"They'll assume we've located the Dart and that we know Lyle is hiding near that dam because he needs power for wherever he's hiding. They'll make plans to catch us all in one operation like fish in a net."

"Why?" she asked.

"Because Paul and his four buddies aren't stupid."

"No, I mean why would Lyle need power? He's stolen information they place tremendous value on. Why not try to sell it back to them?"

"That wouldn't work," Lee said as he placed his knife and fork on his plate. "They'd pay him then find him and kill him. Once they've got him they'll issue us an ultimatum. Surrender to them or they'll kill our families."

"You're missing my point, Lee. Why would a thief who has stolen information need power?"

Lee stared at her and thought for a second. "He intends downloading what he stole on the Internet."

"Yes."

"Alright, Evelyn, I agree with you but another question. Why hasn't he already done that?"

"Because I think what he has stolen is incomplete. He needs more than what he's got to convince everyone who reads what he puts on the Internet is true."

"Well, time's running out for him if the five have what we have," Lee told her.

"Correct, and I have the feeling it has something to do with that 'special lab' I found in the files listed in special information."

Lee stood up and said, "I suggest we get a move on. The quicker we find this guy Lyle the better off we'll be. Don't worry about cleaning up. The robots will do that."

"We use your bike?"

"No. We use the car. It's built for rough terrain and is bullet proof. We should also wear body amour. There's a room in back of the garage that has everything we'll need. All we have to do is stay alive."

"I'm going to get some detailed maps of the area around that damn."

"There's an electric map in the library. Use that to put your maps on, and bring your I-book. And be prepared for a lot of killing."

❦

CHAPTER 30

10 a.m. the lodge

The five of them listened carefully to Sam's voice over the intercom box near the telephone in the breakfast room.

"The Dodge Dart was found in the Danner Woods a mile south of the wilderness area. The plates and sticker are fakes. No human foot prints were found around it because of the recent rain. If the driver of the Dart, whose identity I have not yet learned, went into the wilderness he went on foot or on a bike and he is either living in a tent or a cabin. But no cabins are listed on any maps of the wilderness area north of the Danner Woods. The only thing in that area is an automated dam across the Fork River maintained by robots and checked on once a week by electricians from the Colorado Power Company. There is a power cable coming from the dam to a power plant northwest of the city in the forest preserves."

"Is it the sort of cable that can be accessed by a computer?" Larry asked him.

"No, sir, but the dam has a computer than can be accessed by an outside computer."

"Contact all our trackers in the field and send them into that area around the dam.

Have them search in a circle of five miles, and tell them not be seen or heard," Steve told Sam.

"Yes sir," Sam said. "The trackers are scattered over an area of over two hundred miles, sir. It will take them at least twelve hours to gather in the search area if you don't want them to attract attention."

"Issue them the order to gather in the area around the dam without attracting attention," Paul said.

"Yes, sir," Sam replied.

"Have there been any traces done on the Dodge Dart outside of our own?" Fred asked him.

"I have detected none, sir."

"Evelyn would be smart enough not to leave a trace for us to pick up," Paul said as he stood up. "Notify us immediately, Sam, when our trackers are in the search area around that dam."

"Yes sir."

"I'm going to take a nice walk in the woods, gentleman," Paul said as he walked toward the door.

No one said anything as he left.

Steve was a bit concerned about the casual manner in which they were conducting the search for the man with their information and Lee and Evelyn. They all seemed to think the capture of the man with their information and Lee and Evelyn was a guarantee.

He didn't. He had the feeling things were about to get worse and not better. He got up and headed for his suite to finish a novel he had been reading. There was nothing else he could do.

Larry was happy his computer experts were finally making him appear competent to his friends. He left for the game room where he was going to improve his golf game. He couldn't wait until this mess was over to get back to his private country club. He was certain his golf scores would be the envy of his fellow members.

Fred decided to watch a movie on satellite TV. He hoped there was an old war movie on. He found the wars of the nineteenth and twentieth centuries most interesting—especially those movies about the Nazis. There was something romantic and exciting about them. They were so daring and ruthless with little regard for human life other than their own. Those Nazis reminded him of himself and his four friends. And they were right. Only those who were part of the master race had a right to rule the Earth.

Bruce was a lover of all sorts of music and the lodge's music lounge had an excellent collection of music drives.

❧

CHAPTER 31

12 p.m.

Lee and Evelyn were ready to go. They had packed everything they'd need for two weeks in the back of the black car. Lee had told her if they didn't find Lyle Morton in less than twenty-four hours things were going to get nasty, because he was convinced the five knew about the dam over Fork River and its power cable.

"What do you mean things are going to nasty?" she asked him as they both loaded the car.

"If we don't find this guy Lyle, we're going to have two choices, Evelyn," he said as he worked.

She didn't say anything.

He put the last of the things they were carrying in the back of the black car and closed the hatch. "Did you hear what I said?"

She looked him in the face and said in a cool voice, "We're going to have to arrange a meeting with the five somewhere in the wilderness, or let them find us in a spot we picked and kill them and their trackers to stop them from getting revenge on us by killing our families."

He nodded at her. She understood what he meant by things were going to get nasty.

"You sure that I-book of yours can access any computer or server you want to get into," he asked her as he got into the driver's seat. He had designed the four seats in the car to surround a person's body on three sides, and give back support that protected a person's spine to anyone sitting in them.

"You've seen me use it before," she said. "I can go anywhere with this I-book because it's like that I-pad I used under the Department of Information and not leave a trace. And don't worry I won't be using the servers or computers in your hideout so there'll be no chance of any of the experts working for the five to back track and find it."

"Everything's off a satellite?" he asked.

"Yes, and they won't be able to track our connection through one of them either because my frequency scrambles itself every three or five seconds."

He leaned forward and pushed a button on the dashboard a few inches from the steering wheel that turned on two TV screens in the car. The top one showed what was in front of them. The bottom one showed what was behind them. "Computer, scan the forest for a mile in a circle to find out if you detect any humans or human made objects and tell me."

Twenty seconds passed before the computer responded verbally. "None found."

"You've got an electrical detecting scanner up on that earth roof with identifying vehicular abilities and a heat detector, too?" she asked him.

"I thought you checked the place out from top to bottom."

"I checked it out for comfort not detecting abilities," she said.

"Look up at the roll bar in front of you." He started the engine.

She looked up and saw a rifle attached to the roll bar. She looked to her left and saw the same type of rifle on the roll bar an inch behind hers. "Security assault rifle," she said recognizing both. "Double barrel, too with telescopic sights."

"The extra barrel is an extension with a silencer and flash suppresser. Push the button just above the trigger on the left side of the rifle and the extra barrel comes out automatically and attaches itself to the barrel increasing the rifle's range to over a mile and a half. The telescopic sight automatically goes into play, too. Each magazine has over a thousand charges in it and no more so don't waste them."

"Anything else I should know about?" she asked.

"This car's body is made of a reflective, bullet proof Plexiglas. It can stop regular bullets and electrical bullets, but not rifle fired rockets or rocket propelled grenades."

Evelyn nodded and said, "The Plexiglas reflects the terrain around us. So if someone just glanced at the car as it was moving they'd just see the surrounding terrain. But if they looked close they'd see it moving."

"Exactly. We're not completely invisible." He handed her one of the com-cells he'd taken off the two trackers he'd killed and one of the weapons.

"I've got a semiautomatic," she told him.

"It doesn't hurt to have extra. Keep your energy pills, purification pills, and wits about you, Evelyn. Because if we have a general idea of where Lyle Morton may be hiding they have the same information because they got it the same way we did. Ready?"

"Let's go," she said.

"Open the garage door, computer," Lee said.

The lights in the garage went out, and as soon as the door had opened wide enough for the car to get through it he shot out of the garage.

Evelyn turned around and looked through the back window. "Maybe we should have taken the bike. We're leaving an excellent trail behind us for a low flying aircraft to spot."

"Flying is a hundred times safer today than it was a hundred years ago, and as hard to get a pilot license, too. Any pilot flying an aircraft over anywhere today is going to find Air Security from the World Aviation Administration all over him if he hasn't filed a flight plan in their computers. Our five employers maybe rich and powerful, but the last thing they want is a government agency asking questions they wouldn't want to answer."

"And Mr. Lyle Morton knows why," she added.

"Let's hope we find him before they do," he told her.

"I pray that we do, Lee. I dearly love my children and grandchildren. I wouldn't even want that ass I was married to falling into their hands, even though he seldom made his child support payments on time."

"Yeah," he agreed. "I don't know what they're afraid of losing, but you and I have family." He paused and said, "I wonder why they don't have children? I think they're all married."

"Too busy being rich and powerful and enjoying the fruits that wealth and power bring to have children, I guess."

"But even the rich and powerful eventually die, Evelyn. So who'll get their money?"

She ignored the question. "How long will it take us to reach that dam area?"

"It's over two hundred miles away from us and we'll be traveling through the woods. We can't afford to take a major road. Some cop would spot us and wonder why we're driving a car like this, and right now the five are probably plugged into every cop car radio and computer for a thousand miles."

"So how long?"

"Maybe four hours or more depending upon the terrain we run into."

"So we should make it to this Fork River Dam hours before sunset," she said.

"Yes, we should," Lee said. "Why you ask?"

"It'll still be light out and this reflective car of yours won't be as invisible in daylight as at night," she said.

"Yes, I know, Evelyn," he said. "But do we have the time to wait until sundown?"

"No, we don't," she said.

CHAPTER 32

4 p.m. the lodge

"I think we should go to the area the trackers are heading for," Paul said to the four men sitting in the library.

"Why?" Fred asked. "There are twenty of them out there and well-armed that's more than enough to handle any problem they'll run into."

"How many of the trackers have we left?" Paul asked Larry.

He looked up from the book he was reading and said after a few seconds, "Fifty-four. The ones we sent out to pick up the bodies Lee left us have returned."

"Where are the other thirty-four?" he asked him.

"In their barracks in the basement awaiting orders from us," he said.

"I suggest we take ten with us and send the rest to the lab," Paul said.

"What on earth for, Paul?" Bruce said. "No one in the world knows where it's at."

Paul calmly crossed his legs and said in a deep thoughtful manner, "Lee and Evelyn have to date killed six of our trackers and caused us the trouble of hiding the bodies and cleaning up the mess from the police. We should not underestimate their abilities."

"I agree," Steve said, looking up from the book he was reading.

"You always agree with Paul," Bruce said to him. "I don't think there's any need for us to leave the lodge and go into the wilderness.

It's bad enough that we're stuck here in this damn lodge trying to find ways to kill time until this person with our information has been caught."

"We've forgotten something," Paul mumbled.

"We've forgotten nothing," Larry said. Just to be on the safe side he reached for the intercom box on the table and asked Sam, "Have you managed to get information on who was driving that Dodge Dart?"

"No sir, there were no prints or anything in it that could be used to identify the driver. And I have not been able to get any more information on Lyle Morton from the Department of Information records."

Larry turned off the intercom and leaned back in his chair with a serious expression on his face.

"That expression on your face says you've thought of something, Larry," Steve said.

"I believe Lyle Morton was driving the Dodge Dart and has our information. We must assume Lee and Evelyn know this and they know what we're going to do to them for their betrayal of us once we have the information. We can't take the chance they won't go to the government." He looked at Paul. "I agree with you, Paul. We have to go into the wilderness with our trackers to make sure they do the job properly. And we should send extra security to the lab."

"Going to the government with what little they have wouldn't threaten us in the least bit," Steve said. "Because without proof of the lab's existence and what's in it all they have is vicious gossip."

"You're absolutely right, Steve," Larry said. "But what if they found Lyle Morton and he has the information with him, and they went to the government with that?"

"The Department of Justice would start an investigation," Paul said. "It wouldn't result in anything without proof of the lab's existence. But what would such an investigation to do us?"

"Arouse an intense interest in us by the news media," Steve said. "And one can never tell what those people will uncover."

"And killing some nosy news person sneaking around looking at our backgrounds would only result in more interest in us," Paul added. He looked at the others and asked, "So gentlemen what should we do?" They said nothing and they had blank expressions.

Larry looked at Bruce and Fred.

They looked back at him.

Larry reached for the intercom and said, "Numbers forty through sixty are to report to the lab immediately. The rest of you are to prepare the campers and the intelligence van in the garage to take us into the field." He released the intercom button without waiting for a response.

"How many campers are there?" Fred asked.

"Three," Larry answered. "Paul and Bruce can share one camper Steve and Fred the other one. I'll share with Sam and Troy. The trackers will have pup tents."

"When should we leave?" Steve asked.

"After sundown about nine-thirty," Paul said. "At least we can have a hot meal before we go. I would expect we'd be living out there for a day or two." He stood up and said, "I suggest we go to the supply room and get the proper clothing and footwear."

Fred watched Paul leave with Steve and Bruce and Larry following him. He had never liked Paul because of his air of superiority over them. In fact, he deeply resented him and his resentment had already developed into a very strong dislike of Paul. But he knew there was nothing he could do about it except avoid his company once they had gotten their information back and killed Lee and Evelyn and this damn Lyle Morton. He stood up thinking, *I'm moving to Europe.*

CHAPTER 33

June 6, 6 p.m. Wednesday

"We made good time," Evelyn said as she got out of the car and closed the door.

They were parked in an area surrounded by brush that was more than twelve feet high and so thick a person standing on the outside couldn't look through it and see the car, and where the tops of the trees were intertwined and grew so thick they blotted out the late afternoon sun. Lee had done such a great job of driving the car through the brush he'd done little damage to it. Anyone seeing it would probably think it was the result of the buffalo that passed through these woods. They had passed over a hundred buffalo and antelope wondering around eating plants and drinking water from the four narrow shallow streams they had crossed along with numerous deer and other small animals that paid them no attention because humans were so rare in these woods.

Lee was looking at a terrain map on his com-cell. "The dam's straight ahead about a mile. The Fork River meanders half a mile away to the southeast around this part of the forest. If we walk in a straight line we should be able to spot the dam. And if Lyle Morton is tapped into the power line coming from it, we should be able to follow that line to his hideout."

"How are we going to detect the power cable?" she asked.

"That's your job," he said as he got out of the car and closed the door.

"Oh, yeah," she said, remembering her I-book. "It's programmed to detect unusual power sources."

"Remember, Evelyn, we need to take this guy Morton alive. Our families' survival and ours is dependent upon us knowing what he knows. We maybe able use it as leverage again those five assholes."

"Then let's go," she said. "We've got less than three hours of daylight left."

"I'll lead if you don't mind." He said slipping his night vision goggles over his forehead. He checked the ear radio sticking out of his right ear and said, "You can hear me, can't you?"

"Let's go, I can hear you and I don't mind you leading," she said, hoping they didn't have to wade any rivers or streams—being dry felt better than being wet.

Thirty-five minutes later they were lying on top of a wooded knoll looking down at the dam and small lake behind it and the Fork River that flowed through the dam.

"The river that feed that lake and provides water for the dam comes from northwest but the forest thins out in that direction," he said.

"So Mr. Morton should be east of us where the forest is thicker assuming he's smart," Evelyn said as she turned around and looked at the east. She took the backpack she was wearing off her back and took out her binoculars and hung them around her neck and put the backpack back on her back. She raised the binoculars to her eyes and scanned the forest.

"There's a small concrete building off to the north of the dam," Lee said. He saw what she did and had done the same thing.

"That's the power house where the generators and the maintenance robots are," she said. "An underground cable would run from there in an east south easterly direction if it was going back to the Colorado Power Company. It's located north of the city but south of the Danner Woods forest preserve area. Let's walk east, Lee. I should be able to pick up a power surge coming from it if it isn't buried to deep."

"How close must it be to the surface for you to pick up a surge?"

"At least six feet. Any deeper and I won't be able to detect it."

"Alright," he said. "You check your I-book for power surges and I'll keep a lookout for unwanted company."

They crawled to the eastern side of the knoll and moved carefully down it until they were back in the forest. Evelyn took out her I-book out of the pouch on her left side, turned it on, and pushed a button that activated a program that would detect a power surge. Lee took his rifle and activated it and moved the extended barrel and silencer in place. If he was going to do some shooting, he didn't want his targets to know his or Evelyn's location.

They walked fifteen minutes before Evelyn said, "Got it."

"Where it is," he asked her.

"It's one hundred and ten feet to our left, and not more than five feet down."

"So where is Mr. Morton hiding?" he asked as he raised his binoculars to his eyes and scanned the woods. He activated the heat detector chip in the binoculars.

"He has to be within two hundred feet of this cable," she said. "Unless he's got a power transmitter stuck in the ground just above the cable. Then he could be two or three hundred yards away depending upon the strength of the power transmitter."

"So you look for a power transmitter," he said as he turned in circle scanning the forest for any signs of two legged creatures. Bears usually went about on all four legs. He knew there were no apes or chimpanzees in America except in the zoological parks. The Crown City Zoological Park consisted of four hundred thousand acres, and their animals never escaped. Life was too good for them in the park. "I have a question," he said.

"What?" she asked.

"Why would this guy Lyle need a power transmitter if he's using a modern computer or laptop? They have batteries that can generate all the power he needs," Lee asked. "All he'd need if he wants to download information on the Internet would be a passing satellite he could access."

"If he has an old computer or laptop he'd need a power transmitter to give him power," Evelyn said. "And a generator that's close by to absorb the power so he could plug his computer or laptop into it."

"What makes you think he doesn't have a modern computer?" Lee asked her.

"Why would he be next to a dam and an underground cable if he had a modern computer or laptop?"

"Whoever this Lyle guy is, he's a damn fool," Lee grumbled.

"Not necessary. Antique computers and laptops are impossible to tap into because their software is so primitive. Remember my hideout and that computer in yours?"

Lee didn't say anything.

Evelyn adjusted her I-book to look for a power transmitter. Whether it gave off a strong or weak transmission she knew she could detect it. She started walking to her left. She walked for fifty feet before she turned right and continued walking.

"Why you turn right?" he asked. "Shouldn't we walk over the cable?"

"No, the power surge coming from it would blind my I-book to a transmitter." She walked a hundred feet more before she stopped and took a close look at her I-book then said, "It's to our left thirty feet from the cable."

Lee didn't respond. He was too busy scanning the forest for signs of humans. She looked up at him and asked, "See something?"

"No, and that's what I find odd," he said. "The computer people working for the five had to locate that Dodge Dart like we did. And they knew Lyle wouldn't return to the city. Their trackers would have found him by now. It wouldn't have taken them more than a few minutes to realize he went into the wilderness once he abandoned that Dart and needed power for a computer if they suspect he has an old computer. They would have picked up the dam on their scan of the wilderness area just like we did. So where the hell, are they?"

"Maybe they don't know he has an old computer," she said.

"If he had a modern one their computer people would have picked up on it in a few minutes," he said.

"Maybe they're late," she said. "Because they're calling in the trackers they had out looking for us."

He grinned and nodded as he said, "Yeah, Evelyn that makes sense. The stupid bastards probably had over ten people out looking for us, especially after I killed numbers 23 and 29 and then told Paul when he called me."

"That wasn't very smart, Lee," she said.

"I also told him I'd called the police."

"Why?"

"They'd be too busy picking up their dead before the police arrived to worry about me," he said. He lowered his binoculars and said, "I do believe we've got the jump on them by a few hours, Evelyn. Now all we got to do is find Morton and get him the hell away from here."

"This way," Evelyn said as she moved to her left. She stopped after thirty feet and looked down as the remains of a rotting tree stump infested with ants. "There it is," she said.

"In that tree stump?" he asked with a look on his face that said he didn't want to go digging into a tree stump infested with carpenter ants. The damn things bite and sting.

"No, two feet away." She walked around the tree stump and looked down at the leaf covered ground. "Right under these leaves."

"So he should be within a few hundred feet of this. Right," he asked as he raised his binoculars and looked around the forest.

"Don't waste your time doing that," she told him as she put her I-book back in the pouch on her left side and dropped to her knees and leaned over and began to gently brush the leaves to one side.

Lee looked at her and said, "You act as if that thing could be booby trapped."

"Could have a power discharge chip in it designed to kill anyone who opened it with a few thousand volts of electricity." She looked up at Lee and smiled. "Don't worry, Lee, my gloves are insulated."

"So are mine, but not for a few thousand volts of electricity," he said as he knelt next to her. "Let me," he said as he pushed her hands to one side. "I've defused a few bombs in the past."

"Ever set a few bombs?" She straightened up.

"No, I was just a tracker who killed only when I had to." He brushed the dirt away after he'd cleared the ground of leaves to reveal a plastic covered box the size of the standard size dictionary.

"Stop," Evelyn told him as she leaned over and looked at the transparent plastic cover. She pulled her night vision goggles down over her eyes and said, "Magnify to the tenth power." The goggles immediately gave her a view of the inside of the box. "It's your basic power transmitter box with a counter and a direction gage." She said as she read the counter. "He's one hundred and forty feet away to the north." She stood up and turned north. "Let's go."

"Wait," he said as he began to cover the box with dirt then leaves. "There's no sense in us making it easy for those assholes' killers if they get this far."

Evelyn began to walk slowly north.

Lee stood up and followed her. "Turn on your radio and keep your goggles on. The sunlight is fading and we don't want to run into any surprises Mr. Morton have rigged this area for unwanted visitors." He pulled his night vision goggles down over his eyes and said, "Magnify to the tenth power." The goggle did so.

They walked seventy feet before they saw a cabin surrounded on three sides by trees and heavy brush. The windows were shuttered by rough wooden shutters and no light came through them.

"Think he's in there?" Evelyn asked him.

"Unless this is an illegal hunter's cabin, which I seriously doubt," he said. "No hunter would be stupid enough to build a cabin this close to the city with forest rangers flying over this area two or three times a month during the hunting season."

"Is it the hunting season now?"

"No. This is the breeding season for most animals that's why this isn't some illegal hunter's cabin. This was probably built by someone who liked to get away from the city for a weekend in the woods during the spring and summer. Such cabins are not that unusual this close to the city. Let's get a little closer. Stay behind me, walked in my footsteps, and no noise." He started moving toward the cabin watching where he stepped to avoid stepping on any twigs or crunchy leaves.

Evelyn followed him stepping in his footsteps.

Lee stopped twelve feet from a shuttered window and looked to his left and right. He didn't even see any animals which didn't surprise him. They would avoid a structure a human was living in this close to Crown. "Get down on your belly and cover me with your rifle, and don't shoot me if we have to start shooting."

"Okay," she said as she took the rifle off her left shoulder and lay prone on the ground and aimed at the window.

As Lee approached the cabin window he told the goggles to go to regular vision. When he reached the window, he looked back and saw Evelyn aiming off to his right. He turned back to the window and looked for a crack in the wooden shutters. He saw one and looked through it.

"Living room," he whispered to Evelyn over his ear radio. "Looks clean and there's a book on the table next to the chair facing the fireplace. No sign that the fireplace was ever used. There's a closed door on the left that leads to another room and an open door on the right. Looks like there's kitchen beyond it. I'm going around to the left side. Stay where you are."

A minute later he said, "There's back window here to a bedroom and there's a man sleeping in the bed. The room looks clean and there are clothing on a chair at the foot of the bed."

"That's Lyle Morton," she said.

"If it isn't we've wasted a lot of time," he replied. "I'm going around to the back. You move to your right to where there should be a front door. I don't see a door here."

He moved quietly to his left and stopped when he saw a door a few feet from him. "I see a covered extension coming from the back of the cabin. So there's probably a kitchen door." He turned around and looked into the woods and saw an outhouse attached to the extension and an open pit ten feet away side by side. He saw no one. "There's a garbage pit ten feet from the outhouse the extension is attached to. I'm going to try and get into the extension and see if there's a door. I hope it isn't locked. If anyone comes out the front door shoot for their legs. Make sure it's not me."

"I will," she said.

Lee moved to the side of the extension attached to the house and found a door and opened it. He saw two steps leading up to the door in the back of the house. He looked for any wires that would indicate an alarm system. He saw none and reached up for the door handle. He pulled it down as quietly as he could. The door opened inward an inch. Lee waited for a cry of protest or the barking of dog. He heard none and walked up on the wooden steps, the first step creaked, the second didn't, and entered the dark kitchen with his rifle in front of him. He moved to his right putting a wall at his back and quietly closed the door. "I'm inside," he said. "I'm going to the living room. You come in through the front door. Check for wires on the steps."

Evelyn did as he said and a minute later entered the living room of the cabin. She stopped to check a closed door that was a closet and looked at Lee who was standing at the closed door to the left of the living room.

"Ready?" he asked her.

"Ready," she answered.

Lee reached down and pushed the door handle down and pushed the door open.

The deep breathing of the man on the bed indicated he was sound asleep.

Lee quietly entered the bedroom, looked around carefully for any weapons or triggering devices for explosives—he saw none, and opened a closed door that was a closet then he turned toward the sleeping man. He looked at Evelyn who nodded she was ready if shooting was required. Lee raised his left foot and slammed it down on the wooden side board of the bed.

The sound of Lee's booted foot slamming down on the bed and the shaking bed woke the man up. It took him a few minutes to realize he was looking at two armed strangers dressed in dark jeans wearing body armor with goggles covering their eyes. His first thought was to scream, but he knew that would be a waste of time. Better to save his strength for the horror that was coming than waste it screaming.

Lee and Evelyn stared at the man without saying a word.

He had tanned skin straight black hair and dark slanted eyes that made him look Asian, and his face had only a thin beard. He was five nine and looked to be healthy.

The man cleared his throat and said in a nice baritone voice, "Don't those monsters teach their killers how to speak?"

"We're not here to kill you," Evelyn said.

"No? I'm not surprised those monsters wouldn't want to waste the opportunity to use me as a lab rat in their secret lab," he said.

"What about a secret lab?" Evelyn asked him.

He ignored her and said, "Mind if get dressed? I wouldn't want to meet my maker wearing only my shorts. Not that it would matter to the monsters you two are working for since they have no intentions of ever meeting their maker."

"Who are you?" Lee asked him.

"You don't know?" the man said.

"Answer my question, please."

"Oh, politeness from godless killers how civilize those monster are to teach you to be polite."

"Answer his question!" Evelyn barked at the man.

"Lyle Morton," he said. "Now may I get dressed?"

Lee stepped back saying, "If I see a weapon of any kind, you're dead."

"I don't have any weapons," he said as he setup in bed and pushed the covers back and swung his legs over the left side of the bed. He was wearing boxer shorts with hearts on them. "Hand me my pants," he said.

"Get them yourself," Lee told him as he back farther away keeping his weapon on him.

Lyle got out of bed and walked to the chair where his clothes were. He quickly put on his pants and shirt and sat down and put on his socks.

Lee saw him reaching for his shoes. "Do you have any boots you can wear?"

"Why?" Lyle asked him.

"Because those shoes aren't going to protect your feet very well in the woods."

Lyle looked at him and Evelyn and asked with a curious expression, "Exactly who are you two?"

"Your saviors," Evelyn said. "Now get some boots and put them on. We don't have much time."

Lee looked at his watch. "It's nine o'clock."

"So?" the man asked.

"If we're not out of here in twenty minutes, we're all dead," Evelyn told him.

"Ten minutes would be better," Lee said.

"What type of killers would be concerned with me wearing boots?" he asked.

"Get some boots if you have them and put them on, now," Lee growled at the man.

❧

CHAPTER 34

9:10 p.m.

The convoy of five vehicles had been on the road for only ten minutes and every one of the five was sorry they were a part of it. Ordering killings from five star penthouse hotel suites that cost ten thousand dollars a day was the closest any of them had ever come to being in the field. Even the clothing they wore, even though it was the best money could buy, didn't make them feel comfortable. Boots and camouflage clothing was as unnatural to them as cleaning up after themselves.

They were all riding in Paul's and Bruce's camper sitting around the small kitchen table. Tracker number 30 was driving.

"I don't like this one bit," Fred said. "I still think we could have run things from the lodge."

"We need to be on the scene to make sure our people don't kill this Lyle Morton," Paul said. "We must know exactly how he managed to get our information so we can prevent others in the future from doing the same. A little discomfort is necessary if we are to remain what we are and continue."

Fred looked at Steve and said, "I suppose you agree with Paul."

"Fred," Steve said quietly. "We hired two excellent people to find this Lyle Morton and they quickly figured out once they got him and the information he had we'd kill them and Morton to guarantee our information remains secret. This trip wouldn't be necessary if we hadn't hired Evelyn and Lee."

"I don't recall you protesting when Paul suggested we hire them," Fred replied.

Steve exhaled and started to yell at Fred.

"The one thing we don't need is to fight among ourselves," Bruce said. "And Steve's right, Fred. Like it or not we have to be on the scene to make sure things go right this time. Lee and Evelyn are too smart for us to depend upon them."

"Surely you know we've lost six trackers to them," Larry said. He had a worried expression on his face.

"Why the look of worry," Bruce asked Larry.

"I've the feeling we should have left earlier, or at least sent out our trackers earlier."

"There were twenty trackers in this general area scanning these woods, and by now they've been here for at least an hour," Bruce said. "Maybe they'll find Lyle Morton."

"It took us time to gather them together," Paul told him. He looked at his watch. "They should be within three hours of the Fork River Dam by now."

"What if Evelyn and Lee are ahead of us?" Larry asked.

None of them said anything.

"If they're ahead of us, and we must assume they know about the Fork River Dam by now, they'll reach Lyle Morton hours before we or our trackers do and disappear with him," Larry explained.

"That's possible," Paul said. He still didn't understand Larry's concern.

"Listen to me," he began. "If they get Lyle Morton before we do, he's going to tell them what he took and let them read it. Once they do, they're going to join forces with him and expose us."

"The information we had hidden in the Department of Information amounts to no more than vicious gossip without proof of the lab's existence," Steve said. "We were fools for putting the information there in the first place."

"Until this Lyle Morton showed up our information was safely hidden," Fred said in an unpleasant voice that showed his intense dislike of going into the field. "All we have to do is get those traitors, kill them, and we're safe again."

"But what if we don't get them?" Larry asked him.

"Our people are efficient," Fred said.

"So far Evelyn and Lee have outmaneuvered and killed six of our efficient people and avoided all of our best electrical tracking and tracing equipment. If Evelyn and Lee get their hands on Lyle Morton before we do, they'll disappear the way they did before."

Paul's straight face hid his thoughts until he spoke, "Larry, right. We must do an efficient job of making sure Lyle Morton falls into our hands. Then we can take care of Evelyn and Lee and their families. But if we don't get Lyle Morton—."

"We're fucked!" Bruce said, interrupting him.

"I dislike profanity," Paul said. "And we're not fucked because the three of them would have to get the final proof to support what Lyle Morton took."

"They'd have to prove the lab exists," Larry added.

"But no one knows where it's at," Fred said.

"No one knew about our information in the Department of Information either, Fred," Steve reminded him.

"So what do we do if Lee and Evelyn are ahead of us?" Bruce said.

"The only thing we can do," Paul said.

"Which is what?" Bruce said.

"Go to the lab and await their arrival," Steve told him.

CHAPTER 35

9:03 p.m.

"What do you mean my saviors?" Lyle asked as he walked to the closet and took out a pair of black canvas and leather boots from the back of the closet and walked to a chair and sat down and put them on. He laced up the boots and tightened the laces and tied them.

"We were hired to find you and what you took from the Department of Information about the five," Lee told him. "We knew once we did that we were dead, because you've apparently taken something that threatens them. They couldn't afford to let us live because they knew we'd read whatever you took."

"Why would you do that?" he asked as he stood up and moved his toes around in the boots.

"You're really not too bright, are you?" Evelyn told him.

"I was smart enough to get to this cabin without them knowing about it," he said as he walked around in the boots.

"You left the Dodge Dart in Danner Woods which we found and they did, too. Your social security number belongs to a seven year old girl in Africa, and we're standing here in your cabin on Wednesday night five days after you made your remarkable getaway," Evelyn told him. "Smart, Mr. Morton. No. In my book you're a fucking idiot who should have left things alone, because now you've put our lives as well as yours in danger not to mention the lives of our families."

He stopped and looked at them and realized she was right. "I'm sorry I put your lives and those of your families in danger. But what

I did was necessary if a greater disaster is to be avoided a few years from now. And my family's lives are in danger, too."

"Let's get your things and let's get out of here," Lee said. There was time enough for long talks once they got to safety.

Lyle looked around at the bedroom and said, "I'll need those two suitcases in the closet, and I should pack all of my underwear and socks, though some need to be cleaned. And, of course, I'll need my slippers. I do hate walking about in my stocking feet. It tends to wear out my socks rather quickly, and I only brought a dozen pair with me."

Evelyn looked at Lee with a 'is this guy kidding' expression.

"Get the bags out of the closet, please, Evelyn," Lee said as he stood watching Lyle. He didn't know whether to kill this guy and get the hell out of the cabin, or just leave him. Even though he knew leaving him was out of the question. Their lives and those of the families depended on this absurd man. "Get the fucking clothes you need,

Mr. Morton, and let's go time is running out."

"I don't think we have to hurry," he said. "It will take the five a bit of time to get here."

"But not their trackers, you idiot," Evelyn yelled at him as she slung her rifle over her right shoulder and went to the closet and pulled out two large black plastic suitcases and threw them on the bed. "And they've probably already sent them to that dam. What's in that bag on the floor of the closet?"

"My dirty clothes," he said walking to the closet and pulling the bag out. He walked to the bed and placed the bag next to the suit cases. He opened the suit cases.

"Hurry up!" Lee snapped at him.

Lyle nodded and went to the worn dresser, opened it, and quickly removed his clothes and started putting them in the open suitcases in an orderly manner.

"Aw, fuck this," Lee said angrily and slung his rifle over his right shoulder and walked to the dresser and began throwing the remaining clothes in the suitcases. As soon as they were filled, he said to Lyle, "Close them and let's get out of here while we still can."

Lyle closed and locked his suitcases, picked them up off the bed, and said, "I must get the crystal and my laptop before I leave. Without them I've wasted my time and we will fail."

"Where are they?" Lee asked him.

"In my study."

"There is no study in this cabin."

"It's a corner of the living room I call my study," he explained. "It's a very cozy place to work."

"Let's go get them," Lee said as he grabbed him by the right shoulder of his shirt and threw him toward the door.

Lyle stumbled out the bedroom with his two suitcases in each hand and moved toward the corner of the living room where a desk was with his laptop on it. He put his suitcases on the floor and closed and locked his laptop then calmly picked up a laptop briefcase on the right hand side of the wooden desk and put the laptop in it.

"Let's go," Lee said as he grabbed Lyle by the right shoulder of his shirt and pulled him toward the door.

"Wait!" Lyle yelled. "I must have that crystal on the desk."

"Forget it," Evelyn yelled, looking at the crystal. "It's just a piece of glass."

"No! It's far more than that," Lyle said. "Without it I'm lost."

"You don't need it, it's a fucking paper weight," Lee told him.

"It contains the information the five are out after. Without it I can't expose them."

Lee froze and looked at the piece of glass with a disbelieving expression. Then he walked to the desk and picked it up and looked at it. It was heavy for a piece of glass. He looked down at an open three inch plastic case and asked Lyle, "This goes in there?"

"Yes," Lyle said.

Lee put the piece of glass in the plastic case and closed it and slipped it into his left front pants pocket.

"Give it to me," Lyle demanded.

"No. We're leaving now."

Lee led the way out the front door as he removed his rifle from his shoulder and into the forest with his rifle moving to the left and right. He had his goggles on and could clearly see everything within fifty feet of them in the dark forest. Lyle followed behind him struggling with his heavy suitcases. Evelyn followed him making sure no one was following them.

"It's dark out here," Lyle complained. "I can't see a thing."

"Just stay behind him," Evelyn said a few feet behind him.

"Where are we going? My car is behind the cabin in the woods. We're going in the wrong direction."

"Shut up!" Lee said, turning toward him and pointing the rifle at his throat. "And I'm not going to say that a second time."

Lyle could tell from the tone of Lee's voice he meant every word he said. Lyle decided to be quiet. These two, rude as they were, apparently weren't working for the five or they would have killed him or made a call to the five. Then he remembered what Lee had said to him about being hired by the five, and he felt confused as well as afraid. Was his abduction from the cabin by these two, who seemed to be interested in saving his life, something new those monsters had come up with? Since he didn't know he decided to be quiet and pray to God they weren't going to kill him.

They had been moving for half an hour before Evelyn said, "Lee, we've got to stop. Mr. Morton is about to collapse with those suitcases he's carrying."

"That's what he gets for bringing all that crap," Lee said. He looked back at Lyle and noticed his face was red and he was breathing like he was on the verge of collapse. "We'll slow down, but we don't stop."

They didn't stop until they'd reached the spot where they had hidden the car. When they did, Lyle fell to the ground, breathing like a wounded animal.

"Keep an eye around us, Evelyn," he said as he picked up Lyle's suitcases and carried them to the back of the car.

Evelyn took up a position where she could see anything approaching them.

Lee took a key out of his pocket and opened the rear hatch and threw the suitcases inside. He closed the hatch and went to Lyle. He picked him up by his left arm and dragged him to the door behind the driver's seat, opened the door, pushed him inside.

"We didn't lock the doors of the cabin," Lyle said between mouthfuls of air. "There are bears in these woods." He stopped speaking to catch his breath as Lee buckled him into the seat. "They're always trying to get into the cabin."

"Good, maybe they'll cover our tracks," Lee said as he took off his backpack and removed a plastic cord from it and tied Lyle's hands.

"What are you doing?"

"I don't trust you," he answered as he removed a large camouflaged handkerchief from the backpack, folded it, and wrapped it around Lyle's eyes.

"Is that cloth clean?" Lyle asked.

"No, a bear used it an hour ago to wipe his ass with after taking a shit," Lee said. "Now shut up. Come on, Evelyn."

Within a few seconds they were in the car driving out of the hidden area. Lee headed northwest moving slow.

"Taking a roundabout to the hideout?" Evelyn said, sitting in the passenger's seat.

"I figure their trackers are pretty close. Maybe less than a mile away. If they're spread out we may be able to slip through them without them seeing us."

"If they're smart, they've located that power cable and then the power transmitter," she said. "Once they've got them they'll be in the cabin in minutes."

"Turn on the car's heat detector," he told her. "Most of the large animals have probably bedded down. So you shouldn't pick up anything but the smaller animals."

"Let's hope they don't have equipment to detect body heat," she said as she turned on the car's heat detect and looked at the lower screen on the dashboard. She turned down the glare of the screen till it was hardly visible.

Lee didn't drive fast because he didn't want to make noise even though he could clearly see everything in front of them and on both sides for a distance of twenty feet.

Eighteen minutes later Evelyn said, "Stop. Turn off the engine There are two people about sixty feet ahead of us coming toward us. One's on the right the other on the left about twenty feet apart and they're moving like they're searching for something."

"We're at least a mile from the cabin so they haven't located it yet," Lee said as he brought the car to a stop and turned off the engine and placed his left hand over the center of the steering wheel. He adjusted his night vision goggles to a magnification of five with his right hand and then pulled his pistol out of its holster and clicked safety off.

Evelyn did the same as she told him, "I'll do the shooting while you drive if it comes to that."

"Mr. Morton, be very quiet if you value your life," Lee told him.

Lyle heard what the woman and man said and felt like throwing up. Never in his life had he seen or touched a weapon, and having one fired at him even if he was in a car terrified him. He didn't say a word.

The two trackers moved a few yards ahead then stop, look around, and moved again. Both were wearing night vision goggles and were carrying heavy voltage electric rifles with silencers on them.

Lee and Evelyn didn't say a word as they watched the two men draw closer to the car. All it took was for one of the two trackers to look at the forest being reflected off the Plexiglas of the car and move to investigate. Then the killing would start. And both of them knew if there were two in the woods they probably had plenty of backup not far away.

The tracker on the right approached within twenty feet of the car and stopped and looked in the direction of the car for thirty seconds then moved over to his left a few yards. He was now directly in front of the car. The one of the left moved passed the car, he was over twenty feet away, and never looked in the direction of the car. Then he stopped when he was a few yards pass the car and appeared to be speaking into an ear radio. The one in front of the car suddenly ran forward then turned quickly to the right when he was less than ten feet from the car and ran into the woods in the direction of the one on the left.

Lee and Evelyn turned to their left and watched the two men disappear into the woods.

"Are, are they still there?" Lyle said softly.

"No," Evelyn said in a soft voice. "They're behind us now and moving deeper into the woods."

"Don't you think we should go?" he asked.

"No, not until they're too far away to hear us move," Lee answered.

"They have extremely good hearing and sight," Lyle said. "What they lack is the ability to think critically—specific judgment."

"That's so," Lee replied, paying little attention to him.

"Sorry I spoke," Lyle said to Lee in a nervous voice. "But I was afraid."

Evelyn turned around in her seat and looked out the back window. Lyle was partially blocking her view. "Scoot down a little, Mr. Morton."

He scooted down as far as he could go in his seat while she told her goggles to adjust to a magnification power of ten.

Ten minutes passed before she said to Lee, "They're far enough away not to hear us leave."

"How far," Lyle asked from his uncomfortable position.

"Almost half a mile," she said.

"Wait another two minutes before you leave," he advised Lee.

Lee took his advice and waited.

After two minutes Lyle said, "Now would be a good time to leave."

Lee holstered his weapon and reached down to the steering column and pushed the starter button.

The nice thing about electric powered vehicles is they didn't make a lot of noise when they started up—just a mild electrical purr that quickly goes away as the engine begins to run. In the center of the steering wheel was a small light that went red immediately after the vehicle's engine was turned off then went out after a second. When the engine was started it flashed red for a brief second if the engine was in working order, then went to bright green. After a second or two it faded to a dull green indicating the electrical engine was in perfect working order. If there was a problem with the engine it would flash a bright greenish red warning signal indicating the engine need an electrician to look at it.

Lee shifted the car into gear, when stopped the engine would automatically shift the transmission into neutral, and moved ahead very slowly.

"Don't go fast," Lyle told him. "If they hear us moving behind them they may think it's a large animal. The deer in these woods are constantly moving at night. It's the best time to find food and avoid the few wolves that sometimes come around."

"There are wolves around here?" Evelyn asked him as she holstered her weapon. She was still looking out the back window.

"Yes, they come close to the city because they know deer and other small animals are here because there is no hunting allowed this close to the city." He moved back up to a comfortable sitting position and said, "Of course, coyotes are always around. They've been known to even go into the forest preserves especially during the summer."

"Why?" she asked as she turned to the front.

"People are so careless with their garbage after a picnic in the preserves. They're the same with the public parks in the city. That's why there are so many well-fed squirrels and chipmunks in those parks. Can I remove this blindfold?"

"No!" Evelyn and Lee said as the same time.

Lyle decided to get some sleep since he couldn't see anything.

Lee continued moving slow and quiet avoiding tree stumps and fallen trees and large branches. Twigs and the smaller ones were impossible to avoid. The trees shed useless small branches every spring like deciduous trees shed their leaves every fall. Fortunately, the sounds of snapping small branches and twigs didn't carry very far in the forest because the plants absorbed the sounds. He glanced at the odometer every ten seconds until he saw he was over a mile from the area they had spotted the trackers in then he increased his speed and bounced up and down and leaned left and right as he moved over objects in his path that were less than a foot high.

Evelyn pointed to the upper monitor on the dashboard indicating a paved road that was less than two miles away.

Lee nodded and headed for it. He should have relaxed but he didn't. If the trackers they saw in the woods were anything like him, they'd backtrack for a mile and scan the ground for any signs of humans moving through the woods. If they did, they'd clearly see the marks the car left on the ground and would know the direction he was heading in. He glanced in the rearview mirror and saw Lyle was asleep. "Lyle!" he yelled.

Lyle woke up. "Yes, you called?"

"You said they lacked special judgment. Explain what you meant?"

"I said they lacked specific judgment," he said. "They lack the ability to form complex or simple decisions from bits and pieces of evidence. Meaning they can't look at a series of clues, large or small, and come to a decision about them."

"That bullshit," Evelyn said.

"Oh, no it's not, Miss," Lyle said. "What is your name by the way?"

"Evelyn."

"I'm sorry if I forgot your name when I heard it earlier, but your barbaric companion's brutal treatment of me caused me to forget it. Such as his throwing me into this car, tying my hands, and then blindfolding me. I've even forgotten his name."

"Why do you say those trackers lack the ability to make specific decisions?" she demanded.

"Because they do," he answered.

"How the hell do you know that?" she demanded of him

"Because they were never programmed to do so, they're only programmed to carry out simple orders. But they can never carry out complex orders that require specific judgment because they are clones."

CHAPTER 36

10:45 p.m.

"Sir," Sam said from the expanded van leading the convoy of three vehicles. The van was equipped the very latest in electrical surveillance and computers available on the market. Its satellite accessing equipment wasn't available on the market because it was illegal. Troy was sleeping in a chair that had extended to a narrow bed.

The five men were still in the camper but Paul and Bruce were sitting in the small lounge watching cable TV.

Larry heard him through the intercom system that connected all three vehicles. "What is it?"

"Our trackers have located a cabin in the woods a mile and a half from the Fork River Dam. They also located the dam's power cable and a power transmitter box buried a hundred and forty feet from the cabin."

"Why would Lyle Morton need to be close to a power transmitter box?" Larry asked.

"I do not know, sir," Sam replied.

"All computers have their own power source. If Lyle Morton needed to be next to a power transmitter box it says he needed power his computer couldn't produce," Larry mumbled.

"That's not important, Larry," Bruce told him.

Larry agreed with him and dismissed the question from his mind.

"Did they find Lyle Morton?" Larry asked Sam in an annoyed voice.

"No sir. The cabin was empty, but there were foot prints outside the cabin leading into the woods. The foot prints were those of three humans one was estimated to be a female because they were smaller. The trackers followed them to a place surrounded by trees and thick brush and saw the tracks of a car with wide tires. The car was not there."

"Did they search the area?" he asked Sam.

"Yes sir, they followed the tracks to a dirt road that led to a paved road going north and south. They do not know the exact direction the car went because there was dirt and leaves from the car going both north and south."

"How could that be?" Larry asked.

"Sam," Steve interrupted. "Get a road map of the area where the tire tracks were found and look for any towns close by."

"What's the purpose of that?" Paul asked him.

"Lee would have been smart enough to drive out of those woods going in one direction then back up into the woods and drive out going in another direction to confuse our trackers. He would also have avoided leaving any marks on the road to indicate the direction he actually went."

"Then we've lost Lyly Morton, if he was the person with our information," Bruce said.

"He's the person," Fred said. "And he's with Lee and Evelyn and we don't know what direction they went."

"Let's have Sam access any satellites passing overhead," Larry suggested. "Whether they're in the woods or on a road a satellite will pick them up, and we can follow them to wherever they're headed."

"No, don't tell Sam to do that," Paul said. "We may be able to access any satellite we want without any government agency finding out, but that is not necessary especially now."

"Why isn't it?" Steve asked, looking at Paul.

"They have this Lyle Morton or whoever he is and everything he has about us. And none of it is worth anything without proof of the lab's existence."

Steve nodded his understanding of Paul's reasoning as he said, "Like it or not they will have to come to us, and when they do we will be able to kill them."

"Correct," Paul said. "Instead of us searching for them, they will have to search for the lab. When they find its location, and knowing Evelyn's skills as I do, they will find it."

"Lee will know this," Bruce reminded them.

"Of course, he will," Paul agreed.

"He will also know if they can't find out where the lab is soon, there will be no place on the world they can run and hide we can't go to and find the three of them," Bruce said.

"And when they get close, they'll be deep within the wilderness, and we can have our people kill them without worrying about the police or anyone finding out," Fred said with a smile on his face.

"And this time," Bruce began. "We should be present to guarantee their deaths."

"And we will," Steve said.

"Sam," Larry said. "Head for the lab, and tell our trackers to do the same."

"Yes sir."

"We did not make a mistake in hiring Evelyn and Lee to find this person after all even if they have made fools of us," Paul said. "Because to prove what this person Lyle Morton has on us is true, they will have to come to the lab. And when they get there we will have them all and we can end forever this threat to us and all future threats." He looked at each of them. "Does anyone disagree?"

None of the four said anything.

But Steve was thinking, *if Lee is as foolish as we hope, and Evelyn can't figure a way around our defenses.*

CHAPTER 37

June 7, 12 a.m. Thursday

Lee and Evelyn were desperate to ask Lyle how he knew the trackers looking for them were clones, but they were more interested in making sure the trackers weren't tracking them regardless of what they were.

For two hours Lee had been moving from road to road in an irregular pattern designed to confuse anyone trying to follow them. But he never doubled back once not because he was worried the five were on to his evasive maneuvering, but because he didn't like to do the same thing twice. Twice he'd stopped for fifteen minutes to see if someone caught up with them or was following them and stopped, too. Once on the side of a road running in a diagonal south-east and north-west direction, and once in the woods a hundred feet from a road running north and south. Both times nothing came down the roads in either direction. But still he took evasive maneuvers over a hundred miles from his hideout to be on the safe side. By one-thirty he was sure they weren't being followed, but nevertheless he took evasive maneuvers as he headed for his hideout.

Evelyn silently watched for any vehicles that seemed out of place on the dark isolated country roads Lee took.

Lyle slept, snoring loudly, though all the evasive maneuvering.

At four-thirty Lee backed the car into the garage and lowered the overhead door. They woke up Lyle a few minutes later, removed his blindfold, and took him to a bedroom.

"Does this have a private bathroom?" he asked. "Whenever I wanted to wash in the cabin, I had to use the kitchen sink and the water was cold. And the only toilet was the outhouse behind the cabin."

"Yes," Lee told him as he cut the plastic cord binding his hands.

"Oh, good," he said. "I'm hungry. When do we eat?"

"Later," Lee said as he pushed Lyle into the bedroom. "Don't break anything." He closed and locked the door.

"That man is a savage," Lyle said as he stood staring at the locked door. He sighed and walked toward an open door that led to the bathroom. He looked around it for a few seconds before his eyes fell on the roll of toilet tissue next to the toilet. "I wonder if he's civilized enough to know how to use toilet tissue?" he mumbled to himself. He turned and walked around the spacious bedroom, sat on the bed to test its firmness, was satisfied, and got up and walked to the bathroom removing his jacket as he did so. *That man may be a savage,* he thought. *But for the first time in months, I feel safe.* He decided a hot shower and more rest would be the best thing for him.

Thirty minutes later Lyle got in the bed naked and stretched out his legs. That made him happy, even though he would have preferred some clean shorts to sleep in, but he could at least stretch out his legs. Sleeping in the car had been nice, but a bit cramped.

On June seventh, at ten forty-five Lee opened the door to Lyle's bedroom and asked, "You want breakfast?"

Lyle had been sitting in chair with a large bath towel wrapped about him for the last five hours. The expression on his face showed he wasn't very happy with his situation. "Of course, I want breakfast. And I'd also like my clothes, too, if it doesn't inconvenience a savage like you."

"You call me a savage again, you son-of-a-bitch, and I'm going to kick the crap out of you," Lee told him in an angry voice as he leaned to the right of the open door, picked up Lyle's two suitcases, tossed them on the floor, and closed the door.

"You're too late," Lyle screamed at him. "I used the toilet before I took a shower at five in the morning."

Lee didn't respond.

Lyle got up and walked to the door and tried the knob. He was surprised when the door opened. He closed it and went to his suitcases, put them on the bed, and got some clean clothes out and got dressed. Seven minutes later he walked into the breakfast room and saw eggs, bacon, and biscuits on the table in glass plates under glass covers. He saw there were three sets of dishes on the table, and asked as he stood at the door, "May I help myself?"

"Sure," Lee said, sitting at the table. "But don't forget what I told you."

"I won't," he said sharply to Lee as he rushed to a chair and sat down.

Evelyn walked into the breakfast room dressed in slacks and a matching blouse with slippers on and sat down. "Oh, boy, do I need a cup of coffee."

Lee poured her a cup of coffee and helped himself to breakfast.

Lyle had already helped himself to three eggs, bacon, three biscuits, and was eating like a starving man. He had three cups of coffee with his breakfast and drank a glass of water in twenty minutes and didn't say a word while he ate. Evelyn and Lee ate quietly as they watched him.

"That was delicious," Lyle said as he leaned back in his chair and placed his hands over his full stomach. "It's been almost a week since I've had such a meal."

"Not exactly," Lee said as he got a second cup of coffee. "Today is Thursday you disappeared from the Department of Information on Friday night around 10:45."

"How would you know that?" he asked, getting his fourth cup of coffee. He put three teaspoons of sugar in it before he took a sip.

"You left a trail a first month Cub Scot could follow," Evelyn told him. "If the five hadn't been so busy looking for us they could have found you in less than twelve hours."

"I prepared well for my escape," he said as he put the cup on the saucer.

"Like hell you did," Lee told him. "Fake name with a social security number that belongs to a girl of seven in Africa and that Dodge left in the Danner Woods. You have no idea how lucky you are, Mr. Morton."

He looked at Lee and Evelyn and said, "I suppose I was a bit clumsy."

"You sure were," Evelyn told him.

He looked around the kitchen and asked, "This is a nice kitchen. As I recall from last night we were still in a wooded area. What is this place?"

"My hideout," Lee told him.

"From that hallway, and the bedroom I slept in, I'd say it was pretty large," Lyle said.

"It is," Lee said.

"How large is this place?" he asked.

"Since we're all in the same boat I don't think it'll hurt to tell you," Evelyn said as she looked at Lee.

Lee nodded his approval and said nothing while Evelyn told Lyle how big Lee's hideout was, but not where it was at.

"Now tell us, Mr. Morton, how do you know those trackers we saw were clones?" Evelyn asked him. "Cloning humans has been against the law since the twentieth century."

"So has the production of illegal drugs and moonshine, but people still make and buy both, and there's still a healthy market for them, too."

"There is no healthy market for clones anywhere in the world, Mr. Morton," Evelyn told him. "And if you're as intelligent as you try to sound you should know that."

"Okay, I'll admit moonshine and illegal drugs was a bit of a stretch," he said. "But those men in the woods looking for us were clones."

"Answer her question," Lee told him as he stared at him.

He sighed and decided he had nothing to lose by telling the truth to these two who had saved his life and that of his family, so far. "Twenty-five years ago, while working on historical records from the twenty fifth century in the Hong Kong branch of the Department of Information I stumbled across a hidden file labeled 'The Five'. At first, I thought some computer clerk had made the mistake of filing information from the twentieth and twenty-first centuries in the wrong century. It happens quite often you know. People not paying attention to what they were doing. Everyone makes the foolish mistake of thinking computers can do everything even correct human mistakes. Well, they can't. The darn things have to be programmed with the proper software."

"So, what about this file 'The Five'?" Lee asked him. He wasn't interested in a long lecture on the weaknesses of computers or people.

"Ever since the formation of the World Democracy in 2449 the human race has suffered from reoccurring plagues. The first one began in 2559 one hundred ten years after the formation of the World Democracy and over seven hundred million people died in two years before a cure for that plague was found."

"The new Bubonic Plague," Lee said. He knew about the plague from reading history, a subject he enjoyed reading about.

"Then in 2663 one hundred and four years later another plague hit the people of the world. Only this time it wasn't a new version of the bacteria that caused the Bubonic Plague, but something all-together different and twice as deadly. Two billion people died in seventeen months before a cure was found."

"Another plague popped up in 2787 one hundred and twenty-four years later," Lee said. "It killed a little over two billion people."

"Correct," Lyle said. "Each time the population of the world seemed to be recovering from the horrible losses another plague pops up."

"Then there was one in 2907. It killed well over two billion people," Evelyn said. "I remembered writing a paper on it my first year in college, before I lost interest in history."

"The world' population was close to nine billion when the first one in 2559 occurred," Lee said. "It dropped the world's population to a little over eight billion."

"Go on," Lyle told him.

"The one in 2663 reduced the world' population to about seven billion people," he said. "And the one in 2787 reduced the population to less than six billion people, and the one in 2907 knocked the population down to less than three and a half billion people."

"In an effort to prevent such horrible losses in the future the world government in 2908 began to rebuild the old cities making sure they had safe food and water to drink with proper disposal of garbage. They established wilderness areas all around the world where people were forbidden to build houses, but could go into them for camping and hunting trips. Since it was believed, though there was never any scientific evidence, the plagues were the result of humans coming into contact with wild animals who weren't affected by the bacteria that caused the plagues. The preserves were built around the cities to help reduce contact with animals in the wilderness." Lyle said.

"No one wanted to wipe out the animals in the wildernesses because it was believed, and had been proven that they helped keep the Earth's environment safe for people."

"All of this was done by 2970," Evelyn said. "And there hasn't been another plague. So, what the government started doing back in 2908 was right. The animals in the wilds have increased in number and the places where people live even in small towns and isolated villages are safe from plague."

"So, I thought," Lyle said. "Until I read that Five File and learned that the plagues had all been man-made."

Lee started laughing.

Lyle looked at him and said, "How do you control people, Lee?"

"Through advertisement," he said between laughs.

"No, through fear," Lyle said.

Lee stopped laughing and looked at Evelyn who looked at him and shrugged her shoulders. They were both lost.

"The world has changed since the twenty-fifth century, Evelyn and Lee," he said. "Billionaires are as common as dirt and there are at least fifty people worth over a trillion dollars in the world today. There are no more poor people on Earth. Everyone who isn't a billionaire or worth trillions is classified as affluent or middle class and the middle class is well taken care of. The threat of overpopulation has disappeared because people have fewer children, and the billions that have died because of the plagues. There are no more wars of any kind or size, and people want it to remain like that. And people will do anything to keep the world the way it is."

"Are you saying democracy is threatened?" Evelyn asked.

"Oh, no, those who caused these plagues don't want to get rid of the world democratic government. All they want to do is control the elected leaders."

"And the best way to do that is keep people scared," Lee added.

"You are exactly right, Lee. Keep them so scared they'll keep electing people supported by those five monsters."

"I don't like those assholes, Lyle," Lee said. "But I worked for them years ago—especially Paul. And while he's a ruthless bastard who's not above murder, he doesn't control anyone in the World Government."

"Not directly," Lyle said. "And he and his four friends are the ones who've caused all those plagues just to benefit themselves."

"How did they do that?" Lee asked him, looking directly into his eyes to see if he could detect a lie. "They weren't even alive when the plagues began and they were born after the last plague of 2907 hit."

Lyle picked up his coffee and finished it and sat the cup back in the saucer. He ignored Lee's question as he said, "When I read the Five File, I was shocked by what I had read and decided to gather more information if I could. I learned there were files in the headquarter building of the Department of Information that I could not access from my office in Hong Kong. So, I arranged my death, and a year later using a carefully prepared fake identity I applied for and got a job in the Department of Information's headquarters. Then I spent twenty years working my way into a position where I could start looking for those files."

"You found the special file," Evelyn said.

He looked at her and smiled and said, "You're a very good hacker, Evelyn."

"I'm pretty good," she said.

"Since you located me, I believe you."

"You want us to believe the five are behind the plagues that have killed billions?" Lee asked him.

"Whether you believe it or not, Lee, is your affair," he said. "But as God is my witness it is the truth. And the human race is overdue for another plague by I estimate sixty years."

"That's bullshit!" Lee said angrily. "Not a one of them is over sixty-seven years of age. I know I worked for Paul for twenty years. Anyway, they weren't alive when these plagues hit the world."

"Oh, yes they were," he said.

"Come on, Lyle," Evelyn said. "If they were, they'd be over five hundred years old. Nobody can live that long. I grant you the life expectancy of the average human today is in the mid-nineties and a lot people live to be a hundred and ten. But nobody lives beyond a hundred and fifty years."

"They can if they can clone themselves."

"That's against the law," Lee said. "Even trying to get equipment for cloning requires a federal permit and I doubt if the government has given out fifty of them in the last six hundred years. And when someone did get a permit, they had government inspectors up the ass every second they had the equipment whether they used it or not.

Even the companies that make such equipment are sharply monitored by the government. They have to have a license just to manufacture the stuff, and let's not talk about scientists with the skill to clone. Those people don't even have a private life with government inspectors all over them. That's why most students won't even study cloning science in college."

"Fourteen," Lyle said.

"Fourteen what," Evelyn asked him.

"That's the number of cloning licenses the government has given out in the last six hundred years," he said.

"You got that from the files you found in the Department of Information's main building?" Lee asked him.

"Yes, I did."

"You know who got those licenses?"

"Yes, I do."

"And one of those people works for the five," Evelyn said.

"Dr. Drake Petersen got a license five hundred and sixteen years ago April third of that year." Lee looked at Lyle and couldn't quite decide whether he was looking at a mad man, or a man who had a secret the five wanted him dead for having.

"You know, Lee, what might make what Lyle's saying true?" Evelyn said.

"The fact the five want him dead and us too for finding him," he replied.

"Would you like to see what I've got?" Lyle asked them.

It was a foolish question.

"Yeah, I would," Lee said. "Let's go to the attic computer room."

❧

CHAPTER 38

12:15 p.m. Attic computer room

Lee told the robots to clean up while he went with Lyle to his bedroom for Lyle's laptop case. Then he stopped in his bedroom where he got the case containing the glass crystal from his nightstand where he'd placed it before he went to bed.

"Careless of you to leave it on top of your nightstand," Lyle complained.

"No it wasn't because no one knows about this place but the three of us," Lee told him. "And I trust Evelyn."

"It's nice to know you don't trust me, Lee," he said as he followed Lee out of his bedroom and to the stairs that led up to the attic computer room. Evelyn walked behind him. "By the way you don't mind Lee, do you?"

"If I did you would have known some time ago," Lee told him as he led the way up the stairs.

When they entered the attic, Lyle looked around the computer room at the two desks with chairs and seven other chairs and said, "This is nice. It is far better than that corner in the living room of my cabin."

"All right," Lee said. "Prove to us what you said about the five is true."

"You've never answered my question as to how you know those trackers we saw were clones," Evelyn said.

Lyle put his laptop on one of the two the desks facing the wall, opened it, and sat down took the case containing the crystal from Lee. He opened it, took out the crystal and stuck it into the wide slot on the side of the laptop.

Lee and Evelyn got chairs and pulled them up on both sides of Lyle.

"That piece of glass contains the information that supports your statement that the five and their trackers are clones," Lee said, sitting next to him on his left side.

"That piece of glass as you call it, Lee, is a unique type of flash drive," he said. "It was first invented back in 2590, but it didn't catch on because it was considered to be too thick and fragile compared to the flash drives that were being developed. People thought that it would break if dropped, though it's quite hard."

"But it isn't unbreakable," Lee added.

"No drive is unbreakable, Lee," Evelyn said. She was sitting on Lyle's right side. "How does this one work, Mr. Morton?"

"Call me Lyle since we're all on the death list of the five now," he said. "Inside this piece of glass are twenty thousand facets. Each facet has four sides and a top and bottom and information can be put into it from any side of the crystal, including top and bottom, and removed the same way."

"If one has the code," Evelyn said.

"Yes, that's correct," Lyle said.

"Information bounces around inside it from facet to facet," Evelyn said.

"Yes," he said. "At almost the speed of light and in no regular pattern until a code is entered. Then the information arranges itself in a pattern on the screen of a computer or on a mirror by an invisible beam of light and can be read."

"How many bytes can each facet hold?" Lee asked.

"That's what's wonderful about this crystal, Lee," Lyle said. "Because the information bounces around inside the facets don't hold any bytes they're just reflexed light, electrons, moving around inside the crystal. Making it possible to put over ten trillion bytes of ten bits long inside it."

"How do you know when the crystal is filled?" Evelyn asked.

"It's less transparent."

"It did seem a little cloudy when I first saw it and before you put it in the laptop drive," Evelyn said.

"So how did you manage to steal this crystal from the Hong Kong's Industrial Museum's antiques computer display?" Lee asked him.

Lyle turned and looked at him. "How do you know I stole it?"

"It's hasn't been made in almost five hundred years, and it's not sold on the black market. Something like this would be found only in a museum or a private collection, and you didn't get it from a private collection."

"How do you know I didn't steal it from a private collection?"

"No thief smart enough to get pass the security devices a private collector would have would be so stupid as to hide in a cabin as obvious as the one you were hiding in, and not expect to be found in a few days," Lee answered him.

"He hacked into the museum's security system, blinded it to his presence, shut down the system once he got inside, and used a laser to cut through the display case to get it," Evelyn said, hoping to avoid an argument between the two she knew Lyle would lose considering Lee's rotten disposition toward Lyle. "Didn't you?"

"I decline to answer the question because it may incriminate me," Lyly said. He started typing on the laptop's keyboard.

"I figure you stole it a year before you faked your death and left Hong Kong and your family," Lee told him.

He stopped typing and looked at Lee. "How do you know I have a family?"

"Why fake your death and assume a false identity if you didn't?"

"Let's see what you've got," Evelyn told him. "Put your information on the TV screen on the wall in front of you."

Lyle looked up at what appeared to be a mirror and did as he was told.

They spent two hours reading how the five had learned of Dr. Petersen's cloning process through attending scientific conventions when they were in their eighties. How they had him kidnapped and taken to a hidden laboratory they had secretly set up using some of their vast fortunes and forced him to develop clones for them. To control him Dr. Petersen was forced to first clone guards that only the five could controlled. Once the five were cloned they spent ten years living in the secret lab learning Dr. Petersen's cloning process, and then created a clone of him that retained his scientific mind but not his resistance to them.

The cloning process requires no more than a few hundred cells of the individual to be cloned with its DNA intact. A small patch of skin is more than enough. A scan of the person's DNA determines if the DNA is still in excellent condition. A hundred cells are necessary to guarantee the proper development of an embryo. Once the embryo is developed it absorbs as many of the remaining cells that are not needed as nutrients as it grows. Those cells not used as nutrients die once the embryo has developed—eight weeks—to a point where it can use the nutrients provided it by lab personal in its birthing tube. After two months in its birthing tube, the embryo has developed into a human ten years of age. Another four months and the child of ten will have developed into an adult of twenty years of age because of the enriched nutrients provided it by the lab's personal. The sex of the adult is determined

by adding enriched protein, or by withholding it. Females require more enriched protein than males. But regardless of the sex all the adults are healthy and in excellent physical and mental condition.

Development of the embryo is the only risky part of the cloning process since the embryo must be grown in an environment that exceeds the environment found in the womb of a woman. Once that is accomplished, seventy-two hours is required for the development of a healthy embryo, the embryo can then be placed in a growth tube (birthing tube) but only in a sterile environment to avoid contamination, and the embryo develops into an adult.

Developing another adult requires no more than getting extra flesh from the original donner and freezing them in a nitrogen chamber eight inches in length and three inches in circumference.

"There's nothing here about how they managed to transfer their knowledge from themselves to their clones so they would remain themselves," Lee said.

"Computer, display the mental transfer process," Lyle said.

The mental transfer process is accomplished by accessing the human mind through the eyes. It does not matter if the person's whose knowledge is being transferred has excellent eyesight or is blind, or is

conscious. The Optic Nerve connects directly to the brain and is therefore the best way of transferring the individual's knowledge to the clone. All that is necessary is to activate the Optic Nerve and begin the transfer process. The process takes two hours and is accomplished by the removal of all electrical impulses from the brain of the living person to the brain of the clone while the clone is still in its birthing tube.

All knowledge is nothing but a series of electrical impulses which makes the process of transferring quite simple as long as there is no interference in the transfer process by outside electrical energy.

Evelyn and Lee said nothing after the information ended.

"No questions?" Lyle asked them.

"You found all this in a file in the Department of Information labeled 'special file'?" Evelyn asked him.

"Yes, but only after twenty years of looking," he said. "They had done an excellent job of hiding the information. You have no idea how many blank walls I encountered. I encountered millions of pieces of worthless information before I realized they would hide the information in the one place the Department didn't allow anyone to go without special permission."

"Information from the space probes, ships traveling through space, and the information coming from the Martian Science Station and those Pluto Space Stations." Lee said as he looked at the empty screen.

"Unbelievable," Evelyn said.

"It's bullshit!" Lee said in soft voice.

"No, it isn't, Lee!" Lyle yelled at him.

"Yes, it is, and that's why they put the information among the files on space. They knew no one would believe any of this," he said.

"Then why hire us to find him?" Evelyn asked Lee.

"Before he discovered the one thing that would prove it all to be true," he said. He turned to his left and looked at Lyle. "Well, Lyle, what's missing that makes this information believable?"

"I don't know where their lab is," he said in a soft voice as if he was afraid to speak.

Lee laughed and stood up and began pacing about the room. "We're all up shit creek. And those five assholes know it. They will never stop searching for us until they find and kill us. They will even use our families to force us to surrender to them, then kill them and us." He stopped pacing and looked at Lyle. "And your family isn't safe either, Lyle."

Lyle looked at him and said nothing.

"They already know your identity is a fake, Lyle. How long do you think it will take them to find out where you really came from? Maybe a few days or a week at the most then they'll go to Hong Kong and within a few days they'll know who the real Lyle Morton is and where to find your family." He had stopped pacing.

"No, they won't, Lee," he said. "I faked my death."

"Oh, don't be an ass, Lyle!" Lee told him in a loud voice as he started pacing again. "They'll check every death going back thirty years or more, no matter how the person died to verify there really was a death. And if a body can't be found that was buried or cremated, they'll know one of them is you, and they'll find your family."

"They'll have to check hundreds maybe thousands of death certificates to prove I'm one of those bodies that wasn't found," Lyle said. He didn't believe what he was saying.

"How many people die and completely disappear, Lyle?" Lee asked him.

"I don't know," he said. "But they'll never find me. I'm sure of that."

"Finger prints and DNA don't change, Lyle. Never! And your fingers prints are on file with the Department of Information in both the Hong Kong branch office and the headquarters building in Crown," Lee said as he stopped pacing and looked at him. "And your DNA is scattered all over your office back in the headquarters building along with your finger prints."

Lyle didn't say anything.

"All they have to do is to get the DNA and finger prints of those bodies that disappeared, and then compare them with what they get from your office back in the Department of Information," Lee told him. "I'll give them three days to do that with their cloned experts, if they're using clones."

"Jesus, we're screwed," Evelyn said with the sound of frustration in her voice.

Lee stared at the floor and thought for a few second before he started to speak in a softer voice, "They don't want the information to get out because it would be embarrassing to them and start a lot of questions they'd prefer not to answer. They would lose a lot of their political and economic clout even if the information isn't believed, and that stuff about the plagues is just so much bullshit without evidence."

"We have to find this secret lab," Evelyn said.

Lee turned and looked at her. "Have you anywhere in mind we should start looking?"

Evelyn didn't say anything.

Lee looked at Lyle and asked, "You?"

Lyle lowered his head and looked at the floor.

Lee walked to a chair and sat down. He stretched his legs out and thought aloud, "If I wanted to hide a secret lab, I wouldn't put in it any city, too much of chance it would be found by accident. So I'd put it in the one place there would little chance of anyone stumbling across it."

"The wilderness," Evelyn said.

Lee nodded.

"But far away from any city. And close enough for me to drive to if I had to,"

Lyle said.

Lee and Evelyn turned and looked at him.

❧

CHAPTER 39

June 7, 10 a.m. Thursday

No one would have seen it even if they had been looking for it. A person would have to know exactly where it was if they wanted to find it. It was located twenty-two miles north of the Snake River in the state of Nebraska in an area where cattle were once the main business back in the twenty-first century but had since become a wilderness with hundreds of thousands of square miles of nothing but waist high grass during the late spring and summer and tree covered hills. During the fall it was a brown landscape of dry grass that during the winter was covered by three or more feet of snow. Only wild animals ever came close to it, and even they weren't aware that two hundred feet below the ground was a sophisticated lab that had kept the five living for over five hundred years.

A satellite passed over the area twice a day in the morning at seven and at night at seven, but never recorded its presence because the satellite wasn't programmed to scan for it because the satellite didn't have its presence recorded in its scanning program. And the satellite hadn't existed at the time the five took over the underground complex and turned it into a lab to guarantee them everlasting life. The only thing the satellite was programmed to do was to scan for the movements of the animals that lived in the area or passed through it when the seasons and the weather conditions changed. The passage of the satellite was well known to the five as they were driven at high speeds by the clone trackers to the lab. That was why they had to reach the lab before seven p.m. when the satellite passed overhead one thousand miles up.

If their convoy of three vehicles were recorded by the satellite, the recording would have been immediately picked up by the computers in the Department of the Interior that recorded all movement in the wilderness areas of the world, and someone in the department would have asked why was a convoy of three vehicles travelling north in an area they shouldn't have been in. Not that it was serious violation of federal law, but pouching was still a problem in the world. There was always someone willing to pay a lot of money for a coat, hat, or jacket made from the skins of some exotic animals. Such an article of clothing made quite a fashion statement among some of those who were fashion conscious.

The underground complex consisted of six levels. Each level, except the first one, was four hundred and fifty yards in width and length and separated from the level above by fifty feet of reinforced concrete. Each level was well ventilated as well as heated during the fall and winters, and cooled during the springs and summers.

Level one, two hundred feet below the surface and only eighty yards in width and length, was where the computers and servers were and was divided into two parts. The first part contained the computer and server section with the best and latest computers and servers. The second part was a working area with a dozen desks with less sophisticated computers, and a garage. A simple wooden door connected the two seconds.

Level two was the most secure level in the complex because that was where the labs were located where cloning and other scientific work took place. The very best scientific equipment for the type of work being done was located on level two. All the scientific equipment was illegal since it was for cloning and experimenting with methods of improving the process. That level was divided into two sections as well.

The first section was where the work took place—the man in charge of the complex had his office and private lab in the first section, and a small one-bedroom apartment for himself. The second section was where the embryos and developing clones were kept in stable sterile environments where they could develop without contamination. Steel doors that could only be opened and closed by the computers on the first level separated the two sections, and only the five clones working in the lab and the doctor who controlled the underground complex were permitted pass those steel doors. Admission was by hand prints only—a bit primitive for such a sensitive level. The five also had the privilege of coming and going from level two whenever they visited the lab.

Levels three and four were where the living and recreational quarters were located.

Level three was divided into two sections. The first section consisted of five large apartments each with two bedrooms with baths, a living room, dining room, study with a computer, and lounge in each suite. In the second section there was a lounge, game room with a TV, a library, an and exercise room. Level three was for the five only.

Level four consisted of two game rooms with TV's, two libraries, a large exercise room where the clones were tested for physical fitness.

Level five was where the rest of the clones that worked in the underground complex lived. There were enough rooms in level five for seventy clones, but only the clones that worked in the underground complex lived there and never left it. They were cloned to have no interest in the outside world. The doctor in charge of the complex also had a three-bedroom apartment there which had a study for him. Part of level five was for a kitchen where food was prepared for the clones and the five when they stayed at the complex.

Level six was for storage of food, weapons, and vehicles. Food and weapons were stored in private rooms and only the director of the complex had access to the weapons room. The three clones that prepared meals, they were all cloned to be chefs, could go to the food storage any time when extra food was needed. Level six even had a wine cellar with over five hundred bottles of excellent wine and a hundred bottles of the best liquor money could buy.

Half of level six had maintenance shops for the two clones that worked in the garage to work on the vehicles when needed. Two large elevators, one on the north side of the complex and one on the south side, could take vehicles the size of tanks from the surface to level six. Twelve additional elevators, three on each corner of the complex with stairwells to the left of the three elevators, went from level three to level six. Only one group of three of the twelve elevators went up to level one from the garage. A door in level one led to stairs that connected to the surface. The elevators to level one stopped at level two and required a special code for the elevators to continue to level one. On the right of the groups of elevators was air ducts each six feet in circumference with ladders attached to the sides in case the elevators stopped working. There was even a platform at each level in the air ducts large enough for four people to stop and rest if the elevators weren't working and the stairwells were blocked.

A long tunnel led from an underground missile silo a mile away connected to level three. But the clones were never allowed into the tunnel.

Cameras with motion and heat detectors covered every part of the underground complex. Anyone in level one's computer room could see everything that was happening in the complex with the use of the cameras. There were six computers on each level that could be used to contact each other, and a diagram of the underground complex was on the four walls of every section on every level.

Power for the underground complex came from four huge generators located on level six in a separate room from the garage with a sign on the door that said 'Generator Room'. Disguised solar panels on the surface of the complex provided energy for the generators.

Water for the underground complex came from an underground stream, and was cleaned by filters in a pumping room. All waste, including water, from the complex was recycled and used as energy, or buried once a month and only at night after the satellite had passed overhead in two specially covered pits two hundred yards in width and length two hundred feet from the complex. The clones that worked in the garage were responsible for burying the waste.

Paul was sitting in the passenger seat next to the clone driving looking out the window. But enjoying the beautiful spring scenery was the last thing on his mind. He was thinking that some of his companions had outlived their usefulness.

Fred and Larry were fools as far as he was concerned and could be easily controlled. But Bruce, who was sleeping in the back stateroom, and Steve, who was in his own camper, were intelligent men. And intelligence was dangerous as far as Paul was concerned. Intelligence encouraged deep thinking and deep thinking invariably led to a person evaluating their purpose in life. Humane conduct and compassion for one's fellow humans always followed evaluating one's purpose in life.

Paul had no such thoughts about his purpose in life, which was to live as long as he could and as comfortably as he could with as much wealth and power as he wanted and could acquire. With all the pleasures and comforts that went with the acquisition of wealth and power. What it costs the human race was of no importance to him. They were just sheep anyway. What did it matter to him if a few billion died every one hundred and fifty or so years as long as he remained alive and comfortable?

He looked at the driver and asked, "How soon before we reach our destination?"

"At the speed we're traveling and over such rough terrain another two hours at the most, sir."

Paul looked at the electrical speedometer.

They were traveling at seventy miles an hour.

For the first time he noticed the bumpiness of the ride. He had been in such deep thought he hadn't noticed it before because the camper had a suspension system that absorbed most of the bumps, and his seat absorbed those bumps the suspension system didn't. He rose up and looked at the rearview mirror. The three vehicles were leaving a cloud of dust that was at least half a mile long. It didn't matter since there was no one out here to see the cloud of dust. Paul was wrong.

The government was fully aware that there were a few million people scattered over the globe who preferred to live in the wilderness away from the steel, glass, concrete, and brick of the cities and towns. The only time such people ever made contact with civilization was when they went to some small town for some of the necessities of life they couldn't produce themselves. Medicine and good quality soap were two of those necessities they couldn't produce themselves along with boots and shoes which were better than the moccasins they made from animal skins. And liquor, tobacco and cordite for their primitive weapons.

They preferred projectile firing weapons to the electric weapons. They were easier to maintain and lasted for centuries. Some of them used old muzzle loading black powder weapons from the late-eighteenth century and they were extremely valuable on the antique market. But the people who possessed them never sold them, because they worked just as well as they did when they were first made.

All of such people, no matter what continent they lived on—the south and north poles were uninhabited with automated scientific stations, who lived away from civilization had what could be considered modern devices of communication as well as modern conveniences—modern kitchens and bathrooms. That meant they had com-cells, TVs which accessed programs using the satellites, and laptop computers which were only a hundred years behind those people in the cities and larger towns used. They were also on the dole. They had government issued credit cards which they used when they went to town for supplies they couldn't produce themselves. No one in the government gave a thought to them using government issued credit cards since as a group they seldom spent more than a billion dollars. Pennies considering the government collected nearly twenty trillion in taxes world-wide.

The woman watched the cloud of dust rising behind the vehicles with her binoculars and wondered where they could be going at such a speed. She was dressed in buckskin cloth and wore knee high leather boots and wore a sweat stained formerly tan wide brim ten-gallon leather hat with a wide crease in the back of it to allow rain to run backwards off her hat.

"What are you looking at, Jessie?" her female companion asked as she walked her horse up to Jessie's horse and stopped.

The shade of the trees hid them from view.

"Those cars," she said. "They're going somewhere in a real big hurry."

"Let me see," Cassie said as she leaned to her left and reached for Jessie's binoculars.

Jessie let her have them.

Cassie stared for a few seconds then returned the binoculars as she said, "City people are always in a big hurry to go nowhere."

"Yeah," Jessie said as she put the binoculars in the leather pouch hanging from her neck. "Let's get going. I'm anxious to get home to a hot meal and a hot bath."

"And a good night in bed with your old man, too," Cassie said with a smile. She was ten years older than Jessie and just as anxious to get to their homes in the hills forty miles north of where they were.

They turned their horses around, rode down the gentle incline of the hill to where seven large draft pack horses were waiting. They had gone into the town of Bricker two hundred miles south of where they lived three weeks ago for supplies for the village of eighty-nine people that was their hometown. The horses were carrying a combined weight of two and a half tons of supplies. Enough to keep the people in their village supplied with the necessities of life they couldn't produce themselves until September. In September a dozen people from their village would make the long ride to Bricker with twenty or more of the strong draft horses and four large wooden wagons to stock up for the winter and to buy Christmas presents for everyone in the village. Life in their village, which had no name, was quiet and simple and it could remain that way if three people they didn't know existed, succeeded. If the three failed the eighty-nine people of Cassie's and Jessie's village wouldn't know what hit them.

Cassie and Jessie rode silently for half an hour through a gorge that was a short cut to their village.

"Where could those vehicles been heading?" Cassie asked Jessie. "There's nothing where they were going for over five hundred miles."

"Maybe to Canada," Jessie said. "But there aren't any roads in the part of Canada north of us that connects to a city."

Cassie nodded and said nothing.

CHAPTER 40

12 p.m.

"Okay," Lee said. "But where in the wilderness?"

"Someplace I could drive to quickly," Lyle said as he looked at Lee.

"There are probably hundreds of such places," Lee said.

"Some place not easily recognized," Lyle said.

"Computer, put a map of the wilderness area around Crown on the screen," Lee yelled out loud as he turned to face the screen.

A large map of Crown and the wilderness area around it appeared on the large screen. Crown City appeared as a small red dot in the middle of the map.

"There must be two million square miles of wilderness around Crown you can drive to within eight hours," he said to Lyle.

Evelyn looked at the map and said, "This secret lab wouldn't be next to any major expressways or highways."

"Or local highways," Lyle said.

"What do you think, Lee?" Evelyn asked him.

Lee standing behind them said, "Do I sound like I'm disagreeing with you two?"

Lyle shook his head. Lee annoyed him at times.

Lee looked up at the screen and said, "It wouldn't be above ground, either. That would make it too easy to spot from a plane or a satellite."

"So using a passing satellite isn't going to help us," Evelyn said.

"If they're driving across country to this lab, they'd leave a dust trail," he said.

"Computer, when does the next satellite pass overhead?" Lyle asked.

'The next satellite passes overhead at seven p.m.'

"That's six hours from now. They'd be where they're going by then," Lee said. "And there wouldn't be any dust trail for us to spot if we accessed the passing satellite."

"But they've leave tracks we could see from a passing satellite," Lyle said.

"Not necessarily," Lee disagreed. "Those wilderness areas have large numbers of animals that constantly move about wiping out any tracks the five might leave."

"Yes," Evelyn said. She had a worried expression on her face.

"You've thought of something, Evelyn," Lyle said as he looked at her face.

"I've thought they know we've got to find that lab before we release the information Lyle stole or its worthless trash," she said. "That means even if we find this secret lab they're going to, they will be waiting in it for us to come to it. And they'll have more people and fire power than we'll have."

"But we have the ability to make specific judgments," Lyle said.

"Which isn't going to be worth a damn in a fire fight with dozens of trained cloned killers," Lee added.

"So we're screwed," Lyle said. "I should have just left everything alone twenty-two years ago."

"Yeah, the world needs another plague wiping out billions of people," Lee said sarcastically.

"Maybe they're in the woods about us looking for us," Evelyn said.

"I don't think they are, Evelyn," he said. "But you've got a good point."

"How are we going to know if they're still in the woods looking for us?" Lyle asked him.

"They've probably found the Honda we abandoned, Lee," she said. "And they know we were on foot, because by now they haven't found any vehicles."

"And that encounter I had with two of their killers tells them we're still close to the city," Lee said. "And even if they couldn't track me they know we're somewhere north of where I killed those two killers of theirs."

"You killed two of their killers by yourself?" Lyle asked him.

"Computer has there been any humans within a mile of this place?" Lee asked, ignoring Lyle's question.

'No human presence has been detected,' appeared on the screen.

"That means they're not looking for us anymore, Lee," Evelyn said.

Lee nodded and said nothing.

"And if they're not looking for us, Lee, that means they've gone to their secret lab and are waiting for us to arrive," Evelyn said.

"So what do we do since we don't know where this secret lab is?" Lyle asked.

"Simple," Lee said without looking at him. "We begin to eliminate possibilities."

"What does that mean?" Evelyn said.

"Get on your computer and find out if there have been any unground places built in the last five hundred years." He turned to Lyle and asked, "The Department of Information would have such information, wouldn't it, Lyle?"

"Sure, in the historical records," he said. "Go to historical unground construction, Evelyn. If such a lab was built in the last five hundred years, it would be there."

"Those five have the sort of money where they could have built such a place and no one would know about it," Lee said. "While you search for that, Evelyn, Lyle and I are going to find out if those five ever owned or had an interest in a construction company."

"How did you acquire this place?" Lyle asked Lee as he looked around at the two computers on the two desks and the single server.

"Why do you just assume it's his place," Evelyn told him as she got busy.

"Because of his bossy manner," Lyle said not caring whether Lee liked what he said or not. "And this place doesn't have much of feminine touch to it."

Lee ignored his statement.

"How old is the equipment in this room?" Lyly asked.

"Not that old," Lee told him.

"This equipment looks to be at least seventy or eighty years old," he said.

"Only about fifty," Lee said.

"The best type of equipment to use," Evelyn said. "It can go anywhere modern computers can go and is easily programmed to prevent hacking."

"I can believe that," Lyle said. "No hacker worth the salt in a drop of his blood would think of trying to hack into any of these antique computers and server."

"Let's get busy," Lee said as he walked to one of the two desks and pulled out a chair and sat down. "Come on, Lyle. Let's see how good you really are. Our families' lives and ours are dependent on your skills."

Two hours later Lyle said, "I'm tired and I'm hungry."

"Nothing," Evelyn said. "The world isn't into hiding labs unground anymore."

"The five don't own and have never owned any construction companies," Lee said. "But that doesn't mean they've never had the power to have a construction company build something unground for them."

"Where do you suggest we look, Lee?" Lyle said.

"The lab could be in some old abandoned mine closed up centuries before the world government existed," he said.

"I've accounted for every abandoned mine on this continent, Lee," Evelyn said.

"Okay, Lyle, let's see what we can find about this Drake Petersen guy," he said.

"The only thing you're going to find on Drake Petersen, if there is anything is that he was a scientist," Lyle said. "There will be nothing about him cloning because cloning was illegal when he lived. What I learned about him I learned from the files of the five I stole."

"It won't hurt to try," Lee said as he started typing on the keyboard.

Another three hours and they had nothing on Drake Petersen except that he was a scientist who died over five hundred years ago.

"We're wasting time," Lyle said. "And I'm hungry."

"I'd like a cup of tea," Evelyn said.

"Okay, let's break for lunch," Lee said in a frustrated voice. He felt like they were up a blind alley and couldn't turn around to get out of it.

"It's dinner time," Evelyn said.

"I'll help with lunch or dinner," Lyle said.

Twenty minutes later they were in the kitchen sitting around the table looking at the crumbs that remained of their dinner of sandwiches and tea and coffee. They each had a defeated look on their faces.

Lyle stood up and walked to the coffeemaker and asked, "Does anyone want any more coffee?"

"I'm going to make some punch," Lee said, standing up. "I'm sick of coffee."

Lyle filled his cup from the coffee pot and said, "I wish I had brought my tea kettle with me. It's a real antique. It was made back in 1993 in America and it still works. They made some really fine things back then for household use." He walked back to the table and sat down. "That's amazing too considering how much money they spent on atomic bombs, which they couldn't use for fear of wiping out civilization."

Lee had gotten a container of punch crystals out of the cabinet and walked to another cabinet for a glass pitcher. He filled it with cold water from the faucet and used the plastic scooper from the container of punch to pour two large scoops of dry punch powder into the pitcher then he used a wooden spoon to stir the water and punch. He wasn't paying much attention to Lyle till he heard him mention atomic bombs. He stared thinking as he made the punch and poured himself a glass full. He put the remainder of the punch in the refrigerator and walked back to the table and sat down and asked them. "Have either of you ever heard of MAD?"

"Of course, we've heard of mad," Lyle said. "It means someone is insane."

"No," Lee said. "I mean Mutually Assured Destruction."

CHAPTER 41

12:45 p.m.

The trip over the rough terrain had taken ten minutes longer than Paul's driver had said it would, but now that he was in his expensively furnished spacious two-bedroom three-bathroom apartment in the large underground complex, he didn't give it a second thought. Because he was too busy thinking about how much he hated being in the underground complex. Because it felt like he was buried alive something he feared more than death. Having been alive since 2559 didn't bother him in the least bit, but having to pay a price for living so long while killing so many others made him fear death more than anything. He couldn't shake the felling that he, like the others, had broken a sacred law of God and would pay a terrible price for breaking it once they died. An act he was determined to avoid for as long as he could. Forever if possible.

Paul didn't know if he had a soul and didn't care if he did or didn't. But there was always the nagging thought of what if he did have a soul? What if there was a life after death in a paradise beyond the universe? What if there was a God who judged the souls of people after they died by what they did while they were alive? What would happen to his soul, if he had one, if he should die? Would he suffer punishment for an eternity for his horrible crimes? And what exactly would that punishment be? He dismissed such foolish thoughts from his mind. Death was not for him. He was eternal because Dr. Drake Petersen had been smarter than all the scientists involved with cloning in 2559 and had become smarter—and more important. He had become completely obedient to the demands of Paul and his four companions, and had been so since they learned the secret of cloning ten years after they were cloned, and had cloned Petersen.

They had left his intelligence intact, because they needed that and wanted it to increase but had removed all of his emotional resistance to their combined wills. That way he went on cloning them when they demanded it, and they cloned him when he became old, a hundred years, and showed signs of slowing down. All in all, Paul and his four companions had created a perfect situation of eternal life for themselves.

Paul's com-cell buzzed. He took it out of his pocket and looked at the name of the caller. It was Larry he answered it.

"We've decided to check on Dr. Petersen to make sure he's still functioning as we want him," Larry said. "Are you going to join us in his conference room next to his lab?"

That was a foolish question. If there was one thing Paul was determined never to do, it was to allow his four companions to become more influential than he. To do that would put them in a position where they could dominate him. Maybe even do away with him. It was easier to conceal the cloning of four men who could live forever than five.

"I'll be there in a few minutes," he said and ended the call and immediately left his apartment.

A waiting electric cart with seats for four people was waiting outside the door of his apartment. There was no clone driver. There was no need for one. The cart was automated and programmed to take him, or anyone, anywhere in the underground complex. All he had to do was tell the cart where he wanted to go and the cart would take him there in a few minutes at a hundred miles an hour.

"Petersen's lab conference room," he said after he got into the cart.

The cart remained motionless until he buckled the seat belt around his waist and chest. Then it moved away picking up speed as it quietly took him to Petersen's conference room.

Paul noticed as he rode the brightly lit concrete corridor that it was free of dust and the air had a smell of freshness to it. The camouflaged air intact and exhaust vents on the surface that operated without pumping sounds that came from the generators that provided them with electrical energy did a perfect job of venting any musty smell from the underground complex into the outside. The fresh air only reminded him that he was two hundred feet below ground with millions of tons of dirt, rock, and reinforced concrete above his head. Paul had been thinking for two years of establishing a lab above ground in the Canadian wilderness above the Arctic Circle and closing down this underground lab. He hadn't spoken to the other four about it, because he knew they'd protest. He decided as he rode that once this problem they were facing was solved, he'd kill or reprogram the others to submit to all his demands.

Two minutes later the cart stopped in front of a glass door behind four other carts.

He got out and walked to the glass door that opened automatically and entered a vestibule that led a tan wooded door and entered the room beyond which looked like a small version of a private library with books and papers stacked on tables and shelves covering the four walls, except for where the door was, to the twelve feet ceiling.

The four others were sitting around a small conference table with a pale, expressionless man wearing a white lab coat over his tan jacket with neatly cut and combed brown hair sitting at the end of the table. There wasn't a crease on his blank face or a sparkle in his colorless almost lifeless gray eyes to indicate he'd ever had an emotional feeling in his life. If he had such feeling centuries ago he hadn't had any since he'd been cloned. His smooth, pale hands with neatly trimmed nails rested on the arms of the chair he was sitting in and he didn't move a muscle except for the blinking of his eye lids.

"Why am I here?" Paul asked as he walked to empty chair between Fred and Larry and sat down. He noticed Steve was occupying the chair at the other end of the table facing the pale man.

"Larry told you," Bruce said without looking at Paul. He was looking at the screen in the thin folder on the table in front of him.

The others had open folders in front of them on the table with the same information on their screens as was on the screen of the folder in front of Paul.

"Oh, yes," Paul said as he looked down at the folder on the table in front of him and opened it. The screen inside immediately came on with a detailed health chart on it.

The name at the top of the chart was Dr. Drake Petersen. He read the chart and looked up and said, "Everything appears to be okay with Dr. Petersen."

"Is that correct, Dr. Petersen?" Steve asked the pale man.

"I am in excellent health," the pale man replied. His voice was as emotionless as his face.

They all noted the blood pressure numbers that appeared on the screens and the heart rate. It wasn't the numerical blood pressure or heart rate figures that appeared on the screens that interested them since they didn't know normal blood pressure or heart rates from abnormal ones. It was the word 'normal' that appeared next to the blood pressure and heart rate numbers that interested them.

Paul closed his folder to indicate he wasn't interested in what was showing on the screen. "How do you feel about your life here, Dr. Petersen?"

"My life here is perfect, Paul," Petersen said.

"How is your work proceeding?" Steve asked him. He was like Paul he didn't care about what was on the screens.

"My work is going quite well. I am two months ahead of schedule."

"How are our replacements?" Steve asked him.

"They are in their tubes awaiting activation whenever they are needed. Their pasts have been placed in their brains and they have responded exactly as I expected. All that is left to do is to download your personal experiences into their brains so that each of you can become them. Once that has been achieved each of you will become them ready to resume your lives as completely new individuals and as the heirs of your various fortunes."

"What about your clone?" Fred asked him.

Paul shot Fred a sharp look of disapproval. He disliked the word clone and Fred knew that.

"My replacement is ready," Petersen replied.

"Maybe we should check out the lab," Larry suggested.

"We don't need to do that," Bruce said. "Everything there is fine. If there was something wrong Dr. Petersen would have notified us immediately. What we need to do is prepare for who is coming."

Petersen's face, eyes, and body didn't move an inch when he heard the words 'who is coming'. But his brain immediately registered the words and there was a slight jump in his blood pressure which registered on the screens of folders, and then returned to normal. None of the five, whose folders were still open, noticed the sudden change and return because none of them were watching the screens in the folders in front of them.

"It doesn't hurt to make sure the lab is working properly," Steve said to Bruce.

"Is the lab working properly, Dr. Petersen?" Bruce asked the doctor.

"Yes, it is," Petersen replied.

"Happy, Steve?" he said.

Steve closed his folder and stood up. "How many hours do you think we've got before they arrive?" he asked.

"Who—," Bruce started to say.

"We should be alone when we discuss this?" Paul said. He had never felt that Petersen was as obedient as the others thought. The man was a genius when it came to cloning living things, and one could never be sure of what geniuses were thinking even a cloned one like Petersen.

"Is the lounge acceptable?" Steve asked him.

"Better than Dr. Petersen's lab or this conference room," he said as he stood up.

Ten minutes later they were sitting in the main lounge of the underground complex drinking their favorite drinks and looking as relaxed as worried men could look.

"So?" Steve said to Paul.

Paul turned his head from the nineteenth century French Impressionist painting hanging on a wall that contained a dozen paintings each of a different style by different painters from three different centuries and looked at Steve. "Huh?" he responded.

"We gathered here at your request to discuss how much time we've got before Lyle Morton, Lee, and Evelyn show up," Steve reminded him.

"I was just wondering how we acquired these paintings," he answered as he turned and looked at Steve.

"We got them two hundred years ago when we purchased them at an auction in Rome," Larry told him.

"Ah, yes," Paul said, turning to look at the paintings. "I remember Bruce and Fred bid against each other for three of them. Art critics complained their bidding pushed the prices way above their real value."

"That's not the issue here, Paul," Steve said.

"No it isn't," he agreed, turning to face the four men. "But shouldn't these paintings be arranged chronologically and according to the styles they represent? Having eighteenth century paintings hanging next to twenty-first century paintings seems a bit odd." He looked at Steve and asked, "Don't you agree?"

"We gathered here to determine how much time we have before those three arrive," Steve told him.

"I don't see that it matters," Fred said. "Whenever they come we'll be prepared for them."

"It does matter," Bruce said. "While we may not be in the social registry, we will be missed by those who are, and they may complain to the police about our absence."

"We still have plenty of time left," Paul said as he turned his attention back to the paintings. "We told our wives we'd be gone for ten days, so we won't be missed for another five days. And Lee and Evelyn aren't stupid enough to take more than two days to locate this place." He stood up and walked to the wall length bar to refresh his drink. "By now they know this lab is hidden underground. It won't take them very long to find out where we've hidden the lab."

$$\sim$$

CHAPTER 42

5:30 p.m.

"What on earth are you talking about?" Lyle asked Lee.

"The atomic bomb was developed back in the mid-twentieth century by the United States during a war," Lee answered. "Within a short period of time, after the war had ended, twenty years at the most as I recall from the history I've read six or seven other nations had the bomb as they called it back then."

Evelyn and Lyle didn't say anything.

"There were two competing nations, or powers as they were called, then the capitalists and the communists," he said.

"I remember that from my high school history classes," Lyle said. "The communists were in Russia and Eastern Europe and China. The capitalist were here in America and Western Europe. And they built bombers, big planes to carry these bombs, and ships, too." He turned to Evelyn and said, "You remember, don't you?"

"The only history I liked was the history of computers," she said. "Fashion also interested me, but since I had no talent for it I lost interest. I just read fashion magazines when I want to buy the latest fashions."

"Both sides knew no one could win an atomic war, so they both developed defense systems to guarantee that if the other side started an atomic war they wouldn't win," Lee continued.

"They called it nuclear war, Lee," Evelyn said. "I remember that."

"Okay, nuclear war," Lee said.

"And they were mad for doing that?" Lyle asked him.

"No. MAD. Mutually Assured Destruction was the name of the American defense system to prevent the communists from starting a war. It guaranteed that if the other side started a war with their nuclear bombs they would be wiped out, too."

"I get it," Lyle said. "It was a defense system to guarantee that the other side wouldn't win. Therefore the system was called, Mutually Assured Destruction."

"And this defensive system consisted of three parts," Lee said. "They called it triangle. No, no, eh Triad. Yes. That's what it was called a triad."

"So what did it consist of?" Evelyn asked.

"Three methods of launching atomic bombs," he said. "Or nuclear weapons as they sometimes called them."

"Okay, Lee," Evelyn said. "So what did it consist of and why should we be concerned with some defense system developed by people in the twentieth century?"

"It consisted of three parts," he said. "The first two parts were bombers to fly over the enemy and drop atomic bombs on the communists, and submarines to launch them from underwater in missiles."

"Bombers were what they called their big planes," Evelyn said as if she was asking a question.

"Yes, bombers," Lee said.

"And the submarines were like the scientific submarines that explore the depths of the oceans?" Lyle asked him.

"No, these were submarines built for war, and they could shoot missiles out of them while they were under water. Missiles that had those nuclear bombs on them," he said. "And the third part consisted of missiles, thus the word triad."

"So what," Evelyn said. She didn't understand the importance of what they were talking about.

"The missiles were hidden in silos," he said.

"Of course," Lyle exclaimed, slapping his left hand down on the table. "Grain silos would be a perfect place to hide a lab. Who would think of looking for a secret lab under grain silos? Even though that is a dangerous place to put a lab. Silos have a lot of grain dust in them and that dust can be explosive."

"No, Lyle," Lee said. "Not grain silos. Missile silos. Built underground to hide not only the missiles but the people who would launch those missiles."

"In areas no one would think to look for them," Evelyn said, catching on to what Lee was talking about.

"So, let's go and see what the historical archives in the Department of Information would have on these missile silos," Lyly said, standing up.

Five minutes later after they got Lyle's laptop, they were back in the attic computer room accessing Department of Information servers for information on missiles silos.

"There were a hundred of those silos built by the American Defense Department in the west," Evelyn said as she read the information from her computer.

"Let's see," Lyle said as he typed into Evelyn's screen. The information on her computer screen appeared on his. "The darn things were scattered all over the western plains."

Lee ignored them as he worked on Lyle's laptop and read what appeared on the screen.

"We could search for weeks trying to find which one of these silos has their lab," Lyle said.

"No we won't need that much time," Lee told him.

"How do you know?" Evelyn asked.

"The people who built these silos wouldn't have been stupid enough to put the control centers next to the silos. They would have located the control centers miles away in case the other side found where the missiles were hidden and launched an atomic bomb to destroy them. And they did."

"Where," Lyle asked him.

"One place was in the Rocky Mountains," he said. "Another place was under the city of Washington."

"In the State of Washington?" Lyle asked him as he looked at the screen of the computer he was using.

"In the state capital of the United States," he said. "But we don't have to worry about them."

"Because both are now historical tourist centers," Evelyn said, reading what was on Lee's screen from her own.

"The third place was in the state of Nebraska four hundred and fifty miles northeast of Crown City," Lee said. He was looking at a diagram of the center.

"My God," Lyle said softly as he looked over at his laptop and the diagram on it. "The place is huge."

"Two hundred feet below the surface of the ground in an area surrounded by hills," Lee said. "And it's big enough to provide housing for two thousand people."

"And according to this it was abandoned and locked up in 2271," Lyle said as he read from laptop screen.

"Evelyn, bring up the paths of all the satellites passing over North America," Lee told her. "And get coordinates on that place."

She did so and concentrated her interest on the one that passed over America four hundred and fifty miles north of Crown. "It's due to make another pass at seven o'clock this evening, Lee. That's a little less than an hour and a half from now."

"Get as detail a picture as you can of that area," he told her.

"They might be able to detect her doing that," Lyle warned.

"They probably will," Evelyn said.

"If I were them, and thank God I'm, not," Lee said. "I would have refurbished that place to meet all of their needs. That means there should be air vents on top of it somewhere to bring in fresh air and vent stale air."

"If they detect us using that satellite it means they're using it, too," Evelyn warned them.

Lee nodded his agreement as he said, "Those five wouldn't be so stupid as to have a lab in that underground missile control center and not want to know what's around it. So every time that satellite passes over their computer people can see what it sees."

"If we go there, they'll be able to see us using the same satellite if we get close to that place," Lyle told them.

"How often does the satellite pass over, Evelyn?" Lee asked her.

"Twice every twenty-four hours. At seven in the morning and seven in the evening," she answered.

"So we hide when it passes over," he said.

"Okay, that sounds good," Lyle said. "Now how do we get into this underground laboratory?"

"That's a good question," Lee said as he leaned back in his chair and thought.

"Not necessary," Evelyn said. "All we have to do is prove the lab exists."

"That's not enough," Lee said. "We've got to prove there's cloning going on in that lab and the five are behind it."

"That lab, Lee, will have the best security system in the world and it will be the sort of security system that can detect someone trying to hack into it. And that's the best fire wall any security system can have."

"Then we'll have to figure out a way of getting into the system and shutting it down without it knowing we're doing it," he told her.

She looked at Lee like he was crazy and said, "Oh, sure, why didn't I think of that."

"Lee," Lyle said. "The security system that lab has will be designed to detect anything out of the usual. It will have its own source of power and its only connection with the outside world will be that satellite passing overhead."

"Then we'll have to use the satellite to get into it," he said.

"Lee, the damn thing's been passing over the United States for hundreds of years because it's a simple weather satellite, and easily accessed by just about anyone interested in the weather over America and the rest of the world it passes over. The five will have accessed it, and it will detect and alert them in that place if anything out of the ordinary is received or sent out."

"Look, you two, I don't give a fuck! We have to get in and expose the place to the world and what's been going on in there. Or our families will suffer a terrible fate. So stop telling me how great the fucking security system is. Let's just figure out a way to get into the underground complex and expose it."

Evelyn and Lyle didn't say a word because they knew he was right.

❧

CHAPTER 43

7:00 p.m. Thursday

Troy had slept for ten hours and was fully alert. His attention was on the screen on the wall in front of him and he noticed immediately the blip that indicated someone had accessed the satellite passing over the lab. It took him only a second to indicate the blip had come from a spot fifty miles west of Crown City in the wilderness. He immediately notified Larry.

The nice thing about female clones is they were not only very beautiful and sexy, but they never refused an act of sex. They never engaged in sex with the males clones because the male clones were programmed to have no sexual desire, the females weren't. But their sexual programming was designed so that they never had a desire for sex unless it was suggested by someone. Then they were excellent sexual partners until the person they were screwing was satisfied, then their sexual desires shut down and they never talked about the act even among themselves.

None of the clones were programmed to engage in conversation. Though there was nothing that prevented them from talking and they could speak intelligently. But since they lacked specific judgment detailed conservation on any subject was beyond their ability.

The beautiful red headed clone was dressing when the phone next to Larry's bed rang. He rolled over and picked it up. "Yes?" he asked.

"The satellite that passes overhead was accessed by someone in a wilderness area fifty miles west of Crown City, sir," Troy told him.

"Tell the others to meet me in your office," he said and hung up.

Ten minutes later he walked into the main computer room. Paul was sitting in chair behind Troy looking at the large wall TV screen looking as arrogant as he usually felt. Steve was sitting next to him on his left side with an expression of interest on his face. Bruce sat to the left of Steve his face was a blank. Fred was sitting to the left of him with a worried look on his face. Larry took the chair next to Fred.

"Show me the area where the message was sent from," he said to Troy.

"It's already on the screen," Fred told him.

Larry looked at the screen and saw only wilderness. "Can you give us a more detailed view of the area the message was sent from, Troy?"

Troy touched a key on the keyboard and a white circle appeared on the wall monitor.

"That covers a wide area," Larry said.

"Thirty square miles," Paul said.

"That's small enough for our trackers to swept it from one end to the other," Fred said, looking at the hilly green area. "We should immediately send them there and swept the area. In wouldn't take more than a day to find where they are hiding."

"No," Steve said.

"Why no," Fred asked, looking angrily at him. "It's time we brought this nonsense to an end. The longer we wait the more problems will appear. Better to strike now and end this treasonous conduct of theirs before the authorities find out."

"They will find out if we attack," Bruce said.

"The government, even the state governments don't waste time and money looking at the wilderness areas unless someone is lost in them," Fred said. He was tired of this waiting.

"Locating their hideout would be easy in such a small area," Bruce began to explain. "But getting into and killing those three would result in a vicious fight with a lot of weapons used."

"So what, no one would hear it?" Fred said. "That far from the city guarantees us privacy."

"You're correct, Bruce," Paul said. "But the place is probably heavily fortified with a security system that would notify them of the presence of our people long before they could attack, and Lee and Evelyn would undoubtedly call for help before our people got to them. Even if our trackers managed to get inside this hideout and killed them before help came we wouldn't have time to clean up the scene. All we'd need is the state

of Colorado and the American government wondering why a battle took place in that forest. And it would only be a few hours before the news of the battle got out and that would arouse the interest of the World Government."

"Who gives a damn," Fred yelled angrily. "We'd be long gone before any police or security forces showed up."

"Fred, how would we stop them from revealing what they got on us if they were still alive and fighting when the police arrived?" Bruce asked him.

"Patience is a virtue, Fred," Larry told him. Secretly he agreed with Fred, but he also saw the dangers involved with a fight in the wilderness that close to the city.

"To tell with clichés, Larry," he spat back. "We need to end this mess now. The longer we wait the more precarious our positions become. We have the influence to control the state, national, or world governments."

"But we'd have trouble with the press, Fred," Paul told him. "While we do have a lot of influence with the press we wouldn't be able to control individual reporters from small news networks looking for a great story. And please, Fred, don't suggest killing one of them. A dead reporter would only make the press more determined. Our best strategy is to wait for them to come to us."

"Absolutely," Steve said.

Fred jumped to his feet and started walking toward the door saying in a loud voice, "Well, call me when they come. And if they don't arrive within three days, I'm going home and I don't give a damn what the rest of you think." He kicked the door open and left.

None of the others said a word.

A few minutes passed before Steve stood up and said, "I'm having dinner alone in my apartment, and I don't want to be disturbed until our guests arrive."

The others drifted out one by one until Troy was left alone.

Over five hundred years ago curiosity had driven Drake Peterson in his quest to find a quick way to clone a human. In the process he had learned how to clone different types of bacteria. He could clone harmless bacteria that could benefit the human race and bacteria that could kill billions of people with a ruthlessness known only to the human race. He had even taught the five all that he knew about cloning, and that had been foolish on his part, because they had cloned him to do their bidding, and then killed the real Drake Petersen. But they had not removed his curiosity because they didn't know it was a natural part of his intellect. And that was a mistake on their part.

Petersen had no interest in the outside world, but he did have an interest in the laboratory. It was his world and he wanted to know he controlled it even when the five were present. Which is why he'd programmed the computers in the laboratory, there were exactly a hundred of them, monitoring everything that went on in the underground complex. Even the TV screens were under his control, and he had turned them into two way screens that allowed him to see and hear everything that occurred in the complex no matter where he happened to be.

Petersen was in his bedroom reading a novel on his I-book. He loved reading novels. They were a release for him from his work, because they allowed him to venture into fictitious and mythical worlds beyond the laboratory complex. It had never dawned upon him that novels represented an interest on his part in the outside world.

His computer and com-cell were programmed to let him know what was going on in the underground complex at any time of the day or night. He knew Troy was using a computer at level one to check on the satellite that passed overhead twice a day, but he paid no attention to what Troy was doing until the five gathered in the office Troy was using. Then he stopped reading his novel and listened to what the five talked about and watched every move they made over the com-cell he carried.

He wondered who were these people they were expecting to arrive to the complex? He wondered if they would bring information that would help him in his work. He doubted they would, but maybe they would bring him some new novels. He had only fifty-five novels left he hadn't read. Downloading them from the Internet was such a bother though he never did any of the downloading himself. He had programmed the computer and server in his private apartment to download the types of novels he liked to read using an I-book.

The argument between the five had aroused his curiosity. Why did Fred want to kill some people in the forest around Crown City to stop some nonsense? And who were these people they were waiting for and why? Maybe the guests the five expected would be able to satisfy his curiosity by answering his questions?

❧

CHAPTER 44

Midnight

"I got it! I got it!" Evelyn screamed as she ran out of her bedroom naked into the hallway.

Her screams woke Lee and frightened him and he jumped out of bed and grabbed the electric semiautomatic on the nightstand next to his bed. He rushed into the hallway in his shorts expecting to see trackers from the five coming out of the elevator with electric rifles in their hands and a look of murder on their faces. He was surprised to see Evelyn standing in the hallway screaming, "I got it!"

Lyle came out his bedroom dressed in a long peppermint striped nightshirt looking like some over grown child. He stopped when he saw Evelyn and stared at her.

"Got what?" Lee yelled at her.

"I know how we can get into that underground lab," she exclaimed.

"How" Lyle asked, looking her over with approving eyes.

"Those com-cells you took from the bodies of the two trackers you killed a few days ago," she said.

Lyle turned and looked at Lee who was in white boxer shorts. "You killed some trackers?"

"I told you about that hours ago," he said to Lyle.

"Yes, I remember you did," he said. "But not how you killed them?"

Lee ignored him. "What are you talking about, Evelyn?"

"Those two com-cells you took from those trackers you killed when you went to get supplies," she said. "They probably contain a directory."

"So?"

"They contain numbers that allowed them to contact the five and that lab," she said.

"They do?" Lyle said. "Who are these clones you killed Lee."

"That's not important now," Lee told him. "Explain yourself."

"I woke up an hour ago, and went downstairs to the living room to get those com-cells from that jacket you wore when you went to get supplies. You left them in your jacket pocket. Then I came back to my bedroom and started going over them. They have a short directory listing the names of the five and the lab's phone number."

Lee looked at her face as he said, "You can use the lab's phone number to get into the lab's security system."

"But they don't tell me where the lab is," she said. "But if we get close to it I can use the phone number to get into the security system and maybe shut it down."

"Maybe is a long shot," Lyle said. He ignored her nudity.

"It sure is," Lee agreed with him. "But a long shot is better than no shot at all."

"So what do we do?" Lyle asked.

"Today is Friday. We go back to bed and make preparations tomorrow to go to Nebraska and look for that lab. We leave tomorrow night after ten. Let's hope it's raining."

"Why?" Lyle asked.

"Rain creates a certain amount of static electricity," Evelyn told him. "It'll make it a little bit harder to see us." She looked at her breasts and realized she was naked. "Oh, excuse me." She turned and ran back to her bedroom.

"Go back to bed, Lyle," he said as he turned toward his bedroom door. "We've got a busy day ahead of us."

CHAPTER 45

June 8, 9:50 p.m. Friday

They spent the day preparing for what they hoped would be a trip that would result in the end of the five. They ate breakfast, lunch, and dinner talking about what they'd need and what their chances of success were. All three of them admitted they weren't good, but they also admitted they had little choice. By nine p. m. they were ready to go.

Each of them was wearing heavy work jeans and boots designed for living and walking out doors over rough terrain. They wore long sleeve, dark colored cotton shirts even though they knew the weather was going to get warmer, and over the shirts they wore black leather jackets. Black woolen caps were on their heads and Lee and Evelyn wore the night vision goggles around their necks Lee had taken from the two killers he'd killed a few days ago. Lyle wore a pair Lee had given him around his neck.

Lee was in the garage checking the inventory of the equipment they were bringing with them. He stood behind the heavily built all terrain four door SUV that was in front of the smaller car they'd used to get Lyle.

The four-wheel drive SUV contained four doors plus a tailgate, four-foot high all terrain tires that were self-sealing and eighteen inches wide and bullet proof if they were hit with only small caliber projectiles or low voltage electric bullets. The suspension system was three feet above the ground and built like the suspension system of the tanks in the history museums. The metal sides of the SUV were half an inch thick, the windows were a quarter inch thick, and the engine was surrounded by a solid steel case that was water proof, if they didn't get into water deeper than six feet. Even the wide headlights were covered with thick glass that could stop small caliber bullets and low voltage electric bullets. The SUV was built for violent action as well as rough terrain where roads didn't exist, even dirt roads.

All the seats were designed to recline back so four people could sleep side by side, with limited leg room. And like the car it was covered on the outside with a Plexiglas that reflected the surrounding terrain making it almost invisible at night or in shaded worded areas if a person wasn't looking for it.

"Do we have everything?" Evelyn asked him as she came down the stairs carrying a large canvas bag.

"Hope so," he said as he looked at the list of things he'd put in the car. "We've plenty of firepower with extra charge packs, foods for ten days for four people, bed rolls for each of us, blankets, plenty of water, medical equipment in case we need it, rain gear, extra boots, and clothing. I hope you brought extra underwear and socks with you?"

"I have," she said.

"You check to make sure Lyle has everything he'll need?"

She nodded as she said, "He acts as if this is some adventurous picnic."

"We'll stop fifty or sixty miles from here and see how well he shoots," Lee told her.

"I doubt if he's ever held a gun in his life," she said.

"Well, his life and that of his family may depend upon how well he shoots."

"As well as ours," she added.

Lee didn't reply. Thinking about harm coming to his family upset him and filled him with a rage he knew would cause him to make bad decisions. But he couldn't help but think about his two children. He was glad he didn't have grandchildren he didn't have to worry about like Evelyn did. But he had hopes of having grandchildren one day, if they survived what they had to do.

"Ready to go," Lyle asked as he walked out the door at the top of the garage stairs carrying a suitcase with his laptop hanging from a carrier around his neck. He came down the steps with a bounce like he was on his way to a dinner date with a wife and children he hadn't seen in over twenty years. "I'll be glad when all of this is over so I can get back to my family."

"You've been gone according to you for over twenty years," Lee told him as he looked at him with a disapproving expression. "How do you know your wife hasn't remarried? And your children are probably grown and on their own. They may even have families."

Lyle stopped at the bottom of the stairs and the happy look on his face disappeared. "You know, Lee, I've never thought about that."

"Well, don't start thinking about it now," Evelyn said. "You don't need to be thinking about them where we're going."

Lee folded the paper with the list of supplies and put it in his left jacket pocket as he walked over to Lyle and stopped. "Look, Lyle, this isn't a picnic we're going on. There's going to be killing, and a lot of it. Forget about your life before you found that file in the Hong Kong branch of the Department of Information. Concentrate on one thing and only one thing. What we have to do."

Lyle looked in his face and nodded as he asked, "Can I tell you my real name?"

"Go ahead," he said. "If it'll help you concentrate on the bloody business ahead of us."

"Henry Livingston Norton."

"Mind if we just call you Lyle?" Lee asked him.

He shrugged as he said, "It's been my name for over twenty years."

"What have you got in that suitcase?" Evelyn asked him.

"Change of underwear, socks, two shirts, and an extra pair of pants," he said.

"Put it in the back," Lee told him.

"The roof of this vehicle will do nicely," he said as he walked around Lee.

"No," Lee said. "It'll ruin our camouflage up there. There's room in the back. Wedge it between the weapons and ammo packs." He looked at his watch. "Ten minutes and we're leaving."

Lyle stowed his suitcase in the back and got in the back seat behind the front passenger's seat and strapped himself in. "Ready," he announced.

Lee got in behind the steering wheel and used his com-cell to turn out the lights in the house and garage. "Hope no one left anything burning in the house. I like this place a lot. I'd hate to come back and find only ashes."

"There are no fires burning in the house and the electric stove is back in neutral," Evelyn said. "So let's get this side show on the road."

"Fool's errand would be a better term considering what we're going up against," Lee said as he turned on the SUV's engine and checked the top screen on the dashboard. It showed the forest outside to be dark and quiet except for the usual forest sounds at night. "We're got a lucky start."

"Why do you say that?" Lyle asked him.

"I checked the calendar in my study before I left," he said. "There's no moon tonight and it'll be two days before a quarter moon begins."

"Good," Evelyn said. "We can travel at night."

"That won't stop them from seeing us if they're looking in the right direction," Lyle said. "And don't forget that satellite."

"No, it won't," Lee agreed. "But at least we'll have a narrow edge."

"Thin would have been a better word," Lyle told him as the garage door opened and Lee drove out.

Lyle looked at the surrounding darkness and prayed silently they were successful.

Then he thought of the wife and children he hadn't seen in over twenty years. He dismissed them from his mind.

As soon as they left the garage, the door silently closed and the door looked like it was part of the forest. Only the tracks left in the knee high grass indicated a vehicle had moved through it. Within a few hours the grass would recover from the weight of the SUV on it, and by morning there would be no sign humans had been anywhere in the vicinity.

None of them talked as they moved quietly through the dark forest. Each was thinking of what faced them, and praying they were successful.

CHAPTER 46

12:45 a.m. Saturday

Sam had replaced Troy four hours ago, even though Troy wasn't tired, and had done nothing in that time but look at the TV screen covering the wall in front of him. Thousands of square miles of wilderness appeared on the screen. Miles of forests lined both sides of the Snake River and behind them were hills dominated by prairie grasses that were waist high in some places and higher in others. There were gullies some with grass in them some with brush so thick in them only small animals could pass through. In some places the terrain consisted of gently rolling hills with colorful wild flowers growing everywhere and an occasional group of short thick prairie trees that had managed to survive the buffalo, antelopes, and the harsh winters so common on the Great Plains of North America. Even in the dark the sight, what little of it he could see, should have been beautiful or at least pleasant to look at. But Sam wasn't cloned to appreciate the beauty of the wild Nebraska country. He was programmed to operate computers and look for what the five told him to look for, and when he wasn't doing that he sat and looked at the screen. If he grew tired or hungry or thirsty, or had to use the washroom he was programmed to tell one of them he what he needed. If given permission to leave, he would leave and get food or water or relieve himself. If no one was around to tell him to go and eat, drink, and relieve himself or sleep. He would go and do what he had to do, and then return to his station and review the recordings he'd missed while he was away. Summoning a replacement while he was away even for a few minutes required the ability to think someone should watch the screen while he was away, and he didn't possess that ability.

Once every hour he would change the view on the screen to the wilderness area just west of Crown where someone had accessed the satellite that had passed overhead at seven p.m. on Friday night. This was possible even though there were no satellites passing over the area because Troy had taken a picture of the area and put it in the computer's hard drive. Then he would watch the area looking for any humans or vehicles in the area. But he saw none because there hadn't been any when Troy had taken the picture. He had done that at eight p.m. then at nine switched back to the area around the underground complex. Then at ten he had gone back to watching the area just west of the city until eleven. Then at exactly eleven p.m. he had gone back to watching the wilderness area outside the complex until midnight.

It didn't dawn upon Sam that the area west of Crown he was watching was a picture of the area at seven p.m. and not as the area looked at ten. Like all the clones working for the five, Sam lacked the ability to make decisions on his own because he lacked specific judgment which would have told him he was watching a program of an area that was hours old.

The underground complex had surface cameras, forty of them, that could scan the area outside the complex for a mile in any direction. The cameras also had heat detectors in them which could detect the heat of animals or humans half a mile away. The computer was programmed to analyze the heat signatures the heat detectors picked up to determine if humans or animals had been detected. But the cameras hadn't been raised since the five didn't think it was necessary. There was no sign anywhere of Lee, Evelyn, and Lyle so why raise the cameras?

The five had always been right for over five hundred years, because no one knew about them. There was no reason for them to assume they wouldn't be able to kill Lee, Evelyn, and Lyle once they showed up. Everything was in their favor.

CHAPTER 47

June 9, 1:30 a.m. Saturday

"How far have we come," Lyle asked Lee.

"About seventy miles," he said. "We should be able to make another seventy before we have to look for a hiding place."

"You know, Lee, we're heading into prairie country."

"Yes, I know that," he said.

"This SUV is going to leave tracks in the grass that satellite will be able to see," he said.

"Pray for rain, Lyle," he said. "A nice heavy downpour would be just the thing we need."

Evelyn was working on her I-book. "We should stop fifty or sixty miles from the lab," she suggested.

"They'll see our tracks and know where we stopped," Lyle said.

"Can't be helped," Lee said.

"They'll have the advantage of setting a trap and waiting for us," he said.

"That means we've got to spot it before we walk into it."

"Maybe we'll have a little help, fellows," Evelyn said as she looked at her I-book.

"Explain that, please," Lyle said.

"There are hundreds of thousands of buffalo and antelope on the prairie. They constantly move. Maybe they'll wipe out our tracks."

Lee thought of that while he drove. "We'll be moving at night, Lyle."

"Doesn't matter, they'll still see tracks we leave if they can magnify the telescope of the passing satellite."

"Can they do that, Evelyn?" Lee asked her.

"Probably," she answered.

"But only for an hour," Lee said. "Once that satellite passes they're blind."

"So we'll have twelve hours when they can't see any tracks we leave in the grass," Lyle said.

"That's right," Evelyn told him.

Lyle thought for a while before he spoke. "I would imagine that lab has something that would enable them to spot us miles away."

"It probably does," Lee replied.

"How the hell do we get pass that?" Lyle asked.

"I don't know," Lee said. "I guess we'll have to deal with whatever devices they have for detecting us when we're close to the lab when the situation arises."

"Oh, now isn't that just brilliant," Lyle said in a sarcastic voice. "We could be dead by then."

"You didn't think this was going to be easy, did you, Lyle?" Evelyn asked him.

"No, nor did I think it was going to be suicidal."

"Take it easy, Lyle," Lee told him. "We've time to come up with a plan that might help us."

They rode in silence for an hour before Lyle said, "Maybe we could do something to fool their early warning devices."

"Like what?" Evelyn asked.

Lyle didn't answer. He was looking out the window at the buffalo and other animals wandering around at night thinking. After a few minutes he opened his laptop and began working on it. "Maybe we can use the wild animals that live on the surface around the lab?"

"We're listening," Evelyn said.

"Maybe we should follow the movements of the herds of buffalo," he said. "According to what I just read there are over half a million in Nebraska alone."

"You got information on buffalo on your laptop?" she asked him.

"Yes, when I was hiding in that cabin, I'd download information from the Department of Information about animals and other things. To calm my nerves."

"Listen both of you," Lee said. "They know we're coming and they're prepared for our arrival. Herds of buffalo or any other type of animal isn't going to help us. But using our intelligence just may help us expose those assholes."

Lyle and Evelyn hated admitting he was right so they didn't respond.

CHAPTER 48

June 9, 10 a. m., Saturday

Steve was walking around on top of the underground complex. He didn't want to be bother by the others. He'd had breakfast in his apartment and gone outside for a walk to enjoy the fresh air and the scenery. The last thing he wanted to do was sit in one of the two lounges or one of the three libraries with his four companions. It was alright seeing them once or twice a month for dinner and occasionally golfing or playing tennis with them, he hated golf, at the country club. But being with them every day since the night of June first was more than he could stand.

Paul was an insufferable ass with a false sense of superiority which he hid behind a wall of silence and arrogance and the assumed habits of a gentleman, which he wasn't. Fred was just a fool. Steve was thinking of having Petersen program more intelligence in Fred's clone so the new Fred wouldn't be such a fool. Larry was irresponsible. The man never assumed responsibility for anything. He expected his clones and computers—that he was responsible for, to be able to solve every problem. And Bruce was just the opposite of Larry. While he did have a strong sense of responsibility he seldom used it.

Steve sat down on a rock and looked at the grassy rolling hills with their wooly sides of thicker grasses and a sky that seemed to go on forever. Most people would have considered the sight thrilling. Steve just saw grass and an occasional animal moving across the grassy hills. He decided to relax and let his mind drift. The problems with his companions could be taken care of once Lee, Evelyn, and Lyle were dead and the information they possessed was safe.

"What do you think?" the man asked as he knelt behind a branch that was growing close to the ground.

"Don't see how he got out here without a horse or a car," Dan said to Al.

They were two hundred feet away in a thinly wooded area watching Steve.

Al raised his binoculars and looked carefully over the area. "I don't see no horse or car."

"You think he's from those cars Cassie and Jessie said they saw yesterday?" Dan asked as he looked through his binoculars.

"Must be, but I didn't see any," Al said.

"Think we ought to go down and talk to him?" Dan asked Al.

"Look at how he's dressed?" Al said. "Those are city clothes. They wouldn't last a day in this country. He ain't even wearing boots."

"Want to go down and ask him what he's doing in this country?"

Dan shook his head. "No. I think we should leave him be and get back to our hunting. He probably ain't alone anyway, and he could be up to no good."

"You're probably right," Al said. "Cassie and Jessie said they saw three cars in a line yesterday. They were long campers. Don't nobody come into this country unless they're hunting and that man ain't dressed in no hunting clothes. And the hunting season is months away."

"Let's ride around and see if we can see a camp," Dan suggested. "If he's part of a hunting party he wouldn't be far from the camp."

Two men turned and walked back down the hill to the narrow gully where they had their horses and a pack horse tethered. They mounted up and rode off. Dan held the rope tied to the pack horse. They rode around the hill they had seen Steve on and had seen nothing but the tracks the three vehicles had left. The tracks had ended at the side of a hill. Two hours later they returned to the spot where they had seen Steve just in time to see something they didn't believe. The man got up, walked about thirty feet, and walked down into the ground and disappeared.

"There ain't no caves around here, Dan," Al said as they watched Steve disappear into the ground. "I've been all over this country."

"No, there ain't no caves around here, Dan," Al agreed. "But there's something underground where those wheel tracks we saw ended."

"If the government had put something underground there, we would have seen them working a long time ago," Dan said. "So whatever's down there has been there for a long time."

"Longer than we've been hunting in this country," Al said. "And our people have been in this country for over a hundred years."

"Let's get back to the village and tell everyone to avoid this part of the country."

Dan said.

Al nodded his agreement and the two men left.

"Where have you been?" Larry demanded when he encountered Steve in the halls. He was sitting in a cart.

"Outside enjoying the fresh air," Steve replied as he walked pass Larry.

"That was foolish, Steve, very foolish. What if Lee and those others had seen you? They'd know about the lab complex."

"I suspect by now, Larry, they already know about it." He walked to the cart he'd left in the hallway, got into it, and said, "Take me to my apartment."

The cart moved off.

"Take me to a library that's empty," Larry told the computer in his cart. Like Steve he was fed up with being around the others. "No. Take me to a game room."

He hadn't played pool in years and he wanted to see if he was still as good as he had been years ago.

Larry's cart moved off in the direction of the closest of the four game rooms.

CHAPTER 49

8:30 p.m.

At eight Evelyn and Lee had given Lyle a rifle and let him fire a dozen rounds at a rock fifty feet away. Lyle had hit the rock twice and was delighted with his shooting. Then they gave him an automatic and told him to fire a dozen times at the same rock. He missed it with every shot.

"If we get into a shootout, Lyle, make sure you stay behind us, and don't shot at any of the clones we're going to run it unless they're ten feet away," Evelyn told him.

"And make damn sure you don't shoot one of us," Lee told him.

"I know what you two look like, so don't worry," he told them.

Lee looked west at the sun.

The sun was in the western sky and shadows were already being cast by the hills west of them. The wooded gully they had stopped in was almost dark with the shadows cast by the surrounding hills. They packed up and prepared to leave.

"Let's go," Evelyn said as she placed her bedroll in the back of the SUV. "We're burning night."

"I think the expression is burning daylight," Lyle said as he tossed his bedroll in the SUV next to hers.

"In our case its night," she said.

Lee had been ready to go for ten minutes. "We should be able to make good time with no more trees and stumps to avoid." He looked at the ground they had covered getting into the valley and saw the wide tracks the wheels of the SUV had left in the grass. Traveling over grasslands was easier at night than dodging tree stumps and boulders in the dark in a forest—the SUV's suspension system was high enough to avoid the two feet boulders, though there was no guarantee there wouldn't be larger boulders hidden in the grass. He secretly hoped for rain even if the SUV did leave a muddy trail there was a good chance a heavy rain would wash them away, but June was the beginning of the dry season on the plains.

Evelyn saw where Lee was looking and guessed what he was thinking and said, "Maybe we'll get a nice storm tonight."

"I doubt it," he replied. "This has been a mild season for storms."

"Think we'll make the lab by tonight?" Lyle asked him.

"We covered a hundred and twelve miles last night," Lee said. "We should be able to make maybe a hundred and fifty or more before sunrise even in this country even with these endless hills and gullies."

"Drive carefully," Lyle cautioned him. "Driving into a gully isn't quite like hitting a tree stump."

"Couldn't avoid that one last night, Lyle, it was hidden by tall grass," he said. "Remember we can't use the headlights. Anyway it didn't hurt the SUV."

"Yes, yes, I understand," Lyle said as he looked at the backpacks his suitcase was lying on. "When we reach the place where this underground lab is we're not going to be able to take everything with us, are we?"

"No," Evelyn said. "Just what we need to do what we have to do."

"Then don't you two think we should pack what we need in those three backpacks under my suitcase?"

"Good, idea," Lee said sorry that he hadn't thought of that before they left his hideout. He had put the backpacks in the back of the SUV for that purpose, but he had been so interested in finding the underground lab he hadn't thought of anything but that. "Check our position on the map to make sure we're heading in the right direction, Evelyn, while I pack out backpacks."

She nodded and took her I-book out of the pouch on her left shoulder.

"Why don't you use my laptop," Lyle said. "It's on the back seat. It has excellent maps in it with numbers on them to determine coordinates and even elevation lines."

"Use it inside the SUV where the glow from the screen can't be seen," Lee told her.

Evelyn got into the SUV and got Lyle's laptop and started to work. By the time Lee and Lyle had packed their backpacks with what they hoped they'd need she had finished determining their position. "We're at least three hundred and thirty-eight miles south of that missiles complex, Lee."

"Good," he said as he turned around and looked east down the gully they were in.

"Let's see if your aim has improved over the last half hour, Lyle." He turned back toward the SUV's bed and took out a rifle and a semiautomatic.

"I don't really like guns," Lyle said. "That's why I didn't too well with that handgun."

"Neither do I, but where we're going—you're going to have to use one, so now is the perfect time to see if your shooting has improved. I should have stopped last night and let you shoot, but I didn't so now you shoot a second time." He walked twenty feet from the back of the SUV and stopped. "Come here, Lyle."

Lyle walked over to him and stopped. He seemed nervous.

Lee handed him the rifle. "Hold it like you're going to shoot, and calm down."

Lyle raised the rifle to his right shoulder, got a good grip on the weapon, and waited for Lee to tell him to shoot.

"You remember how to remove the weapon's safety?"

"Yes, I know," Lyle said as he started to lower the rifle and look at the button.

"No, feel with your right thumb," he told him. "In a shootout you're not going to have time to look and see if the safety's on." Lyle did as he said.

"See that half dead tree in front of you," Lee told him.

"The one far away?"

"Yes. Aim at the part where that large dead branch joins the trunk and squeeze the trigger. Don't pull it like you did half an hour ago. Just squeeze and don't think about the rifle concentrate on the target."

Lyle did as he was told and hit the branch. He lowered the rifle and smiled at his excellent marksmanship. "Right on target with the first shot this time, Lee," he said.

"Yes, right on target," Lee agreed as he took the rifle from Lyle and gave him the semiautomatic. "Now do the same with the semiautomatic and remember don't lock your elbow. This weapon doesn't have the kick that projectile weapons have, but it doesn't hurt to follow the same rules. Relax and squeeze."

Lyle did the same and missed. "Damn!" he cussed.

"Don't feel bad. That tree is probably over fifty feet away. It's a hard target to hit with a handgun in this declining light. Where we're going the targets are going to be closer, and not stationary like that tree and they will be shooting back."

"That I know," he said as he engaged the safety and handed the gun to Lee butt first.

"Keep it. Get use to carrying it, and don't forget you've got it. And one other thing," he said. "Identity your target before you shoot. Let's go."

Lyle walked beside Lee putting the automatic in the front of his belt.

Lee saw what he did. "Don't forget to remove the weapon from your belt before you remove the safety and put your finger on the trigger or you might shoot yourself."

"If I've got to do any shooting, I intend having this weapon in my hands long before I have to shoot it," Lyle said.

"Use the handgun as a backup weapon," he said. "The rifle has a larger voltage than the semiautomatic."

"I suggest we head west for ten miles, Lee," Evelyn said. "Then turn east when we reach the latitude the lab's on."

"Why?" Lyle asked. "Going straight for the lab seems the best plan."

"The terrain's rougher with more gullies and woods. We can use them to mask our movements if they have electrical equipment scanning for us."

"And if they do?" Lee asked her.

"Then every time we get on high ground they're going to see us."

Lee nodded his understanding as he opened the passenger door and got in the SUV. "You drive, Evelyn. When you get tired, Lyle can take over. One of us can sleep while the other two remain awake."

Five minutes later they were driving across country heading west.

CHAPTER 50

9 p.m. Saturday

Steve was back on top enjoying the coming night and the stars that were beginning to appear in the dark sky. He was lying on his back on the large rock he was sitting on and looking at the sky. His mind was free of all thoughts and for the first time in days he felt relaxed. He didn't want to think about what he intended doing once Evelyn, Lyle, and Lee were dead and their information was secure. He raised his left arm and looked at the luminous hands on his watch. *They should all be asleep in an hour.* He lowered his arm and breathed a sigh of relief.

The four others were so busy with their private interests none had paid any attention to him. That gave him time to wander about the huge underground complex without being notice. The clones, especially Petersen were either asleep or busy doing what they were programmed to do, allowing him to go to the computer room and program the computers that controlled their clones.

Producing a clone was easy today compared to what it had been in the 1980's when some scientist in Britain had cloned a sheep. It had taken that scientist and his helpers a year of hard work to get numerous strands of DNA from a sheep, grow them in test tubes with nutrients in them till a few developed into cells. Then carefully monitor the cells until one eventually became an embryo that grew into a sheep. The sheep had survived only a few years before it died. Today the entire process took only nine months, from DNA to fully

276

developed adult human. Even the transfer of a person's mind into the clone's brain took only two hours. That way it wasn't necessary for them to spend years in school learning how to be responsible adults in a modern world. They'd come out of the seven feet by four feet glass tubes in the cloning room with the same minds they'd had before they were cloned.

The only difference between the five of them and the other clones is they had the ability to think in a complex manner. They were real humans in every sense of the word except they hadn't spent nine months in woman's womb and twenty years in school learning. They even had normal human feelings which the other clones didn't have because feelings weren't programmed into them since as slaves, which they were, they didn't need such feelings. Only the ability to obey without question was all they needed.

The five of them were resistant to every disease known to attack humans, as were

they clone slaves, and if some new disease came along by the natural process of nature which they could not resist they could be cloned again once a cure was discovered. Basically the five of them were immortal. They had been alive since 2559, and they would continue to live as long as they desired, as would Petersen who was constantly improving on the process of cloning.

Steve smiled when he thought of what he'd done in the computer room that controlled the cloning process.

Steve had spent years studying inherited diseases that turned people in their sixties or older into helpless humans, dependent upon modern medicine to give them normal lives.

Steve wasn't as concerned with developing the cultured background of Paul, Fred, Bruce, or Larry. But he was as cultured as they were and as socially acceptable as they. What he possessed that they also possessed was the knowledge that one man could live forever or as long as he wanted with Petersen's cloning process and not attract any attention. But five risked the secret getting out. The society columns of the various newspapers, magazines, and Internet had already noted that the five of them came from wealthy parents who'd been rich since 2559, and had escaped the plagues that had killed billions of others. And they had all inherited their wealth during the plagues that killed their parents. That had to change once Evelyn, Lyle, and Lee were dead.

And Steve had started the change when he was in the computer room that controlled the cloning process. He had simply programmed the computers to put within the brains of the four an electric spark that would destroy some of the brain tissue of the other four once the mental exchange process started. Once the exchange was completed the four would seem as normal as he. But by the age of forty they would begin to develop into mental vegetables with no knowledge they'd ever been cloned, and die.

Only he would remain normal. He'd made plans for his blood line to come to an end. It was time he disappeared as Steve Gamble and became someone completely different. A distant relative unknown to anyone, especially his four companions, would be found living in some isolated area and inherit most of his wealth. He'd made plans for a fourth of his wealth to go to his clone, more than enough with his knowledge of how to make money to recreate another fortune as great, maybe greater than the one he now possessed. The rest would go to charities since he had no heirs.

Steve raised his left arm and looked at his watch and smiled and thought, *who would have thought the program to destroy my companions was in the base of a cheap watch.*

Paul had wondered why Steve was avoiding him and the others. *Well,* he thought as he lay in bed. *I'll find out as soon as we've taken care of those three fools.*

CHAPTER 51

June 10, 2 a.m. Sunday

Evelyn was in the back asleep. Lee was in the passenger's seat looking out the window into the darkness as Lyle drove. The SUV bounced along over the rough terrain. He looked to his left at the terrain map on the bottom screen on the dashboard and noticed they were driving through a narrow valley.

"Computer," he said. "Show the weather conditions in this part of Nebraska."

"Hoping for rain?" Lyle asked as he drove. He was enjoying himself. Driving at night without headlights was something he'd never done in his life because he thought it was insane and he'd never had a reason to do so. But in the wilderness it seemed like the most intelligent thing to do considering where they were going.

Lee didn't answer as he looked at the weather report on the bottom of the screen.

"Not a breeze out there," he said. "Dead calm."

"We're not going that fast," Lyle said as he glanced at the speedometer. "Twenty miles an hour. I didn't know we were traveling that fast. I'm going to slow down."

"You do that, but I don't think our speed is the cause of an absence of wind," he said. "Computer, how far are we from our destination?"

Two hundred and twenty-eight miles appeared on the screen.

Lyle saw it and said, "Pretty good. We've traveled over a hundred miles in a little over five hours. You know we'd be there by now if we didn't have to go through all these gullies to avoid being seen."

"Yes." Lee agreed. Traveling a hundred miles in five hours across country where the closest thing to a road was a flat piece of land that had no breaks in it for the SUV to bounce over, wasn't bad. "That satellite passes overhead in another five hours. Increase your speed by another ten miles."

"I don't know, Lee, not in this terrain," Lyle said. "We could end up running into a gully or small stream."

"Computer, show what's five hundred feet ahead of us and the terrain we're traveling over, and what's fifty feet on both sides of us," Lee said.

A detailed picture of the surface of the land five hundred feet in front of them, and fifty feet on the sides in the darkness appeared on the top screen.

"Pretty flat except for those lumps of grass and brush," Lyle said.

"Show the heat of all objects that are above seventy-five degrees." Lee said to the computer.

Every object warmer than seventy-five degrees appeared on the screen.

"I like this SUV," Lyle said a big smile on his face. "Where did you get it?"

"It's almost twenty-five years old," Lee said. "An ex car thief Paul wanted me to kill because he stolen an antique car Paul owned put it together for me."

"Then you killed him?"

"No, I took Paul's precious car back to him and told him if the thief ended up dead the police would start asking questions."

"And he let the guy live?"

"The five don't like attracting the attention of the police, and the guy was well known to the police as a thief of antique cars. A lot of rich people like to collect antique cars."

"That's surprising considering their power," Lyle said.

"One of the reasons the five are as powerful as they are, is they keep out of the public eye. They've never been in any society or gossip columns, and they don't associate with people who regularly appear in such columns. Their power is based upon what they've got on powerful, greedy businessmen, and stupid politicians who accept money from them under the table for their campaigns and don't realize the five have recordings of them accepting the money. If the information about them you stole gets out, they'd lose a lot of their clout even if no one believed it."

"Why would their clout desert them?" Lyle asked him.

"Politicians don't like dirt coming out about them in the form of pictures and recordings that appear on the Internet. It aids their opponents and scares away people who want to appear as good people to the general public, even if some of them aren't."

"Those five monsters are really in a bad situation, aren't they?"

"If it became known they are clones who engineered the plagues that have killed billions, they would be destroyed. Clones aren't considered to be real people, and have no rights. Every religion in the world denounces cloning as a violation of God's sacred law of human life. Even the people who follow those religions believe that."

"They would be considered devils," Lyle said.

"If the information you have on them is correct, that's exactly what they are."

"I wonder what would happen to their estates."

"I don't give a fuck what happens to their estates," Lee said. "All I want to do is protect my family from them, and survive to live a peaceful quiet life."

"Why did they hire you and Evelyn? They have their own trackers."

"She's one of the best hackers in the world and I'm a fairly good tracker." Lee didn't like talking about his natural skills as a tracker.

"And they needed someone who could think other than just take and carry out orders like their clones."

Lee didn't say anything.

"So the five hired you two, and both of you immediately knew that if you found me they would have to kill you because they couldn't guarantee you wouldn't read and report the information to the government."

"That's it. But we knew nothing about clones and specific judgment."

Large bright warm lumps appeared on the top screen on the dashboard with smaller bright lumps scattered among them four hundred feet ahead of them.

"What are those?" Lyle asked as he quickly glanced at the screen.

"Avoid them by at least two hundred feet," Lee told him. "They're sleeping buffalo. The smaller lumps are probably deer or antelopes."

Lyle dropped his speed and steered around the bright lumps.

"Do you trust Evelyn?" Lyle asked him.

"Yes, just like I trust you."

"Why?"

Lee glanced at him and said, "It's time for you to do some specific thinking, Lyle."

"What do you mean?"

"We have to trust each other or we die and our families do, too. And we have to succeed, too. Or a whole lot of people we'll never meet are also going to die within the next forty or more years. If the information you got on the five is correct."

"Oh, it's correct alright, or they wouldn't be interested in catching and killing us."

"Computer, show the weather conditions on the bottom screen," Lee said.

'Wind zero miles per hour, temperature 80 degrees, humidity 55 percent.'

The high humidity and dead calm struck Lee as odd. "Looks like we might get rain." Then he said to the computer, "Show weather conditions for two hundred miles around us."

"We're far from any radio or TV stations, Lee," Lyle reminded him.

"Radio, and even TV waves, bounce off the upper atmosphere. Even out here we can pick them up." He was looking at the bottom screen when he heard a slow rumbling sound. He looked up at the top screen. "Those buffalo and antelopes are moving north."

"Maybe they're heading for water," Lyle said. "No streams or rivers appear on the map."

Lee wasn't paying any attention to him because he was looking at the weather report. "The same conditions exist a hundred miles west of us."

"Now that these animals are moving I can pick up speed," Lyle said as he increased his speed to forty miles an hour. "We should be within fifty miles of that underground lab before six at the speed we're traveling. Assuming, of course, we're on course."

"What does these weather conditions usually mean?" Lee asked the computer.

'Such weather conditions are usually present before a wind storm develops.'

"What type of wind storms?"

'Powerful wind storms with rain. Possibly sleet. Tornados are commonly produced by such weather conditions.'

"Is this SUV tornado proof?" Lyle asked. He's seen what was on the screen.

Lee ignored his question. "Is there a storm approaching us?"

'A rain storm one hundred and seventeen miles away with winds of over thirty miles an hour is approaching this position out of the west at twenty-two miles an hour.'

"That gives us a little over five and a half hours," he said. "How fast are you going?"

"Forty miles an hour," Lyle said.

"Increase your speed to fifty-five."

"Over this rough terrain?"

"The tires and suspension system can handle it. Just avoid any gullies. Especially the deep ones. We don't want to end up upside down in a deep gully in a rain storm. We could drown."

"We'll reach the coordinates of that underground lab within less than four hours," Lyle warned him as he increased his speed to fifty-five miles an hour. "If we don't kill ourselves first."

"A powerful storm might be in our favor," Lee said. He looked at Lyle. "If you can't handle this SUV at that speed, I'll take over."

Lyle hit the brakes and brought the SUV to a sudden stop. "Please, do. I've never driven in a rain storm with winds over thirty miles an hour."

"It's not here yet," Lee told him. "Just crawl in the back and strap yourself in."

Lyle quickly crawled in the back next to Evelyn and buckled his seat belt around himself. Lee moved over into the driver's seat and started driving the SUV. He'd reached sixty miles an hour in five minutes. He glues his eyes to the terrain map, because it was too dark for him to see more than a foot pass the hood, and avoided lumps in the ground that were too high for the SUV's high suspension system.

By five o'clock they had traveled ninety-seven bumpy miles. Evelyn had woken up half an hour after Lee started driving. She couldn't sleep with the bouncing of the SUV and Lyle had a look on his face that indicated he was more afraid of a crash than the approaching storm.

Evelyn looked at her watch and said, "The sun should be rising in half an hour."

"We've got a powerful storm approaching us. It's about fifty-one miles away. And we're less than a hundred and twenty-six miles from that underground lab."

"We should start looking for a place to hide," she said.

"No. If you can look at the lower screen," Lee told her.

She leaned forward without unbuckling her seat belt and looked at the screen. "Winds in excess of forty miles an hour and increasing. That's a pretty powerful wind."

"I suspect it's developing into a tornado, Evelyn."

"Then we should find a nice deep gully to hide in, Lee," she said.

"No. Tornados are unpredictable. They can move in any direction in a moment. We get hit by one and we're finished. We've got to reach the coordinates of that lab before the tornado, if one is developing, reaches us."

"And if one does hit us when we reach those coordinates?"

"We're finished."

Evelyn settled back in her seat. "We've got less than two hours before that satellite passes overhead, Lee. If we aren't hiding when it does, we will be finished after they send their clones after us."

CHAPTER 52

5:30 a.m. Sunday

Petersen had little need for sleep. Four hours and his body and mind were good for at least twenty hours. It gave him plenty of time to work or read his novels. When he wasn't working or reading, he was eating, cleaning himself, or walking about the underground complex making sure everything was working perfectly. He had been following the same pattern for nearly five hundred years and never once was he bored because he was curious about everything.

The surface cameras recorded the movements of large herds of animals moving over and around the complex when the cameras were up and operating. The herds of animals were always moving. They were driven by instinct. During the fall they moved south leaving the land around the complex almost devoid of life except for those animals that lived below ground. Most of them hibernated during the long, cold winters. They would mate during the fall and then go to sleep. Once or twice a month each winter they would awaken from their hibernation to go outside to hunt for food and then return to their underground nests and sleep for another the three or four weeks and repeat the process until spring. Then they would give birth and get on with the business of living.

Petersen knew their habits and those of the migrating animals so well he could predict the seasonal changes by simply looking at the electric calendars included in the clocks on the walls of every room in the complex.

It was the weather that was unpredictable. Sometimes the prairie was green with spring rains and the melting of winter snow. Sometimes the winter was mild and little snow fell and the spring rains weren't as heavy as they should be and the prairie would be brown during the spring and almost desert like during the summers. And storms came and went when he least expected them. But they never surprised him since the surface cameras could detect them miles away.

The movement of the herds to the north indicated a powerful storm was coming. Regular storms didn't bother the animals of the prairie, but powerful ones frightened them and they moved as far away from them as possible.

What Petersen found odd was the five didn't know how powerful the surface cameras were. If they did they would have known about the people on horseback who occasionally rode over the complex hunting animals. Petersen knew they came from a village fifty-seven miles southwest of the complex, and knew nothing about the complex. He always had two cameras up, and he had programmed the cameras to alert him when they were around the complex. He liked watching them, and wondering why in the modern world anyone would want to travel by horseback and bath in the river that flowed a few miles west of the complex. He didn't tell the five about them because they hadn't asked if anyone ever came to the complex, and he was programmed only to answer their questions.

This morning Petersen had decided to walk to the silo. He hadn't done that in seven months and he felt a need to change his routine. And the one-mile walk down the round concrete tunnel was somewhat pleasant. It gave him a chance to look around the operational chamber where the concrete tunnel began beyond a seven-foot high three-foot thick steel door and pass another steel door into the concrete tunnel as he casually strolled to see if the robots kept the operational chamber and the four rooms attached to the operational chamber in perfect condition. He knew they did since he monitored all the activities of the robots in the underground complex every day and the robots always did as programmed.

Petersen didn't know why he enjoyed the mile walk as much as he did. All he knew is he felt relieved when he made the walk and looked over the operational chamber and the four rooms as if he were outside enjoying fresh air.

The one-mile tunnel from the complex was built just as solidly as the complex but it was only a hundred feet below ground and connected to the silo. The silo had a movable ten ton concrete square slab twenty feet thick and forty feet wide and long covering the top. The slab moved on well-oiled steel wheels that were two feet in height and width and it covered a missile which the five demanded remain in operational condition. Petersen didn't know why they wanted the missile operational but he did know what had once been incased in the five containers on the top of the missile. He hadn't looked at the missile in four hundred years. There was no purpose in looking at it. It sat on its launching pad as it had since it was put there in 1975. The robots that cleaned the lab also kept the missile clean and operational.

When he reached the one hundred feet circular silo the missile was in, he noticed there wasn't even dust in the one hundred feet high silo, and walked around the steel catwalk that surrounded the missile to a flight of stairs and walked up the stairs to a ten feet tall, five feet wide heavy steel door that connected to the outside. He opened the steel door with a minimum of effort, its hinges were well-oiled like every hinge in the complex and there was no squeaking noise, and walked and up a flight of twenty stairs to a steel door that led to a cave that lead to the surface. With the exception of the computer attached to the wall at the bottom of the stairs in the silo there were no cameras in this part of the complex. It had never dawned upon him in the five hundred years he'd been making this walk that the lack of a camera to detect movement in this part of the complex was an oversight.

He walked to the cave opening and looked east and saw the rising sun. The sight would have been lovely to any normal human, even with the dark storm clouds rapidly gathering in the west, but Petersen was a clone and beauty meant nothing to him. Neither did the gathering storm in the west.

$$\sim$$

CHAPTER 53

6 a.m.

The sun was in the eastern sky above the horizon but the sky above them was almost as dark as the night as the storm moved eastward gathering speed and power with every passing second. The winds were howling and hitting the left side of the SUV with such force Lee had to steer into the wind to stop it from being toppled on it right side.

"Lee, the wind is also twenty-five miles an hour," Evelyn yelled at him. She was leaning forward and looking at the bottom screen.

"Maybe we should find some safe gully to ride out the storm," Lyle suggested in a loud voice. He looked west out his window and saw nothing but the darkness coming with the storm.

"There is no safe gully, Lyle," Lee yelled at him over the roar of the rapidly approaching storm.

"But its madness to continue driving in this storm, it's only going to get worse," Lyle told him. "We need to get out of this wind."

"We have to reach those coordinates first," he responded. "I can't look at the screen. How far are we from them?"

Evelyn leaned back and reached down between her feet and pulled Lyle's laptop from the case it was in. She quickly brought up a map that showed where they were and the location of the underground lab. "About sixty-eight miles."

"We've traveled fifty-eight miles?" Lyle asked him.

"If that's what your laptop shows," Lee said.

"You think we can make it?" Evelyn asked him.

"I sure hope so."

"We can't keep bucking these winds, Lee," Lyle said. "It's only a matter of minutes before we flip over."

"Is there a low spot we can get into that'll get us out of this wind and keep us going north?"

"Give me a second," Evelyn replied as she started typing on the laptop. "Why don't you have a voice activated laptop, Lyle?"

"Because I didn't need a voice activated laptop," he answered.

"Hurry up!" Lee yelled.

"Turn right and go down between these hills on our right. We'll be heading east but there's a narrow valley nine miles away that connects to this one that'll take us north again."

"Brace yourselves." Lee told them as he moved toward a slopping hill and began to move down it.

The wind hit the back on the SUV like a giant hand and began to push the SUV down the side of the hill into the valley between the hills. Lee put his right foot on the brake pedal and turned the steering wheel left and right to avoid being flipped head forward onto the roof of the SUV. The tires gripped the slippery grass and just as the SUV seemed as if it was about to flip over on its left or right side or top Lee would turned the steering wheel left or right to prevent it. The wind got under the rear end of the SUV and raised the back wheels off the ground.

The three of them held their breaths and prepared for the worse.

The thick steel front bumper dug into the ground throwing dirt and grass on the windshield and steading the SUV and preventing it from flipping over on its roof. The rear end dropped back to the ground, the rear wheels got a good grip on the slippery grass, and the SUV continued its slide into the narrow valley. Suddenly the wind got under the SUV and was about to flip it head over heels onto its roof when the SUV hit the ground between the hills and bounced like a rubber ball on its large, thick tires. But it was right side up and sitting still.

Lee looked back at them and grinned as he asked, "Bet you never been on a roller coaster like that?"

"Punch it," Evelyn told him. She, like Lyle, didn't consider the slide down the hill to be a roller coaster ride.

Lee immediately started driving again. The push of the wind against the SUV was

much less and he increased his speed.

Lyle turned around and was looking out the back window. "I see a bright sky between the dark clouds and a black wind tunnel that looks like its thousand or more feet high. And it's moving toward this valley."

Lee didn't say anything. He just kept driving as fast as he could. The SUV was bouncing over the rough terrain like a rubber ball bouncing down stairs. He turned the steering wheel left and right to avoid large objects in the path of the SUV. Twice he scrapped the left and right sides of the SUV as he maneuvered pass trees and large rocks. His maneuvering blew most of the dirt off the windshield and allowed him to see what was in front of him. *And I always thought the Great Plains was just a grassy treeless rock free prairie,* he thought as he drove.

Silence settled in the SUV as Lee drove. The only sound was the howling of the wind over the hills as if it were angry at not being able to get to them. The sky was a mixture of bright morning and clouds so dark in some places they seemed almost black like they were clouds of dirt. The only good thing about the wind whipping into and out of the narrow valley was that it kept the windshield free of dirt. Lee was happy about that. If he had turned on the wipers he would have turned the windshield into a streaky black mess he couldn't see through.

Forty-five minutes passed before Evelyn who was leaning forward looking out the windshield in spite of the bouncing saw the valley that would carry them north again. "Can you see it, Lee?" she yelled over the wind. "It's off to the left."

"I see it," he replied as he looked out the windshield and hoped the valley had fewer obstacles than the one he was in. He moved to the right and prepared to make a wide turn. A sharp turn with the wind hitting the SUV would flip them over. He touched the brake once with his right foot to slow down the SUV just as he reached the turn and swung the SUV in a wide slow left turn.

The SUV made the turn as if he was turning from a four-lane street onto another four-lane street. As soon as he made the turn the powerful wind dropped to no more than a pushy wind. The valley was as narrow as the one they had left. Lee could see a stream forty or more feet ahead with tall trees and thick brush growing on both sides of it. Lee smiled when he saw they weren't the only living things in the valley. He didn't know if there was fish in the stream and didn't care since a fish dinner was the last thing on his mind. On both sides of the steam were deer, antelope, buffalo, and a small herd of horses. They looked at the intruders and back away from the stream.

"The sky seems to be clearing," Lyle said as he looked out the back window. "Hopefully the tornado is heading west or south."

"What are they doing here?" Evelyn asked when she saw the animals.

"Instinct told them this was a safe place from the storm," Lee said. "So it should be safe for us."

Evelyn got back on the laptop. "Lee, it's seven o'clock. We're still at least forty miles maybe more from the coordinates of that underground lab."

Lee dropped his speed to ten miles an hour and eased the SUV into the stream, hoping it was just what it appeared to be a flat stream with no hidden deep spots they couldn't drive out of if they drove into one. He moved close to the right side, east, where the trees were thicker and were growing over the stream casting morning shadows on the sparkling waters.

"We should look for a hiding place," Lyle suggested.

"Let's hope these trees provide us with some cover," Lee said. "Because at the moment, Lyle, there is no such thing as a place to hide."

Lyle's spirit dropped like a rock and his stomach felt like it had turned into a rock. He was more afraid than when Lee and Evelyn surprised him in his cabin. He didn't say anything because he knew Lee was right. There was no place to hide.

CHAPTER 54

7 a.m.

There was no reason for the five men to gather in the main computer room of the underground complex. Whatever Troy got on his screen from the passing satellite they could see on the wall screens in the studies of their apartments. The constant presence of each other since June first had put their nerves on edge, and gave each of them a strong dislike of being together. In the last five hundred and sixteen years the only time they had spent so much time together was when they were in their late nineties and in the lab waiting to be cloned into new people.

After they were cloned, and they were never cloned at the same time. They were each cloned a few years apart. Someone in the news media would have found it odd that five wealthy and politically influential men died at the same time. The world news media was filled with ambitious young people looking to further their careers with a story that would guarantee not only newspaper headlines but also the lead stories on the cable and TV news channels. The problem with a united world was there were no more stories of wars, uprisings, and civil unrest to guarantee ambitious news people a chance to further their careers with exciting stories of bloodshed and suffering. But thank heaven there were still natural disasters and crime among the rich and beautiful people that still got headlines and lead stories on the cable and TV news reports.

Paul was always cloned first making him six years older than the last one cloned. That was always Bruce. He didn't complain because it gave him a few extra years of life in his old body and the chance to see and hear how the world would react to the deaths of the other four. The others always learned of the world's reaction to their deaths after they were cloned. And since they had always made it a point to avoid publicity, since their first cloning, few people among the general population knew them or cared whether they were alive or dead. As for the rich and politically powerful, they didn't care what happened to them either as long as they made money from their business deals with the five or kept receiving the fat campaign contributions that got them reelected from the five's estates.

Once they were cloned their former bodies would be returned to their homes by loyal clones where the bodies were found the next morning by a servant. A doctor would be summoned, an examination made, and it would be announced by their doctors or lawyers they had died of natural causes in their late nineties or early hundreds.

The problem was with their estates. A relative no one knew about would come forward or be found by investigators hired by the executors of their estates in some isolated town in the back country on one of the continents and inherit their estates once blood relations through DNA had been established two or three years after their deaths. To avoid the suspicion that they were the same person, the clones never looked exactly their former selves. But there was enough physical resemblance to prove the heirs were related to the deceased. But the same knowledge and memories had been passed from clone to clone for over five hundred and sixteen years.

The world news media never paid any attention to these occurrences because by the time the inheritance had taken place the news media had lost all interest years ago.

Another reason was the plagues. They had always occurred a few years before they inherited their estates. The plague of 2907 had killed so many people no one cared who inherited the estates of the five. Ninety percent of the people in the world had lost a loved one, close relative, friend, or neighbor. That made it possible for them to inherit their estates in 3008 without another plague. The world population was still recovering from the plague of 2907 and wasn't interested in rich people inheriting estates worth hundreds of billions of dollars.

Paul sat in his study looking at the screen on the wall opposite his desk.

"The storm has prevented a clear view of the area around the complex for a hundred miles," Troy's monotone voice said over the computer screen in Paul's study. "It is still possible to detect through heat any humans in moving vehicles in the area since the electric engines produce heat."

"Have any been detected?" Larry asked from his study. The others heard the question.

"Just one, sir, at exactly seven a.m. It was an SUV moving through a narrow valley forty-seven miles southeast of the complex."

"Show it!" Bruce demanded from his study.

The recorded film of the SUV appeared on the screen. It was hard to see because it kept appearing and disappearing as the storm moved overhead.

"Clear up that picture," Larry ordered Troy.

"That is as clear as it can get, sir. The storm is extremely powerful and blowing dirt and other debris is clouding the picture."

"What color is it?" Paul asked calmly.

"Impossible to determine because it appears to have reflective panels on it that reflect the surrounding terrain."

"Camouflage," Steve said. "That's them alright. Lee would have the intelligence to use a vehicle to reflect the surrounding terrain.

You've used him in the past, Paul. Would he be smart enough to use an SUV that has camouflage abilities?"

"Seeing and hearing but not being seen or heard is one of his tactics," Paul said.

"We should send out our people to kill them now that we know where they are," Fred said.

"What type of storm is that?" Paul asked.

"A powerful wind storm that has developed into a tornado," Troy said.

"Is there rain?"

"A rain storm is following the tornado, sir. The tornado is moving in an erratic manner. The rain storm is moving east at speed of twelve miles an hour. It will be over this area by eight o'clock."

"Then we send out our trackers to find and kill them as soon as the tornado has passed," Fred said.

"I agree," Paul said. "They're in the valley to avoid the tornado. And they won't go very far even if that SUV is an all-terrain vehicle."

"Hopefully they'll be killed by the tornado," Steve said.

"Can we detect them if they should survive the tornado and get close?" Larry asked Troy.

"Yes sir. We have hidden detectors in the cameras on the surface that can detect all movement by animals or humans for a distance of fifty miles."

"Good," Bruce said. "By this time tomorrow we can all return to our normal lives."

"We should verify they are dead and we have any computer equipment they have with them before we leave," Fred said.

"Exactly," Larry said. "We want to make sure they are dead and not wandering around out there on the prairie trying to break into the lab."

"Don't worry," Fred assured Larry. "Our trackers will find their bodies and make sure they are dead. Finding any equipment they've brought with them should be easy."

"Notify me, Troy, when the tornado and storm have passed," Paul said before he turned off his computer and returned to his favorite Sunday morning cable show.

The other four men turned off their computers and went about their private business.

Petersen heard everything they said over his com-cell. He brought up a picture of what Troy had on the screen in the computer room he was working in. *Why are the people in that SUV so important to the five gentlemen?*

CHAPTER 55

7:15 p.m.

"Think they've seen us?" Lyle asked Lee and Evelyn. He was afraid.

"Yes," Evelyn said. "I'm hoping they won't send out their killers until after this tornado and storm passes."

"Where does this stream go, Evelyn?" Lee asked her. They had run out of trees and were driving through the stream with nothing to hide them but the dark clouds of the tornado and tall grass on both sides of the stream. But those wouldn't stop the powerful lenses of the satellite from seeing them. And if the satellite saw them the five saw them.

Evelyn looked at the laptop. "It dead-ends in a small lake in a boxed canyon five miles ahead of us. After that we have two choices. Stay in the canyon and wait till the tornado and storm passes, or take our chances out in the open."

"Chances?" Lee asked her. "Like we got any?"

"None," Lyle said in voice filled with the sound of failure.

"Don't give up until you're dead, Lyle," Lee told him hoping to boost his spirit.

"What the hell," Lyle said. "If we're going to die, we might as well make those bastards work hard at killing us. Let's get out of this valley and head for that lab regardless of the weather."

Evelyn looked at him and smiled and said, "I'm with you, Lyle. Let's make the bastards work."

Lee looked to the left and right and decided the left side was the easiest way out of the valley. "Get ready. I'm leaving this valley." He turned the SUV to the right when he saw a slope he knew the SUV could climb. Then turned left again and headed directly for the slope. He floored the accelerator forcing the electric engine to produce all the power it could produce.

The SUV hit the slope, bounced once, and began a rapid climb out of the valley as the tires dug into the wet grass and dirt. As soon as it reached the top, Lee turned the steering wheel to the right so the wind could hit it on the right side. And the wind did just that rocking the SUV from side to side like it was a child playing with a swing.

"Head north, Lee," Evelyn said as she looked at the laptop. "We're less than forty miles from the lab. Maybe this wind will help us out a little. It's coming out of the south."

"That's where I'm heading," he told her.

Lyle turned around and looked out the back window. He could see the tornado a mile away moving east. "The tornado is moving east away from us."

The sound of rat-tat-tat filled the SUV as the rain blowing east horizontally hit the left side of the SUV.

"Glad we're not out in that," Lee said. "It would knock us down."

"I just thought of something," Lyle said still looking out the back window.

"What?" Lee asked him.

"There are probably detectors of some sort on the top of that lab. The kind we won't be able to see because they'll look like the surrounding terrain." He turned to face the front.

"Cameras hidden among the tall grass designed to look like grass. Probably simple antennae that move with the wind and can detect everything that moves human or animal for miles around," Evelyn said.

"That means they now have us on their screens, and don't need the satellite" Lee said in a gloomy voice. The rain was coming down so heavy he had to turn on the windshield wipers to be able to see. "The damn thing is probably east of us anyway."

Evelyn and Lyle said nothing. There was nothing to be said. They all knew what they were heading into. A battle with obedient clones they couldn't win in a straight forward fight.

The SUV was doing sixty miles but the wind and rain made it feel like they were going only twenty miles an hour. They rode in silence for an hour.

"We're less than twelve miles away," Evelyn said as she looked at the map on Lyle's laptop.

Lee thought of using the detectors in the SUV to see if he could detect anyone approaching them, but decided against it. The five's clone computer experts would detect his scan, and pinpoint their position. For the first time in his life, he felt like he had failed his children and himself.

A strong wind slammed into the back of the SUV and pushed it forward thirty or more feet.

Lyle turned around and looked out the back window. "The tornado has changed direction and moving directly toward us."

Lee looked in the rearview mirror and saw the tornado and decided what the hell things can't get any worse. He pushed the accelerator to the floor and the SUV shot forward leaving the tornado behind.

For twenty minutes the SUV bounced over every obstacle in the way, and thank God none were higher that a few inches off the ground.

"How close?" Lee asked Evelyn.

She looked at the map on the laptop screen and said. "It's less than eight miles to the west."

The tornado suddenly picked up speed and headed directly toward the SUV.

"It's coming directly at us," Lyle said.

The tornado suddenly took a sharp right east and raced pass them as if they were standing still.

"It's moving off to the east," Lyle said.

"Are there any gullies around here, Evelyn?" Lee asked her.

"No. We're on a plateau. There's a drop off about a mile in front of us."

"Shit!" Lee cursed as he headed north keeping the petal to the floor and pushing the SUV for all the energy it had. The rain has reduced his vision even with the windshield wipers working at top speed to ten feet beyond the hood.

It was dark enough outside to be twilight.

"It's coming back toward us," Lyle said, watching the tornado.

"That damn tornado acts as if we've done something to it," Evelyn said, turning around and looking out the back window just in time to see the tornado moving toward the SUV.

"How close is it to us?" Lee asked.

Lyle didn't have to tell Lee the tornado was on them. He felt the powerful winds of the tornado sweep under the SUV and pick it up like it was leaf and push it forward. Lee didn't look left or right or back. There was no need to since he'd lost control of the SUV to the tornado. He saw the edge of the plateau rushing toward them like it was moving. For a moment he didn't know what to do then he slammed his right foot down on the brake. The SUV actually slowed down even with the tornado carrying it. The SUV dropped to the ground like a rock, bounced three times on its large, wide tires and went over the edge of the plateau carried by the winds of the tornado.

For a few seconds it floated in the air and everything inside the SUV that wasn't tied down floated, too. The equipment in the back of the SUV floated to the ceiling like they were in space and then suddenly dropped with a bang on the floor of the SUV. If they hadn't been wearing seat belts, they would have floated and dropped too.

Lee didn't know how high the plateau was but he soon found out as the winds of the tornado released it and the SUV dropped like a rock to the ground below. The impact was jarring and the SUV rolled ahead for a yard then flipped over on its right side like a great beast that had just given up the fight for its life and died.

"What do we do?" Evelyn screamed.

The tornado sounded like a giant train rushing down upon them.

"Get out and find some shelter," Lyle yelled back.

"Where's that?" she asked him with a scream "Over there," Lee said, looking through the windshield which hadn't cracked.

"Looks like a cave about twenty or more feet away." He unbuckled his seatbelt and felt into the passenger's seat then struggled up on his feet standing on the passenger door.

"Can we get out?" Lyle asked as he reached for the buckle of his seat belt. He touched it but didn't unsnap it because he knew he'd fall on Evelyn if he did. "Unsnap your seatbelt, Evelyn, and crawled forward before I undo mine."

Evelyn unsnapped her seatbelt and fell off to the right on the door, and with some effort got to her feet.

"Grab the backpacks in the back, Evelyn, if you can." Lee told her as he unlocked the driver's door and pushed against it with all his strength. The door felt like it weighted a ton and he wasn't as strong as he used to be twenty years ago.

Evelyn turned around and crawled over the back seat to the back of the SUV and grabbed her and Lee's backpacks and tossed them over the seat next to Lyle who was still strapped into his seat.

Lee managed to get the door open with a tremendous amount of effort and pushed it back till the hinges locked it into the open position. He kept his right hand on the door to make sure the wind didn't blow it shut. He was surprised to find out the wind was holding the door opened. But he still kept his hand against it just in case the wind changed direction and pulled the door shut. He looked around and saw a cave off to their left behind them.

Evelyn climbed back over the seatback and tossed the two backpacks over the passenger seat to the dashboard. Then she crawled over the seat and stood next to Lee.

"Unsnap your seatbelt, Lyle," she yelled at him over the sound of the howling wind.

Lyle did so and fell on the right window. He got to his feet within seconds and picked up his laptop from the floor, it didn't appear damaged, and quickly shoved it into its carrying case.

Lee climbed out of the SUV onto the rear passenger's door and reached down for the backpacks Evelyn was holding up to him. He grabbed them one at a time and dropped them on the side of SUV then reached down and pulled Evelyn up onto the edge of the roof. "Run for that cave behind us," he told her.

The rain was coming at them like watery hail and stinging their faces and hands.

She slid over the windshield and dropped down on the ground and ran around to the left side of the SUV and grabbed both backpacks off the side of the SUV and ran for the cave using the backpacks to protect her face from the wind-blown rain drops.

Lee helped Lyle out and told him where to go.

Lyle slid pass Lee onto the ground and ran for the cave. He used his laptop to protect the left side of his face from the rain coming out of the west.

Lee jumped down and followed him holding his left hand and arm up to protect his face from the stinging rain. Once he got inside the cave he turned around and looked at the SUV. Beyond it he could see the tornado moving once more toward the disable vehicle like it was a dead animal the tornado wanted to tear apart.

"Get farther back in the cave," he told Lyle and Evelyn as he turned to follow them. He stopped and turned around in time to see the tornado grab the SUV and lift it high in the air like it was a helpless animal and take off heading east. Lee felt bad as he watched. The SUV was good sturdy reliable vehicle, though old, and would be missed now that they were on foot. He turned and walked into the cave, glad to be alive, and sorry at the loss of the SUV.

They walked back into the dark cave not caring whether there was already an occupant in the cave. All they wanted to do was get away from that tornado and the stinging rain. Farther back in the cave they dropped to the floor and said silent prayers of thanks to God.

Evelyn used one of the two backpacks as a pillow and stretched out on the floor.

Lyle did the same.

Lee just leaned back against the wall and was glad he wasn't leaning against some pointy, sharp rock. He closed his eyes and within a few seconds he had drifted off to a sound dreamless sleep.

CHAPTER 56

June 10, 7:45 a.m. Sunday

The passing satellite had picked up the SUV for a few minutes just before the satellite passed on and the SUV was no longer within range of its powerful telescopic lenses.

Troy had notified all of them when he saw the SUV flying through the air ten minutes ago. And they had all rushed to the main computer room on level one even though they could have seen everything Troy had seen and recorded on the wall screens in their studies.

"This is an accurate recording?" Paul asked in concerned voice. He was hoping they weren't watching some long abandoned SUV being carried by the tornado.

"Yes, sir," Troy said.

"How do you know?" Steve demanded. He was standing next to Paul looking at the long, wide screen with a look of hope on his face.

"This recording was made at seven-twenty yesterday evening, sir. I compared it to the recording of the SUV moving through the valley forty-seven miles southeast of here ten minutes before this recording. It is the same one. It even possesses the same reflecting panels that act as camouflage."

"Did you get a license plate number on the one in the valley?" Larry asked him. He was standing to the left of Steve.

"No, sir, the satellite couldn't scan the back or front of the vehicle because it was looking straight down at it. All it saw was the roof and the hood."

"Back up the recording and magnify," Bruce told him. He was on the left end next to Fred who stood next to Larry.

Troy did as he was told.

"Why do that?" Fred asked.

"If those three were in that SUV with the doors open like that they would have been thrown out," he answered. "Even wearing seatbelts wouldn't have stopped the force of that tornado from pulling them out."

"What was the force of the tornado, Troy?" Paul asked him.

"The winds were moving at a speed of one hundred six miles an hour, sir."

"Such winds would not only have pulled them out of the SUV, but the force of their bodies against those seat belts would have killed them, or at least cause them sever injuries," Bruce said.

"And without medical help they would all die within minutes," Paul said.

The five of them watched silently as the tornado ripped open the doors of the SUV and flung everything in it that wasn't bolted down out into the swirling winds of the tornado.

"I saw no bodies," Bruce said. "When did you record this?"

"Both recordings were made yesterday, sir as the satellite passed overhead."

"Why weren't we notified then?" Bruce asked him.

"Because the computer didn't make the comparisons until ten minutes before I notified all of you, sir."

Troy's explanation was an intelligent one and they didn't complain.

"You think they could have gotten out of that SUV alive?" he asked Troy.

"I do not know, sir."

"In winds of a hundred and six miles an hour?" Paul asked. "Even if they had managed to get out of the vehicle the wind would have picked them up and carried them away and eventually flung their bodies out to slam into the ground or some object that would have killed them instantly. Look at what that wind did to the SUV, no human or animal could survive winds of that force."

Larry started to laugh.

"Is that laughter of success, Larry?" Steve asked him.

"What we couldn't do Mother Nature has done for us," he replied. "Our problem has been solved."

"I agree with you, Larry," Paul said, feeling happy for the first time in days. "Where we failed Mother Nature has succeeded. But it would be prudent to send out our people to look for their bodies after the storm has passed."

"Of course," Larry agreed as he turned toward the door, but he didn't start walking because he turned toward the others. "But for the moment I suggest we all go back to our quarters and get some sleep. This matter has done a lot to deprive us of sleep."

"I agree," Steve said with a broad smile on his face. "Our problem has been solved, and I for one would like a good country breakfast and another six hours of sleep."

Larry turned back toward Troy and asked, "How long before the storm passes?"

"Weather reports indicate that by noon there will be clear skies, sir," Troy answered.

"Shall we gather here at noon, gentlemen, or wait till after lunch?" Paul asked them. For the first time since June first his voice had a friendly sound to it.

"Before lunch would be better," Fred said. "That way we can eat lunch and discuss what we intend doing when we get home."

"Good idea, Fred," Bruce said.

"Troy," Larry said. "Have the cameras with the detectors in them on the surface scan in all directions. Make sure they're on maximum range, and look for anything that might indicate a human presence."

"Yes, sir."

Larry was the first to leave the main computer room. The others followed him in various moods of happiness. For the first time in ten days they engaged in idle small talk with each other about their lives back home. They took the second of the three elevators to the accommodation floor and separated as they each walked to the electric carts that had brought them to the elevators and went to their separate apartments.

Petersen had heard everything they said, but didn't care because he was in his private apartment reading an adventure novel. He knew a scan of the area for fifty miles wouldn't reveal any human presence because the horseback riding people were intelligent enough not to be away from their village during a tornado. A thought passed through his mind to check the stairwell outside the missile silo, but he dismissed it as unimportant. Because no one could survive being in a tornado. But he did wonder if the people in the SUV were the people the five had talked about arriving the first day they arrived at the complex.

CHAPTER 57

4:30 p.m.

The cave they were in was slanted down and outward making the part of the cave they were in dry. Any water from the rain storm that had accompanied and followed the tornado that had managed to get into the opening of the cave hadn't gotten into the part they were in and had quickly flowed out. They slept, and all three of them were exhausted, in a dry cave with only the dying sounds of the dissipating tornado and the pitter patter sound of the rain in the rain storm making it into the cave. Hungry awoke them.

"I'm hungry," Lee said. He had slid to the floor on his right side and in his sleep had turned over on his back. He had been awake for only a minute.

"Me, too," Evelyn said. She was lying on her left side with the backpack still under her head. She had been awake for half an hour, but hadn't moved because she was still resting. Getting out of the SUV and into the cave had taken a lot of her energy.

Lyle, lying on his back with the other backpack under his head, snorted twice and opened his eyes. He blinked his eyes twice before he spoke. "I can't see a damn thing."

"We're in a cave, remember," Lee told him.

"Oh, yes, I do," he said as he sat up and stretched. "Oh, God, did I sleep."

"We all did after fighting that tornado."

"There's food in the SUV," Lyle said as he started to stand up. His legs were still asleep and it took him a minute to wake them up.

"Forget about it," Lee told him. "I saw the tornado pick up the SUV and carry it away just before I ran back into this cave."

Evelyn sat up and got to her feet and stretched. She turned toward the opening of the cave and said, "I see light."

Lee stood up saying, "I doubt if the sun's set." He raised his right arm and pushed the light button on his Timex watch. "Four thirty-one. We've been asleep for over eight hours."

"Sleep we desperately needed," Evelyn said as she started moving toward the opening of the cave.

"Be careful," Lee warned her. "We're close to that underground lab."

"I remember," she said as she walked to the edge of the cave and stopped and looked out at a beautiful blue cloudless sky. She gave a sigh of relief thankful that she was still alive and free in spite of her growling empty stomach. She thought a cup of hot black coffee with a teaspoon of sugar would be just the thing she needed, and she knew she had no chance of getting one. *A drink of water would do just as well,* she thought and looked out at the terrain. All she saw was endless grass a few short prairie trees and rolling hills. *Not a stream of water for miles I bet.* She looked down at her feet expecting to see mud and noticed she was standing on flat hard, smooth ground. She found that curious.

"What do you see?" Lyle asked as he walked up to her and stopped by her side.

"Flat ground," she said.

"What?" Lee asked as he walked up to Lyle's left side and stopped.

She turned around and looked at the ground behind her she could see. "It's flat and hard."

"That's usual for ground in most places, Evelyn," Lee told her.

"I don't think this is a cave, at least not a natural cave," she said as she looked at the ground. "The ground is too flat and there's a diamond pattern cut into it like for traction."

"I wondered as we were running for the cave would there be any animals in here taking shelter from the storm," Lyle said.

Lee instinctive turned to his right and looked at the wall. It was smooth except for a few small cracks. He walked over to it and touched it with his left hand. "This wall is smooth. Check the other wall, Lyle."

Lyle walked over to the wall to his left and looked at it for a second before he touched it with both his hands. "This one is smooth, too like something cut through it."

"This isn't a natural cave, Lee," Evelyn said.

"No, it isn't," he agreed. "That's why there were no animals in it. They avoid this place even in a storm. This cave is man-made. And this isn't concrete, it's stone. Only an industrial laser could cut stone as smooth as this. Let's get the backpacks there should be a flashlight in both of them." He turned and walked back into the cave and found the first backpack, opened it, and took out a flashlight. He turned it on and shined it on the walls of the cave and the floor. "There are groves cut in the floor next to the walls for drainage and the floor is slighted slanted toward the opening. Plus the floor is arched just a bit to prevent water from gathering in the center."

"That would weaken the floor over a period of time if it wasn't removed even if it's stone," Lyle said. He had walked back into the cave and stood next to Lee. "Have you notice also the cave has a slight right turn to it."

"That's why the daylight didn't wake us after the storm passed," Evelyn said as she walked back toward them.

"How far were we from the coordinates of that underground lab?" Lee asked her.

"Where's the laptop?" she asked.

Lee scanned the floor with the flashlight till he found it lying next to the backpack Lyle had slept on. "There. Hope it isn't broke. It took quite a beating in the SUV when that tornado grabbed us."

"It's old but it's well built," Lyle said as Evelyn knelt down, picked up the case it was in. She removed it from the case, sat it on the ground, opened it, and turned it on.

"He's right," Evelyn said. "It's still good to go. And the map of this area is still on it." She looked at the coordinate numbers on the screen. "According to the laptop, gents, we're a mile east of the coordinates for that underground lab."

"Then something is wrong, or we're damn lucky," Lyle said.

Lee looked at him. He could see his face in the glow of the flashlight. "You're right. If they had known we were here we'd be in custody. And any detectors or sensors they've got on top of that lab wouldn't have been damaged by the storm. They would have been withdrawn into the ground, and they would have picked us up and alerted them. That storm must have passed us hours ago."

They stared at each other for a few seconds before Evelyn said, "There are no sensors in this cave if it's a part of the lab."

"Maybe they don't know it's here," Lyle said then quickly added. "No that's stupid. After five hundred years they'd know everything about this country for five hundred miles in all directions. What's on top and what's underground."

"Then tell me why we're not in custody or dead?" Lee asked him.

Lyle thought for a few seconds, shrugged, and said, "Maybe this cave really has no sensors in it."

"Turn off that laptop, Evelyn, they might be able to detect its electric output," Lee said. "If they don't know this cave is here and we're in it, no sense in informing them."

Evelyn closed the laptop shutting it down, put it back in its carrying case, and stood up and looked around. "I'll bet the walls of this cave are too thick for them to detect any electrical output, Lee. Let's look around this cave."

Lyle got the other flashlight out of the other backpack.

"Let's stick together while we look around," Lyle suggested. He patted his stomach and felt the semiautomatic still in his belt. "I've still got my gun."

"Me, too," Lee said, feeling the weight of the weapon stuck in his belt on his right hip. "What about you, Evelyn?"

"I've got mine," she said as she looked around the dark cave. The light from Lee's flashlight provided her with just enough light to see the walls. She looked up at the ceiling. "This definitely isn't a natural cave because the ceiling is flat and free of stalactites, and there are no spider webs or dust strings."

"Something keeps this man-made cave clean," Lyle said. "Because if it hasn't been used in years' dirt would have blown into it over the years and fungi would be growing on the floor."

"Let's see what's at the end of it," Lee said as he shined his flashlight down the dark cave and started walking back into the cave.

It took them less than thirty seconds to discover the steel door twelve feet away at the end of the cave. They stood in front of it looking at it.

"Looks to be in good shape," Evelyn said.

"And very large, too," Lyle said.

"This underground complex was built back in the nineteen seventies for defense purposes," Lee said. "This whole cave and this door wouldn't look this good after a thousand years not with all the moisture that falls on this plain every year. The opening to this cave should have been blocked with thick brush and maybe even a few of those prairie trees, this steel door would have turned into a pile of red rust, and there should be all sorts of insects in here and spider webs everywhere, but there aren't. There aren't even any bat droppings on the floor and they always seek caves to nest in."

"No, there isn't," Lyle said, looking at the ground. "With exception of the opening of the cave there isn't even any dirt on the floor. That says this place gets regular weekly care."

Lee and Evelyn didn't say anything.

"So, what should we do?" Lyle asked them.

"Do we have choices?" Evelyn asked him.

"No, we don't," he replied.

CHAPTER 58

"We've still got our weapons," Lee said as he reached for his electric semiautomatic.

"Yes, we do, Lee," Lyly said, touching the semiautomatic in his belt.

"I've got mine," Evelyn said as she bent over and picked up the case the laptop was in and looped the strap of the case over her head and pushed it to her left rear.

"Well, let's see what's on the other side of this door." Lee reached for the handle and moved it down without hearing any squeaking sound. The door didn't move.

"Push it," Evelyn said.

Lee pushed and the heavy steel door easily opened an inch. He was surprised when the door moved without a sound.

Lyle shined his flashlight on the three hinges of the door. "Those are hydraulic hinges. They're made to hold a lot of weight. This door must weight a ton or more."

"It's at least ten feet high and half that wide," Evelyn said, looking at it.

"And at least a foot thick," Lyle said as he looked at the edge of the door.

"You were right about this cave getting weekly care, Lyle," Lee said as he leaned forward and examined the hinges and sniffed. "There is the smell of some lubricant on these hinges."

"Well, we got the door open," Evelyn said. "We might as well go inside."

Lee pushed on the handle and the door silently opened to the right, and lights went on inside the room behind the door.

Lee dropped to the floor like a rock, pulling his weapon out of his belt, and pointing it forward to start shooting.

Lyle ducked to the right pulling his weapon out of his belt and up to point in the direction Lee's was pointing.

Evelyn moved to the left pulling her weapon out of her right jacket pocket and pointing it inside the room.

Petersen may have been a clone, but his body still required food and liquids. He put a plastic book mark, he had learned over the centuries they lasted longer than paper book marks, and could be used for years before they became worn and had to be recycled. He stood up and walked toward the dining room in his apartment where one of the clone chefs had left his dinner on the dining room table a minute ago. Just as he walked out of his study a message flashed on the screen on the wall facing his desk.

'The cave door to the silo has been opened.'

After ten seconds it went out and the screen became blank again. It was the first time such a message had appeared on the screen. Four hundred years ago the silo and its contents had been renovated and improved by the five for emergency purposes. No emergency had ever arisen for its use and the five had forgotten about the silo and its contents.

They remained in their ready positions for a minute.

"Maybe opening the door turned on the lights?" Evelyn whispered to Lee and Lyle.

Ten seconds passed before Lyle spoke. "Yeah, the lights come on automatically when the door is opened."

"I go first," Lee said as he got up. He hesitated for a second then realized he'd taught himself for years never to hesitate in a dangerous situation. He walked into the room and stopped on a steel platform. "There are stairs here. They lead down. You two wait until I call you." He started down the steps cautiously. His muscles were tight and he was ready to start shooting the moment he saw someone, or one of the five. He stopped and stared at what he saw in the center of the silo when he reached the bottom of the stairs. *What the hell.* Was the only thing he thought as he stared at the sight that greeted him. After ten seconds he turned around and said to Evelyn and Lyle. "Come on down and bring the backpacks. You two aren't going to believe what's here."

A few seconds passed before Lyle started down first with one of the backpacks on his back followed by Evelyn moving just as cautiously as Lee carrying a backpack. When he reached the bottom of the stairs, he stopped and looked at what Lee was looking at.

Evelyn, behind him, asked as she looked at the strange object. "What the hell is that?"

"I think it's one of those twentieth century missiles," Lee said as he looked up at it.

"We're on a catwalk," Lyle said as he turned his attention to where he was standing. "And it goes around this missile thing."

Evelyn walked to the railing around the catwalk and said, "This walk must be over a hundred feet in circumference." "It goes around this missile," Lyle said. He looked back at the missile. "That missile, if that is what it is, must be thirty feet around."

"How tall is that thing?" Evelyn asked as she looked up at the tip of the missile then down at the bottom of the silo.

"Must be eighty or ninety feet," Lyle said, leaning over the railing and looking at the bottom of the silo. "This silo must be a hundred feet high because the missile doesn't reach the top, and we must be at least fifty feet from the bottom."

"There's a round stone covering at the top of this silo," Evelyn said as she looked beyond the tip of the missile to the covering. "And it looks to be pretty thick."

"Why is it here?" Lee asked as he started to walk to his left on the catwalk around the missile.

Evelyn followed him. "Notice this silo is just like that cave. Clean. There's not a speck of dust or dirt on anything. Even with that door closed if no one was taking care of it there should be dust on everything. It's like that missile was built this week and put in this silo yesterday." She looked down at the catwalk. "Even this catwalk is in excellent condition. Look at how the metal has that new look to it."

"Well, it isn't new," Lee said.

Lyle had gone in the opposite direction. "There's a big steel door here," he said.

Lee and Evelyn walked over to where he stood.

"Think we should open it? Notice the hinges are the same as on that other door and on this side."

"We're in a position, Lyle, where the only way we're going to get out of it is to open doors," Lee reached down for the heavy metal handle and pushed it down and pulled back. The door didn't move. Lee, holding the handle down, pushed it.

The door opened just as silently as the other one.

Fluorescence ceiling lights came on lighting the hallway beyond it. They saw another steel door at the end of the hallway.

"What do you think?" Lyle asked them.

"Might as well," Evelyn said. "We've got nowhere else to go."

Lyle led the way down the hallway. He opened the door at the end, which opened inward and just as silently as the other too, and walked into a circular room with two leather chairs sitting in front of two control panels on two desks on walls ninety degrees apart. On the wall in front of both desks was a series of six lights. With the words 'start count down' 'open silo' and 'launch weapon' next to each of the three top lights. The other three lights near the bottom had the words 'test' 'check' and 'test completed' near each light. Above the lights on the walls were maps of the world showing it from the north-pole behind a sheet of glass. On the Asian continent was a red dot with the word 'target' written next to it next to a city on the map.

Everything in the room was clean.

Evelyn walked over to one of the control panels and read what was written on them. "Titan ICBM launch control," she said.

Lee walked to one of the chairs, pulled it from under the desk, and sat down. He was surprised in didn't collapse under his weight, and it still had the soft feeling of a chair recently bought. He looked at the control panel on the desk in front of him and said, "We've come upon an antique that has been well preserved."

"We have?" Lyle said.

"Yes, we have, Lyle," he said. "That missile is a part of the twentieth century MAD defense system of the old United States of America, and this is where the missile was launched from."

"What does ICBM mean?" Evelyn asked.

"Intercontinental Ballistic Missile," Lee said. "And this map shows its destination. That place on the map marked target was the city that was supposed to be destroy with an atomic bomb."

"That missile in that silo flew around continents?" Lyle asked.

"No, it flew to the target marked on this map on the Asian Continent," Lee said as he looked up at the map. "And it flew over the north pole."

"Why over the north pole?" Evelyn asked him.

"It was the shortest route to its target," Lee answered.

"So who's been keeping this place is such a pristine condition?" Lyle asked.

"The clones who work for the five who want us dead and their information back."

'It doesn't make sense," Lyle said. "Even if that missile can still be launched it wouldn't hit anything because it would be detected by the World Security Forces and blown out of the sky by a laser weapon before it got twenty thousand feet in the sky."

"The World Security Forces have laser weapons?" Evelyn asked.

"I guess they do," Lyle shrugged as he spoke.

"Unless it has something in it like a computer with a firewall that could stop it from being detected, or at least electrically confuse any laser weapons pointed at it," Evelyn said.

Lee nodded his agreement. "Whatever it's for the five don't know we're here because we're not being attacked. And that means we still got a chance, a slight chance I grant you, of succeeding."

Evelyn looked around the room and said, "People were assigned here to wait a launch order over those control panels."

"Yes," Lee agreed.

"From who?" she asked.

"I don't know," Lee said. "Some general, I suppose."

"So there should be a bathroom around here with running water."

"How can you be so sure?" Lyle asked her.

"Because everything in this silo is clean and probably operational, and that means a bathroom with running water." She turned around looking for a door. She saw one and walked to it. "And people, even those waiting to kill others on another continent, need a bathroom."

"Maybe there's a way to get into the servers of the underground lab from these control panels," Lee told them.

"I was right," she exclaimed after she'd opened the door and looked into the room behind it. "There's a bathroom here. It even has a shower."

"Oh great, we can clean up before we attack," Lyle said in a sarcastic voice.

Evelyn walked into the bathroom and over to the face bowl and turned on the faucet that had an H on top of it. "Hot water, too." She looked in the direction of the toilet. "And there's toilet tissue."

Lee turned from the desk and looked around the room. *Why would someone maintain this room as if it was to be occupied?* He stopped when he saw an intercom box with a numbered pad underneath it. "Evelyn, come here."

She walked out of the bathroom with what could pass for a smile on her face considering their position.

"Can you get into that and from there into the servers in this place?" he asked pointing to the intercom box.

She walked over to the intercom box and looked it over. "This is a twentieth century intercom box with a numbered pad for dialing the specific box you want. This thing is primitive."

"Can you get into a server from there?"

"Well, it operates on the same basic principal of modern day com-cells, and if it's connected to the electrical system of that underground lab, I don't see why not? But I'm not making any promises."

Lee looked at his watch then turned around and looked up at the wall behind him.

There was a plain round face white military clock with twenty-four black numbers on it and the red second hand was moving. "That clock is working and it says five twenty-five. That's sixteen hundred hours and twenty-five minutes according to the clock. And it's accurate."

"It could be battery operated, Lee," Lyle said.

Lee stood up and walked over to the desk and leaned on it with both hands to see if it could hold his weight. It felt strong enough. He climbed up on the desk and pulled the bottom of the clock an inch from the wall and looked under it. "There's a wire going from it into the wall."

"I'm not surprised," Lyle said. "Everything in this silo is ancient and working like it's all new."

"Can we eat before I start?" Evelyn said. "I get nervous when I'm hungry and we haven't eaten in more than twenty-four hours."

"Open up those backpacks, Lyle. There should be some energy fruit bars inside both of them and a few packs of instant coffee," Lee told him as he got down off the desk. "Run a basic check on that intercom box, Evelyn, while I see if that hot water in that bathroom gets hot enough for a decent cup of coffee."

"Give me one of those com-cells you took off those two tracker/killers you killed, Lee," she said. "I'll bet there's a number in them for the lab."

Lee reached into one of the backpacks and took out one of the com-cells and walked over to Evelyn and handed it to her.

She turned it on and brought up the directory on it. "There're only two numbers in the directory. And both have five letters and five numbers mixed together."

"That's a ten-digit code," Lyle told her.

"Get busy on the coffee, Lee," she said as she put the com-cell in her pocket and pulled the cover off the intercom box and located the two wires that transmitted and received information. She took the com-cell out of her pocket and removed its cover and connected the two wires to its processor. She worked quietly for ten minutes before she said, "This intercom box is connected to the wiring system of the lab. And that's probably connected to any servers in the lab. Now I need to use the laptop to see if I'm right."

"And if you are?" Lee asked her from the bathroom where he was running the hot water.

"Then I can get into their servers."

"And the battle begins," Lyle said.

"After coffee and energy bars," Lee added.

CHAPTER 59

6:34 p.m. Sunday

Lee's thorough search of the three small rooms inside silo control room had revealed a small pantry with plastic covered food in it that was a thousand and one hundred years old and was dust in the original shape of the food because not a breeze had disturbed it. Another room contained two single beds and a nightstand between them. All were perfectly preserved, but dusty, because moisture and wind had not been able to get to them. The third room was a kitchen with an electric hot plate, a table with four chairs, and an electric coffee pot that still worked, and four cups.

Lee used the coffee pot to make coffee for the three of them after he had rinsed it out while Evelyn worked on getting into the servers with the laptop.

Lyle simply walked around the rooms shaking his head in a confused manner.

"Coffee's ready, Evelyn, Lyle," he said to her as he filled two cups for them.

She ignored him and continued working.

Lyle walked into the kitchen and picked up one of the cups. He took a sip of the coffee and said, "Its good, Lee."

"Thank you," Lee said as he walked out of the kitchen and over to Evelyn, looked over her shoulder, and asked, "How are you doing?"

"The trick to getting into a sophisticated server, Lee, is to do so without alerting the server' fire wall. And I'm sure this place has the best server with the best firewall money can buy. But all firewalls have a weakness."

Lee did say anything. He just stood over her watching her as she sat on the floor with her legs crossed typing on the laptop's keyboard.

"And that weakness is to prevent anyone from getting into the server without a specific password. The firewall has to scan all incoming messages to make sure they're not a virus sent by a hacker to break into the server, and that is its weakness. All I've got to do is convince the firewall that what I'm sending is just a normal incoming message, and I'm in the server." She raised her hands from the keyboard and watched the blank screen.

'Access permitted,' appeared on the screen in white letters.

"What did you do?" Lee asked her.

"I asked the server to run a check on the missile in the silo to make sure no damage had been done to it by the storm."

"Isn't that foolish," he exclaimed in a worried voice.

"No, Lee, it isn't foolish. This missile control room is connected to the server in the underground lab. The server monitors everything in the lab including this control room and that missile. Any message concerning this control room and the missile would be analyzed by the server to determine if it was an incoming virus. Once it analyzed the message was coming from this control room, it would allow the message into the server and respond."

"Has it?"

"Look at the screen."

'Wait for scan of missile and control room.' An empty rectangle appeared next to the message. A red mark appeared in the left side of the rectangle and quickly moved to the right side. 'Scan complete.'

Evelyn started typing again. "Download diagram of the underground complex onto this computer with all sensors displayed."

Two seconds passed before 'Download complete' appeared on the screen.

Evelyn then typed, "New code for this computer." She typed the word 'White602'."

"Are you in?"

"Wait a second."

'Accepted,' appeared on the screen.

Evelyn breathed a sigh of relief and said, "Now all we have to do is hope they don't run a check on codes in the server."

"If they do, your code is going to pop up and one of the five's computer clones is going to wonder who put the new code in the server."

"I wouldn't worry about a clone informing them of a new code in the server, or any of the servers if this place has more than one server," Lyly said. "Remember what I said about them lacking specific judgment?"

"Yes, I do," Lee said. "They don't have the ability to form opinions on their own."

"They can't wonder why a new code is in the server Evelyn put it in," Lyle said.

"So the clone won't tell one of the five about the new code?"

"Not unless they ask the clone if there's a new code in any of their servers, if this place has more than one server," he said. "If they do, the clone will answer the question truthfully."

"They'll know immediately we're here if they didn't order a new code put into the server," Evelyn said, closing the laptop and getting up. "Where's my energy bar and coffee?"

"On the desk over there," Lee said, pointing to it.

"And our mission is to expose them to the world," Lyle added. He was sitting at the other desk. "How does what you've done help us do that?"

"We'll know what the lab looks like," Lee said, following Evelyn to the desk.

Evelyn sat in the chair facing the desk and picked up the cup of coffee and took a large swallow. "That makes my stomach feel much better."

"Will one of you answer my question?" Lyle demanded.

"The answer is simple," Lee said. "We get into that lab and get into one of their computers and download everything we can get onto the Internet. Then get the hell of out here."

Lyle shook his head and mumbled, "What seemed so simple years ago has become extremely complicated and very dangerous."

"Let's go to the kitchen and sit at that table and take a good look at that diagram of the lab," Lee said as he picked up the laptop and walked toward the kitchen carrying it.

Half an hour later they had each eaten an energy bar and had a second cup of coffee and scanned every inch of the lab diagram on the laptop.

"There are six levels to the lab," Lee said, looking at the diagram on the laptop.

"The top level is where the computers and servers are located."

"How many servers are there?" Lyle asked him.

"Four," he said. "The second level has a lab in it and some sealed room, but nothing about what's in it or the lab. The third and fourth levels have accommodations, three libraries, four game rooms, and a gym. The fifth level is like a barracks with rooms and bathrooms for a hundred people, and a storage area like a pantry for food and drink, and a large kitchen. Level six is a garage with a generator room, storage rooms for weapons and more food and drink. But mostly it's a garage with a dozen heavily armored antique vehicles. Bathrooms were also scattered about on all six levels and clearly marked."

"Why those old armored looking cars?" Lyle asked.

"This place was built for a nuclear war," Evelyn said. "The original occupants would have wanted to defend it if it was attacked on the surface by ground forces."

"You think they still operate after a thousand years?"

"Yes, but only if their gasoline powered engines have been replaced with electric engines," Lee answered. "Just like I bet this missile control room is still capable of launching that missile?"

"But why and at whom," Lyle asked. "There are no more warring countries."

"Maybe those five men like to amuse themselves knowing they have an active missile," Evelyn said.

"I seriously doubt, Evelyn, if there's an active atomic bomb on top of that missile," Lyle told her.

"Maybe they just keep it to amuse themselves," Lee suggested. "No one knows about this place so why get rid of it?"

"But, Lee, this lab's been here over five hundred years. Who wants to keep a five-hundred-year old missile that's not worth anything except in a museum?"

"Notice how wide the tunnels are?" Lee said pointing to the tunnels displayed on the laptop diagram. "Wide enough for those armored cars to drive through. And there are three elevators at each corner of this complex and a large one at the north end of the complex and another large one at the south end, and both look large and strong enough to carry those armored cars to any level."

"So how do we get to the servers in that main computer room?" Lyle asked, staring at the diagram on his laptop as if the answer would appear by magic.

"There are six levels," Lee said. "The main computer room is at the top two hundred feet below the surface, and its computers and servers are probably connected to every sensor and detector in the entire lab and the control room and that missile."

"There are three hundred of those sensors scattered throughout the complex according to this diagram as well as cameras on the surface," Lyle said. "All placed where they overlap each other. Making it impossible to get pass one without alerting another. They must have picked us up when we were fifty miles away with the sensors, cameras, and detectors on the surface."

"But they also picked up the tornado and the storm," Lee said. "And if they picked us up they must have seen what that tornado did to the SUV. They probably accessed that satellite looking down and seen everything that happened."

"It would have been overhead when the tornado hit us. Visibility would have been terrible but they would have certainly seen enough to see what happened to the SUV," Evelyn said. "The question is did they see us get out of the SUV?

Lee looked around the kitchen and said, "We've been here a long time and we haven't been attacked."

"You think they believe we're dead?" Lyle asked her as he looked at her face.

"If they do they won't be interested in searching for us. And if they don't look for us we've got a slim chance of succeeding. But there's one other thing you two haven't considered," she said.

"What's that?" Lee asked her as he stared at the diagram on the laptop.

"That top level where the computers are is the most important room in this entire underground complex, because those computers control everything in this complex and the servers have all the codes and can access any computer in the complex."

"They'll send out their trackers to find our bodies, or something to indicate we're dead," Lee said. "We do have a chance but not much of one."

"So we get into that main computer room and see what information we can get on them being clones, and send it out to the world," Lyly said.

"The best place to start would be the sixth level," Lee said.

"Why there?" Lyle asked him.

"Because it's the best way to get into that top level." Lee pointed to tunnels under each level. "Those are probably access tunnels. The people who built this place probably ran their cables through those tunnels. Notice how they run under each level and connect at the end of each level in a tube and go up to the next level, and eventually to the top of the complex. And all the wires go to the same tube which is right next to the stairwell. That tube is not very wide, but wide enough for me to crawl through it. But first we'd need a diversion."

"Wait a minute, Lee," Evelyn said. "Look at those air ducts next to the elevators."

He looked at them. "What about them?"

"There are two on each side of the groups of three elevators next to the stairwells," she said.

"Yeah, I see them," he said.

"Notice they have ladders in them attached to the walls and a platform every fifty feet," she said.

"Yes," he said. "So?"

"All of them go all the way up to that top level, and there's a small door on each level that allows anyone in those ducts to get out on each level."

Lee looked at them and understood what she was getting at. "A long climb with rest stops, and better than crawling up a tube with cables in them."

"We could all go through one of them," Lyle said.

"Yeah, Evelyn, you're right," Lee said. "Those ducts would be the best way to reach the top level."

"So what kind of diversion do we need?" Evelyn asked him.

"Could you activate all the sensors so they'd all go off at the same time, Evelyn?"

"Easy." She was looking at the bottom of the third level. "The source of power for this complex is probably solar."

"Probably," Lee agreed.

"See that room at the sixth level labeled generator room in the far eastern corner, the one where an air duct goes all the way to the surface?"

"Yes what about it?"

"There's probably a small solar disk on the top of this complex that pops up once every few days to get solar energy. The energy is probably shot down into a generator through fiber optic cables in that generator room and then magnified to keep this complex going for days."

"With fiber optic cables running from it to every computer and sensor and detector in the place," Lyle said.

"That's the place to create a diversion. Find the main fiber optic cable that channels energy to where it's needed by the generator in that room and stick a reflective object in it. The alternating energy would continue to flow, but not in an even manner.

Every security system and computer in this place would start to malfunction."

"What type of reflective object?" Lee asked her.

"Fiber optic cables carry only electrons in the form of light," she told him. "All we'd need is something that would reflex the light back up or down. Something small like a polished safety pin or needle might do it."

"Or the blade of a knife?" he asked her.

"As long as it can reflex the light in the fiber optic cable."

Lee reached into his pants pocket and pulled out his pocket knife and opened the large blade. "Would this do?"

Evelyn looked at the shiny blade and said, "Perfect."

"When do we start?" Lyle asked them.

Lee looked at his watch. "It's eight now. I suggest we wait until midnight. By then the five will probably be asleep."

"If they think we're dead," Evelyn added.

CHAPTER 60

June 11, 2:30 p.m. Monday

"How long have our people been outside searching, Sam?" Paul asked him. He was standing behind Sam looking at the screen on the wall of the control room.

He had replaced Troy at noon. "Since the storm passed at nine-thirty in the morning, sir. Troy sent them out with instructions to look for bodies."

"And nothing has been found?"

"Only the SUV and the debris thrown from it."

"What type of debris?" Larry asked, sitting in the chair next to Sam.

"Can food, medical equipment, blankets, extra clothing, a suitcase, and bottles of water."

"Were there plates and a sticker on the SUV?"

"The windshield was gone, but the plates were intact."

"I suppose they were fakes?"

"Yes sir. The numbers were a collection of numbers than belonged to seven other SUVs in Asia, Africa, and New Zealand."

"But no bodies were found?" Steve asked from his position on the opposite side of the desk Sam was working at.

"No sir."

"How usual is it for bodies not to be found after a tornado has struck a village or town?" Fred asked. He was sitting on a couch against an opposite wall looking at the wall screen.

"Bodies of victims are always found under the wreckage of buildings, or within a mile of where the tornado struck," Sam said.

"There have never been cases where bodies were not found?" Steve asked him.

"I don't know, sir," Sam replied.

"We should find out if there have ever been cases where people disappeared in tornados," Bruce said.

"And where are we to look for such information, Bruce?" Larry asked him.

"The Federal Emergency Assistance Agency," Paul said. "Every nation in the world has such an agency to help people in case of natural disasters. And they all keep records going back centuries."

"Access that agency's computers here in the United States, Sam," Larry ordered him. "And find out if bodies have ever completely disappeared after a tornado."

"Yes, sir," Sam replied and started typing on the keyboard.

The five men waited silently while he accessed the information.

"There have been five instances in the last twelve years when bodies were not found after a tornado struck a village," Sam said.

"Maybe they were carried miles away and dumped someplace no one bothered to check?" Fred suggested.

"Have bodies ever been carried farther away than a mile?" Larry asked Sam.

"I will check, sir," Sam replied and started typing again. After a few minutes he spoke reading what was on the TV screen. "Tornado don't last very long, sir. Maybe twenty minutes at the most though twenty years ago one lasted thirty-three minutes and killed a hundred and seven people when it struck a large town in northern Mississippi. When they break apart they drop whatever is in them where they break up. There has been only one case recorded where a body was found six miles away a week after the tornado wrecked a home,"

"We would be foolish to assume this is one of those rare instances," Bruce said. He was standing next to Paul.

"How many people have we got out looking for their bodies?" Steve asked.

"Twenty, sir."

"How large an area are they searching around the complex?"

"Three miles."

"How many people are there in the complex?" Paul asked.

"Counting the laboratory workers thirty-nine, sir."

"How many lab workers are there?"

"Five including Dr. Petersen."

"Send out everyone who isn't a lab worker or working in the kitchen and expand the search area to include seven miles," Paul ordered him. "Make sure they are all wearing goggles that can identify a human body part."

"And equipment that can detect human DNA," Steve added.

"Yes, sir," Sam replied obediently and issued the order to the remaining clones that weren't lab workers or kitchen workers.

"How could they have possibly survived a tornado, Sam?" Fred asked.

"Many people over the centuries have been known to survive being caught in a tornado." Sam replied as he read the information from the screen. "Last year a five-year-old boy was picked up by a tornado in Asia and survived after being carried a quarter of a mile before the tornado broke up and dropped the boy."

"We must assume that Evelyn, Lee, and Lyle somehow got out of that SUV and found a hole in the ground to hide in," Paul said. "Until their bodies or parts of them have been found and identified by DNA as theirs then they are still alive and a threat to us."

"All our people are armed?" Larry asked Sam.

"Yes sir."

"It appears, gentlemen, we may be here a little longer than we had hoped this morning." Steve said.

"We can't go anywhere until those three are confirmed dead," Fred said.

"Make sure our people do a yard by yard search, Sam," Paul told him.

"They are doing that sir," he replied.

"Then I suggest we go to lunch, gentlemen, since we can't do anything but wait for a confirmation of their deaths by either the tornado or our people," Larry said.

They all silently left the top level feeling depressed, and hoping for the worse for Evelyn, Lee, and Lyle.

CHAPTER 61

12:01 a.m. Monday June 11

"You two ready?" Lyle asked Lee and Evelyn as he sat at the desk and checked his weapon.

Lee looked at him and smile as he said, "You've come a long way from being a clerk in the Department of Information, haven't you, Lyle?"

"I was never a clerk," he said. "I was a senior investigator and analyst making sure the information that crossed my desk was accurate. That's why I was capable of getting the information on those monsters, though I must admit I stumbled across it. I hid my actions behind my job requirements."

"We go out that door over there," Evelyn said, pointing to it on the diagram. "And go down the tunnel behind it until we get to a door security pad. When I've gotten into it, I can blind their sensors and detectors to our presence by telling them we're just lab personal."

"It's that easy?" Lee asked.

"Only if the lab personal are allowed to freely move about this complex."

"And if not," Lyle asked her.

"Then we fight our way to the main computer room and download what we've got on them and the location of this lab."

"Let's go," Lee said, standing up. His stomach wasn't empty after two energy bars and four cups of coffee, but the butterflies of fear he felt in it made it feel like it was empty. He kept his face hard looking to hide his fear.

"Aren't you scared?" Lyle asked him noticing his hard expression.

"Damn right I am," he said in a voice he hoped was devoid of fear, but he knew it wasn't. "All I can think of is what will happen to my children if we fail."

"You're not alone in thinking that," Evelyn told him. She handed him one of the two com-cells he'd taken from the two trackers he'd killed. "This isn't going to be much help, but we'll be able to check our location with them. I've downloaded the diagram of the lab into them. Lyle, you stay with me if we get separated."

Lee activated the com-cell and looked at the diagram of the lab on its small screen. "Okay," he said and headed for the door.

As soon as they walked through the steel door into the tunnel the lights in the corridor came on.

"How long a walk to do you think we've got?" Lyle asked, looking down the long corridor.

"According to the diagram a mile," Evelyn said. "Let's hope everyone's asleep."

"Don't count on it," Lee told them as he led the way walking as quietly as he could on the stone floor.

They tried to relax as they started the mile walk to the door at the end of the tunnel, but neither of them was. They were quiet, because there wasn't anything they could say to boost their spirits. All they could do was to have confidence in their plan.

The steel door at the end of the long tunnel was like the others on oiled hydraulic hinges that made it easy to push silently open. As soon as they left the long tunnel lights came on in the room they'd entered and went out in the tunnel.

"Think those lights contain sensors?" Lee asked Evelyn.

"I didn't detect any on the diagram," she said, looking up at the lights as she stood behind Lee with her I-book open. It was easier to carry than the laptop which hung from her left shoulder in its carrying case. "What I'm worried about is are the lights being detected as they come on and go off."

"Isn't that odd they wouldn't contain sensors?" Lyle said, looking up, too.

"Maybe not if that tunnel we just left and the silo control room are an extension of the lab and not a part of it," Lee replied as he increased his speed.

"Why a missile," Lyle asked. "It doesn't seem to have a purpose."

"The missile was here when they took over this complex. Why waste time removing a missile no one knows is here?"

"Why keep it in such good condition? Why the oiled hinges on the doors and lights in the silo and rooms and tunnel if it has no purpose?"

"We can answer those questions, Lyle, after we've done what we can here to do," Evelyn said. "So let's just forget about it and concentrate on what we've got to do."

"Where are we now, Evelyn?" Lee asked her. "I didn't see this room on the diagram."

"It's an annex room, and it was on the diagram, Lee," she answered as she looked forward and saw an elevator. "That elevator should take us down to level six."

"Why not just take this elevator up to the top level?" Lyle asked.

Evelyn studied the diagram again. "Because it doesn't go higher than level three the level we're on. And it has a double door that opens on this level."

"We don't want to go there," Lee said. "Even if those five are asleep, they may have guards out. Remember that house we met the five in, Evelyn?"

"Yeah, trackers in the woods across the street watching our every move," she said, walking to the elevator. "Get ready."

"Step to one side before you push the call button," Lee told her as he moved the com-cell from his right hand to his left, and took out his weapon and flicked the safety off. "You get on the other side with me, Lyle, and get ready. But don't start shooting unless you have a target."

Lyle nodded and walked to the right side of the elevator door behind Lee while Evelyn moved to the left and pushed the call button.

The elevator door opened immediately.

Lee quickly glanced into and drew back. It was empty. "All clear," he said and quickly moved into the elevator Evelyn and Lyle joined him.

Evelyn turned around and looked at the elevator panel and saw four buttons with a number on each one. She turned around and looked at the door behind them and saw the buttons on the left side that opened that door. She turned back around and looked at the buttons on the panel and reached down with her left hand and pushed the button with the number six on it.

The door closed and the elevator started to move down.

"This elevator's movement is being registered on one of those computers in that top level, isn't it?" Lyle asked.

"Yes, it is," Lee said.

Troy was sitting in a chair in front of the desk that faced the large TV screen on the wall. He saw a message flash on the bottom left side of the screen. 'The elevator from the annex room to the launch room tunnel is moving down.'

He did nothing because the orders he had been given by Larry when he replaced Sam was to wait for a contact from one of the trackers outside the underground complex searching for the bodies of Evelyn, Lyle, and Lee. But he did remember the message about the movement of the elevator.

The elevator quickly and silently went down to the sixth level.

"Let's hope there are no clones down there waiting for us," Lee said in a calm voice.

"Can't you scan for people at the sixth level?" Lyle asked Evelyn as he looked over her left shoulder at the I-book she held.

"No, all I've got on this I-book is a diagram of the complex," she told him. "I'm not tapped into any of this complex's sensors."

Lee looked at the fifth button as it flashed white and said, "Get ready. Next stop level six."

They moved to the sides of the elevator, with almost no cover for them if someone outside started shooting, and waited for the door to open.

The door opened on a black room.

"If there was anyone here, even a clone, the lights would be on," Lee said as he breathed a sigh of relief. "Let's go." He walked quickly out of the elevator and moved to the left to keep a wall at his back.

Evelyn and Lyle followed him doing the same thing.

The lights in the room came on showing a large garage with a dozen antique armored vehicles parked in the middle of the room with four in three neat rows.

"This place is huge, Lyle said as he looked out at the large garage. He looked up toward the ceiling. "And high. That ceiling must be a good fifty feet high."

"Where to now, Evelyn," Lee asked her.

She looked at her I-book for a few seconds and said, "To the generator room. That's where we'll find the optic cable we need to neutralize the sensors. It's to our right in the center of the wall." She started walking rapidly toward her right.

"Keep the wall to your right," Lee told her and Lyle. "If we get attacked by someone, we want them coming at us from only one direction."

They walked as rapidly as they could to the wall in front of them then moved along it till they came to a metal door with the words 'generator room' written on it in six inch black letters.

Troy saw the message stating the lights at the sixth level were on in the same part of the screen he'd seen the message about the elevator. Again he did nothing but obey the orders Larry had given him.

Lee moved in front of Evelyn and started to reach for the doorknob. "Stop," Evelyn told Lee.

He stopped and turned around to face her as she moved forward pass him.

"Notice the key pad to this door isn't off to the side on the wall near the door, but on the door itself."

"That mean something," Lyle asked.

"Yes. It means this door has a sensor on it. Force that door open and you break a circuit. Touch one of those numbers or letters on that keypad that isn't part of the code and an alarm goes off," she said, stopping just in front of the pad and looking it over. "See this plastic cover just below the keypad?"

Lee and Lyle looked at it and said nothing.

"It's nonmagnetic." She looked it over for a few seconds then reached into her jacket pocket and removed a small, plastic jackknife and opened it and slid the sharp hard blade under the bottom edge of the cover and pulled up on the knife raising the plastic cover. She removed the cover and handed it to Lyle and leaned forward and looked closely at the electrical parts exposed. "See this round, flat piece of metal."

"The operating chip," Lee said.

"It's the processor, and electrically connected to a main server in that main computer room." She reached in with her right index finger and thumb and gently grabbed the processor and gently removed the chip and waited.

"What?" Lyle asked.

Evelyn smiled as she put the chip in her jacket pocket and closed her knife and put it in the same pocket. She grabbed the door handle and pushed it down and opened the door. It opened outward without a sound.

"You think it set off an alarm in that computer room?" Lee asked her.

"Not with the processor removed," she told him.

No alarm went off, but a message appeared on the same part of the screen Troy was watching as the other two messages.

'Generator room alarm has been deactivated.'

Troy ignored it.

A dark room appeared in front of them.

"We're going to need our night vision goggles," she said. "I hope they're in the backpacks."

"What did you do?" Lee asked her.

"I deactivated the alarm that's why the lights didn't go on in this room," she told him. "If I have punched in the right code the alarm would have been shut down and the lights in the room would have come on automatically."

Lee and Lyle took their backpacks off and opened them. Lyle found one pair of goggles for himself. Lee had the two he'd taken from the two trackers he'd killed in his backpack. He gave one to Evelyn then put his own.

She slipped the night vision goggles on over her head and down over her eyes as she said, "Now we move fast, because somewhere in this complex a maintenance robot has been alerted that the processor to the door has malfunctioned. And it is probably being sent by a computer to repair or replace it."

Once they had their goggles on they walked as fast as they could into the dark room. The goggles made everything in the dark room seem as bright as a cloudy day.

Troy saw the message that a maintenance robot had been sent to repair the faulty processor in the door of the generator room and thought, *I have no orders about maintenance robots and faulty electric processors.*

Evelyn looked around the room for a few seconds then moved quickly to her right toward a large generator that sat close to a far wall between two smaller generators. All three were emitting a humming sound indicating they were working.

"One of you keep an eye out for a maintenance robot," she said. "It's probably down at this level in some closet."

"Help her, Lyle," Lee said as he moved to one side of the opened door.

"What you want me to do?" Lyle asked Evelyn as he moved up to her left side.

"This large generator probably supplies power to the others, so look for a large plastic cable coming from the back of it and going up into the roof," she said as she looked at the end of the generator and then looked up. "There it is." She pointed up with her right hand toward the ceiling. "That's what we want." She put her I-book in the pouch and jumped up on top of the generator and walked to the wall the cable was attached to. "Lee, have you got that knife you spoke of?"

"Yeah," he answered.

"Go get it, Lyle and bring it to me," she said.

Lyle ran back to Lee and asked, "Where is it?"

Lee reached into his left pants pocket and took out a small jack knife and handed it to Lyly saying, "Make sure the blade is shiny."

Lyle took it, pulled both blades out of the knife, and decided the larger one would reflex better than the smaller one. He closed the smaller blade as he ran back to Evelyn moving both sides of the larger blade over his left sleeve to make it shine better. "Here, I've polished it a bit." He held the open knife up to her.

"Have you got a knife I can cut through this plastic covering with?" she asked him.

"Why not use this one?"

"I need that one to reflex the light back up the optic cable inside this larger cable," she said. "Look in your backpack, or Lee's there should be a larger knife in one of them."

Lee heard what she said and took his backpack off his back. He had remembered putting a large hunting knife in one of the inside pockets of the backpack. He quickly ran his left hand along the inside of the backpack while he looked for any approaching robots. He found it and saw a robot walking toward the room. "I've got one, Lyle, and there's a robot coming," he yelled back at them.

Being quiet didn't make much sense now.

Lyle took a few steps back toward Lee and yelled, "Toss it!"

Lee threw the knife in the direction of Lyle's voice and dropped his backpack on the floor and took aim at the robot's head with his semiautomatic.

Lyle saw the knife in its sheath flying through the air and caught it and ran a few steps back to Evelyn and handed her the knife.

"Don't shoot that robot, Lee," Evelyn screamed at him. "Step back from the door and let it examine the keypad. When it notices the processor is gone it will go and get another one."

I sure hope you're right, Lee thought as he stepped back from the open door and waited.

The robot walked up to the opened door, stopped, scanned the electrical part below the keypad with its electrical eyes, and turned around and walked off.

Lee let out a loud breath as he mumbled, "You were right, Evelyn."

"Told you so," she said as she removed the hunting knife from its sheath,

dropped the sheath to the floor, and cut into the plastic covering. She cut a rectangle into the covering and peeled it back and looked inside at the optic cables. It took her only seconds to locate the main optic cable.

It was as thick as her little finger with faint light moving through it.

"Now let's hope this works as I'm hoping it will," she said as she put the point of the large blade of the jackknife against the plastic of the main optic cable and pushed hard against it.

The blade easily went into the optic cable and instantaneously reflected some of the light back up the cable. Nothing happened.

"Did you do it?" Lyle asked her.

"Yes. The blade is in the cable and some of the light is being reflected back up the cable," she answered him.

Lyle looked up at the ceiling and saw the lights were still off. "Nothing's happened?"

"Let's hope something did happen," she said as she got down off the generator and picked up the sheath for the hunting knife and stuck the knife back in its sheath.

"What do you mean? Shouldn't the light in this garage have gone off?"

"Not necessarily, Lyle. What we want to do is to screw up the sensors so they don't detect us," she said as she started walking back toward the door.

"So, we don't know if the sensors are shut down, or screwed up, do we?" he said, following her.

"We will soon," she said as she approached Lee. "Let's get out of this room, Lee.

And leave that open." She walked out of the room pass Lee giving his back his knife.

"Everything go alright?" Lee asked Lyle as he grabbed his backpack, put the knife in the pocket, and waited till Lyle walked out of the room.

"I don't know," he said as he walked out of the room behind Evelyn. "But I sure

as hell hope so."

Lee slung his backpack over his left shoulder and followed Lyle. "Where to now?"

"To the closest air duct that will take us up to the main computer room and the top of this complex," Evelyn told him as she pushed her night vision goggles up to her forehead and took her I-book out of its pouch and looked at it.

Troy didn't notice anything wrong, because there weren't any more messages flashed on the TV screen he stared at.

Petersen got out of his bed, he'd been sleeping for four hours and that was enough sleep for him, and walked into his study and looked at the laptop on his desk as he had done for over five hundred years. He saw all the messages that had been flashed on the TV screen in front of Troy, and a message that said the power system that controlled every camera, sensor, computer and server in the entire underground complex was malfunctioning.

That's never happened before, he thought. *I must have one of the computers in the main computer room check it out. I don't think the five gentlemen would like it if there was a problem with the complex's security system.* He looked at the gold and silver clock on his desk Paul had given him over five hundred years ago. He didn't know why Paul had given him the clock all he remembered was Paul had given it to him.

The time was one thirty-three in the morning.

But first I shall bath, shave, and have breakfast.

Petersen turned around and walked toward his bathroom thinking about what he should have for breakfast.

Lyle and Lee pushed their goggles up to their foreheads as they followed Evelyn over a hundred feet to a narrow door next to one of the four groups of three elevators. She stopped at the door, looked at it for a second then at her I-book.

"This air duct will take us up to the main computer room on level one," she said as she looked at her I-book. "We should come out in the southwest corner of that room."

Lee looked around the garage and said, "But, Evelyn, we're in the northern part of this garage."

"Yes, but the computer room on level one is much smaller than this garage, and it's on the northeastern side of this garage. Meaning we should come out of this air duct on the southwest side of the computer room on level one," she explained.

"Well, let's stop standing and talking and get into this air duct," Lyle said as he looked nervously around the garage. He saw a robot walking toward the door of the generator room. "That robot's coming back to repair that security lock on that door."

"Okay, let's get into this air duct," Lee said as he looked down at the door for a doorknob and saw none but he did see a lock with an opening for a key. "This damn door has a regular lock on it."

"Can you open it?" Lyle asked him.

Lee took the hunting knife out of the pouch on his backpack, and put his weapon in his right jacket pocket.

"What are you going to do?" Lyle asked him as he watched him.

"Jam this knife's blade into the keyhole and turn it," he told him.

"What if it doesn't work?"

"Pray it does, Lyle, or we're finished and—,"

"I know, our families," he finished.

Lee jammed the blade into the keyhole as far as it would go, and twisted the knife to the left. He heard a popping sound and felt the door give a little then he pushed against it, and it opened.

They felt a rush of cold air going up the duct.

"This must be an exit duct," Lee said he looked in the dark room and saw a ladder attached to the wall directly in front of him. He pulled his night vision goggles down over his eyes and walked into the room and looked up.

Evelyn followed him and Lyle followed her closing the door. He pulled his goggles down over his eyes and looked at the lock and saw that the blade of the knife had gone completely through the lock.

"This lock is ruined," he said. "We can't lock this door behind us."

"Maybe we can jam something under the bottom of it," Evelyn said.

Lyle looked at the bottom of the door and said, "I think I've got what just might work." He took off his backpack and opened it.

"We'd need something strong to prevent the door from being easily opened," she said.

"No, just something to jam under the door and the floor that will prevent someone from opening it easily," he said as he took a pair of socks out of his backpack.

"You think that'll work?" she asked him.

"It should," he said.

She turned around and looked at Lee putting his knife in the pouch, and looking at the ladder asked, "Think that'll hold the three of us?"

He reached out and grabbed the ladder and pulled against it with all his strength. "Yeah, it's solid steel and anchored to the wall by steel bars. This ladder could hold a couple of tons." He stepped back and looked up at the ladder and saw it disappear far above them. "How far do we have to go before we reach that room on level one?"

Evelyn looked at the diagram of the underground complex on her I-book. "This level is fifty feet high and there's fifty feet between each level and the other levels are only twenty feet high. Four hundred and thirty feet before we reach level one."

"Then let's get started," he said as he started climbing it. "You get in the middle, Evelyn, and you bring up the rear, Lyle. We stay at least ten feet apart. That way if I fall you two will have time to get out of the way to avoid being hit by me."

"What about me?" Lyle asked as he partially unrolled the pair of socks and stuck them at the corner of the door on the floor and pushed the door close.

"You'll be like Evelyn and I, if you fall," Lee said as he climbed the ladder. "On your own till you reach the bottom, and pray the fall kills you if you fall. You don't want to end up an injured man in the hands of the five. Your death would be far worse and much more painful."

Lyle didn't like hearing what Lee said but he said nothing as he watched Evelyn close her I-book and put it into the pouch on her left side and start up the ladder ten feet behind Lee. He waited until she had gone up ten feet before he started up looking at her ass thinking *at least the view is better.*

They climbed a hundred feet to the first platform before they stopped and got on it to catch their breaths.

"That wasn't so bad," Lyle said as he looked around the round air duct.

"This platform isn't smooth," Evelyn said as she ran her hands over the parts on both sides of her hips. "It's made up of three wedges and we're sitting on one of them."

Lee looked at the two wedges on the other side of the air duct as he ran his hands over the one they were sitting on. "I think they're supposed to move together to form a solid platform."

"Why?" Lyle asked. He was running his hands over the walls of the air duct.

"To stop someone from doing what we're doing," he said. "I doubt if these platforms form an air tight seal across this duct."

"This air duct is made out of solid steel," Lyle said. "And like this platform its round."

"These wedges are probably controlled in that control room on level one," Lee said. "Push a button on some panel and all the wedges in this duct come together preventing someone from using the duct to get to the control room."

"The people of the twentieth century must have been a pretty paranoid group to build this complex," Evelyn said.

"Not from their point of view," Lee told her.

"Lee, anyone who'd build something like this underground complex and that silo with a missile in it are paranoid," she told him.

"Not when you live in a world where you have enemies all around you who want you dead," he said. "We don't understand them today, because the nations of the world aren't out to destroy each other to gain more wealth and power." He stood up. "Imagine living in a world with the constant threat of nuclear annihilation hanging over your head?"

"I don't imagine it was nice," she said as she watched him start his climb to the fourth level.

"How far to the next rest stop," Lyle asked her.

"Seventy feet," she said as she started her climb.

He waited until she was ten feet ahead of him before he started to climb. "Have you noticed there's little dust on this ladder?"

"Whoever is in charge of this complex when the five aren't here does a good job of making sure the robots clean it," she said.

"Less talk more climbing," Lee said.

They stopped three more times before they reached the second level and stopped again on a platform.

"One more level to go then into that computer room," Lee said.

Lyle and Evelyn looked at him and said nothing.

"Drink some water from those water bottles you've got," he said as he took his backpack off his back and opened it and took out a plastic bottle of water. He opened the bottle and took three large swallows of water and returned the bottle to his backpack.

Evelyn and Lyle did the same thing as Lee had done.

"I don't know what we're going to run into when we enter that computer room," Lee began. "But if I know Paul and his four friends, there'll be a clone on duty in there. That's why I go first. I've had more experience lately in killing their clones. When I say clear you both come up quickly."

Lyle and Evelyn nodded their understanding.

"While Lyle and I get something to block the door, you, Evelyn, get on one of those computers and find out what's in them and the servers."

"Think we'll have a lot of time?" Lyle asked him.

Lee looked at his watch. "Its two fifty now, Lyle. Once we get in that computer room we'll have ten maybe twenty minutes before they come at us with every clone this place has. By that time Evelyn should have some idea of what's in those computers and servers and can start downloading it on the Internet. After that it's a fight to stay alive as long as we can, and frankly, the odds are against us."

"The first thing I'm going to do, Lee, is to shut down every elevator in this complex," she said. "That way when they come at us it'll have to be through the stairwell and there's only one that leads to level one."

"Good idea," he said. "It's easier covering one door that two or three elevators."

The three of them looked at each other in silence for a minute.

"You ready?" Lee asked them.

"I'm ready," Lyle said, patting his stomach where his weapon was in his belt.

"Yes," Evelyn said, smiling to alleviate her fear.

"Remember identify your targets then shoot to kill," Lee said as he stood up and started up the ladder to level one. *I should have checked those doors on the other levels to see how hard they were to open. It's too late now.*

Troy raised the cameras on the surface and had them go to maximum magnification and heat detection and scan in a three hundred and sixty-degree circle. He programmed them to look for only human heat signatures for a distance of fifty miles. For twenty minutes he saw and watched the TV screen seeing only the heat signatures of the clones out searching for Lee, Evelyn, and Lyle.

The tracker/killer clones had found the remains of the SUV and most of the contents in it three and a half miles east from the complex, but not any humans. Any normal human would have thought they had just disappeared from the earth, but Troy wasn't a normal human, and he did not understand why the bodies or parts of the bodies of the three humans hadn't been found. That should have caused him concern, but being concerned wasn't programmed into him when he was in his birthing tube. All he was expected to do was to carry out the orders Larry or one of the other four men gave him.

But Troy did have extremely sensitive hearing and the computer room was quiet even though all the computers and servers were working.

Lee stopped outside the door on the platform outside of level one room and looked closely at the handle on the door. He smiled and saw no lock.

Evelyn and Lyle climbed up on the platform next to him and saw his smile.

"What?" she asked.

He put his left index finger to his lips cautioning her to be quiet. He turned to his right and looked at Lyle with his finger still to his lips.

Lyle nodded and said nothing.

Troy heard someone say something behind him to his left, but he didn't look in the direction of the sound. His orders were to scan with the cameras and their heat detectors for the three humans. Not to listen to anyone but one of the five or all of them.

Lee looked over the door and saw that it opened outward. He put his left hand on the handle, flicked the safety off his semiautomatic with his right thumb, and pushed down on the handle and pushed the door open. He jumped into the room with his weapon held in front of him and looked over the room. He paid no attention to the four desks with computers on them, or the walls above them with large, wide TV screens on them, on the four servers in the middle of them. All he saw was a man with fair skin and short black hair sitting at a desk in front of one of the large TV screens.

Troy heard the handle of the door being pushed down and the door opening, and turned around toward the sound in time to see Lee jumping into the room. He may have been a clone who lacked specific judgment, but he knew instantly the man dressed in a black leather jacket, jeans, and boots with a black woolen caps on his head and night vision goggles over his eye was the man the five men who gave him orders wanted.

He started to turn around to push an alarm button on the desk next to the keyboard to alert the five, but he was too slow.

Lee, without hesitating, aimed and shot Troy three times in the chest.

All three electric shots hit Troy in his chest and ripped into his heart. He may have been a clone, but three shots of five hundred volts each killed him instantly, just as it would a real human and his body went limp in the chair.

Lee quickly moved to the right then to the left looking for anyone else in the room. Only when he was certain the clone didn't have backup did he yell, "Okay, come in. It's safe."

Lyle came out of the air duct first with his weapon in his right hand and a look of determination on his face.

"Take it easy, Lyle," Lee said. "There's no backup, and the only clone here I've killed."

"We heard the shots," he said as he walked over to Troy's body and looked it. "I've never seen a person who's been shot to death."

Evelyn came out of the air duct seconds after Lyle and stood at the door of the air duct and looked around for ten seconds before she rushed to a desk next to the one Troy's body was in front of and sat down in the chair. She looked at the keyboard in front of her on the desk and at the TV screen on the wall in front of her and mumbled, "Where are the fucking codes that would allow me to control this computer control room?"

'What codes would you like?' appeared on the TV screen.

For a moment she said nothing. She was too surprised that the computer had answered her question then said, "The main code that allows access to every program in all these computers and servers and this underground complex."

The word 'evolution' appeared on the screen.

Stupid code for five assholes who've been around for five hundred years because of cloning, she thought as she typed the word 'evolution' into the computer and pushed enter.

A list of fourteen codes appeared on the screen with an explanation of what the codes did next to the words.

Lyle and Lee stood watching her.

Evelyn smelt the odor of human waste and turned and looked at Troy's body and asked, "Now that he's dead and has released all his body wastes could one of you get rid of it?"

"What are we going to do with it?" Lyle asked her.

Lee looked at the open door to the air duct and said, "Let's dump it down there."

Lyle turned around and looked at the open door to the air duct and shrugged.

Lee walked over to Troy's body saying, "I'll take his legs, Lyle."

Both of them picked up Troy's body and carried it to the air duct, pushed it inside on the platform, then pushed it from the platform. Neither said anything until they heard a mild thud of the body hitting the bottom level in the air duct.

"What we just did was rather barbaric even if that man was a clone, Lee," Lyle said in a depressed sounding voice.

Lee closed the air duct door and looked around at the room. He saw four closed doors. "Let's see what's behind those doors, Lyle."

"You don't think there are any more clones in here, do you?" he asked as he followed Lee a door.

"Damned if I know," Lee responded as he walked to the left side of one of the doors and stood with his back against the wall and reached for the doorknob.

Lyle had stopped in front of the door.

"Do you really want to be standing there if there is another clone behind this door and he has a gun?" Lee asked Lyle.

Lyle immediately moved to one side and got ready to shoot anything behind the door that was human. "I'm ready," he said.

Lee opened the door with his nerves on edge ready to kill.

Nothing came from behind the door.

"There's no one in there," Lyle said, leaning to his left and looking in the room. "It's dark in there and it looks like there are a lot of guns in it." He was still wearing his night vision goggles.

Lee glanced quickly in the room and saw guns. He ducked into the room, moving to his left to keep a wall behind him, and looked around the dark room. All he saw with his night vision goggles was racks of weapons.

"Let's check the other three doors and see what's behind them," he said, coming out of the room.

One was a completely furnished bedroom with an attached bathroom. The other one was a kitchen with everything a person would need to prepare a meal for themselves.

The last one was a small clinic with medical supplies for giving first aid and equipment for preforming minor operations.

"How are you doing, Evelyn?" Lee asked as he walked back to the first room pushing his night vision goggles up to his forehead.

"I'm in the system, Lee," she said as she removed a cable from her pocket and plugged one end into her I-book and the other into the USB port of the computer she was using. She pushed her goggles up to her forehead.

"What does that mean?" he asked.

"That means I've got every code in this place on my I-book," she answered as she looked at the information being downloaded from the computer to her I-book and hoped there was enough space on the hard drive for all of it.

"Those weapons in that arms room looked old," Lyle said, walking over to Lee and Evelyn.

"Probably," Lee said standing behind Evelyn. "This entire complex was built back in nineteen seventy-five, and those weapons were put here to be used by the people assigned here to defend it."

"What were those things with tripods on them?" Lyle asked. "Some sort of drilling equipment?"

"Didn't you have history in high school?" Lee asked him. "Those were machine guns, that could fire hundreds sometimes thousands of projectiles at the speed of sound every minute."

"And these boxes against the wall?" he asked.

"They contain the projectiles. Bullets."

Lyle walked back into the room and leaned down and read the words on the side of one of the boxes, saying in a loud voice, "Fifty caliber armor piercing bullets five hundred to a box. Manufactured by the Smith and Wesson Arms Company."

"Don't open them," Lee told him. "Some of those bullets were explosive."

"This stuff's been here more than a thousand years, Lee," he said as he straightened up and walked out of the room. "I doubt if they're still dangerous."

"I still wouldn't open them," Lee said. "Our ancient ancestors were very good at building weapons of mass destruction. They weren't worth a damn at taking care of the poor, though."

Petersen, having spent over five hundred years in the complex, knew it better than he knew how to clone people, and he was extremely good at that. He walked out of his bedroom fully dressed saying, "Something's not right."

He walked into his study and pushed a button on the laptop on his desk and saw everything that was displayed on the computer in the control room Evelyn was using. He pushed another button on the buttons at the top of the laptop's keyboard and activated the cameras in the control room. He saw Evelyn at the desk working on the computer and Lee and Lyle standing behind her.

These are probably the people Paul and the others talked of coming here, he thought. *I shall go and greet them.*

He took his com-cell out of his pocket and called the kitchen and said, "Forget about my breakfast. Have a robot meet me at the elevators with coffee and donuts for six people."

"Yes, sir," a clone replied.

Petersen walked out of his apartment toward the elevators. He decided not to awake the five until after he'd greeted their guests.

"I wonder how much all this cost?" Lyle asked as he looked at the screen over the desk.

"The lives of thousands of poor, starving people." Lee answered.

"All of those guns were built by that Smith and Wesson Company?"

"I guess so," Lee answered.

"What primitive barbaric people our ancestors were," he said. "They built all of these weapons and bullets when they could have used the money to feed people who were starving. The twentieth century must have been a terrible century for humanity."

"It was one of the bloodiest centuries in the history of the human race," Lee told him.

Lyle angrily shook his head at how barbaric the people of the twentieth century were.

"What have you got, Evelyn?" Lee asked her.

Lyle was on his right side.

"The second level. The clone room," she said as she looked at the screen.

Lyle and Lee stared at the screen and saw a dozen seven feet glass tubes with fully formed human bodies inside them.

"The security system is screwed up?" Lee asked her.

"One way to find out," she said as she sat in the chair and pushed enter on the keyboard and looked up at the screen.

A second passed before the word 'working' appeared on the screen.

"You're in the security system?" Lee asked her.

"Yes, and I doubt if anyone in this complex beside us know it."

CHAPTER 62

3:20 a.m.

In the center of the main computer room was a tower of glass with eight sides to it. Each side was a computer screen six feet wide by eight feet high. At the base of the tower were four five by four feet servers that had only two lights on each one, green indicating the server was working properly, and one red indicating there was a problem in the server. If there was a problem in one of the servers, the other three would quickly analyze it and correct it or show on all of the screens what the problem was and how to fix it. A simple fluctuation in the flow of electrons had never occurred and the servers immediately identified it as a problem, but just as quickly analyzed the problem as not important when the flow of electrons continued a second later without another fluctuation. The servers continued doing the jobs they were designed and built to do without any trouble.

One of the reasons it wasn't noticed by any human eyes is everyone working in the underground laboratory complex was asleep except those clones working in the kitchen preparing breakfast for the five when they awoke. But there was a problem, because fifty years ago while updating all the computers and servers in the complex Petersen had put a program in the servers that analyzed any problem that occurred in the computers and servers no matter how insignificant it was. When the servers weren't capable of solving the problem a small transparent question mark would appear in the lower right hand corner of each of the eight screens. Such a question mark appeared on the eight screens.

Evelyn was working on trying to determine which of the servers had the information about the five in it when she saw a statement flash on the computer screen on the wall in front of her. 'An elevator from level three is coming to the computer room.'

"Can I get a picture of who's in that elevator?" she asked aloud as she looked around the keyboard and wondered what keys she had to push to get a view of the inside of the elevator.

'Yes.' appeared on the computer screen.

"Then show me," she demanded.

A picture of Petersen and a robot with a covered serving cart appeared on the screen.

"Company's coming," Evelyn yelled out.

Lee standing behind her asked, "Who?"

"A guy with a covered serving cart and a robot," she answered.

Lyle and Lee looked at the screen.

"My God," Lyle exclaimed in a soft voice. "I know that man."

Petersen had been programmed to contact the five when anything unusual happened. Nothing unusual had ever happened in the five hundred years he'd been in charge of the underground complex, and he'd never had any reason for contacting them. But today was different. The five's guests had arrived and it was his responsibility as head of the underground complex to contact the five and informed them their guests had arrived. He used the intercom box in the elevator to call the phones in their rooms and inform them.

Fred answered his call first.

"Who is this and what's wrong?" he asked in a sleepy voice as he held the receiver to his left ear.

"It is I, Petersen, and nothing's wrong, sir," Petersen said. "I'm just calling you to inform you your guests have arrived and they are in the computer room on level one."

It took two seconds for what Petersen said to register in Fred's brain.

Fred sprang out of bed and pushed the button on the base of the lamp on the nightstand turning on all the lights in his suite. "Computer!" he screamed. "Wake the others and tell them the three are here in the computer room."

Evelyn shook her head as she looked at the list of codes on the TV screen on the wall in front of her and said, "Computer, shut down the intercom system."

"Why are you doing that?" Lee asked her.

"That man pushed a button on the elevator panel that operates the intercom system," she said.

"That guy is calling the five?" Lee asked her.

"I suppose so. I can't hear what he's saying, but I saw his lips move," she answered.

"That guy is Dr. Drake Petersen," Lyle said. "He's the one who five hundred years ago cloned the five."

"Are you serious?" Lee asked him as he looked at him with a surprised expression.

"Ask him if he's Drake Petersen when he gets here," Lyle replied.

Fred was dressing as quickly as he could. "Computer," he yelled. "Have you notified the others on this level?"

There was no response.

"Damn you, computer, answer me," he yelled.

No response.

Fred didn't yell anymore because he knew why the computer wasn't responding. He ran out of his apartment to the one closest to his and kicked open the door and ran inside.

The door being kicked opened awoke Steve immediately and he grabbed the electric semiautomatic pistol on the nightstand next to his bed and sat up and pointed it at the door of his bedroom. He didn't know which of his five companions had kicked open the door to his suite, but he knew no clone or Petersen would have done such a thing. They weren't programmed to kick open doors any of the five were behind.

"Wake up, Steve," Fred yelled at him. He wasn't stupid enough to rush into the bedroom of one of the others after he'd kicked open the door of their apartment.

"That you, Fred," Steve asked, recognizing his voice.

"They are here and in the control room," Fred yelled from the living room.

The expression 'My God' didn't issue from his mouth. He didn't believe in God because he'd been alive for five hundred years and it was science that had kept him alive all those years. Not God. He sprang out of bed screaming, "Wake the others!"

He didn't have to scream that, the noise of Fred kicking open the door to Steve's apartment had awoken the other three.

Steve was dressed in half the time it took Fred and was walking out the door of his apartment when Paul, Bruce, and Larry walked out the front doors of their apartments dressed in silk pajamas and looked at Steve and Fred.

"Why all the noise," Bruce asked.

"Those three are in the main control room," Fred told him.

"How do you know that?" Paul asked him in a demanding voice.

"Petersen called me a few minutes ago and told me our guests have arrived."

"Where are they?" Paul asked. There was a sinister sound to his voice.

"The main control room on level one," Fred repeated.

"That's impossible," Larry said. "Troy's up there. If they had tried getting in there, he would have sounded an alarm."

"Ask the computer," Fred told him.

"Computer is Troy still in the control room?" Larry asked.

The computer didn't respond, but Petersen's com-cell picked up the question, and he started to answer it as he walked out of the elevator followed by the robot pushing the covered serving cart.

Lee was standing off to the left side of the elevator. As soon as Lee saw the robot walk out of the elevator he aimed and fired at its head.

His volt hit the robot in the glass circle that went around its head and immediately deactivated it and it froze in a standing position with its hands on the handle of the covered serving cart.

"Why did you do that?" Petersen asked Lee with his com-cell in his left hand and a foot from his mouth.

"Come forward, Dr. Petersen," Lyle said. He was standing off to the right side near the desks with his weapon pointed at Petersen. "And don't make any foolish moves or you will die."

The computer didn't answer Larry's call and he instantly knew that meant trouble.

"Call in all our trackers now," Paul told Larry as he turned around and went back into his apartment to dress.

"That might not be possible with them in control of the computer room," Steve said.

"I can contact them by com-cell," Larry said as he walked back into his apartment.

Steve and Fred followed him.

"Can you get a message through all this concrete and steel?" Steve asked him.

"Yes, if they haven't shut down the transmitter on the roof," he said as he walked into his bedroom and over to the nightstand next to his bed and picked up his com-cell. "All of you trackers return immediately to the compound. That's an order."

"Yes," was the only response Larry heard.

Evelyn shook her head in anger. She had heard Larry's call to the trackers over the computer speakers. She should have shut down the transmitter the moment she sat at the desk. She mumbled, "Lee, I screwed up."

"What did you do?" he asked as he slowly approached Petersen. "Give me your com-cell," he said to Petersen.

"I didn't shut down the transmitter," she said. "I thought we'd need it to download the information in these servers. And now they've called in their tracker/killers."

Petersen stared at Lee as he approached him with his weapon pointed at him.

"That robot was harmless. All of the robots here are harmless. They are only cleaning and service robots. They are not programmed to harm people."

"I didn't know that, did I?" he said as he took the com-cell from Petersen's left hand. "Find something to tie the guy up with, Lyle, or I'll kill him, too."

"Don't do anything foolish, Dr. Petersen," Lyle said as he looked around for something to tie him up with. "Are there any ropes or wires in this control room?"

"No, there are no ropes or wires here," Petersen said then added. "There are only wires that connect the computers and servers."

"Go to the washroom and see if there are any towels in it," Lee told Lyle. "If there are, cut or tear them into strips and tied him up." He walked behind Petersen and pushed him with his left hand toward an empty chair. "Sit over there, and no trouble."

While Petersen walked to the chair Lyle rapidly walked to the washroom.

"Why are you here with weapons?" Petersen asked him. "I am no threat to you and there's nothing to shoot in this room." He looked around the room. "Where is the clone called Troy?" He sat in the chair.

"He's in level six," Lee told him.

"Why is he there?"

"Don't worry about him," Lee told him.

Evelyn started typing on the keyboard of the computer in front of her.

"The computers in this compound can respond to speech," Petersen said, looking at her.

"Yeah, I know that," she said as she accessed all the surface cameras.

"How many people are still in the compound?" Lee asked Petersen.

"Twenty-three," he answered.

"That includes us?"

"Yes, and five lab workers, five kitchen workers, three garage workers, and the five gentlemen and Troy."

"Are those lab and kitchen workers trained as tracker/killers?"

"No, they were cloned to be lab workers and cooks." He looked at the covered tray. "I had them make coffee and donuts for you."

"Real nice of you, Petersen."

Lyle came out of the washroom tearing two large towels into strips.

"Your hands will be tied behind you and your legs and arms will be tied to the chair you're sitting in," Lee told him. "Take my advice and don't resist."

"I am programmed to run this underground complex and the laboratory on level two," he said. "I am not programmed to fight. But I do like reading novels."

"What kind?" Lyle asked him as he started tying Petersen's hands behind his back.

"I like all kinds. I have no definite preference. I read anything that is interesting to me."

"Do you remember what you once were?" Lyle asked him as he tied his legs and arms to the chair.

"I am a professor of microbiology and genetics. I am an expert at cloning humans."

"Do you remember having a family?"

"No."

"The bastards programmed that out of his mind when they cloned him," Lyle said.

"Lee, this is Paul," came over the com-cell in Lee's left hand.

Lee looked at the com-cell and wondered if he should answer.

Evelyn turned around and looked at him and said, "Might as well answer him. They know we're here and we're trapped in this room."

Lee raised the com-cell up to his mouth and said, "I hear you, Paul. Or would you prefer Mr. Simpson?"

"Whatever you like," he said.

"So what do you want?"

"To tell you not to download any information about us being cloned," he said. "Because if you do you will release information to the world that you and Evelyn are also clones."

"What?" Evelyn asked.

CHAPTER 63

5:30 a.m., Monday June 11

"You're full of shit," Lee replied in a hard voice.

"Have Evelyn check the lab records on your dates of birth," Paul said. His voice was calm with just a touch of friendliness in it. "You'll learn you weren't conceived as an act of love between a woman and a man or born of a woman like normal people."

"We're not clones, Paul," Evelyn said. "We both have families."

"Check the records on your dates of birth," Paul said. "You'll find information on the dates when you were cloned and when you came out of your cloning tubes."

"So we can waste time while your killers return to break in here and kill us?" Lee said. "Nothing doing. We're going to download all the information about this complex on the Internet and you five will be finished."

"Are you afraid to check?" Steve asked him.

"Who the fuck are you?" Lee was angry at being told he was a clone.

"You know me, Lee, you've worked for me a few times in the past," he said. "And all you have to do is check. Not only will you find written information about your cloning but a visual record as well."

"Check," Lyle told Evelyn. He was looking at Lee and Evelyn with eyes that held the look of disbelief.

"That's the voice of Lyle Morton, isn't it?" Bruce said.

"Just check," Lyle told Evelyn. "It's the only way to prove them wrong."

"You are a foolish man, Mr. Morton," Bruce said. "You didn't think we'd check and find out who you were, did you? You thought you'd done a perfect job of hiding your true identity from us. Well, you haven't and your family will suffer."

"Lee and Evelyn can't afford to expose us without also exposing themselves as well," Larry said. "Lee, kill him now and protect yourself and Evelyn from being exposed as clones, and all of your recent acts will be forgiven."

"Forget those assholes, Lyle," Lee told him. "They want us to waste time checking on bullshit while they work out a plan to get in here and kill us."

"Suppose they're telling the truth, Lee," Lyle told him. He looked at Evelyn whose face was pale with uncertainty and a fear they could be right. "Check and prove them wrong."

Evelyn turned toward the computer and said, "Computer, my name is Evelyn Summers I was born on January 3, 3013 is there any information on me in the servers?"

'Yes.' appeared on the screen.

"Show it," she said.

'Evelyn Summers, female, emerged from her birthing tube on January 3, 3013 at seven forty-five p.m. Birth certificate shows she was born to a Julie and Crag Summers. Both parents had died six months before she was born.'

"Oh, my God," she exclaimed softly in a depressed voice. "I came out of a birthing tube like some clone."

Evelyn stared at the information on the screen as if it was a monster out of her worse nightmare.

"Now you, Lee, if you have the courage to face the truth," Paul said. His voice had the sound of mockery in it.

Lee turned toward the computer and said, "I was born July 10, 3015 show information on a person born on that day by the name of Lee Adams."

'Lee Adams, male, emerged from his birthing tube on July 10 3015 at six a.m. Birth certificate shows he was born to a Ruby and James Adams. Both parents had died six months before he was born.'

Lee dropped to his knees on the floor like he had been shot. He felt sicker than he'd ever felt in his life. A moan emerged from his dry lips. "I didn't know."

"Expose us and you expose yourselves," Fred said. "Now kill Lyle and let us in that control room."

"Something's wrong," Lyle said, staring at the information on both of them on the screen.

"Just you, Lyle Morton for being a damn fool to think two clones we created to serve our needs would help you expose us," Steve said. "And because of your foolishness you and your family will die. But you will die quickly. I can promise you they will scream and beg for death for days before they finally die."

Lyle turned to Petersen and asked, "Why are their birth parents names listed if they were cloned?"

"Who are you talking to?" Paul asked him.

"None of your business," he replied.

"Answer my question," he demanded of Petersen.

"Because they are not really clones," Petersen said.

"Is that you, Petersen?" Larry screamed over his com-cell.

"Yes, I came up here to greet them because I heard the five of you talking about them coming in my study the first day you arrived," he said. "I brought them coffee and fresh donuts."

"Shut your fucking mouth! That is an order."

"Okay," he replied.

Evelyn looked at him, her face pale and sickly looking, and asked, "Do you have to obey all orders given you by the five?"

"Yes. That is how I am programmed."

"Petersen say no more," Larry screamed over the com-cell at him.

Lee knew they were trying to hide something. He turned off the com-cell in his hand and stood up and asked him, "Are we really clones?"

Petersen looked at Lyle, Lee, and Evelyn and said, "Not really."

"Then what the fuck are we?"

"You two were very successful experiments I was ordered to carry out by the five gentlemen," he said.

"What type of experiments?" Evelyn asked.

Lee stood silent.

"You are real humans except you were developed in test tubes before you were transferred to birthing tubes."

"We were developed in test tubes from DNA taken from our parents?" Evelyn asked him.

"No, from sperm and an ova taken from them while they were still alive," Petersen answered with a blank expression on his face.

"Damn you, Petersen," Paul screamed over his com-cell. "Don't say anything."

"Stop wasting your energy," Steve told him. "If Lee's turned off the com-cell he was using to talk to us, Petersen can't hear you."

"Where the hell is Troy?" Larry asked.

"Probably dead," Bruce answered.

Larry punched the code for Sam into his com-cell and said, "Sam, get up, get dressed, and come to this location as soon as possible." He waited for a reply. Thirty seconds passed before he said, "Sam, can you hear me?"

Ten seconds passed before he heard, "Yes, Mr. Davis, I can hear you."

"Come to this location immediately and bring a laptop with you," he demanded.

"Yes, sir," Sam replied.

"What good is that going to do?" Fred said. "They've got control of the control room, and there's no way we can get into it except by force."

Paul raised his com-cell to his lips and said, "Who is in charge of the trackers outside looking for Lee, Lyle, and Evelyn?"

"Ray 39," Sam said.

"Ray 39, how close are you to the compound?" Paul asked over his com-cell.

"Twenty minutes, sir. Ten others are only five minutes away, sir," Ray 39 replied.

"They might as well be on one of those Pluto Space Stations for all the good it will do us," Fred said. "By the time they reach here Petersen will have told Lee and Evelyn the truth about themselves and they will begin the download."

The doors of the elevator they were standing next to opened and Sam walked out holding a laptop in his left hand.

"Those three people we've been looking for are in the control room, Sam," Paul told him.

Sam nodded his understanding.

"Sam, is there any way to stop those people from downloading information onto the Internet from the control room?" Larry asked him.

"A moment, sir," Sam said as he sat down on the floor, crossed his legs in Indian fashion, and put the laptop on his legs and opened it. He started typing on the keyboard.

The five stood looking at him with expressions of fear and worry on their faces.

"No, sir," Sam said, looking up at them.

"We're finished," Fred moaned and turned around and started walking toward his apartment.

"But it can be delayed by half an hour at the most, sir," Sam said to Larry.

Fred stopped and spun around and asked in a loud voice, "How?"

"I can tell the servers to carefully examine all the information in them for viruses before downloading."

"Do it now," Paul said as he looked at his watch. "More than enough time for some of trackers to return and break into that damn room and kill all of them."

Sam started typing on the laptop's keyboard.

"With minutes to spare to stop the download," Steve said with a smile on his face.

"Can you get our trackers into the complex?" Paul asked him.

"When the servers start checking for viruses, I can access the complex's security system and order the doors to open to allow them to enter."

"What doors?" Paul asked him.

"There are two doors that lead directly to the control room from the top," Sam told him.

"Can you do that without them knowing?" Steve asked him.

"Yes, sir, if the people in the control room aren't aware of what I'm doing."

"Get control of those doors now!" Paul told him.

"Can you let us see and hear what's going on in the control room?" Steve asked Sam.

"Yes, sir, but they will be able to detect the accessing of the cameras and shut them down." Sam was typing on the laptop to get control of the doors.

"But will they know you've gotten control of the security system?" Bruce asked him.

"Not if they are trying to stop me from getting control of the cameras, sir," he answered.

"Get control of the security system now," Paul told him.

"Yes, sir."

"How did they do that?" Lee asked Petersen as he began to regain control of himself.

"The process is quiet simple," Petersen said in a voice without emotion.

"Explain it," Lyle demanded. He didn't know why but he didn't feel an ounce of fear in spite of what Lee and Evelyn had learned about themselves. He knew he should have since he was the only person in the entire underground complex who had been born of a woman by the natural act of sex, impregnation, and birth nine months later.

"A living ovum and live sperm were taken from both of their parents and placed in a test tube till one of the sperm implanted itself in the ovum, and then given the proper nutrients for development into an embryo, and then the embryo was placed in a birthing tube for further development," he explained. "The entire process took place in the sterile environment on the second level."

"And nine months later a baby is taken from the birthing tube in both of their cases," Lyle finished for him.

Evelyn's and Lee's crushed spirits began to rise again.

"Oh, no, it didn't take nine months to develop them into living humans. Six months was all that was required, and a full grown educated human twenty years of age emerged from each birthing tube."

"So, we are clones," Evelyn moaned, feeling like she was something despicable and inhuman.

"Don't believe that crap," Lyle told her. "Both of you are just like me. You had a mother and father just like I did. You just didn't know them."

Lee looked at Petersen, he felt like killing himself just before he released the information on the five, and asked, "Are we just like him?"

Petersen turned in the chair and looked at Lyle who standing on his left side and asked him, "You are the product of a sex act between a man and a woman, aren't you?"

"Yes, I am," he said, trying not to sound like he was better than Lee or Evelyn.

Petersen turned to his front and looked at Evelyn and Lee. "The only difference between you two and this gentleman is instead of coming out of your birthing tubes as babies, you came out as twenty-year-old adults."

"How was that possible?" Lee asked, wanting to feel he was as human as Lyle.

"I simply increased the amount of enriched protein nutrients given to both of you, and increased the environment in both your birthing tubes to resemble a natural environment as you both developed. And using mental transference from a computer I educated both of you so that by the time you emerged from your birthing tubes. You both had an education equal to that of a normal person." He looked at both of them then at Lyle and added, "Educating you two was my major concern, though it was a bit easier with you, Lee."

"What do you mean?" Evelyn asked him. She was beginning to feel better but she still had the feeling of being a freak.

Petersen looked at her. "You were my first experiment in the development of a normal person by increasing the speed of development through enriched protein and mental transference. I was a bit worried about over doing the mental transferring. I didn't want to make you into some mental freak of nature but a normal person." He leaned forward and looked in her face. "I do think I did well with you, Evelyn." He looked at Lee. "You were much easier than Evelyn because I had perfected the process by the time your embryo was placed in a birthing tube."

"So everything we remember about our past was implanted by you?" Lee asked him as he looked at him with hate building inside him.

"Just up until you were twenty years of age," Petersen said in a logical voice. "After that you were released into the world as a normal person, and any experiences and knowledge you two acquired was through the natural process of living and working in the world."

"So our skills in tracking and hacking we acquired on our own after we were released?" Evelyn asked him.

"Yes," he said. "I would have liked to watch and record your development after you two left the complex, but the five gentlemen refused to allow me to do that."

"Did we have implants in us that allowed them to track us?" Evelyn asked Petersen.

"No, because they didn't know about you," he said.

"Then how the hell did they know we came from birthing tubes?" Lee growled at him.

"Three years after you left, Lee, they came here to check on my work and learned about my experiment with both of you."

"How did you manage to get sperm and ova from our parents?" Evelyn asked him.

"I had eight clones kidnap the two women and two men who made up a small hunting party seventy miles south of the complex, and render them unconscious. I had them brought here and removed ovum and sperm from them, then I had the clones dispose of them," Petersen answered.

"You had our parents killed?" Lee asked him.

"Yes, once I got live, healthy sperm and ovum from the two women and two men I had no further use for them."

Lee looked at Evelyn and said softly, "I would have liked to know them."

Evelyn looked at him and said, "Yes, that would have been nice."

"Oh, I implanted in your brains as much as I could get from their brains while they were unconscious into the computer. So what you know about your parents is true."

"Lee," Evelyn said. "I know both my parents died in an accident when I was nineteen."

"Mine died when I was the same age," he replied.

"But you were both separated by two years," Petersen told them.

"I used money I inherited from my parents to set up an apartment for myself in Crown City, and go to graduate school," Lee said.

"Me, too," Evelyn told him. She looked at Petersen and asked, "Where did our inheritance come from if you had our parents killed and buried somewhere on the prairie?"

"I set up accountants in banks in Crown in both your names from money I had available here," he told her.

"Did you inherit a million dollars, Evelyn, like I did?" Lee asked her.

"Yes," she answered.

"And no one knows about any of this except you and the five?" Lee asked Petersen.

Petersen turned his head and looked at Lyle and said, "He does now."

"When did you two start working for the five?" Lyle asked them.

"I was twenty-five," Lee said. "I worked for them for twenty years then I told them to go to hell."

"I was twenty-three," Evelyn said. "I stopped working for them at forty-seven."

"So they hired both of you after you'd left here and been in the world for a few years as normal humans," Lyle said. He looked at both of them carefully.

"What are you looking at, Lyle?" Evelyn asked him.

"They didn't kill you two after you left their employment because they had this information they could use against you anytime they wanted to," he told them.

"Well, no more," Evelyn said. "Even if we have to be exposed and die, too."

"You two still haven't gotten it have you?" Lyle asked them.

"Yes, we have, Lyle," Lee said, looking at Petersen with hate in his eyes. "We're the results of experiments conducted by this Professor here."

"No, you're not," Lyle told him. "With the exception of your conception and early development, you're as normal as any human in the world. You even have families and grandchildren. Real clones don't." He turned his head to the right and looked at the screen. "We have trouble."

Evelyn looked at Lee and said, "You know, Lee, Lyle's right. We are really just like everyone else. We are the product of normal human fertilization except we developed quickly in birthing tubes if the professor is right."

"I never lie, because I've been programmed not to lie." Petersen told them.

Lee looked at her and smiled as he said, "You're right, Evelyn."

"What are you smiling at?" she asked him.

"I was thinking about a good looking redhead I know," he said.

"I said we have trouble," Lyle yelled at them as he watched the screen.

Evelyn turned to her right and looked at the screen and saw ten men approaching the complex from the north. "They can't get in," she said. "I've shut down all the entrances."

"What's that in the right corner of the screen?" Lee said as he looked at the screen.

"What?" she asked.

"In the lower right hand corner of the screen a flashing light," he told her.

She looked at it for a few seconds then said to the computer, "Explain the flashing light in the lower right hand corner."

'Virus scan of all the servers,' the computer replied.

"Who ordered that?"

'Operator Sam.'

"How, only I have control of the servers and computers?"

'Operator Sam is using a laptop to order a virus scan.'

"You're right, Lyle, we've got trouble," Lee said as he watched the ten trackers heading for the northern entrance.

"Where are those trackers headed?" Evelyn said as she looked at them.

'For the northern entrance to the control room,' answered the computer.

"What northern entrance?" Lee asked. He turned and looked at Petersen. "Is there a northern entrance to this control room?"

"Yes, two hundred feet above us there is a door with dirt and grass on it that leads to stairs that lead to another door."

"What other door?" Lyle asked him.

"The door that leads to this control room," Petersen answered. His face was expressionless and there was no sound of concern in his voice.

"How can we see this northern entrance?" Lee asked him.

"The cameras on the surface will show you."

"Computer, show the northern entrance."

The northern entrance appeared on the screen.

"The damn door is open," Lyle said. "What do we do?"

"Go and greet them," Lee said. "How do we get there, computer."

"There is a door on the north side of this room that leads to stairs that lead to the northern entrance," Petersen said as he looked at the screen. "It has never been used."

"Evelyn, try and close that door while we hold off those killers," Lee said as he started walking toward the northern part of the control room. "And keep an eye on the professor. Yell if you need us."

"Don't worry, Lee, he's not going to do anything, but answer any questions I have."

Lyle followed Lee with the expectation of doing something he had never done in his life, killing other people even if they were clones.

The five were standing around Sam looking over his shoulder at the screen of the laptop.

"Very good, Sam," Larry said as he and the others watched the ten trackers move toward the open door. "They should be able to get into that control room within minutes."

"If Lee isn't aware they're coming," Steve added.

"He's too busy being upset over being a clone," Paul said. "Our problem will be solved in minutes, gentlemen."

CHAPTER 64

6:15 a.m., June 11

"Thank God this is a steel door," Lee said as he opened the control room door.

They could see light coming into the control room from outside.

Outside the steel door was a small steel platform and a flight of steel steps that led to a steel landing just above a wide alcove that steps from the outside door lead down to.

"What do we do?" Lyle asked in a worried voice.

"Follow me and do as I say," Lee told him as he ran out on the platform and down the steps. When he reached the landing he looked at both ends of the landing and said, "This is a good position to be in. We'll have the high ground, and can hold them off till Evelyn can shut that door."

"So we just stand here on the steps and shoot them as they come through the door?" he asked Lee.

"We're two hundred feet below the surface according to that diagram we saw on your laptop," Lee said. "That means that outer door is probably a hundred feet or more away from where we're at. Those clones will have to come down those steps at the end of the alcove to reach that alcove at the bottom then come up these steps." He looked at the alcove. "And there's nothing in that alcove they can use to hide behind. See the steps at the other end of the alcove, Lyle?"

"Yes, I see them," he said.

"Once they reach the bottom of those steps they'll have two choices come for us or go back," he said.

"Well, they're not going to go back, Lee. They're clones and will do as order by those five."

"You take the right side and lie flat on your stomach with your weapon just at the edge of the landing," he said. "I'll be on the left." He moved to his left.

Lyle moved to the right and lay down as Lee told him.

"Make sure your weapon is on maximum power," Lee told him. "And shoot only those that come down the steps to the alcove. And remember aim and shoot, and don't think about who you're shooting. They're clones with no feelings of remorse. Kill them or they will kill you. And don't hang over the edge you'll make a better target for them. But aim."

"How do I adjust this weapon for maximum power?" he asked in a nervous voice as he aimed his weapon.

"There's a small switch on the right side of the semi-automatic push it all the way down. You'll have less ammo, so don't waste it and don't throw up because you'll have to lie in your vomit. Now be quiet and still and fire when I fire. Good luck."

Lyle adjusted his weapon for maximum power and cleared his mind of everything except killing the clones that were coming to kill them.

Lee didn't tell him that if these clones were trained to kill, they would be crack shots, and they were probably wearing body armor. There was no sense in upsetting him more than he was already upset. He waited.

"The end is near for those traitors," Bruce said, looking at the ten clones approaching the open door.

The clones were in two lines with ten feet between the lines and six feet between the ones in front and behind.

"They must kill Lee first," Steve said. "The other two don't have his survival skills."

"Don't worry, Steve, we have more than enough people to do the job," Bruce told him.

"Yes," Larry agreed. "We've got forty-four others coming as fast as they can. Even if they manage to stop these ten we will eventually overwhelm them."

"There's no sense in us remaining in this hallway. I suggest we go to the library, gentlemen, where we will be comfortable," Paul said. "We can also have breakfast while we wait for the rest of our people."

"Can you use the computer in the library to do what you've done with that laptop?" Fred asked Sam.

"Yes, sir," Sam replied.

"Then I suggest we retire to the library," Larry said. "We can have breakfast brought for Sam as well."

"Yes," Paul agreed as he turned and started walking toward the library. "Considering what he'd done for us this morning Sam should have the honor of eating with us."

All Steve could think was, *I hope we're right.*

Lee glanced over at Lyle and thought *I hope he doesn't fall apart when those bolts start hitting the wall behind him and the ceiling above him.*

The first two clones to reach the door stopped on both sides of the open door and glanced inside. There was no one on the steps and they couldn't see the bottom of the alcove from where they were.

"I'll go first," the one on the left said. "You cover me."

The clone on the right nodded and got ready to cover the other one.

The steps and the alcove were like a cave and echoed their voices to Lee and Lyle so they heard what they said and prepared themselves for the fight that was coming.

Lee knew they would come down the steps in pairs on both sides of the stairs one covering the other. The advantage Lee and Lyle had was they would see the clones before the clones were in a position to look up and see them. He looked at Lyle and saw a frightened but determined look on his face. He looked back at the bottom of the stairs that lead to the outside door and waited for the clones to arrive before he started shooting.

The first clone moved quickly through the door and headed down the steps one at a time on the right side while the other one moved to the opening and started coming down the steps two yards behind the other one on the left side of the stairs. Before he reached the bottom of the steps the first clone started shooting his weapon moving it back and forward to frighten or kill anyone hiding at the bottom of the steps.

Lee held his fire.

Lyle swallowed his fear and waited for Lee to start shooting. He kept his eyes and attention focused on the steps leading from the alcove up to the outside.

The first clone came down the stairs and headed for the stairs that lead to the landing and the second one followed a few yards behind the first one, but he didn't do any shooting.

Lee waited until both clones were in the alcove and moving toward the steps before he took aim at the chest of the second one and fired two shots.

Both shots hit the clone in the chest, went through his body armor, and dropped him instantly.

Lyle following Lee's example aimed and shot the first clone in the chest.

The clone fell to the floor and rolled over on his left side and fired to his right in the direction of Lee. His bolts of electricity hit the wall behind Lee high above his head.

Lyle took his time, he was scared, and shot the clone in the forehead.

Two other clones came down the steps into the alcove firing wildly up high to frighten away whoever had killed the first two and running for the stairs.

Lee dropped both with double shots to the chest. *You five should have given these clones better body armor,* he thought.

Four other clones rushed down the steps two by two toward the alcove but didn't fire until they reached the alcove. They knew where Lee and Lyle were because of the shots they had fired but they couldn't see them. The door began to close behind the last two clones before the first two reached the alcove.

"Lee, the light from the outside in dimming. The door is closing!" Lyle screamed.

"Shut up and shoot!" Lee replied in just as loud a voice.

One of the clones' shots nicked the landing an inch from Lyle's left wrist.

The close hit upset Lyle and he jerked the trigger of his weapon and threw his aim off as he fired and hit the floor just in front of the clone.

The clone ran for the stairs and jumped three feet and landed on the second step from the bottom high enough for him to see Lee and moved his weapon in Lee's direction. He was a little too slow.

Lee fired a quick shot hoping to startle the clone and hit the clone on the left side of his face opening his cheek to the bone and ripping his left ear from his head.

This time Lyle didn't fire wild and his shot hit the clone in the throat and knocked him back down the stairs. His body slid to the floor at the bottom of the stairs preventing an easy access to the stairs by the other clones.

The door had closed and the only light in the alcove and on the stairs and landing was from the lights in the ceiling.

The other clone on the left ran to the stairs and foolishly grabbed the body of the dead one by his left arm and pulled his fellow clone's body from the steps. By doing that he had to turn around. The last two clones came down the steps into the alcove with their weapons held up high.

Lyle fired and hit him in the center of his back where his body armor was thick and the bolt didn't penetrate.

The clone turned around with a blank expression on his face and raised his weapon to fire at Lyle. His shot missed Lyle's head by more than a foot and hit the stone wall behind him.

Lee fired twice and both shots hit him in the face killing him.

The last two clones looked up at the same time and saw Lee and Lyle and came at them without hesitation.

Lee and Lyle both fired six shots each and hit both clone twice in their heads and four times in their chests.

They dropped like rocks.

The last two clones outside the door stopped and called for their companions to open the door. Their calls were in vain. The door was steel and an inch thick with at least a foot of dirt and grass attached to the outside of it.

Lee waited with his weapon pointed at the door expecting the clones to force it open. When the door didn't move, he breathed a sigh of relief and relaxed.

"Lyle, how are you?" he yelled at him without looking at him.

"Scared," Lyle replied in a soft voice as fear moved back and forth in his body. *I never thought I'd be able to kill like I've done. Not even clones. What has happened to me?*

"Lee, Lyle, the door is closed and locked!" Evelyn screamed at them. "But the outside cameras show forty-four others coming."

We'll never stop that many, Lee thought. *They'll come at us from at least two or three directions in groups of three or four. We'll be overwhelmed. We need another plan of survival.* He carefully looked at the clones lying on the stone floor at the bottom of the stairs to make sure they were dead and not faking death.

"Can the others outside open that door?" Lyle yelled to Evelyn.

"Not unless they have explosives," she said.

"If they had explosives these dead ones would have used them," Lyle replied.

"How close are they?" Lee asked as he got up. "Let's go Lyle." He started up the stairs to the control room.

"We can take'em, Lee," Lyle said in a courageous and positive voice as he sprang to his feet and followed Lee.

"No we can't," Lee told him as he started up the steps to the control room.

"They're about two miles away and approaching fast," Evelyn told him.

"In cars or trucks?" Lee asked her as he walked up behind her and looked at the screen.

"Eleven four-wheel drive all-terrain vehicles that look heavily built," she said.

"Don't worry, Lee, we took out eight on the stairs we can take these others out, too," Lyle said, walking over to Lee's right side.

Lee swiftly turned around and said in an angry voice, "You did good, Lyle, real good. But there are forty-four other clones coming to this complex and they've probably got heavy voltage weapons that'll cut through anything we can put up before them. And they won't be coming at us two at a time. If we don't figure out how to get out of this damn control room we're dead."

Lyle's confidence began to drop as he asked, "So what are we going to do?"

"Can you download everything in these servers and computers on the Internet, Evelyn?" Lee asked, turning around to look at the screen.

"Not as long as that virus scan is operating," she said as she pointed to a bar at the bottom of the screen. "There's twenty minutes left."

"Why so long?" Lyle asked her.

"The larger and more complex a computer system is the longer the virus scan takes, Lyle. There are four servers here with vast amounts of space on their internal hard drives plus four computers. Every drive will be scanned for a virus and the information in them before the scan stops."

"Can you do anything while that's going on?" Lee asked her.

"I just did," she said as she typed on the keyboard. "I closed that outer steel door and the one that leads to this room. But there are other entrances to this complex and I'm trying to get to the program that controls them to shut them down as fast as I can."

"Can't you stop the scan?" Lyle asked her.

"No, I can't. Whoever this Sam is he's very good because he ordered the scan to continue without interference."

"I just thought of something," Fred said as they walked into the library.

"What have you thought of, Fred?" Larry asked him.

"What if they manage to stop the scan?"

"They can't, sir," Sam replied, following them.

"And why can't they?" Paul asked. He was again worried.

"I told the servers not to stop the scan until it is finished."

"Can they work their way around the scan and download information?" Steve asked. "We mustn't forget Evelyn is an excellent hacker."

"No, sir, but they can still control the complex."

"Does that mean they can lock all the doors to the complex?" Bruce asked him.

"Yes, sir."

"Open every door to the complex and order our trackers to enter by different doors four at a time and converge on the control room," Steve told him. "Breakfast will have to wait."

"Yes, sir," Sam said as he walked to a desk with a computer on it and began to do as Steve ordered.

"How many entrances are there to this complex?" Paul asked.

"Six, sir, including the one to the control room," Sam said. "And all of them are opening up. And the trackers have been given their orders."

"There are only three elevators to the control room and a stairwell," Larry said. "Once our trackers are in the complex I'll have them converge on those three at the same time. They won't be able to kill the other forty-four. Where are the ten that were close?"

"One moment, sir, while I access the cameras over the outside door they used to get into the control room stairwell from outside."

The five men stood watching him.

"Eight of the men are not visible, but two are still outside and both the steel inner door and steel outer door are closed and locked."

"That's good," Larry said.

"No it isn't," Paul disagreed in a harsh voice. "If those two doors are closed, it means the eight that got inside are dead. Tell them to use the closest door to get into the complex, Sam, and to report to you."

"Yes, sir," Sam replied as he sent the message to the surviving two clones.

"How much time is left before the virus scan is complete?" Fred asked.

"Fifteen minutes, sir."

"How close are the forty-four others?" Paul asked him.

"Less than a mile and a quarter away," Sam said.

"It'll take them more than fifteen minutes to cover such a distance over rough terrain no matter how fast they drive," Steve said. "Can you expand the scan time?"

"I'll try, sir."

"Temporarily stop the scan, Sam," Larry ordered him.

"Are you crazy," Bruce yelled at Larry. "They'll download the information when the scan stops."

"No, I'm not crazy, Bruce," Larry said calmly. "They can't download anything until the scan is complete or is permanently cancelled. By temporarily stopping it the scan will lock down the system giving our trackers time to reach the complex."

Paul walked up behind Sam and looked at the large screen on the wall. "Temporarily stop the scan, Sam, and then try and access the cameras in the control room."

Sam started doing as he was ordered.

A minute passed before Paul spoke, "There they are."

The other four men looked at the screen and saw Evelyn sitting at a desk working a computer and Lee and Lyle standing behind her. Petersen was tired to a chair with a pleasant look on his face as if he were watching an interesting TV program.

"Can we see what she's typing on the keyboard?" Paul asked Sam.

"No, sir, their bodies are blocking the cameras."

"Lee and Lyle wouldn't be standing behind her if the eight that got into the stairwell were alive," Steve said.

"They have no heavy voltage rifles," Fred said. "I wonder why not?"

"That isn't important, Fred," Larry told him. "What's important is we can now see what they are doing."

"Maybe Evelyn will start talking to the computers and we'll be able to hear her and block her moves until our trackers get into that control room and kill them all," Fred said.

They saw Lee turn around and look at the four cameras in each of the four corners of the room. They saw a serious expression on his face then watched him raise his semi-automatic and shoot out each of the cameras.

"Damn that man," Paul hissed in a frustrated voice.

"So we wait until the rest of the trackers arrive and go in that room and kill them all before they can download any information on us," Steve said.

CHAPTER 65

7 a.m., June 11

Evelyn was busy working on the computer and unconcerned with anything Lee and Lyle were doing.

Petersen sat and silently watched and wondered when he would be able to have breakfast. Never in the five hundred years he'd been in the underground complex had he gone a day without breakfast. Some mornings he had a late breakfast because he had spent the night working on the proper development of the clones for the five, or a new form of deadly bacteria they wanted him to develop. Then he'd wake up late.

Lyle and Lee were busy silently thinking of what tactic they would use when the forty-four other clones reached the complex and joined forces with the two clones they hadn't managed to kill and the five monsters.

Lyle heard his stomach growl and realized he was hungry. "Why don't we eat those donuts Petersen brought?"

Lee looked at him then at the door that had the room of antique weapons and ammunition in it. He didn't say anything because a plan was forming in the back of his mind.

"A little food in our stomachs won't improve our situation, but it certainly won't worsen it," Lyle said. "It may even help us think up a way out of this room we're trapped in."

Lee shrugged his shoulders and didn't say anything because Lyle was right. He got up and walked to the serving cart that had the coffee and donuts on it, and removed the cloth covering the cart.

"We've got two dozen donuts of various kinds stacked on a glass plate, and six cups with saucers and spoons, six small plates, and a large pot of coffee. And there's cream and sugar," he said as he looked at the large glass covered plate of donuts. He turned to his left and looked at Evelyn. "You want a couple of donuts and some coffee?"

"Yes," she said as she continued typing. "If those five are smart, Lee, they'll try to shut off the water in this control room. Why don't you take those canteens we have in our back packs and fill them with water from the bathroom faucets?"

"I'll do it," Lyle volunteered as he turned around and walked to the backpacks on the floor.

While Lyle got the canteens Lee poured coffee in one of the cups for Evelyn. "You take cream and sugar?" he asked her.

"Black, please, and a jelly donut if there are any," she said. "Make it two, I'm hungry."

Lee did as she asked and brought the coffee and two sugar covered jelly donuts on a small plate to her. "What are you doing?" he asked as he sat the coffee and donuts on the desk next to the keyboard.

"Destroying all that stuff about us in the hard drives of the servers and computers," she answered.

"How do you know they don't have paper files on us?" he asked. "Once the Justice Department gets into this place they're going to go over this complex with a very fine tooth comb and find everything."

"There are paper files in here on cloning and developing bacteria that's specifically developed to kill people, but everything on us and the five are in the servers."

"How do you know that?"

"Because I asked the computer to search the servers and the hard drives of the other computers for such information and the one I'm working on. Apparently Petersen over there likes to make paper copies of important work."

"And we're not that important?"

"Like he said, Lee, you and I were experiments and nothing else."

"Yes you were," Petersen said, breaking his silence. "I don't mean to belittle you two as humans but the only part of your development that was important was the rapid growth of your bodies, and the transmission of knowledge into your brains."

Lee turned toward him and asked, "What sort of knowledge?"

"General public school knowledge and certain childhood experiences," he said as he looked at Lee.

Lee started at him wondering if he should hate him.

"I had to give you some childhood experiences, or you would have had only knowledge about your public school education. And that would have made it impossible for you two to blend into society. Not having a past beyond college other than a public school education makes a person a bit noticeable to regular people"

"I don't remember much about my childhood experiences," he told Petersen.

"I'm not surprised," Petersen told him. "My study of reports on people's childhood experiences indicates most people only remember those things about their childhood that has a direct bearing on their adult lives."

"I remember I liked playing computer games," Evelyn said as she stopped typing and reached for her coffee. She took a large swallow, put the cup down, picked up a donut and bit into it. "Mmmm, this is a good donut. Really sweet plum jelly, too." She returned to typing.

"We have clones that were programmed to be excellent chefs," Petersen told her. "And we have an excellent wine collection, too."

"All the comforts of home, huh," Lee said.

"Yes," Petersen said.

"How do you know about regular people?" Lee asked him. "The five let you leave this complex every now and then?"

"I haven't been out of this complex in five hundred years," he said. "I access the Internet during my leisure time and study reports done on people by psychologists and psychiatrists."

"What sort of life did you have before they cloned you, Petersen?"

"I don't remember, and it's not important. Only my work in the complex is important."

"I've filled the canteens," Lyle announced as he walked out of the bathroom and over to the two backpacks and put them back in the backpacks.

"Get something in your stomach," Lee said as he walked to the door with the

room of antique weapons. He opened the door, turned on the lights inside, and walked into it and began to look around. Then he started examining the boxes of ammunition. He knelt down and opened one of the metal boxes and looked at the ammunition inside it. An idea began to form in the back of his mind as he looked at the ammunition in the box he'd opened. He stood up and walked out of the room. "Petersen, what's on top of that missile in the silo?"

"Oh, you've seen the missile," he answered.

"Yes, we saw it now what's on top of it?"

"A warhead. That's what the people centuries ago called those things they put on top of missiles," he said. He turned as best he could being tied to the chair and looked at Lee. "Do you know what type of missile it is?"

"Yeah, an ICBM."

"Very good, Lee," he said. "Now do you know what those letters stand for?"

"Intercontinental Ballistic Missile."

"How do you know that?"

"I like to read history."

"That's what makes you a real human, Lee," he said in a voice that had just a touch of excitement in it.

"Because I wasn't programmed to like history?"

"You and Evelyn weren't programmed for anything while you were in your birthing tubes."

"We were just given a basic elementary and high school education," he said.

"And some facts about your parents. I decided it was necessary that you should know personality traits about your parents."

Evelyn stopped typing and turned around and looked at Petersen. "I remember my parents as being kind and loving who had a love of the outdoors."

"And you, Lee?" Petersen asked him.

"Yeah, I remember the same thing about my parents," he said.

"That's very good to hear," he said. "You two should have kept in touch with me so I could update my records on your mental development after you left the complex. But that's my fault. I didn't give you the compound's address. Because we don't have an address you two could have written to." He looked closely at Lee and then at Evelyn. "Now that I've met and spoken to both of you, I know my experiment in rapidly producing two normal humans was successful."

"Maybe you'll win the Noble Prize for Biology," Lee told him. "Now what type of warhead is on that missile? An atomic bomb?"

"No, such a weapon has a limited killing range," he said. "The five gentlemen wanted a warhead of bacteria that would become air born once the warhead opened and released its contents. The fact that you both know your parents were kind and loving with a love of the outdoors indicates a biological transmission of certain mental traits carried in their DNA from their minds into their sperm and ova. And those mental traits developed within both of you."

"Why?" Evelyn asked him as she returned to the keyboard.

"Because your parents were wilderness people."

"What do you mean wilderness people?" Lyle asked him. He had a mouthful of donut. He was sitting at one of the desks.

"People who live in the wilderness in small villages away from towns and cities. I had the eight clones capture and drug them, it was a mild sedative that didn't harm them, when they were asleep and brought here to the lab where I removed sperm and ova from them. Then combined them to make both of you?"

Lyle took a swallow of coffee and said, "Then you had them killed?"

"I couldn't release them back where they were found," Petersen said. "The five gentlemen demand that this underground complex remains secret."

"What type of warhead was originally on the missile?" Lee didn't like what he heard, but there was nothing he could do about it now.

"The same as were on the other three missiles in the four silos that surround this complex."

"What were they?" Lee asked them.

"Atomic bombs as you said. Four per missile."

"Where are the other missiles and warheads?"

"The five gentlemen had no use for four missiles so those other three silos were filled in and the warheads were buried somewhere in the wilderness."

"So there are sixteen atomic bombs buried somewhere outside this complex?" Lee said. He decided to help himself to coffee and donuts. He had a plan forming in the back of his mind and he knew he'd need some food to keep his mind going. He walked to the cart and got himself a cup of coffee and two plain donuts.

"No, just fifteen. One is down in the garage area in a secure room."

That's when Lee knew what he had to do to get out of the complex. "We may have a chance to escape," he said as he walked to a desk with his coffee and donut and sat down.

Lyle stopped drinking his coffee and asked, "We do?"

Lee nodded and started eating his donut.

"Well?" Lyle said. "Explain yourself."

Lee swallowed and asked Evelyn, "What have you been doing?"

"After I removed everything about us from the servers' and computers' hard drives I started putting up firewalls to stop this Sam guy from getting control of this room," she answered.

"Can you locate this secure room where that atomic bomb is located?"

"I suppose so," she answered. "I've got control of the entire computer system of this underground complex for now."

"Then do it," he said as he finished one of the donuts and started on the other one.

She started asking the servers and computers where was the secure room with the atomic bomb in it?

"What exactly have you got in mind, Lee?" Lyle asked.

"We got almost no chance of winning when those other clones arrive, and they're probably close by now," he said. "That means we've got to do something to stop those assholes from launching that missile with the bacteria in it. And detonating an atom bomb is the best way to stop them, Lyle."

"That's insane!" he replied. "I don't know much about those atom bombs they built centuries ago, but the damn things are very destructive."

"And there is radiation," Petersen said then quickly added. "But most of the deadly radiation dissipates within two or three weeks."

"I've found the room, Lee," Evelyn said.

"Petersen are there instructions with that bomb?" Lee asked him.

"Yes, we kept those," he answered.

"Why?" Lyle asked him.

"I don't really know," he said. "But I suspect it was for destroying everything in the complex if the five gentlemen had to abandon it."

Lyle looked at Lee and said, "What's your plan?"

"What about those armored antique vehicles down in that garage?" Lee asked Petersen.

"What about them?"

"Do they still work?"

"Only the electric powered ones. Those that operate on liquid fuel are useless, because there is no liquid fuel. The fuel in their tanks evaporated a few centuries ago."

"Those armored antiques all operate on liquid fuel, Professor," Lee said.

"No, there are two that are electrically operated," he said.

"How is that? Powerful electric engines weren't developed until the middle of the twenty-first century," Lee said to him.

"I had the clones remove their internal combustion engines and replace them with electric engines," he answered.

"Why?"

"I wanted to see if they would work with electric engines in them, and they did. Quite well, too."

"Did you ever take them outside and drive them around?" Lyle asked Petersen.

"Both of them but only once."

"So what good are they, Lee?" Lyle asked. "There are no batteries to operate the weapons. They're probably those old kind that fired projectiles."

"Are they, Petersen?" Lee asked him. He finished his coffee.

"Yes, but the projectiles are still good. In that dry environment at the sixth level the explosives are still good, but not as effective as they once were."

"All right, Evelyn, this is what I want you to do," he said. "Open that room but don't let the five know."

"That's easy since I've still got control of this control room," she said. "But this Sam clone they've got working for them is very good. So whatever you're planning we might as well start now."

"We get down in that garage, set that bomb to explode, and use one of those armored vehicles to get into one of those special elevators and get the hell out of here," he said.

"It just might work," Lyle said in a hopeful voice.

"If we can set that bomb to detonate after we leave this complex," Evelyn added. She didn't want to tell them the moment the five and their clones got into the control room it would take them only minutes to get control of the complex again and trap them inside the elevator until their clone killers found and killed them.

"The moment we leave this room those five are going to know in less than a minute, Lee," Lyle said. "And they'll use these computers and servers to stop us from leaving this complex."

"Maybe," Evelyn said.

CHAPTER 66

7: 30 a.m. library

"The trackers are here, sir," Sam announced.

"Yes, we can see them," Larry said, looking at the screen on the wall.

Thirty-eight well-armed men and six women were waiting outside the five entrances to the complex. Nine were outside four of the entrances eight were outside the fifth. The two from the ten were still outside the door that led to the control room.

"Open the doors and let them enter," Paul said.

"It will take some time to get pass the firewalls the people in the control have set up," Sam told them.

"How much time," Steve asked.

"I don't know, sir," Sam answered.

"Guess?" Bruce ordered him.

"I don't know how to do that, sir?"

"Ten minutes," Fred said.

"Possibly, sir, maybe fifteen minutes," Sam said.

"It doesn't matter if it takes an hour," Paul said. "They're trapped. We have control of all the exits. No matter where they go we shall have them."

"Can they contact the outside world," Steve asked Sam.

"No, sir," Sam answered.

"Why not," Steve asked him.

"I have shut down the long range transmitter."

Paul smiled as said, "You see, gentlemen, they are trapped. They can't go anywhere and time is against them."

"I wouldn't be so sure," Steve said. "Remember we didn't think they survived the tornado, and we didn't suspect they could get into this complex and overpower Troy. But somehow they did."

"All of that is true, Steve," Paul said. "But they're trapped now with no way out and no way to transmit the information they found in those servers and computers. We will have them all in a few hours at the most."

"As of this moment Lee and Evelyn are working on a way out of the trap they're in, and I have no doubt it's something we won't suspect until it's too late," Steve said.

"Stop being so pessimistic, Steve!" Larry shouted at him. "We will win and by tomorrow we will be home."

"And if they kill Petersen?"

Paul turned and looked at Steve and said in a reassuring voice. "We have a clone for him in a birthing tube, Steve. If they kill him, two or three of us can remain here for six months to clone a new Petersen with all the skills of the one they've captured."

Steve turned around and walked to a chair and sat down thinking, *I wonder what plan of escape Lee has these fools don't believe he has.*

"What do you mean maybe?" Lyle asked Evelyn.

"They'll have to get pass the firewalls I've instanlled to get control of the computers and servers in this control room, and I don't care how good that Sam clone is it's going to take him at least ten minutes to get pass those firewalls once he gets into this room."

Lyle nodded his agreement as he said, "That may be enough time for us to do what we have to do."

"All right, Lee, we've got fifteen minutes at the most," Evelyn said, pushing her chair back and standing up. "Let's go."

"What about Petersen?" Lyle asked as he stood up and grabbed one of the backpack.

"Leave him for them," Lee said as he put his backpack on his back and moved toward the door leading to the stairwell.

"We're using the stairs?" Evelyn asked him.

"If we use one of the elevators would they detect one of them moving?" Lee asked her as he opened the door to the stairwell.

"Yes, they would even if they couldn't stop it," she said. "The stairs are the best way down. Even if the doors are electrically monitored they won't be able to stop us from opening them."

"Before we go I want to ask Petersen a question," Lyle said.

"Hurry up," Lee said harshly.

"Dr. Petersen, there have never been any reports of some missile exploding on Earth for five hundred years. So how did the five spread those bacteria than killed billions over the years?"

"Clones were sent to certain places with the bacteria in vials which they opened, and then left to return here," he said in a calm voice as if he was talking of planting a garden.

"Let's go," Lyle said. "Those five monsters have to be destroyed and this damn complex with them."

Lee pulled his night vision goggles down over his eyes, took out his weapon, and entered the stairwell.

Lyle and Evelyn did the same thing.

"Be careful," Lyly warned them. "We've got over four hundred feet to go, and we don't want to fall.

Lee set a fast but safe pace down the steps avoiding taking two or three at a time.

He hadn't done that in years anyway.

"I have the ability to open all the doors except the one to the control room," Sam announced.

"Do so," Fred ordered him.

"Yes, sir," Sam said and opened all five entrance doors to the complex.

The forty-four clones rushed into the complex in two-by-two formations to protect each other moving their weapons from left to right and up and down.

"Go immediately to the control room all of you and capture or kill everyone in the control room as soon as the door to it opens," Paul ordered them over his com-cell.

"How shall we go?" asked one of the clone trackers.

"Use the elevators," Bruce told them. "Nine of you go to the control room elevators. A sign above them will tell you which ones. The rest of you go to the other elevators."

"Are the elevators available, Sam?" Paul asked.

"In two minutes, sir."

Running down stairs wearing night vision goggles even in a dark stairwells was easier than climbing a ladder in an air duct, and seven minutes after they left the control room they were approaching the garage.

"Hold," Lee said as he reached the door to the garage. He was breathing hard and his legs were a little tired. He had never run down over four hundred feet of steps in his entire life. He approached the door, grabbed the handle, and slowly opened the door, and quickly looked out. "All clear," he said and walked out into the garage and the light sensors immediately detected his presence and turned on all the lights.

"Go to the right, Lee," Evelyn said as she followed him, pushing her night goggles up on her forehead. "There should be a sign on it."

"Why? No one comes down here," Lyle said as he followed her pushing his night goggles up on his forehead.

Evelyn admitted he was right and said, "It should be only fifty feet from the stairwell."

Lee pushed his goggles up on his forehead and ran to his right and stopped in front of a plain steel door. "This it?"

Evelyn stopped next to him, took her I-book out of the pouch hanging from her left arm, turned it on, and looked at it. "This is it, Lee, and it's unlocked," she said a few seconds later.

Lee grabbed the handle and pushed it down and pushed against the door. It opened without a sound and the lights inside the room came on.

There was a metal table in the center of the room and nothing else except a large wooden travelling trunk with tarnished handles on both ends in the far right corner. Lee and Evelyn entered the room.

"Is that it?" Lyle asked, walking into the room behind Evelyn and Lee. He was looking at the wooden trunk.

"That's what I saw on the screen on the wall in the control room," Evelyn said as she looked around the room for a camera. She saw one in the left corner high on the wall. "I saw it through that."

Lee walked over to the trunk and looked around the room. "I don't see any instruction books." He leaned over and looked under the table. "Nothing."

"I doubt if the people of the twentieth century would leave an instruction book for how to detonate something as deadly as this lying on the table or floor, Lee," Lyle said as he walked to the front of the trunk and saw two brass clamps. He put his weapon in his belt and pushed the two clamps up.

The metallic sound they made startled Lee and Evelyn and they both jumped back.

Lyly looked at them and said, "What's in here is not a fire cracker. Jumping back wouldn't help any." He raised the lid and pushed it all the way back.

Strapped to the top of the lid on the inside was a booklet that had 'Instructions to Arm the Weapon' written on the front cover. Lyle pulled the booklet free of the straps and opened it as Lee and

Evelyn walked up on each side of him. Lyle began to read the words on the cover.

"This is a twenty megaton bomb and has the destructive power to destroy everything within a circumference of fifty miles."

"What does ten megaton mean?" Evelyn asked.

"Probably how much power it has," Lyle said.

"You're right, Lyle," Lee said as he read the information at the bottom of the cover. "Megaton means one million tons of TNT."

"Is that like the TNT that's produced today?" Lyle asked him.

"I don't think so since the companies that produce TNT today have probably improved it," he answered.

"This is an extremely powerful weapon, gents," Evelyn said.

"Go to the arming instructions." Lee said. "If it can destroy an area of fifty miles it can destroy this entire underground complex."

"But Lee, it means we've got to be farther away than fifty miles, or we won't survive the explosion," she told him.

"You know these things produced a lot of terrible radiation that could kill people who survived the explosion," Lyle said.

"Go to the instructions, Lyle," Lee said.

"The elevators are available, sir," Sam said.

"All of them?" Larry asked him. He was standing behind Sam looking at the screen on the wall.

"Yes, sir, all of them."

"Good," Paul said with a smile on his face. "In a few minutes, gentlemen our problem with Lee and Evelyn and that damn Lyle Morton will be over and we can begin our revenge against their families."

"It is a pity no one will know but us," Fred said. He wasn't smiling but his voice had a happy sound to it.

They watched quietly as the first nine of the clone trackers went to the three elevators that went to the control room and pushed the buttons summoning the elevators.

"Will they all arrive at the same time?" Bruce asked as he stood next to Paul.

"Yes, sir, I've programmed all the elevators to arrive at the same time and open at the same time," Sam said.

"That is excellent, Sam," Larry said as he reached out and patted him on the right shoulder.

They watched as the doors to the three elevators to the control opened and three clone trackers entered each elevator with their weapons ready to kill. The five of them watched as the doors closed and the elevators began to move up to the control room.

"In less than two minutes we will be safe again," Paul mumbled softly.

Steve sitting in a chair watching them wasn't so sure. He had never liked Lee or Evelyn, but he didn't underestimate their intelligence or abilities. They had already proven they were skillful in the use of both. Even Lyly had proven to be smarter than any of them suspected. Acquiring their information from the Department of Information without their people working for the department knowing what he had done had proven that.

Lyle went to the table of contents of the thin booklet and found the page the instruction for arming the bomb was on. He turned to it.

"Instructions for arming the weapon," Lyle read the heading of the paragraph.

Lee and Evelyn looked over his shoulders and they all read quietly to themselves.

Raise the plastic cover on the keypad and push the red button on the right side of the keypad at the top. A seven-digit number will appear in the rectangular screen above the keypad. That is the arming number. Punch all seven digit numbers on the keypad as they appear on the screen this will make the weapon ready to be armed. Then push the green button on the left side of the keypad at the top and the bomb will be armed.

ARMING THE BOMB DOES NOT MEAN IT WILL DETONATE. A DETONATION CODE HAS TO BE ENTERED AND THEN A TIMING CODE.

"Where is the detonation code?" Evelyn asked.

Lyle quickly scanned the page. "Not here." He went back to the table of contents. "Nothing here refers to a detonation code."

Lee saw the word Annex at the bottom of the table of contents. "Go to Annex at the end of the book, Lyle," he said.

"Why if there nothing about a detonation code listed there?" he asked.

"Annex means to join together. Maybe the detonation code is a way of joining the parts of the bomb together to get it to explode."

Evelyn looked at her I-book. "We'd better hurry there are three tracker/killers in each of the three elevators going to the control room."

"How can you see that?" Lyle asked her.

"I programmed one of the servers to put on my I-book everything this Sam guy working for those five sees, and he's watching the tracker/killers in those elevators."

"We should have killed Petersen," Lyle said as he turned to the page of the booklet Annex was on. "He'll tell them where we are."

At the top of the page was a seven-digit number in a red rectangle with the words 'Detonation Code' above and below the rectangle. Below it were instructions. They began to read.

> *To detonate the bomb punch the seven digit code in the red rectangle on the keypad as it appears in the rectangle once the weapon had been armed then push both the red and green buttons at the top within two seconds of each other. THIS WILL NOT CAUSE THE BOMB TO EXPLODE! A TIME SCHEDULE FOR THE BOMB MUST BE ENTERED FOR THE BOMB TO EXPLODE IF THE BOMB IS ON THE GROUND. IF THE MISSILE IS LAUNCHED WITH THE BOMB INSIDE THE NOSE CONE BOTH THE ARMING AND DETONATION CODES WILL BE AUTOMATICALY ENTERED ONCE THE MISSLE REACHES THE PROGRAMMED ALTITUDE OVER ITS TARGET. AN ALTITUDE CODE WHICH WILL DETONATE THE BOMB WILL BE IMMEDIATELY SET BY THE MISSILE'S ONBOARD COMPUTER ONCE THE MISSILE HAS REACHED THE TARGET ZONE.*

> *To set the timer push the red button on the right side at the top of the keypad and six zeros will appear in the screen. Then push the buttons to set the exact time for the weapon to explode on the keypad. Then push the button at the bottom of the keypad. The weapon will be set to go off at the time entered and the countdown will begin.*

> *WARNING!*

*This weapon has a destructive range of fifty miles.
The minimum safe distance is sixty-five miles from
the destructive range. Be under cover to avoid the
radiation.*

"Who wants to set the detonating code?" Lyle asked.

"Me," Evelyn said. "I'm the computer expert in this group." She reached down and pushed the buttons that armed the bomb. "How much time do you think we'll need to get away?"

"Do those large elevators that take those armored vehicles to the top still work?"

Lee asked Evelyn.

"Everything in the complex works, Lee," she answered.

"Wait here while Lyle and I find one of those electric powered vehicles Petersen told us about we can use," he said as he turned toward the door.

"Why are we going to do that before we set the timer?" Lyle asked as he gave the booklet to Evelyn and followed Lee.

"Don't forget me," Evelyn yelled at them.

"We don't want that bomb going off with us in here unless we have no choice."

Lee was running toward the line of armored vehicles. "I won't," he yelled back at Evelyn.

"How do you know these things still work? Just because they're electric powered doesn't mean the batteries are charged."

"Petersen said two of these vehicles work because he drove around in them outside this complex. I'm just hoping the maintenance robots and clones in this place were programmed to keep their batteries charged and the vehicles in working order." He stopped next to a tank and looked it over.

"Petersen's been here for over five hundred years," Lyle said. "He could have had the robots in the place make the changes to the two armored vehicles over a century ago, Lee."

"Well, if you got a better idea for getting out of this damn complex, Lyle, I'm sure listening," Lyle stopped next to him. "Which one should we take?" He didn't have a better idea.

Lee looked down the row of vehicles and said, "One with wheels. These tracked vehicles probably make a lot of noise."

"Lee, in ten minutes or less they're going to know we're down here and send those killers after us," Lyle said. "Noise isn't something we have to worry about."

"Start looking for a wheeled vehicle with inflated tires."

Lyle moved among the vehicles till he came to one that was long and had six four feet high two feet wide inflated tires on it. "Here's one," he yelled. His voice echoed around the garage.

Lee ran over to him and started climbing on top of it from the front using the lift rings. He got up to the hatch, moved the handle to one side, and the hatch sprang open two inches. He raised it, took off his backpack and tossed it inside, and got down inside and sat on a cloth covered seat. The ceiling lights in the garage provided him with enough light to see the dashboard of the vehicle.

Lyle used another hatch on top of the gun turret and tossed the backpack he carried into the armored vehicle and dropped down onto a dry leather seat that creaked under his weight. "This is a gun," he said as he looked around and saw a cylinder with five holes in it under a metal block.

Lee ignored him as he saw a switch that was pointed to off. He reached down and turned it to on and was surprised when nothing happened. "Damn, the batteries are dead."

Lyle leaned down and looked at the dashboard. "No they're not. Look at the dashboard it's lit up."

Lee looked at the dashboard and smiled when he saw a dial with an arrow on it pointing to the letter F. "The batteries are fully charged," he said.

"That dial doesn't refer to the batteries, Lee, that's indicates the fuel tank is full," Lyle said, looking at the dashboard. "I've read about old gasoline powered cars and F means full. E means empty."

"Liquid fuel," Lee asked him. "Petersen said there was no liquid fuel in these vehicles."

"Apparently he was wrong," Lyle said. "Or maybe the robots replaced the liquid fuel with a type of gel that acts like liquid fuel."

"There's gel that can do that?"

"Yeah, back in Hong Kong there was a rich guy who collected antique cars that used liquid fuel but he had to use a gel like substance because liquid fuel was impossible to get," Lyle explained. "The fire department forced him to have all sorts of fire control devices in the special garage he had them in because that gel substance he used was very explosive. He had to get special permission from—"

"Tell me how it works, Lyle. Not a history lesson on a rich guy with antique cars."

Lyle looked over the dashboard. "There should be a starter button on the dashboard somewhere."

Lee looked at it and said, "Just above the switch." He pushed it and the engine roared to life. "Damn these engines make a lot of noise."

"This thing probably has an old electric engine. They tended to be a bit noisy when started," he said as he leaned back and rose up out of the turret and screamed,

"Evelyn, start the counted down."

Evelyn heard him and reread the instructions then punched in the detonator code. She rushed to the door and screamed, "I'm giving us forty minutes." And rushed back into the room and punched in forty minutes and pushed the button at the bottom of the keypad to start the countdown and ran out of the room pushing buttons on the keyboard of her I-book.

Lee looked at the steering wheel and at the accelerator petal and brake petal and gently pushed down on the accelerator and moved the armored car out of the line of vehicles and using the brake petal stopped and waited for Evelyn. He raised his head up out of the hatch and saw her running in their direction and screamed, "Over here!"

Evelyn turned toward them and ran up to the vehicle and stopped and said, "Open the door."

"Haven't found one," Lee told her. "Climb up on top and use the hatch next to that gun."

Holding tight to her I-book she did as Lee said and slid down the hatch on top of Lyle. "Sorry," she said.

"Which way," Lee asked her as he dropped back down to his seat and reached up and closed the hatch.

"We're facing east and the elevator we need is north. Turn left and don't run into anything. I don't know how to stop the count down."

"We really must stop living on the edge," Lyle said, as Evelyn got off him and took a seat under another hatch to his left. He looked around the inside of the vehicle and saw two dozen tubes filled with projectiles. "I hope we don't run into any of those damn killer clones of theirs because I haven't the slightest idea how to use this gun."

"Can you drive this thing?" Lee asked him as he turned left and moved at a slow speed northward down the aisle between two rows of armored vehicles.

"Of course, I can drive," Lyle said. "It's probably operates on the same principal as electric cars. It has an accelerator petal and a brake petal doesn't it?"

"That it does," he said.

Evelyn looked at her I-book and said, "Their clones are entering the control room. I can't see inside the control room, because you shot out the cameras, Lee. If this Sam person is with them, it won't take him more than a few minutes at the most to work through the firewalls I've set up."

"They'll know where we're at?" Lee asked her.

"They'll access every sensor in this place and know exactly where we're at in less than thirty seconds," she answered.

"Petersen will tell them where we've gone, and they'll know instantly what we're up to," Lyle said. "We should have killed that man."

"Can they shut down the countdown?" Lee asked Evelyn.

"I doubt it," she said.

"Why do you doubt it?"

"Because I have the instruction booklet for that atomic bomb with me," she told him. "So they can't stop the countdown unless they have the shutdown instructions in one of those servers or computers in the main control room."

Good, Lee thought. *They'll have to take us alive to get the booklet and stop the count down and that I will not permit.*

"Let's switch places, Lyle," Lee said.

∾

CHAPTER 67

7:15 a.m., the library

"Our people are in the control room, sir," Sam announced. He was watching the clones leaving the elevator.

"Have them kill those three traitors," Paul said. His voice had the sound of success in it.

"Yes, sir," Sam replied and issued the order to the clones.

"Only Dr. Petersen is in the control room," one of the nine clones said. "And he is tied up."

"They are not there, sir," Sam said.

"What?" Bruce said.

"They are not there," Sam repeated.

"Where the hell are they?" Larry demanded as he looked at the screen. All he could see was the interior of the three elevators and a small part of the control room just outside the elevators. "Only Petersen is there and he's tied to a chair."

"Do you have control of all the exits leading from the complex?" Steve asked as he stood up and walked up to the screen and looked at it.

"Yes, sir," Sam said.

"What about the cameras with their sensors?" Fred asked, standing next to Paul.

"No, sir," Sam said. "There's a program in place in the servers that prevents me from accessing the cameras."

"Remove it," Larry ordered him.

"I can't do that from here, sir," he said. "I must have control of the servers in the control room to do that."

"Put in a code that locks down all the exits," Steve told him. "Then we must go to the control room and find them. They have to be somewhere in this complex."

"How the hell did they get pass our people if they didn't use the elevators?" Fred asked. He answered his own question. "They used the stairwell next to the elevators. What fools we were not to send trackers into that stairwell."

"Do not despair, gentlemen," Paul said in a light hearted voice. "Wherever they are in this complex they can't get out. Let's us go to the control room."

"Has anything been downloaded from the servers to the Internet?" Steve asked Sam.

"No, sir, the long range transmitter isn't working."

"Come, gentlemen, to the control room where we can end this problem of ours within half an hour at the most," Paul said as he turned and started walking toward the door.

The others, except Steve, followed Paul. He stared at wall screen for a few seconds then turned and followed the others thinking aloud, "Why would they abandon the control room before downloading our information on the Internet?"

"Don't concern yourself with such insignificant thoughts, Steve" Paul told him as he walked out of the library and turned toward the elevators that lead to the control room. "We shall find out what they've been up to in a few minutes."

"Sam's virus scan prevented them from downloading anything on the Internet, Steve, and he shut down the transmitter," Larry told him. "They knew our clones would be in the control room long before the scan was complete."

"And remember, Steve, the virus scan was on temporary stop," Fred said. "Until the scan was completed or cancelled all they could do was sit and wait."

"They got into this complex by some way we weren't aware of for the purpose of downloading our information on the Internet," Steve said in an angry voice. "If they've abandoned that purpose, it's because they've done something else that is just as harmful to us."

"You overestimate them, Steve," Larry told him. "All of their plans have failed, and they'll be in our hands in an hour."

"Unless they've planned something else we don't expect," Steve disagreed.

The others ignored him as Sam, carrying the laptop, stopped in front of the elevators and pushed the call button.

"There's the elevator we want, Lee," Evelyn said as she looked through one of the three small periscopes in front of her. "That one directly in front of us with the large, wide overhead steel door."

"Lyle, take my place so I can learn how to use that gun," Lee said as he brought the armored car to a stop. He got up out of the seat, picked up his backpack and tossed it into the back of the vehicle and move back past Evelyn so Lyle could take his seat.

Lyle moved to the driver's position and dropped into the driver's seat and looked over the dashboard and said, "This is just like a modern car except it has an old electric engine."

"How old is the engine?" Evelyn said as she returned her attention to her I-book. "If they're smart, Lee, and they are far from being dumb, they'll spot us and have their killers at the top where that elevator opens to the outside."

"Once we get in that elevator and start it moving to the top," Lyle added.

"That's why I'm going to learn how to operate this gun," he said as he took the seat behind the gun and began looking over the small panel to the right of the gun. He looked at the cylinder to the left of the gun then turned around and looked at the two dozen tubes with projectiles in them behind him. "This thing is like those ancient revolvers of the old western days here in America."

"Where does that elevator stop?" Lyle asked as he started driving the armored car. "And, Evelyn, I have no idea how old this engine is. I'm just glad it works."

Lee leaned over to his left and saw a long rectangular shaped hole under the gun.

"Fill those cylinder holes with those projectiles, slide the cylinder into that square hole, and-," he leaned over and saw a lever that had the words 'locking lever' on the handle. "Pull this lever down and lock it in place." He looked at the two control handles on the small panel. He grabbed the right one with his right hand and felt a trigger an inch from the top. "And start shooting." He grabbed the left handle with his left hand and felt a trigger on it. "For lefties and righties," he said. "Now how do I aim this thing?"

"About fifty feet from the top is a long corridor that leads directly to a stone door that opens on the outside," Evelyn told Lyle. She wasn't paying any attention to what Lee was saying. *I sure hope this Sam guy isn't smart enough to figure out my code.*

He smiled when he saw a rubber lined periscope two feet above the panel. He raised his seat using the handle on the right side under the seat leaned forward and looked through it and saw darkness. He looked at the panel and saw a switch pointing up and pushed it down. A whirring sound came from the panel, and he looked through the periscope again. He could see the steel door of the elevator in front of the vehicle with a target pattern imposed on the screen. It took Lee less than five minutes to load six projectiles into the cylinder and push it into place. "Alright, let's get her ready to rock and roll as the ancients use to say."

"Can you open the elevator, Evelyn?" Lyle asked her as he approached the high wide elevator door.

"No problem," she said as she used her I-book to open the elevator door.

"I hope the maintenance robots down here kept everything operating or this is going to be a very short trip, and we've going to have a very violent end," Lyle mumbled as he drove into the elevator and stopped.

"Within thirty-five minutes," Evelyn added looking at the countdown on the bottom left side of her I-book.

"Thirty-five minutes what?" Lyle asked her.

"That's what we've got before that bomb explodes," she told him.

Steve didn't say anything as they rode the center elevator up to the control room. He was too busy trying to figure out what Evelyn and Lee had done that would cause them to abandon the control room and their plan to download the information on them onto the Internet.

The elevator stopped and the door opened and Sam led the way out into the control room. He walked to the same desk Evelyn had used and sat down in the chair and used the keyboard to access the computer's hard drive.

Paul walked out and saw Petersen tied to the chair next to the desk Sam was sitting in front of and said, "Are you alright, Dr. Petersen?"

"Yes, I'm quite well, but I'd like to use the washroom," he answered.

"Untie him," Paul said to the closest clone.

The clone tracker did as he was told.

Petersen stood up, said, "Thank you," and walked rapidly toward the washroom.

Larry stopped behind Sam and asked, "Find out everything they did and undo it."

"Before you do that, Sam, make sure every elevator in this complex is shut down," Steve said.

"I can only do that, sir, after I've got control of the servers and computers in this room."

"Get control of the servers and computers, Sam," Paul said. "Then check the information on us to see if it is still coded and in place."

"Listen all of you!" Steve yelled. "We've got to find out where those three are and stop them before they leave this compound. Checking on our information can wait since we know they didn't download it on the Internet."

"Once Sam has control of the servers and computers, Steve, that can be easily done," Larry told him. Steve's demands were annoying.

"Aren't any of you thinking?" Steve said in a strong voice.

"Of course, we are, Steve," Bruce said. "We understand the importance of finding out where they are in the complex. Once Sam has control of the servers and computers we will find and kill them."

"We must make sure our information is still intact in the servers first," Paul said as he walked to a chair and sat down and crossed his legs as if he were preparing to engage in a discussion on modern art with a group of art lovers.

"I'm getting control of the servers and computers, sir," Sam told Larry.

"Very good, Sam," Larry said and patted Sam on his right shoulder with his right hand.

"But I'm detecting the presence of another program in the servers," Sam added.

"What program?" Fred was leaning against the wall behind Sam with a bored expression on his face. He felt a calmness he hadn't felt since he woke up this morning.

"I don't know, sir," Sam said. "It appears to be an interference program."

"A program designed to stop you from gaining control of all the servers and cameras in this complex?"

"Yes, sir."

"They're somewhere in this complex they don't want us to know about," Larry said.

"That is obvious, Larry," Paul said. His nerves were back on edge.

"They're heading out of the complex," Steve said.

"That's foolish," Bruce said. "They can't get out. All the exits are locked down."

Paul turned and looked at the steel door leading to the stairs that led to the door that opened on the outside. "All the other exits are being covered by our people, aren't they?"

"All of them," Larry told him.

"There's no way they can get out," Paul said.

"No, there's no way they can leave this underground complex," Larry told him.

Petersen walked out of the washroom and stopped next to Paul.

"Dr. Petersen, what did they do just before they left this room?" Steve asked him.

"They asked me questions," he said.

"What sort of questions?"

"The missile in the silo and what happened to the warhead on top of it," he answered.

"How would they know about the missile in the silo?" Paul asked.

"Because, Paul that's how they got into the complex," Steve said.

"Oh, don't be foolish, Steve," Paul snapped at him.

"If all of you will remember, that wrecked SUV of theirs was found a few hundred feet from where the underground silo is," Steve told them.

"So, what," Bruce said.

"Somehow they found a way into the silo from a cave on the surface and from there into this complex while we were all asleep," Steve told him.

"Impossible," Fred said. "There is no way into that missile silo from outside and from the silo into this complex, because there is no cave."

Paul turned to Petersen and asked, "Is there?"

"Yes," he answered.

Petersen's answer shocked Fred and he gasped, "How could they have gotten into the silo from outside, Petersen?"

"When this underground complex was built centuries ago, the builders put a cave in the side of the hill that leads to the silo, and there is a tunnel that leads from the silo control room directly into the complex."

"What else did you tell them about the missile, Dr. Petersen?" Paul asked him.

"I told them about the warhead on the missile, but not about the type of bacteria in it."

"Is that all you told them?"

"No, that wasn't all I told them."

"What else did you tell them, Dr. Petersen?" Steve demanded.

"They asked me about the atomic warhead that was originally on the missile," he said. "I told them it was down in a special room in the garage."

Steve stared at him with his mouth open.

Bruce, standing next to Steve, noticed his expression. "You think there's something important about that?"

"Are there instructions with that warhead?" Steve asked Petersen ignoring Bruce's question.

"Yes, in the wooden box with the warhead, but they did not ask me about that and I did not tell them," Petersen said.

"We should have programmed the ability to lie into Petersen when we've had him cloned centuries ago," Steve said.

"Don't be a fool, Steve," Paul said. "We didn't want Petersen lying to us. That's why we programmed him to tell us only the truth."

Steve looked at Paul and said, "My dear, Paul, Evelyn, Lyle, and Lee aren't in this control room because they're down in the garage in that special room programing that atomic bomb to detonate. And if it does everything in this underground complex laboratory of ours is going to be destroyed, including us and them."

"I don't think they'll do that," Fred said.

"Yes, they will," Bruce said. "We've made it quite clear to them what we'll do to their families if we survive."

"By destroying us in this complex they protect their families from our revenge,

even if they die with us," Fred said.

"Sam, how many people have we still got?" Paul asked him.

"Forty-eight," Steve answered for Sam.

"And they are all covering the exits from the complex, except the nine in here. Let's send the nine here to the garage and that special room." He looked at Petersen.

"Where is it?"

"To the right once you leave one of the three elevators," he said. "It is the only door in the garage that doesn't have a sign on it."

"One of us should go with them," Fred said. "Remember our clones carry out our orders without question, but they lack the ability to make judgments."

"He's right," Bruce said. "If that atomic bomb has been set to blow up, they won't be able to deactivate it."

"I agree," Paul said. "But if we have the ability to access the intercom system I suggest we let those three know we know about the bomb."

"Can we access the intercom system, Sam?" Larry asked him.

"Yes, sir, we can," he answered.

Larry looked around for another computer and walked to it. "Give me control of the intercom system, Sam."

"Yes, sir," Sam said as he typed a message into the computer giving control of the intercom system to Larry.

"I'll go to the garage and read those instructions and deactivate that bomb," Bruce said as he walked to the elevator. "You nine come with me," he said to the clones standing in the control room. They immediately followed him into the open elevator the five had used to reach the control room.

"Computer, let me be heard over the intercom system," Larry said.

'The intercom system is operating,' appeared on the screen.

"Your plan to blow up this complex with an atomic bomb has failed, Lyle, Lee, and Evelyn," Larry said.

Evelyn started the elevator moving as soon as she'd closed the door behind them.

"They're on to us," Lyle said as he waited for the elevator to reach the top level.

"Let's hope they don't detect the movement of this elevator until we're in that corridor leading to the outside," Evelyn said.

"If the door in the corridor that opens to the outside is as thick as this elevator door is it won't matter, because we'll be trapped," Lee said.

"Answer them one of you," Lyle told them.

"Why?" Evelyn asked him. "What good is that going to do?"

"It'll keep them busy," he said.

"He's right, Evelyn," Lee agreed with Lyle. "If they're busy listening to one of us, they may not be able to detect what we're doing."

"Don't count on it you two. Those guys may not be real humans, but they aren't stupid, but I'll try," she said as she punched transmit into her I-book and spoke. "Who are you?"

"You may call me Larry, Evelyn," he said.

"Your momma and daddy give you a last name other than asshole?" she said.

"My parents died nearly six hundred years ago, and my last name is Davis," Larry said. "You may call me Mr. Davis or Larry which ever suits you best."

"How about inhuman monster," she said.

Larry laughed and said, "Only one as ignorant as you would fail to see the good we've done the human race."

"Good!" she exclaimed in a loud voice. "Killing billions of innocent people with genetically alerted bacteria so you and your four fiends could stay alive for five hundred years and pass your wealth along to yourselves is not my idea of doing good for anyone."

"We've prevented overpopulation, and by doing so furthered the cause of science," Larry told her.

"Bullshit!" Lee said.

Larry heard Lee's comment.

"Only a mindless fool such as you would make such a statement, Lee. There is no more poverty, war, or starvation. The world is united under one world government that has eliminated violent competition between the nations and made war a thing of history. Would any of that have occurred with unlimited growth of the human race? I think not, Lee. This world would be a dead world if we hadn't released microbes into the air that killed millions so billions of others could eventually have better lives."

"You five are in damn terrible company," Lee said. "Every two bit ruthless dictator throughout history who has murdered millions has made the same claim. 'I did what I did for the good of all people.' It was bullshit centuries ago and it is still bullshit."

Evelyn turned off verbal on her I-book and said, "We're near the top. Another few yards and we're in that corridor that leads outside."

"If you three are hoping that atomic bomb in that special room in the garage you set to detonate will explode I suggest you stop hoping. We know about it and will stop it from exploding within a few minutes," Larry told them.

Evelyn turned on the I-book's verbal again. "Not without the instruction booklet you won't," she said.

"What!" Paul exclaimed in a loud voice.

"I have their location, sir," Sam announced.

CHAPTER 68

7:45 a.m., control room

"Where are they?" Steve asked Sam.

"They are in a large elevator in the northern part of the complex heading to the top."

"Can they get out?"

"Yes, sir. I have not yet established complete control over the servers."

"Send all of our people to that elevator and tell them to stop them from leaving that elevator," Paul ordered him.

"Yes, sir," Sam replied and sent an order to all the clone trackers to the tunnel that elevator opened on to.

"We will lose a few more people," Paul said. "But they will be dead the moment the elevator door opens."

"At the speed the elevator is moving, sir, they will be in the tunnel a minute or more before our people reach the tunnel," Sam said.

"You still have control of the doors to this complex?" Fred asked Sam.

"Yes, sir, but if there is a special program in the servers, they will be able to open the door."

"Find that damn program now!" Paul ordered him.

"I am looking, sir."

"Bruce, did you heard what Evelyn said?" Steve asked.

"Yes, I am entering that special room. I've ordered four of the trackers to get one of the armor vehicles down here and follow them."

"Do you think you can deactivate that bomb?"

"I don't know," he said. "I'm opening the case it is in."

"And?"

"Wait," he said.

Steve waited a few seconds before he asked, "Can you deactivate that bomb?"

"We have twenty-two minutes before this antique bomb explodes."

"How do you know?" Paul asked him.

"There is a timer on this bomb on a keypad and it is counting down."

"They probably have an armored vehicle, too," Petersen volunteered.

Larry turned toward him and asked, "How do you know?"

"They asked me about them," he answered.

Steve walked to an unoccupied desk and sat down in the chair. The others were fools. He knew Evelyn well enough to know she'd probably set the timer on the bomb so it couldn't be stopped. Trapping and killing her, Lyle, and Lee in the corridor wouldn't prevent their lives from coming to a violent end.

Paul looked at him. "You have the look of failure on your face, Steve."

"I'm thinking," he lied.

"About what?"

"Sirs, there is a program in the servers that is set to transmit information to the Department of Information the moment it is activated."

"Can you stop it?" Larry asked him.

"I don't know, sir," Sam answered. "It's attached to another program."

"We've found your program, Evelyn," Paul said.

"So what?" You don't have the code to shut it down," she told him.

"You're smart enough to know there is no such thing as an unbreakable code."

"You don't have that much time," she said.

"Even if we can't break your code there will be no information transmitted from this complex because the transmitter is shut down," Paul told her.

"We're in the tunnel," Lyle said as he drove the armored car out of the elevator into a wide, round tunnel with a flat stone floor. "The people who built this missile control complex centuries ago sure did a lot of engineering."

Lee turned around and looked through the periscopes behind him as he asked Evelyn, "Are there any doors leading to this tunnel?"

"I don't know, Lee. I didn't have time to check."

"Yes, there are," Lyle said.

Evelyn looked through one of the three periscopes in from of her and saw what Lyle meant. "There are four of those clones in front of us, Lee."

Lee turned around and looked through the target finder and saw them. "I wonder if this tunnel was built to have a battle fought in it."

"We don't have a choice now," Lyle told him as he saw the four clones raise rifles and fire at them.

The four electric volts slammed into the front of the armored car with enough of an impact to rock it back on its back wheels.

"You okay, Lyle," Lee yelled as he took aim with the armored vehicle's cannon at where two of the clones were lying on the floor next to the wall on the right.

"Yeah, but I don't think this armored car can stand a lot more direct hits."

"Fuck it," Lee said as he hoped the tunnel was built to withstand a battle in it and fired at the two clones. A loud banging sound filled the interior of the armor car.

The armored car rocked back as the shell left the barrel and slammed into the floor just in front of the two clones. It exploded sending rock and body parts flying in the air.

"People long ago fought with noisy weapons like this?" Evelyn yelled out over the noise.

"They fought with a lot of things," Lee said taking aim at the two clones on the left. He pulled the trigger and the gun boomed again and a shell shot out of the barrel rocking the armored car backwards again.

The shell hit the wall between the two clones and blew them into two large chunks without arms or legs attached to the bodies, along with some of the wall, landed in the middle of the tunnel floor.

Lyle slowed down to almost a stop.

"What are you doing?" Lee yelled at him.

"The bodies are lying in the middle of the floor," Lyle answered.

"They're dead!" Evelyn told him.

Lyle didn't answer. He just increased his speed and rolled over the remains of the four clones and the debris. The armored car rocked from side to side as it rolled over the bodies crushing them into the floor. *Lord, our ancestors were a violent bunch.*

Lee turned around and looked behind and saw six more clones approaching from the rear. "There must be doors into this tunnel." He traversed the gun and aimed at them and fired another shell.

The shell exploded next to two of the clones killing them instantly and wounding another. The other three threw themselves to the floor and started firing at the armored car. The heavy volts slammed into the back of the car and made it rock forward.

"Can you open that door at the end of this tunnel?" he asked Evelyn.

"I'm working on it," she replied as she typed on her I-book.

7:46 .a.m.

"Can you stop her?" Paul asked Sam.

"I don't know, sir. The programs in the servers are very sophisticated."

"Bruce, what are you doing?" Larry asked him.

"Coming back to the control room," he said. "I can't stop the count down and we have nineteen minutes before the bomb explodes. You should start downloading all information on flash drives and get out of the complex before the bomb explodes."

Steve immediately turned toward the computer on the desk he was sitting at and said, "Computer, put all information concerning cloning on your hard drive and eject it when finished."

"What are you doing?" Fred asked him.

"What we should have been doing along," he said. "This complex is finished. We can setup another somewhere else, and when we've been cloned again we can seek revenge against them and their families. You have failed!"

Paul smiled and said, "Brilliant, Steve."

"What about the blast from the bomb?" Larry asked.

"The bomb in under more than four hundred feet of earth and concrete the complex will absorb most of it if we can get a few hundred yards away," Fred told him.

The three of them heard what Steve said.

"Can they do that?" Lee asked Evelyn as he took aim at another group of seven clones coming for them from behind.

Six heavy volts slammed into the back left side of the armored car and pushed it into the wall. The loud sound of metal scrapping against stone filled the interior of the car.

Evelyn looked at him and grinned and shook her head.

"You prepared for them doing something like that?"

"They can download everything they want on the computers' hard drivers. But getting away is a different matter all-together."

"The door, Evelyn," Lyle yelled. "It's only a few hundred feet in front of us."

She returned to her I-book as she said, "Patience, patience, Lyle. Remember Rome wasn't built in a day."

"At the moment, I don't give a fuck about when Rome was built. I just want that damn door open because we're doing forty miles an hour."

Lee took careful aim at a group of seven clones—nine more clones were coming out of door near the elevator, and fired putting the shell between them.

The shell hit the floor and exploded knocking all seven down and forcing the others to drive to the floor to avoid as much of the impact of the exploding shell as possible.

Two more shells left then I'm going to need help reloading. He glanced at Evelyn and hoped she'd get that door open before he ran out of ammunition.

Not one of the seven clones he'd fired at got up, but six of the nine did and started firing as fast as they could at the car.

Two volts missed but the rest hit the car in the back and caused it to bounce like a rubber ball.

Lee didn't like the feel of that because it meant one or both of the rear tires had been hit. "Keep driving, Lyle, no matter what!" he yelled at him.

"The door—," Lyle started to say and stopped.

The door was opening, but slowly.

Lyle started to slow down.

Lee felt the car slowing down. "Don't do that."

"I have to or we run into the door," he replied.

"Can you make it move faster, Evelyn?" Lee asked her.

"The damn thing probably hasn't been opened in over five hundred years, Lee," she answered. "It's not going to move like the door on your garage. Give it time."

The heavy steel door rose slowly revealing as it rose a wall of plant life so thick the sunlight couldn't penetrate it.

"We're not going to make it," Lyle yelled as he saw the wall of brown and green in front of them.

Lee turned around and looked through a periscope in front of him at the wall of brown and green plant growth, and knew Lyle could be right. That wall in front of them appeared to be more than a foot thick and most of it looked like the trunk of trees or woody plants. He knew instantly there was only one thing to do. He turned around and moved the barrel of the gun to the front and said to Lyle, "Give it all she's got, Lyle. It's our only chance. And brace yourselves." He aimed at the wall of brown and green plants and fired his remaining two shells into it.

The two shells blew a hole in the wall of plants about five feet wide.

Lyle knew just what he had to do. He floored the accelerator and headed straight for the five feet wide hole. It wasn't until the armored car was inches from it that he thought, *what the hell is on the other side?* He didn't think about his question. He was too afraid there might be nothing on the other side of the wall but open space and maybe a thousand feet to the ground.

The car slammed into the wall of plants at top speed and went through it like it was a simple hedge along a green lawn. But the impact, mild though it was, jarred the hell out of them.

Evelyn dropped her I-book and reached for the lever of the hatch above her to steady herself and planted her feet on the foot rest of her seat. Lyle just held onto the steering wheel and kept his right foot on the accelerator and his left foot on the floor. Lee held onto the trigger handles of the gun and let his legs fly free.

Lyle didn't think anything or say anything as the armored car crashed through the green and brown wall of plants and ended up in midair.

The car moved forward in midair for twenty feet then dropped like a rock to the ground. Fortunately for them the ground turned out to be a gully filled with woody brush. The car hit the ground with a loud bang as the suspension system and three axles of the car gave out a loud metallic scream in defiance of the weight of the car. A loud squishing sound followed by the sound of breaking wood as the six tires of the armored car went almost flat under the impact then shot the car six feet into the air. The car hit the ground again, bounced three feet in the air, then hit the ground a third time, and bounced only a foot in the air. It landed on the ground a fourth time and the tires took over crushing brush beneath them and the car shot forward through the gully.

Evelyn's head hit the hatch above her, but not with much force because she used her arms to stop herself from hitting the hatch with much force. But pain shot through her head and she screamed, "Hell!" in pain. She dropped back down in the seat and bounced each time the car bounced.

Lee shot forward and turned his face to the left. The right side of his face slammed into the target finder of the gun and he felt a sharp pain in the right side of his face. He threw himself back in the seat hoping he hadn't done any serious damage to his face, and bounced as the car bounced. His legs flew up and down in front of him.

Lyle, holding on to the steering wheel hit the hatch above him with the top of his head—he felt like he'd been hit in the head with a tennis racket, but not as hard as Evelyn and his feet and legs didn't hit anything because he kept his feet planted solidly on the floor and the accelerator. But he bounced in the driver's seat each time the car bounced.

As soon as he felt the car was on solid ground he looked through the periscope in front of him and saw the gully turned left. He turned left, too. He screamed, "We're free!"

"In what direction are we headed?" Evelyn asked him.

"I don't know," he shot back at her. "Away from that damn underground laboratory complex."

"Keep going," Lee yelled at him. "Remember what the instructions said about being far away from the explosion."

"At least sixty-five miles," Evelyn said.

"Well, we aren't going to make five miles," Lyle replied.

"Slow down so I can get my I-book," Evelyn said. "I put the timer on it."

"No!" Lee yelled. "Keep going as fast as you can."

Lyle kept his right foot on the accelerator and the armored car shot through the gully like water in a flash flood.

"Maybe they were right about the complex absorbing most of the blast, Lee,"

Evelyn said.

"Right or wrong we go as fast as we can from that complex," he replied. "The more miles between us and that bomb the better."

7:55 a.m.

As soon as the computer flashed a sign indicating the hard drive was free of it, Steve pulled it out. "Let's use the door in the control room that goes outside," he said as he jumped to his feet and rushed toward the door.

"Open that door, Sam," Larry ordered him in a loud voice as he moved toward the door.

Paul was in front of him behind Steve and Bruce and Fred followed him.

Petersen sat down and watched them running. His empty stomach was rumbling and he wanted his breakfast.

"I can't," Sam replied in a calm voice as he remained seated in front of the computer.

The five of them stopped yards from the steel door and turned toward Sam.

"Why can't you?" Fred asked him.

"Because there are five programs in the servers that prevent me from opening the outer door to this control room, sir."

"Get rid of them," Larry ordered him.

Sam didn't reply.

"Did you hear me, Sam?" Larry asked in a loud voice.

"I have three of them down, sir," he said. "But the fourth one has a transmit code attached to it."

"Is that the transmit program you spoke of?" Paul asked him. His usual calm, arrogant voice was filled with fear.

"Yes, sir, it is."

"Remove it and the fifth one, too," Paul told him. For the first time in over five hundred years Paul was sweating because he was afraid.

"Yes, sir," Sam replied.

Bruce looked at his watch and said, "Hurry, we've only seven minutes left."

"The last program will be gone in less than two minutes," Sam told him.

"Come, let's prepare to leave," Paul said as he walked to the steel door and grabbed the handle. He pushed down on it and smiled when the door opened. He pulled it open and started running down the steps.

The other four ran after him leaving Sam at the computer to face death without them. They ran down the steps to the alcove and toward the steps that lead to the steel door that opened to the outside, ignoring the eight dead clones lying on the floor, and up the steps to the outside door. Paul grabbed the handle and pushed down on it. It didn't move.

"Pull up on it," Steve told him.

Paul pulled up on the handle and it didn't move. He threw his right shoulder against the door and tried to force it open.

The door didn't move.

"Help me," he cried to the others.

They all rushed forward and began pushing on the door.

It didn't move an inch.

"Oh, no," Larry whined as he back away from the door.

"Sam, open this door!" Paul screamed at him, He was terrified, but not of death. He was terrified that his life of over five hundred years was about to end and he would finally find out if there really was life after death. If there was life after death, he would have to face God and explain his actions for over five hundred years, and that terrified him far more than a violent death.

Sam didn't respond. He was busy working on the computer to get the doors open.

Steve turned around and walked back down the steps to the alcove and through the alcove to the steps leading to the control room and sat on the bottom step. He looked at the hard drive in his left hand and tossed it away. It was useless to them.

"What can we do?" Larry cried as he pushed against the door.

Steve heard him and said in a calm voice, "Await the death we've managed to avoid for five hundred years."

"Try pulling," Bruce suggested. "We've still got a few minutes. If we can get outside before the bomb explodes we might survive it."

"What time is it?" Paul demanded of him as he stopped pushing on the door.

Bruce glanced at his expensive platinum and gold watch and said in a soft terrified voice, "We've got three minutes before the bomb explodes."

"Yes, let's try pulling," agreed Fred as he pushed Paul aside and grabbed the handle and tried pulling on it.

Larry helped him.

The door remained closed and locked.

Fred gave up and walked back down the steps and through the alcove and up the stairs into the control room.

Steve got up and followed him though he didn't know why.

Paul, crying like a baby, turned and walked down the steps, through the alcove, and up the stairs to the control room. Larry and Bruce continued pulling on the door.

"A bit late for tears, isn't it, Paul?" Steve asked in a voice that was surprisingly calm as Paul walked pass him. He walked to the desk he'd been sitting at and sat down.

Paul stumbled to another desk and sat in the chair as he cried, "I don't want to die. I don't want to meet God. I don't want to pay for the sins I've committed. I don't want to die. I'm afraid of meeting God."

Steve ignored him and looked at the clock on the wall above the center elevator. It read 8:09. "Time should be up within a few more seconds," he said as he wondered why time passed so fast when one was in a hurry.

Sam was still busy working at the computer.

Petersen was still wondering when he could have breakfast. He was really hungry.

None of them heard the explosion of the antique atomic bomb, and they didn't feel anything.

CHAPTER 69

8:09 a.m.

"When was the bomb supposed to explode?" Lee asked Evelyn.

She dropped to her knees and picked up her I-book and looked at it. It was still operating. She looked at the timer she'd put on it in the bottom left hand corner. "About now," she said.

Lyle heard her and didn't say anything. He just kept driving down the gully as fast as the armored car could go.

Lee was thinking, *at least those five monsters won't survive this disaster.*

8:10 a.m.

Within less than two seconds the interior of the underground laboratory complex reached a temperature equal to that on the surface of the sun. From level six to the control room on level one everything in the complex was first destroyed by the blast resulting from the explosion then reduced to liquid by the tremendous heat. Steel, glass, plastic, and even some of the rock became liquid because of the heat. The bodies of the clones in their cloning tubes were reduced to atoms. Nothing survived the blast and the heat except the information in the servers and computers. All of it left the complex three seconds before explosion and went directly a communication satellite six hundred miles above the Earth and from there down to the servers in the Department of Information in Crown City.

Evelyn had put a program in the servers that was attached to the program that opened the outer door in the complex's control room and the long range transmitter. The moment Sam tried opening that outer door her program began to operate. And Sam knew nothing about the program because he didn't know the code word she'd given the program to reveal itself.

Work began in the Department of Information at nine a.m. when people settled down to their computers and laptops with their favorite after breakfast drinks, if they had breakfast—the summer was coming and lot of the employees in the Department of Information were dieting so they'd look attractive in their new summer wear.

The servers and computers accepted all of the information and registered the time and date when the information arrived as well as where it had originated. Today was going to be a most unusual day for the Secretary of the Department of Information.

The Bureau of Geology in the Department of the Interior was operated twenty-four hours a day seven days a week because Earthquakes were always occurring around the world somewhere, and the Bureau wanted to know if there was anyone living in those areas who might need assistance, also received information. Every seismograph in the department as well as over two hundred around the world registered the explosion and

recorded it as a nuclear explosion. The program in the seismographic machines that analyzed Earthquakes hadn't done that it over six hundred years. Many people working in the Bureau weren't even aware there was such a program in their seismographic computers. When the nuclear explosion in the complex occurred, no one knew what the hell could have caused a nuclear explosion.

But those on duty who read the computer displays knew the exact location of the explosion.

The people living in the wilderness village forty-eight miles north of the complex felt the ground tremble and wondered what could have caused the earth to tremble. A second later they heard the sound of the explosion escaping from the ground and were frightened. They rushed out of their houses and small businesses that served the community, and looked in the direction they thought the sound had come from. All they saw was a cloud of smoke in the form of a dust cloud far to the south of them that was quickly blown eastward by the westerly winds. Some suggested using their radios to call the government in the state capital to report it, but others suggested doing nothing. If they had heard the explosion, the people in the state capital two hundred miles southeast of them had heard it too, and would send people to investigate. The investigators would stop by the village—the state medical people knew where it was, to see if everyone in the village was okay. All the adults in the village agreed and they went back to their usual work. The children in the school returned to their school work with something to talk about after school as they walked to their homes.

Lee, Evelyn, and Lyle not only heard the tremendous explosion, they felt the shaking of the ground—even though they were a mile away, and thought only one thing.

We're all dead.

Lyle kept driving the armored car as fast as he could think it was a waste of time and energy, but he didn't know what else to do.

Lee expected the ground under them to collapse and suck them back down into the complex, which he was certain was in complete ruin. He looked through the periscope in front of him and admired what little of the beautiful sunny day he could see.

Evelyn, bouncing around in her seat with the bouncing movement of the armored car was looking at her I-book and wondering why they were still alive.

For ten minutes neither of them said a thing then Lyle spoke.

"How long do you think it'll be before the blast reaches us?" he asked Lee and Evelyn.

"I don't—." Lee started to say.

"It won't," Evelyn said, cutting him off.

"Why not," Lee asked as if he was disappointed it wouldn't.

"The information in the booklet said to be a minimum of sixty-five miles away when the bomb went off," she said.

"Well, we aren't that far away," Lyly said in a depressed voice.

"No more than two at the most, Lyle," Lee agreed.

"Sixty-five miles away if it was a surface explosion," Evelyn told them.

"Of course," Lee exclaimed. "The explosion was underground. That control room must have been at least a hundred feet below the surface, and that garage the bomb was in at least four hundred or more feet below the control room. And like one of those five said the complex would absorb most of the explosion."

"Most of the explosion was absorbed by the ground around the complex?" Lyle asked. He sounded very hopeful they wouldn't die.

"We were at least a mile away," Lee said. "With millions of tons of rock and dirt between us and the explosion. That's why we weren't killed. Even the sound of the explosion didn't bother us because of the millions of tons of earth between us and the explosion. All that earth absorbed most of the sound, too."

"And the steel of this car," Lyle added.

"What about that fallout stuff from an atomic explosion in the history books?" Evelyn asked them.

"I don't recall reading a lot about that," Lyle said. "I was never really interested in the violent twentieth century when I was in school."

"Well, I was," Lee said as a big grin began to spread across his face. "They called it radiation, and it was supposed to be really deadly if it got on you. It could kill you in hours or days depending upon how much you got on you, and I don't think we got any on us."

"Because the explosion was underground," Evelyn said. "That fallout stuff or radiation would have been contained by the ground around the explosion."

"So we can stop and get out?" Lyle asked him.

"No," Lee said. "We keep driving until we're sixty-five or more miles away."

"What about our injuries?" Lyle asked. "I feel blood on the top of my head and it hurts."

"Me, too, Lee," Evelyn said.

Lee felt the right side of his face with his right hand and twitched with pain. "I got a cut on the right side of my face when I slammed into the target finder. Slow it down a bit, Lyle, so we can stop bouncing around. I'll see if this thing has a medical kit in it."

Lyle dropped the speed of the car from forty miles an hour to twenty.

"If it does it isn't worth a damn, Lee," Evelyn said. "I doubt if the robots who took care of this car updated the medical kit."

Lee turned around and looked behind him and saw a medical box. "There's one on the wall just above these projectile containers. The medicine is probably all dried up, but maybe there are some bandages we can use. I've got a medical kit in my backpack. The medicine in that hasn't expired." Lee eased out of the seat and reached back for the metal medical box attached to the wall. The box wouldn't move, it was bolted to the wall, but he managed to undo the latch on the door and opened the box and saw basic first aid medical equipment. He looked at the medicine in the plastic bottles.

The medicine in the plastic bottles had long ago turned to dust, but the packages of bandages still had a fresh look about the paper covering the bandages even though it was yellow with age and looked very brittle.

"This stuff is real old," Lee said as he removed one of the bandage packs. The dried yellow paper began to flake away the moment he put any pressure on the pack. "I sure hope this pack didn't have valuable information on the inside of it, because the moment I touched it the paper began to fall apart."

Evelyn turned around and looked at the open medical box. "Just instructions on the use of it," she said. "Open that package in your hand, Lee."

He did and looked at the thick gauze bandage. "It feels dry, but it might still be of use."

"Use the kit in your backpack, Lee," Lyle advised him. "No sense in escaping from that complex and atomic blast just to die of an infection from five-hundred-year-old bandages."

Lee decided Lyle was right and put the bandage back in the medical kit and closed and locked the lid and got off his seat and got his backpack. He opened it and took out the medical kit.

After bandaging himself and Evelyn he bandaged Lyle.

"How far do you think this thing will go on these batteries?" Lyle asked Lee.

"Your guess is as good as mind. I've never driven an armor car before," he said. "If it has a recharger attached to the engine, it can go around the world a dozen times before the batteries dry up."

Lyle looked at the mileage gage on the dashboard of the armored car and asked, "What was the mileage on this thing when you first got in it, Lee?"

"I wasn't interested in the miles this vehicle had been driven, Lyle, just if it still worked."

"The mileage meter reads five miles," Lyle said. "I don't think we've travelled that far."

"In what direction are we headed?" Evelyn asked.

Lee opened the hatch above his head and looked out.

It was a beautiful day with a bright sun and a clear blue sky as far as he could see.

He turned around and saw the sun in the eastern sky. "We're headed west," he said. "Let's keep going for another few miles before we stop and get out and walk around a bit."

"What are we going to tell the government people?" Evelyn asked. "As soon as we drive into some town in this antique every cop in town is going to be all over us."

"We tell no one anything," Lyle said.

"What do you mean," Lee asked him.

"No one knew about us and our mission but those five and their clones, and they're all ash or atoms if that bomb did what it was built to do."

"It did what it was built to do," Evelyn assured him.

"Then we're the only people on Earth who know about the explosion," he said. "We don't talk to anyone or we'll be asking questions of government investigators until we die of ripe old age."

"Every earthquake detecting machine in the world recorded that explosion. And right now the people in the Geology Bureau of the Department of the Interior are sending

planes and helicopters to the area where the explosion occurred," Evelyn said.

"You think they know it was an atomic explosion?" Lee asked her.

"Well, they certainly know by now it wasn't an earthquake," she said. "And the satellites flying over this planet with the ability to detect radiation are registering the radiation count over that complex and sending it down to some government office."

Lee didn't say anything.

Lyle drove silently.

"You two haven't anything to say?" Evelyn asked after a few minutes of silence.

"Lyle's right, Evelyn," Lee said. "We don't talk about what we've gone through to anyone, or our private lives are destroyed. I don't know about you two but I don't want to end up on the cover of any magazines as the man who set off a five-hundred-year-old atomic bomb."

"We'd end up on the morning talk shows all over the world, Lee," Lyle said. "We'd probably make millions and be able to screw some of those skinny, sexy talk show women."

"I don't want to make millions, and I damn sure ain't interested in fucking some over paid talk show asshole no matter how sexy he is," Evelyn said. "I just want to go back to my private life."

"So we drive this armored car south as close to some town as we can get and get out at night and walk the rest of the way to the town, and take transportation home," Lee said. "If we're asked what we were doing in the wilderness we tell who ever asks us we were camping."

"They're going to want to know how we got this deep into the wilderness, Lee," Evelyn said.

"Let me think," Lee told her.

"Why not tell them we were camping in a SUV when that tornado forced us to leave it and hide in a gully," Lyle said. "And the tornado picked it up and destroyed it."

"That might work, Lee," Evelyn said.

"What if they find my SUV?" Lee asked.

"There's no way to trace it to you, is there?" Lyle asked him.

"No, there isn't," he said. "I got it the last time I worked for Paul."

"So, we just tell anyone who asks us we were camping and lost our van to that tornado," he said.

"That might work," Lee said. "What do you two think about it?"

Lyle and Evelyn thought over what Lee said and agreed with him.

"You guys got any money?" Lyle asked.

Lee took his wallet out of his pocket and pulled out the credit card the five had given them and Evelyn had changed to make it impossible for them to be traced. "I got two hundred and fifty in cash plus that credit card the five gave us and my own credit card."

"I got two hundred and my personal credit card," Evelyn said after going through her pockets. "And the same type of credit card Lee has."

"I've got twenty dollars on me," Lyle said. "I didn't plan on any long distance traveling. I just wanted to stay alive."

"Think we should risk using the five's credit card?" Lee asked Evelyn.

"No. It'll probably take the FBI a few days to find out all they can about the five if—," she paused and picked up her I-book and checked to see if her download program worked. "My program worked, you guys. Everything in those computers was downloaded to the Department of Information."

"We ditch these credit cards the five gave us now, Evelyn," Lee said as he removed the card from his wallet and tossed it out the open hatch.

Evelyn did the same thing.

"I used that credit card to buy food and clothing at the country store my first day in my hideout," Lee said with the sound of worry in his voice. "The FBI and the World Police Department are going to check everything about those five, and the people in that store saw me."

"If we can get back to your hideout in the next two days, Lee," Evelyn began. "I can use the computers in the attic to remove any record of you buying anything in that store. They've probably been paid by the bank that issued the card by now. So the FBI and the World Police Department won't be able to track your purchases."

"And we go about our private lives," Lyle said.

"You got a problem, Lyle," Lee said.

"No, I don't," he said.

"You died over twenty-two years ago. You suddenly pop up alive, it isn't going to take the police very long to connect you to that explosion."

Lyle said nothing as he drove. Then he said in a sad voice, "Looks like I'll have to stay dead with a new identity, because I can't go back to being Lyle Morton. By now the security people in the Department of Information know that was a fake name."

"You're paying a hell of a price for destroying that complex and the five," Evelyn said.

"Yeah, I am," Lyle agreed with her. "But it was worth it to stop millions of more people from dying of their killer bacteria."

"I wonder how the government is going to release the information to the public about what those five did," Evelyn asked.

"Not our problem, Evelyn," Lee told her.

Twelve hours of driving at thirty miles an hour, after three rest breaks, they abandoned the armored car in the woods five miles outside a town after wiping their prints from everything they touched, and walked to the town. They got a hot meal, a map to tell them where they were and spent the night in a small country motel in separate rooms where they each had a hot bath. The next morning, they took a cab to the closest town with a train station and took the train back to Crown. A few hours later they were in Lee's hideout where Evelyn removed all evidence of Lee having bought supplies in that country store he went to his first day in his hideout. All three of them were safe, free, and invisible to the government.

$$\sim$$

CHAPTER 70

June 30, Sunday

Once the director of the building the Department of Information was in had read the information downloaded from the complex, she knew she couldn't release the information to the public without the World President knowing about it first, but she didn't think it was her responsibility to take it to the president. So she went directly to the office of her superior, the Secretary of the Department of Information, and dumped the information in his lap. As soon as he read it, he took it to the President and dumped it into his lap. And there the buck stopped.

After reading it, the President realized to release such information to the world would cause uncontrollable rage on the part of the people. Even though racial and ethnic prejudice were irrational emotions of the past, he knew it would only be a matter of hours before people jealous of another nation for any number of reasons would start pointing at that nation and accusing them of the horrible plagues that had been released on the world by the five. He called a meeting of his top advisers and presented the problem to them, and they came to the same conclusion he had arrived at before he called them. Release the information to the public and every scientists doing work on bacteria and genes would face the wrath of an enraged public, in addition to national prejudices raising their ugly heads.

There could be no information released to the public about the plagues of the past beyond what the public already knew. All the information would have to be gathered together on the flash drives that contained the information and buried in some isolated unknown government warehouse hundreds of miles away from the nearest population center. All the servers and computers that received the information would have to be scrubbed clean of the information to guarantee that it never got out, and then sent to a recycling plant.

As for the explosion the public was told an ancient nuclear bomb in a silo that had been forgotten for over five hundred years went active because of the tornado that stuck the area the silo was in, and the timing device on the bomb was activated and trigged the explosion the day after the tornado had struck the area where the silo was located.

When the public was given the story the President and his advisers came up with the public thought it was all so very exciting and over a hundred thousand people from Crown City planned to visit the area during the summer. The government told people the area was off limits for at least two years because of the dangerous radiation levels. A thousand federal security officers were stationed in a circle thirty miles around the area three days after the explosion to prevent the determined from visiting the area anyway. A hundred and twelve people were arrested in August and fined a thousand dollars each for trying to enter the area where the bomb had exploded for acts hazardous to human health.

There was even a plan by a few ambitious business people to build motels in the area so people could visit it the moment radiation levels were safe. A few stupid people, over two thousand, actually wanted to become radioactive so they could show themselves at parties and get in the sandal magazines. The fools didn't realize they could contaminate others with radioactive and eventually die painful deaths. But the security forces kept them out of the area.

The Department of Health sent a number of investigators to the village north of the radioactive area to check the people in the town to see if they were contaminated. None were and after a few days the investigators left the small village and the people went back to their normal lives.

By September school had begun again and parents were more interested in their children making good grades than they were in a radioactive area in the wilderness.

The wives and girlfriends of Paul, Steve, Bruce, Fred, and Larry were worried their husbands and boyfriends had met with foul play when they didn't show up after a few weeks and reported their disappearance to the police in Crown. They didn't suspect for a moment they had died in the nuclear explosion, because they knew their husbands wouldn't be so foolish as to venture into the wilderness.

The women were never aware the President ordered a quiet investigation of the women to see if they were involved with any plagues and exactly how old each of them was. The investigation cleared all of them of any suspicion, but the World Police Force and the FBI kept the detailed reports done on each of them.

They were foolish for going to the police to complain about the disappearance of their husbands because the special police investigation into the disappearance of Paul, Steve, Bruce, Fred, and Larry uncovered political and business corruption going back almost five centuries.

The Statue of Limitations prevented the Justice Department from doing anything about corruption that was more than twenty-five years old, but the Justice Department could investigate and arrest people involved in corruption and violation of laws that had occurred within the twenty-five years. Over three hundred businessmen and women world-wide went to prison for terms of five to twenty years. A third of the members of Congress had to resign their positions in Congress and face the possibility of being arrested, tried, and going to prison if they were convicted. Prison was a terrible, terrible prospect for men and women who had known nothing but a life of luxury and power.

The wives of the four men weren't charged with anything, because they hadn't done anything illegal. But three-fourths of their wealth was confiscated because it had been earned illegally, and fines and back taxes took three-fourths of the remaining fourth. The wives of the five that were married were far from being poor, but they didn't inherit the hundreds of billions of dollars each of their husbands had been worth. To most people inheriting over a hundred million dollars was a gift from God. But to the wives of Paul, Steve, Larry, and Fred it was almost like being poor. They had to sell half of the seven homes each man had owned, and nearly all of their billion dollars art collections.

Larry's girlfriend got only the townhouse, the cars, and jewelry he had bought her. The rest of his estate, since he left no will and had no heirs, went to the State of Colorado. The citizens of the state demanded that all the money from his estate go directly to the public schools and hospitals. The governor and the state legislature spent weeks dividing his two-hundred-billion-dollar estate among the public schools and hospitals. A group of concerned citizens in the state made sure not a penny went to any politician.

Reporters following the investigation into the wealth the five men had found it odd that for over five hundred years that the men who had inherited the fortunes of their grandfathers during the plagues looked almost identical to their grandfathers. Further investigations by determined reporters uncovered the fact that the heirs of the vast fortunes were always found in out-of-the-way places where the plagues had done their worst killing. It caused many people to wonder if the five had something to do with the horrible plagues, but far worse than that, it ruined the social lives of their widows and girlfriends. Bruce's girlfriend got a job as an actress. No one among the rich wanted anything to do with them. All they had was each other and they quickly grew to hate each other. So they stopped visiting each other.

Lee and Evelyn returned to their private lives and families, Lee started dating the redhead across the street. No one, especially the government, suspected they had anything to do with the nuclear explosion, and there was nothing in the downloaded information about them.

The abandoned armored car was discovered a year later by government officials going over the area checking on animals to see if any had been contaminated by radiation. By the time the car was discovered it had been taken over by birds as a safe place to build their nests. The excellent condition of the armored car convinced the government officials it hadn't been left there centuries ago, and they knew the wilderness people hadn't been using it. A report was written up on it with the words 'No explanation for the condition of the armored car or its location'. The government officials let the bird keep their home.

Lyle returned to Hong Kong, but never made contact with his family. He saw them on the streets of the city, and knew where they lived and they were happy. His wife had remarried as Lee had told him she probably did, and his children were married with children of their own. There was no place for him in their lives because he'd died twenty-three years ago and became another person. All he could do was to use his skills and knowledge of the Department of the Information to establish a new identity for himself and live a quiet, peaceful. It was a terrible price for him to pay to stop five monsters from killing billions of innocent people so they could continue living.